Lineberger Memorial Library

REFUGE

Refuge

—— *a novel* ——

DOT JACKSON

CHARLOTTE 2006

REFUGE: A NOVEL
by Dot Jackson
NOVELLO FESTIVAL PRESS, CHARLOTTE, NORTH CAROLINA

©2006 by Dot Jackson

This is a work of fiction and any resemblance to real persons
or events is purely coincidental.

ISBN 0-9760963-5-8

    Library of Congress Cataloging-in-Publication Data

Jackson, Dot.
  Refuge : a novel / by Dot Jackson.
    p. cm.
  Summary: A Charlestonian woman escapes her husband and returns to
her family's abandoned homestead in the Appalachian mountains.
  ISBN 0-9760963-5-8
  1. Wives—South Carolina—Charleston—Fiction. 2. Appalachian
mountains—Fiction. 3. Domestic fiction. I. Title.
  PS3610.A349R45 2006
  813'.6—dc22

                2005035875

Printed in the United States of America
Book design by Bonnie Campbell
SECOND PRINTING

~

To my people, who told the stories,
and to Aunt Bird Montgomery, who swaddled the newborns
and closed the eyes of the dead, and in between, taught us how to live.

~1~

SOME KIND OF SIGN

I THANK YOU THAT YOU'RE HERE, BELOVED BIRD. WE NEED TO HAVE A talk. There's something in the wind—I've not ever had such a feeling as has come over me today. I was sitting here sewing on this baby quilt a while ago; you were out fishing, tearing up ducks, whatever—which I thank you also for eating outside. Feathers and bloody mess scattered all over is not what we need this evening, on account of what I am about to tell you.

Which is, well, I don't quite know. A while ago I made this little fire. I go down for wood and I see it is running out, which is the first time that has happened, that it's not stovewood enough I'd say to get us through a week. And when the wind blew so hard a shower of rocks fell down the chimney; I know we ought not to use this fireplace but it got so chilly I was cold to my bones. That wind!

I get the fire going and I sit down here and must have, just a little bit, dozed off to sleep. And that old mournful wind howling down the gap, moaning in the hemlocks, playing the deep strings.

And I hear Isolde singing.

Now, I've heard plenty of strange singing on this place; heard it down the chimney, and out amidst the briers. But this was something else again. Nothing like that other. I've not heard Isolde in I guess thirty years, and now she wakes me with a jolt. Oh, it was glorious. I woke up with the tears just streaming.

First thing I thought, "It's my mother." Aw, no—my mother is lying dead for years and years, somewhere in France, beside that last old man she married—the tenor. I never can bring back his name.

Fact is, when I thought about it, my mother never was this good a singer. She tried. She aspired. But beside this she'd sound like a wind-up canary. And now it dawns on me: it's Pet. It's my daughter. Although you would never put us together. Pet is big-boned and blond—big chest. She has this Isolde voice my mother would have died for. And I bet she has (excuse me) pissed it away, in that snobby Episcopal choir. Maybe this was just the ghost of dead possibility.

Whatever else, my dear friend, it is a sign.

You have never seen my daughter but I think that's fixing soon to change. She has been real put out with me for quite some time, as I have probably told you. She thinks it is not civilized the way I live. I am an embarrassment, a family disgrace. The crazy old woman.

Can't say as I blame her. But since I put my dimestore glasses down somewhere I can't see to write worth a toot. If that nice old guy can't get up here with his logging truck, I can't get any mail and can't send any. I know it's been at least a month now. And Pet's off down there in Charleston with her step-ins in a wad.

Odds on, it's her all right, in my dream. I'll give you ten to one she's out there, wroth as the Queen of the Night, rolling this way. Pet and her sweet, fat man are in their big car, heading for a showdown. And this time I may be just too spent to fight her. Plus, she's got reason to act up. Last letter I got I made out that she is fixing to have another baby, at way past forty and her two girls nearly grown. Didn't sound thrilled. Maybe she does need me. Do you think I'm too absolutely crazy to be of any use?

Which brings up the saddest point: this may be goodbye for us, my dearest, best bird. You can have no notion what your companionship has meant to me. It is not just the fish and rabbits and things that you have brought to keep me alive. It's not just that you've literally saved my life more ways than one. All that was certainly a blessing these last years. That and having something live, something wise and kind as you to talk to. Without you I think I might have lost the power of speech. Maybe the rest of my mind, too.

Now, whether or not I wish it—and I can't say whether truthfully I do or do not—a change is on the wind. If you come home one evening soon and find your window closed, please understand a rumpus is going on, and just go on back into the birch grove, and make your life where my heart will always be.

What I have to think of, from this moment, is what I'm going to say to humankind. How will I explain a lot of things? Down in Charleston I have two granddaughters that I do not know at all. And another baby coming. Folks in high society. What will they make of this old wraith? What on earth do I say to them?

By their lights, nothing but softening of the brain would bring someone back up here to live this way. And they don't know the half of it. Am I to tell them why? Am I to tell them what it was I did? Bird, I did a dreadful thing. I came here desperate, and I thought my heart would break for the love of what I found. And then I would not rest until I destroyed it.

And you want to hear the worst? I would do it again. Oh yes, oh yes, I would do it. God forgive my soul, but I don't think I could help it.

Now, how am I going to put this so those girls will not despise me? And it still be every bit the truth? Go on to sleep, beloved. I have to study about this. I have to think.

~2~

THE WILDERNESS

I SAW THIS PLACE FOR THE FIRST TIME WHEN I WAS NEARLY middle-aged. The reason why it took so long was a bitter pill to swallow: the bare idea that I might belong here just mortified my mother. What is so strange now is seeing the thing played out again, with my own child and her children. Which seems to be the way. Kind of like a mechanical fountain, same old water under the bridge, again and again.

My daddy was Ivan McAllister Steele, born here in this house, like all the Caney Valley Steeles except me. Like none of the others, my daddy left. All the same he loved this house. Talked to me about it while he rocked me on our piazza, watching ships go out to sea. Of course, even little, I wondered why he left so magical a place, or why he never took us and went home. But he would never say, directly.

My mother explained it for him once. "There is nothing there for anyone who has ambition and intelligence," she said. Her nose tilted up when she said things like that. My daddy just raised his eyebrows and smiled a little smile at me. He knew what he was dealing with, with Mama. She had no idea what she was dealing with, in him.

She called him "Mackey." I did too—it was probably the first word I ever said, and if it bothered him he never did let on. He was a quiet man. Big tall handsome man. He had an open, good-hearted sort of face, broad and strong at the chin, wise about the eyes. If something got his goat you hardly ever knew it; he kept his feelings—hard ones, especially—to himself. I suspect that bored my mother. He seemed to have another life inside his head that she would never get to; that's why she kept clawing and hammering away. Better she should hurt him, to her way of thinking, than to be shut out.

My father was an artist. He built sailing ships, in his Charleston dry docks. His office had windows that opened on the Cooper River, nearly at the sea. It smelt of leather and salt air and smoke; it had paintings on the walls of schooners with their big sails full of wind; and a model of a clipper in a five-gallon jug up on a stand. His desk was always covered up with diagrams of whatever the carpenters were working on. People came to him, fishermen and sportsmen and people dripping with money; they brought their dreams and watched them materialize, first on paper, from his pen, and then in wood, from the ribs out, in the yards.

How he chose to go that route he never told me. He went away from here to go to college. When he left here for the last time he went into the Navy. He must have been stationed at Charleston because somehow he got to know the owners of the yacht works. It was an old business, not tremendous in the way of the big ship-yards, but very particular, very respected. Eventually he ran it and was part owner. When he died, somebody took down the brass plate from his office door that said IVAN MCALLISTER STEELE, PRESIDENT, and gave it to Mama. It ended up in my little cedar box of very private things, with the rainbow-dyed hair ribbons and dried gardenia buds.

I know one thing was so: he had to be making money when he married Mama. He bought her a big house SOB, "south of Broad," the southern part of Charleston where the only poor folks were the ones that waited on the rich.

My mother's entire concept of the earth was SOB. No, that's not quite true—her parents left her the house on James Island where she was raised, but that didn't do much to broaden her perspective. Her father was a lawyer who never worked at it a lot; he spent thirty-two years in the state legislature.

My Charleston grandfather's name was Henry Seneca Twyning. I never knew him except by his portrait, ruddy and hook-nosed and stout and stern, in his gray waistcoat, with a whoosh of fine white hair making wings out from his temples. He was up in years when my mother was born; his first wife died childless when they were middle-aged, and he married an old maid, a German immigrant named Maria Hardmann, who had been his first wife's nurse.

I remember Grandma Twyning just a little bit. She had some wasting disease that made her look even older than she was; she sat on pillows in her chair with a shawl over her lap and had her hair braided and knotted up so tight it looked like agony, to me. Her face was thin and sharp, her eyes were dull blue and clouded under the hoods of papery-thin eyelids. She was like a fragile, sweet old bird. I am not sure she ever knew me.

My mother was Natalie Twyning, those two old people's only child, brought up by ancient aunts and nursemaids to be one of the belles of Charleston. She was a little spoiled. It would make her very mad when my father told somebody how he had met her—so it pleasured him to tell it, several times. Before he got married, Mackey lived at Miss Charnley's Residence Hotel. Miss Charnley had a butler named Campbell Hillhouse, a virtuous mortal if one ever drew breath, but out of Miss Charnley's reach he sure could pick the banjo. I need to say that whatever else my father did, what he did the best was fiddle. He and Camp Hillhouse made a friendship that lived as long as they did. In the evenings after supper, Camp retired to one black alley or another, where he was kin to people who played music. Mackey took to going with him.

One rainy night real late they were in a buggy coming home from one of these events, and they came upon a surrey that was down with a broken axle. There was a young couple in it, coming all dressed up from a fancy party. The gentleman didn't want to get wet and dirty so they had been sitting there for quite some time when Camp and Mackey stopped to help. Well the young man may be there yet, but the lady was annoyed and ready to go home. Camp was always skinny; he scrooched down on the footboard, at Mackey's feet, and gave the girl his seat. Mackey had his funny little fiddle case beside him, and she noticed.

My daddy teased her about it ever after; he would put on this high voice with dimples in it and say, "Oh, sir! You play the VIO-LIN!" Well, no, Mackey didn't "play the violin"—he was a fiddler. But that was lost on her.

"After a fashion," he said to her.

It was only the polite thing that when he had escorted her to her door and safely into the care of her mother, she invited him to a recital the next Saturday. She was going to sing. To refuse her anything at all would have been rude and cruel.

Seven weeks later, they were married in the Twynings' parlor. The bride was barely eighteen, round and blond and extremely pretty, with half a bloodline blue as indigo. The groom was well past thirty, a fine-looking man as silent as he was clearly solvent. But he was also from a family and a place on the dark edge of the universe, so far from SOB that if either his home or his family might be shown to actually exist, on a map somewhere, it would still be of no consequence at all.

These were my parents. The only thing they ever had in common was me. When I was born, a year after that wedding, Mama named me Mary Seneca, for her mother and daddy.

In one thing, my daddy had his way. Before he brought my mother into their new house, he sent for Camp Hillhouse and his wife, Mittie, to come live in the servants' quarters, on the alley. Aunt Mit began to wait on Mama and do the cooking. Uncle Camp actually ran the house and did everything else for us.

Secretly, Mackey and Uncle Camp played a game between them that I dearly loved. My mother went to lots of teas and meetings of the Daughters of the Confederacy and sang for something at the Episcopal Church every time the doors were opened. Mackey would drive her anywhere she wished to go, then find pressing business elsewhere until it was time to pick her up. The "business" was most always in our kitchen.

As soon as Mama was safely delivered, Camp would come trotting in the kitchen door with his banjo in a croaker sack and Mackey would get his "violin" and the stolen Culture Hour would get underway. Oh, it was wonderful. Camp wore a grin, the livelong time, flashing his gold tooth. Mackey's face would give off light like he was seeing Heaven. He wouldn't let Mit put me to bed till time to go get Mama. "It's the only chance she'll ever have," he said one time. There was something sad about the way he said it.

What we did, those nights, was dance. In a certain way. "Now pretend you and me are up at Caney Forks, and this is a Saturday night," he would say. And he would get Camp to pick "Bile Them Cabbage Down," and he would hold my hands in his, expecting me to follow. "Don't go braggin' this around the neighborhood," he'd say behind his hand. "And don't show it off to your mama."

She must have caught on about it; she at least suspected. Not long after I started to school, a woman came to town and set up a dancing studio. She called herself "Madame Alexandra." Mama sent me to her. The first day, Camp drove Aunt Mit and me over in the carriage. Mit went in with me. On the way back, after I had spent an hour with some other little girls squatting and waving my arms, one of us was as mystified as the other.

Mit sat with her mouth poked out and finally she said, "What kine a' dancin' do 'e be, when 'e ain' fuh make no noise?" We decided not to ask my mother that question, lest she ask us some. The last thing I ever wanted to do in all my life was to cause Mackey Steele any more trouble than I knew by instinct that he had already.

If it was not over one thing, it was over something else. One thing that drew brimstone from my mother was what he called "valley talk." It was the primary language of Big Caney; he spoke it comfortably to Camp, who talked so comfortably to him in Gullah. Each fully understood by the other. It was a language that probably would have slowly died, at our house, if "valley talk" had not come so easily to me.

Oh, my. She would catch us. One time, I must have been four or five, Mackey was helping me get ready to go to Sunday School. And I said to him, "I ain't a-goin' to wear them old white shoes that pinches."

Mama was standing in the door. She glared at him. "I had hoped," she said, "that my child would never have to KNOW that she is half po' buckra — much less show it." Mackey didn't swat her. Don't know why; he just looked bland and amused and went on pulling up my socks.

But she won. I never saw this valley or any of my father's "buckra" family until I had two children of my own. My mother never saw it. Her vision of it was enough: it was a foul, incestuous backwoods place, diseased and preyed upon by wolves and bears, landlocked and ignorant and so far from the crab-pots that no dinner could possibly be safe. Wilderness, dreadful, like in the Bible. A dwelling place of savages.

Mackey had a different idea of what was Wilderness.

IN THE EVENINGS he would hold me close to him, we would rock and watch the ships move up and down the channel, watch the gulls dipping for their supper, flocking and circling in the sundown light. What I loved the best was the stories he would tell. Sometimes he would need, I think, to tell about what all he had loved and left behind.

Big Caney River was something mystical to him. He was raised in the big woods up and down this river. I had never seen such woods as these; I had never seen a swift, clear river you could play in and not think of dark things lurking at the bottom. All of that was twice as wondrous to me. So were the people. He talked about his mother—it seemed to please him that I looked like her, even if Mama did call me "my little darkie" because I had black hair.

Mackey's father was a great fiddler; his name was Ben Ivan Steele. His mother's name was Daisy and she had a sister named Panama. With the accent in the middle. Pa-NAM-a. I thought that was funny. I thought it was funny about the old woman that climbed out on the roof and crowed to wake the roosters, every morning, and the little boy that sneaked out in his long nightgown at night to ride bareback on his daddy's fire-breathing dragon of a mare. Oh law, I envied that little boy; I envied the freedom and the daring.

Mackey sang to me a lot. Never when my mother would hear it; she was the real singer and would have had unpleasant things to say. She rarely ever sang to me herself because I was too little to appreciate it. But Mackey rocked and sang old songs. Valley songs. One of them kind of said it all. It went, "We'll stay a little while in the wilderness, in the wilderness, in the wilderness. We'll stay a little while in the wilderness. Then we'll be goin' home. . . ."

There was something in the tone of voice, a loneliness and isolation that said way more than the words. Our neighborhood there in Charleston, our stuccoed, porticoed house with its camellia garden and wisteria bower, all the traditional niceties and the restraints and intrigues, all the odd little feelings of separation, of being a fragment forever parted from the whole, that was my father's Wilderness.

In that Wilderness he died.

If there were things about Mackey that nobody knew, they didn't bother me. I didn't need to see his people or the place where he was raised; they were as real to me as Moses in the bulrushes or the Water Babies swimming. I knew them. I knew he missed them. There were times when he was so blue he was absolutely silent. That made Mama furious. I would hear her yelling at him, sometimes, when their door would be closed. She would go around days at a time all puffed up pouting and her eyes all red.

One time, I remember Mackey cried. I was maybe five years old. It was over a letter, I think it was from his mother. He came in from work and got it and went outside, out of Mama's sight, and sat on a bench under the wisteria and drooped his head down in his hands and sobbed. He stayed to himself a long time after that. He didn't even fiddle.

It was the spring after I turned nine that something really happened. He got a letter from Caney Forks, and Mama forgot to tell him. It lay on the secretary with a pile of social mail he'd never look at, till one day I was helping Aunt Mit dust and came across it. That other-worldly return address. When I showed it to him he looked real anxious and sat down and opened it at once. It being from that exotic shore, I hung over the arm of his chair and read it.

"Mack, I am at the end of my rope," it said. "There is nothing I wouldn't do to get us clear. But it looks like we are going to hell at a gallop. Give me advice, soon as you can, please Cousin. Panama sends love." It was signed "Devotedly, Ben Aaron."

Mackey closed his eyes and put his hand to his head and sat there with the letter in his hand. When Aunt Mit called us to supper, he said to go on without him. When he finally did come he didn't eat, he just sat there messing his dumplings around with his fork. That night I heard him and Mama talking. Or mainly I heard her. She was topping cotton.

"What do you think there would be in that place for ME?" She was yelling. "How can you be so selfish?" She commenced to wail.

"What kind of life would there be for that poor child? What kind of society? Every Saturday a dog fight? Cruel!" she shrieked. "CRUEL!"

Things were not right with Mackey the next day. Nor after. That was in April, 19-and-9. A couple of days after that put-to, Mama had some ladies in, and he and I went out for a walk. He hardly said a word. We walked along the Battery, holding hands, and I knew he didn't feel very well, he looked sort of gray. We came back while it was still light. And when we got to the house, he couldn't get up the steps. He sat down and leaned his head back against a pillar, and closed his eyes. "I've got the headache, Mary Sen," he said. "Go get Mit to give you the camphor."

Well, I went back to the kitchen and told Mit, and she got the camphor bottle down and came with me, fast as we could go. When we got out there she put the camphor under his nose, and then he just slumped forward. He sighed a huge sigh and I grabbed at him, and Mit went screaming around the house after Camp, he was hoeing in the back, in the flowers, and he came running, with the hoe in his hand, and Mama came running, with the ladies hurrying behind her, holding up their skirts.

And Mackey was fallen over, on the step, with his head down, and my arms around him, and he was dead. I remember clinging onto him, and somebody, I guess it was Camp, pulling me away. I remember the horror of my hands being pulled away from him. It was like, if I let go of him, he's gone.

I remember Mama lying across the bed, then, with her face down, choking with sobs, beating her head against the mattress, and the doctor sitting by her telling her over and over that apoplexy was nobody's fault. "An act of God," he said, "an act of God . . ." And the ladies sitting around the room stiff as pokers, and their faces sad and helpless, some of them wet with tears.

The rector came, in his black suit and white collar, and assured Mama that it was not her sin that had cost us Mackey; it was indeed an accident of nature, though the thought was hinted at that Mackey had been a rare communicant and incurably Presbyterian.

All of Charleston came, it seemed. People would squeeze me, and their tears fell on me, but I shed none at all. My eyes were so dry they were gritty. I couldn't blink. My nose bled all that night, down the front of my white apron. I had a big smear where I rubbed it on my sleeve.

I remember somebody saying, "Hadn't we better notify his people?" But Mama wasn't hearing anything. "What was that little town he came from?" somebody said. They talked around and nobody could remember. And I couldn't speak a whisper.

I remember the casket sitting in the parlor, and there were flowers all over, and people sitting up all night. And we were getting ready to go to the church, for the funeral. Aunt Mit put a white dress on me with a white organdie pinafore, and I was out in the yard, wandering around, when the undertaker drove up with the hearse and a team of black horses. I had picked up a butterfly wing out of the grass. I had seen it glistening blue, in the sun, it was something precious, and I put it in my pocket and went into the house. The grown people were standing around talking. So I went and stood on my tiptoes and leaned over Mackey. I curled his hair around my fingers, I never forgot how it felt stiff, and I slipped that butterfly wing under his hands, on his chest, before they got me away and closed the lid.

One night that next summer, in a hotel in Paris, I had a horrible nightmare that Mackey had died, and I woke up screaming. Mama got up, she was real puzzled, but she held me all that night, and let me cry.

Being a widow of fair means, Mama was not exactly doomed to sorrow her life away ragged and hungry, or lonely. There she was at twenty-eight, surrounded by the world of the living. A three-hanky funeral, a week of heart-rending mourning and that was about all she was good for. Mackey had been buried six miserable days when she blew her nose with finality, plastered her eyes with sliced cucumbers to cool away the red, arose and had Mit do up her hair, and in resplendent weeds, commanded Camp to drive her to the steamship ticket office.

Almost overnight she and Mit put wardrobes together and packed new trunks bought in a frantic round of shopping. She and I sailed first for New York and then for Europe. We spent the rest of that spring and all that summer in Italy and Germany and France. Mainly we spent it in opera houses, watching large ladies sing themselves to death. Sometimes I would go to sleep before the mortal cough and thud.

But it was not all bad; in Paris I saw where Madame Alexandra had sort of got her idea. Pavlova and Karsavina and Nijinsky were there, dancing with the Diaghilev company. We saw them dance in *Les Sylphides.* I kept that program under my pillow, and then in my suitcase, till I could get it home to the little cedar chest of special things. It was like, ever after, I shared some wondrous secret with those wispy, floating ladies in their painted moonlit woods. I just couldn't quite figure what it was.

We went home to spend an empty winter, then, in Charleston. Bleak. I remember mercifully little about it. Dutifully, Mama still wore black dresses all the time. They were real cunning, with bodices that fitted like skin. Paris black dresses.

We were not far enough away from the churchyard that I couldn't go down there in the afternoons after school, and sit on the bricks around Mackey's grave, and watch the beards of moss wave in what I decided was the breath of God. Aunt Mit would make up her mouth and shake her head about that. She'd frown and say, "Miss Nat, ol' Plat-Eye gwine git dat chile, hangin' round all dem dead peoples." Ol' Plat-Eye carried off bad and reckless children regularly; they were always from the other side of town, though; nobody whose name would ring a bell.

And Mama would say, not real concerned, "Stay 'way from down there, Mary Sen, it'll make you have bad dreams."

I did have dreams. That winter I had one, over and over. It didn't seem to mean anything at all; it certainly wasn't bad, it was so beautiful I hated to wake up. It was about someplace I was sure I had never been, and it was like I was with somebody, it seemed like it was Mackey, only that was kind of vague. And it was real early morning, and there were mountains on both sides of us, and ahead of us, and it was misty, and the sun was just up and the air sort of shimmered. We were going down the road, into the sunrise, into the morning. Just two ruts, the road was, and there were flowers blooming in the middle and in the fields on either side. You could smell the cool and the fresh. But it was perfectly quiet. There was no sound in this dream. And it was terribly real. It was like I would be there a while, even after I was awake. But I didn't tell anybody; there was nothing to tell. I mean, nothing happened.

There was another dream like that a while later. It was happy, too. All it was—and I could see it exactly, when I closed my eyes in the daytime—it was a man that might have been Mackey, only somehow I didn't think so. This was a big tall man and he had on a red checkidy flannel shirt, and he was sitting on a barrel, in this big old rough boarded up-and-down room, playing the fiddle. Only you couldn't hear this either; it was a silent picture. And I didn't know why it was anything so joyful, but it was.

Well, it was a couple of years later, it was the winter I stayed in the boarding school in Paris that I had the bad dream. It had nothing to do with ol' Plat-Eye or the graveyard. It was somewhere I hadn't been, either. It was in a piney woods. A dreary kind of place. There was not any railroad track there but I could hear the engine coming, coming right toward me, going *chug-chug-chug* and I couldn't move. And I could see it then, coming. It was horrible. And all of a sudden fire shot out of it, and the thing rolled over, and there was one man on the ground burning. And there was one hanging in a tree. Years and years after that I could see him dangling in that tree.

Well, I woke up absolutely terrified, it was so much worse than it sounds. And there was nobody to tell. I had to lie there till morning, stiff as a board. When it got light I knew the cooks would be up so I crept down to the kitchen; I didn't know how to tell them I was afraid of a bad dream, but I did know how to say I didn't feel good. So they let me sit on a stool in the corner, they thought I was homesick, and I sat there all that day. It scared me for a long, long time. It was too real. Until many years later when I learned what it meant— and then only partly—I had to pray and take deep breaths before I could get near a train. Piney woods were pure terror, and the sound of a steam engine puffing would set me to shivering. I only tell you these things because of some other odd things that would happen later—when the other shoe would drop.

That first winter back in our house without Mackey was a lesson in how lonely a child could be. Children in books had families. They had grannies and all that. Even poor little Grandma Twyning had faded and gone, the summer before Mackey died.

Well, I had Mit and Camp. They were love and law and comfort. I will say, too, that Mama got to be a little bit more interested, if not real motherly. I know now that she was terribly lonely, too. Especially back in that house. We did have all the things we saw that summer, though, to talk about for a long time after. And some things we didn't talk about at all.

I remember when a year or so had gone by I asked her if we would ever get to see Mackey's folks. She was sitting doing up her hair, and she looked very thoughtful, in the mirror. "I don't know them," she said. "I think they probably felt they weren't our kind." I felt very timid about this, somehow, but I finally asked her if they ever knew that Mackey had died.

"I wrote them but they didn't come," she said. "Here—I hear the veg'table man. Run see if he's got some nice fresh peaches. We'll have Aunt Mittie make a pie."

I do know—and this was years after Mackey died—one day Mama got a letter from Caney Forks. I got the mail that day and took it to her, just jumping up and down to know what was in it. "Just business," she said. I fought the devil all that day to keep from sneaking it off her dresser. But righteousness prevailed. When I tipped in to get it she had hidden it, or thrown it away.

Just a little while after that we went off to Europe again anyway. That was the time we stayed a year and a half, and I went to the boarding school. Mama had made up her mind she was going to be a great, celebrated singer. She set out to find a teacher who could work that miracle, and somebody she met in Paris told her about one who was right then in Bayreuth, coaching a Wagnerian soprano.

We went to Bayreuth. Oh, my. So many hours a day we sat there being entertained by those big ladies trumpeting from the mountaintops and rattling their spears. Mama had bought this book that had all the goings-on in English. Before we would go to the opera house we would lie on the bed at the hotel and read the day's installment. Wagner moved a lot faster toward certain doom in print than he did on the stage. But you know, it was fascinating. All those mixed-up kinpeople; it was much worse than Charleston, brother and sister falling in love and the baby coming, and Brunnhilde marrying her own nephew. There was something about it, though. Something grander than life. I felt such a huge, ecstatic sorrow—does that sound right?—when their world burned down, even though they were such a mess.

Mama was thrilled she had got herself in with the singing teacher. His name was August Rehnwissel. He was a little wooden soldier with gray hair that stood up like the bristles on a brush and he had a little pointed gray goatee. He was a wizard. Right off I could tell that. In his presence, for a little while, my mother was quiet and real humble.

But then one morning he came up to our rooms. I was in the bedroom brushing my hair and I heard him singing to Mama, "Guten Morgen, schöne Müllerin. . . ." He sang on and on, about her little blond head, and blue eyes like flowers, like morning stars. (That is what Mama said it was later, sighing.) His voice was sort of crackly; he was not young. But something about him was terribly touching. It was exquisite. Such was the whole life and substance of Dr. Rehnwissel. Early in September, Mama married him.

They would move around; he worked with singers who were like butterflies, lighting in one city and then another. So I went to the boarding school and when they would be in Paris, I would see them. There were several English girls at the school; it was not like I would be in total isolation until I learned a little French, Mama said. "Spend your time on cultivated things," she said. "When you marry a rich man some day you will want him to be proud of you." Mama's aspiration for me, from my very birth, was that I grow up worthy of "the best catch in Charleston," whoever that privileged fellow turned out to be. It never looked like all that broad (or wonderful) a field, to me. I hardly think it ever occurred to her that when this prize was hooked I might have to support him. But, time would tell.

Another thing was, being immersed in cultivated things didn't necessarily mean one would absorb much. There were so many things not to be good at. Like painting, and needlework, and "expression." Oh, that was awful. There was one good thing, and that was going to dancing class; I worked it out with the teacher that I could go every morning. "You are utterly daft," one of my English friends said. I reckon it did seem odd.

It was this elderly, really ancient Russian lady that taught us. Madame Wolinskaya. She had regular satchels under her eyes and a long crooked nose. She was ear-to-ear wrinkles and she never cracked a smile. And she held her head back and made a long neck.

It was the same thing in there every single day. The piano player looked like a mummy. Some people said he was wound up with a key. He played the same thing, the same way, every class. He never read from music and he never took his eyes off us and he never changed his expressionless expression. He and Madame never spoke to each other. Nobody spoke to anybody. She would only croak out orders, and beat on the floor with her stick and he would commence to play and sometimes with no comment at all she would swat one of us about the legs. When the hour was up we bowed to her and cleared out fast.

But there was a kind of perfect, higher order in it. Some security. On the last day, when we were leaving to come home, I ran after Madame and threw my arms around her and cried on her neck. I was never so surprised in my life as when she kissed me goodbye, and her wrinkles were full of tears.

The Turks and the Serbs and the Bulgarians and a bunch of other people were at each other's throats and in Paris and Vienna and Milan people were talking and worrying about it. Even people like Mama and Dr. Rehnwissel. It distressed him because Germany was wearing its horns and clacking its spears, and when he would be safely in Paris he would wag his finger and expound. "Der Kaiser, der Kaiser! He vants only de verrlt, tank you. Hang der Kaiser, und ve have peace." The wisest thing Mama ever did was to get homesick for Charleston in the fall of 1913.

Our homecoming caused some social ripples. We were not unpacked when Mama put on her first Saturday afternoon musicale in the parlor, to show off the trophy from her European hunt to the artier lions of Charleston. She reveled in the flood of invitations. She would have dragged the poor man to a rooster fight if anybody there would have admired him. She called him coyly, "the Doctor."

"The Doctor" was not a social creature. He was a refugee. He went along with her in a disoriented daze. Behind the blank look in his eyes lay the catalogue of Brahms lieder, detailed to every breath-mark, every whoop of the Valkyries and all Isolde's moans and sighs. In his heart he had stored every measure, every nuance of the full gospel of his great god Schubert.

There he sat, politely, probably thinking of kraut and dumplings, while a lady of "The Muses Club" laboriously rendered a piano selection called "Ben Hur's Chariot Race," and another sang "The Palms." There was a buxom matron—I can see her now but I can't bring back her name—who treated him to a dramatic recitation called "Oh, Dat Watermillion" at one soiree, and again at the next, by popular request. Though not his.

Upon these pagan altars he refused to lay any but the brass among his treasures. At the musicales he would play for Mama to sing Strauss waltzes ill-fitted up with words, and stuff from Lehar operettas. It satisfied them both. She loved them; he despised them. The guests applauded. When the house was empty, he would shut the French doors of the parlor and soothe his wounds with the salve of Schubert.

Inevitably, starting with several other ladies of the Episcopal choir, pupils presented themselves. He would get exasperated with them sometimes, but I never knew the man to be really unkind. Not in English. I am not as 'shamed as I ought to be to say that I got to where I could mimic these lessons admirably, only at low volume, in the safety of the kitchen. I could make the proper tremulous tones by holding the table and jiggling my leg, and interrupt that artistry with explosions of "Himmel, fummon! Breet! Breet! Mit der belly breet!" Aunt Mit tried to keep a respectful face. "Dat ol' man, he gwine ketch you," she would say. But Camp would laugh himself double, till the tears would flow.

Sometimes for the Doctor's salvation we would spend a season in New York. That would brighten him. One thing that plagued him, he was arthritic and his fingers hurt.

In one of the real old houses in our neighborhood there was a family that Mama had always known. Their name was Lamb. Actually, the man of that house, Mr. Hubert Pettigrew Lamb, Senior, was absent and presumed deceased. By some. Stamped clearly on my mind was the day he turned up missing. I remember

Miss Lilah, his wife, laid back on the settee in our sun room, with her arms flung out and her eyes rolled back, just prostrated. Somebody had seen Mr. Lamb, who was a cotton broker, walking toward his office that morning, with his valise. And strangely, and suddenly, he had turned and started running for the railroad, just as a slow-moving freight hit the crossing. No, he was not ground to pieces by the wheels. The witness reluctantly reported that Mr. Lamb had saved himself by grabbing hold of the ladder, on the side of a car, and swinging on, with his free hand. His hat had blown off, in that act of desperation, and was returned to the "widow."

"Snatched away! Just snatched away," Miss Lilah lamented. "Criminals have got him in they clutches, right this minute. Po' Mister Lamb. . . ."

Courageous Mr. Lamb, Mackey said, when Mama and Camp had seen Miss Lilah sadly home. Mackey detested Miss Lilah. He called her "harmless as a serpent and wise as a dove." It must be noted, but behind one's hand and only once, that Miss Lilah had "married up." As dressmaker to the ladies Lamb, she was often in that household, when Mr. Lamb was young and easily misled. The advent of Louise, who turned out to be a blue-blood, clearly, when her mother, clearly, was not, confirmed that matrimony by coercion had probably been justified.

But, then, Mama's uncle had been married to Mr. Hubert Pettigrew Lamb's half-sister Margaret. So we were connected. And whether we cared much for Miss Lilah or no, she and her issue were due some loyalty.

Her issue were two. The baby was about two years older than I was; he was named Hubert Pettigrew Lamb for his father, but outside the sanctity of his home he was generally known as Foots. That was one of the sidelights of everybody in a family being named the same thing; it didn't matter what your name was, you probably weren't ever called that anyway. Foots was Foots; it was just his lot. But I remember a mammy was still pushing him in a baby carriage when I was walking to the candy store all by myself. Miss Lilah didn't want him to have to walk. I remember my father saying, with her very same expression, "Him little foots mus' nevah touch de groun'."

I guess Foots was about seven or eight when his father crossed the bar, so to speak. His sister Louise was nine years older. Louise was my friend. She was very thin, she had dark reddish hair that curled but she pulled it back tight into a bun, on the back of her neck, and she had great, beautiful gray sad eyes.

Louise played the piano extremely well. Never in public; she rarely ever went out in public, and when she did, she slipped around as quietly as a shadow. Miss Lilah cautioned her constantly about her heart. Like, "You know Louise you cain' nevah tell when yo' heart will make you faint."

Louise was an epileptic. That was a disgrace.

Well, she was in her mid-twenties when Dr. Rehnwissel came on the scene, and timid as she was, they got to be great friends. In a little while he had her playing accompaniments for his pupils, to spare his crippled hands. He suggested then she take some piano students on her own. He also suggested that she teach them in our parlor, after he had made the curious observation that she never had a spell anywhere but at home. So she did, she took just two or three students.

I liked having her in the house more. She was eleven years older, but she was closer than any friend I had that was my own age. She just seemed so wise. I told her all kinds of things I would never have thought of telling Mama. Things like about being in love.

There was this boy named Siggie Bonenblume. Siggie had eyes like melted chocolate. His parents owned the biggest dry-goods store in Charleston. He played the violin. Oh, so soulfully he played the violin. We would meet each other at the ice cream parlor, and we went for walks along the Battery. We had long talks about life. When we were about seventeen we began to plan our great adventure. We would go to New York. He would go to a better music teacher than Miss Rothbard, who played with her eyes squinted and her tongue out the side of her mouth. And I would go to dancing class every day. Mostly though, we would just go to New York and get married. We were out walking one day when we decided that. Once it was agreed to, he led me behind some myrtle bushes and kissed me. It left us panting, and right sweaty.

Aunt Mit watched things happen and took the matter to Mama.

"Miss Nat, dat chile be talkin' to dat boy. He dis won' DO, Miss Nat. Dem peoples dey don' believe dat Jesus Christ is riz."

Well, Siggie did play the violin, and it was a good bet, in Mama's calculating mind, that he would never be poor. Her moral stance in favor of the Resurrection was pretty weak. "It might be better if you would not get serious," she told me, discharging her Christian duty.

Nothing was going to stop us. We walked into the store one day, hand in hand, to announce our intentions to Siggie's mother. She was sitting on a stool behind the counter, putting down figures in a ledger. When she looked up and saw us, through her big thick glasses, her eyes looked like cold water under ice. "Mama . . ." Siggie said. She never said a word. She just looked. He never said another.

Siggie's mother wanted him to be a doctor.

When I went to the ice cream parlor the next afternoon Siggie did not meet me. I got very embarrassed standing in the doorway, waiting, trying not to look abandoned. Then I went home and sat on the steps and watched for him to come along on his bicycle. It was drizzling rain when Louise came. I told her I was watching the gulls. But something they were doing was making tears in my eyes, and she sat down beside me, with her parasol over us, and finally I tried to tell her, and she put her arm around me, and dried my face with her handkerchief.

"He was not the right one," she said, making it so simple. "When the right one comes nothing will keep you apart." Louise herself, I knew, must be waiting for the right one. Nobody yet had discovered how beautiful she was, locked up in her problems. Maybe nobody ever would. She took me to the picture show that night to see Charlie Chaplin.

But I did not feel good for months. My stomach hurt. I had sore throats. It was not all love-sickness; it was the times. That spring and summer we went to war with Germany. Boys I had known always were going to the Army. Our house was depressed.

Dr. Rehnwissel wore his own sorrow like a shroud. He was cut off from the lifeline of his intimates at home, and not being the most reasonable man in the universe he could see no end to it. Besides, it was not the most popular thing, right then, to be a German national in Charleston. Tacky people, who could not separate politics from art, would ask him point blank where his sympathies lay. Mama hung a big American flag on the front porch but at Halloween some bad ugly boys egged the house, anyway. The Doctor refused to be consoled that they had egged some other people's, too.

Those things hurt him. One thing made him furious. Some of the ladies held a charity tea at our house, one day, and one of his pupils, Annie Sloan, the bank president's daughter, was going to sing. She picked two songs by Schubert. The doctor played for her. She sang in German, sort of a reckless thing to do. After the first one, when the polite clapping had died down, one old biddy turned to another and in a voice like a goose honking she said, "You'd think since he's a guest in ouah country he'd have mo' respect." Well, there was this stricken silence. And then the Doctor rose, bowed low, and said to the singer, "Annie, for this lady now you sing 'Old Black Joe.'" And he sat down and with thunderous ripples and flourishes he rendered an introduction. Annie stood there a minute and turned and fled, just mortified.

Oftener and oftener, we would hear him singing, himself, in the shut-off haven of the music room. He had a favorite hopelessness song; it was Schubert's "Trockne Blumen." Dead flowers. He could put more splendid tragedy into the last line of that song than in all the rest of his repertoire. "Der Mai ist kommen, der Winter ist aus." He sang it rasping and crackling and booming. He sang it for a lie. May was not coming. Winter was forever. Louise and I picked it up between us. In the pits, we would cry out to one another, "Der Mai ist kommen. . . ."

Louise knew the pits real well. She lived there. Her brother Foots — Hubert — had the Army breathing down his neck. Miss Lilah was hysterical. It was real strange — here she was so ashamed of Louise having epilepsy, and yet I do believe she'd have sworn Foots had syphilis if it would have kept him home. She couldn't palm him off as her sole support because he'd never worked. She thought about sending him into the ministry, as an emergency measure. But no divinity school would have ever believed he was sincere. Amid the weeping and wailing, Foots had to go. Not far, just down a little way in the swamps, to a training camp. Onto those little foots that had never (or rarely) touched the ground they put some old rough army boots. Foots was always very particular about his food; he wouldn't eat this and that. He liked pretty things; he had his mother's habit of turning a piece of china over, at somebody else's house, to see who had made it. Now there he was standing in line to dip his mush out of the pot, into his tin plate, like common people. He wrote his mother about the leaky tent and the mucky cot he slept in, and the coarse harshness of the people in charge. He had been assigned the duty, with some others, of digging privy pits. Miss Lilah would bring his letters to read to Mama. Miss Lilah was almost prostrated with grief.

I was generally feeling sorry, at that time. I was sorry for Dr. Rehnwissel. And Louise. I think mainly I was being sorry for me, about being rejected by the whole world (which was one boy); just so alone. I was even right sorry for Foots. Foots couldn't help the way he was. He was not an unattractive person. I mean in his looks. He was dark and thin and sort of angular. His features were sharp; he had been so little in the sun his skin was milky pallid, set off all the more by his black curls and deep-set black eyes. He was very vain about his clothes. Louise and his mother could be downright dowdy, but never Foots—a tailor sewed for him. In his pettedness, Foots was almost pretty. Only always it seemed like he held his mouth in a twist of shrewish discontent. It was strange. Somehow his perpetual dissatisfaction made it a challenge to please him.

Oh, that I might never have known the effect a mosquito could have on my life. But, about six weeks after he was shanghaied away to camp, a mosquito bit Foots. Or apparently it did. Anyway he started having fevers. He shook and shivered until the Army despaired of a cure and sent him home. He had earned in that brief career—or at least he had been paid—the sum of thirty dollars and nine cents per month. Having contributed thus to home and country, he could in all good conscience retire, and devote himself to not recovering from his illness.

When he was settled back into his room at home, his mother gave herself to attending the fallen hero until she herself collapsed. The household fell then upon Louise. They had help only irregularly, as it was circulated around the colored town that Miss Lilah was neglectful of settling her accounts. So I went sometimes to help Louise.

She had another helper when it came to taking care of her brother. Foots had a long-time friend named Denby Turnham who was very devoted. They were logically matched; whereas Foots could be volatile, when crossed, particularly since the fevers, Denby was soft-spoken and serene. He played the organ at the Episcopal Church. In this hour of need he sat long evenings, reading to the patient or mopping his brow.

And sometimes it fell to me to feed poor Foots, or to fetch for him. We had some amusing conversations; he disliked a great number of people and could talk about them wickedly. To be liked by Hubert Pettigrew Lamb was such an achievement as to be an ostrich feather in one's cap. We had known each other always, of course, but had not spent such intimate times together. He seemed to be making a genuine effort to be nice.

Only coincidentally, I noticed that the lifestyle in that household was in most ways terribly austere. The sheets were patched and fragile. Louise wouldn't let me help her with the laundry; she hung it in the attic, and once when I went up looking for a towel there were a few shreds of female underwear hanging on the line, just tatters. Every scrap of food in that house was managed like it was gold.

And also coincidentally, my father had set things up so that when I turned eighteen I would begin drawing income from his estate, on my own. The stock he owned in the shipyard had done very well, during the war. None of that was a deep dark secret from our friends.

I can't reconstruct what happened, exactly. I couldn't have said what was going on, quite, at the time. I just know one day Louise and her mother were both sick to death with the flu, it was a terrible winter for the flu that year, and I was too low for a germ to come near me, so I had fixed them all some soup. And I took Foots his, and he looked so forlorn, with nobody to cater to him, and I sat down by him, in a chair by his bed. And he told me all about how awful it had been in the swamp, about the frightful corns his boots had made, and the shovel-blisters on his hands that got infected. And about how horrible it was to be night and day with men so crass and common. I had never known anyone crass or common; the experience did sound tragic.

And I was moved to share the story of my own recent sorrow, of love and disappointment and rejection. There was no future for me, I said. No, and none for him, either, he said. He was troubled for his mother and his dear, afflicted sister. Now that he was incapacitated, what would become of them? And we sighed, and with a faint flutter he reached out his thin pale sensitive hand, and our futureless prospects were welded.

Late that winter I married Foots. Friends our age were dying in the war; neighbors were dying of the flu. Propriety spared us the horror of a big flashy wedding. I remember standing in front of the preacher, in the archway between the parlor and the music room, answering what I had to answer, and all the while I was thinking right there in that corner is where they had put Mackey's casket. It was like I could see it; it distracted me. Maybe it was all the flowers that reminded me. All the somber people. Louise stood up with me; I could hear her valiantly trying not to cry out loud. Denby Turnham stood up with Foots and cried out loud. But then Denby cried at baptisms and installations of the vestry. Miss Lilah sniffed dutifully into her hanky. My mother did not cry at all; she had fretted in suspicion that Hubert was not solvent. But then, there was no bluer blood in Charleston than came down through the departed Mr. Pettigrew Lamb.

I would have a good name at last. A very good name.

My mother owned that nice house on James Island that had come from her family. She and Dr. Rehnwissel moved into it and let us have the house where I grew up. We didn't live in it alone, of course. The week we came back from Palm Beach the creditors moved in on Miss Lilah, discreetly, and the old Lamb place became the property of the Bank of Charleston.

I didn't know much about what to expect out of being married so I didn't expect much. So for a while we got along fairly well. There did seem to be a good many things Foots needed; he went right away to the tailor's and had him make some new silk shirts and summer suits. He had never had a car and it occurred to him that he needed one. A friend of their family died; Foots paid a duty call upon the widow and bought himself the old man's Cadillac. Camp had to teach him to drive the thing; the happiest I ever saw him, though, was when he would sit in the back and have Camp drive him places.

He mostly spent his days at the Bon Homme Club, smoking and talking big money and playing cards. He spent a lot of evenings at Denby's. We did go to a good many parties; he was a good dancer, and the ladies found him droll and entertaining, especially the ones who didn't know him well. At home he tended to be restless; boredom was his hobby. He was not a reader; no interest much consumed him, except gossip. He spent a good bit of his time, I found, studying the mirror, polishing expressions of aloofness and shrewdness and disdain, pulling in the waist seams of his jacket and sucking in his cheeks.

As for our private encounters, they were not particularly rewarding. Not to either party, I am sure. And not terribly private, either; Miss Lilah had assigned herself the next room so she could appear in an instant, should Foots be "stricken." Appear she would, often, and with no warning. "I-o-wa thought I heard Hubut mekkin' a noise," she would say.

"He was snorin'," I would say, as was generally the case. Come to think of it, he was oddly free of "fevers" for the first few weeks. He was the picture of health until one morning I got out of bed feeling horrible, myself, like I had swallowed a bug in my sleep. I didn't get to the bathroom till I'd thrown up in the floor. Foots raved, he was so disgusted. His mother came gallumping in and stepped in the mess and howled. "Louweeeese! Louweeeeeeese! Call fo' de doctoah! Hubut's lost his stomach!"

About a week of awful mornings later I went to the doctor, privately, and found out what was the matter. I had to go home and tell it, but I couldn't believe it. Neither could Miss Lilah. "I don't believe Hubut could . . ." she commenced, in shock. But he was sitting there and she thought better of it. Foots caught it and smiled wickedly. "Oh, no, it couldn't be mine," he said. Louise was absolutely stricken.

"Oh, my poor little sister," she said, gathering me into her arms.

I was not anticipating a joyous experience. So I was not disappointed. Very shortly Foots woke me up one night, he was mumbling and thrashing around in the bed, wrestling the covers and kicking left and right. I raised up and put my hand on his head. And he flailed out and back-handed me in the eye. Well, 'course I yelled, and here comes his mama. "It's his fevah! It's his fevah!" she was hollering. "Get a col' rag fo' his head!" He felt cool as a mullet to me. But he muttered and thrashed and I went and got two cold rags— one for his head, and one for mine, and sat in a chair the rest of the night.

When I went downstairs the next morning Mit threw up her hands and yelled, "No, Jesus!" It was an accident, I said. But I don't think we were either one convinced. At dinnertime that day, Louise was sitting across the table, having to look at me, trying to make pleasant talk. All of a sudden she excused herself, weakly. She made it into the hall before she fell; it was the first seizure she'd had, when I was with her. That afternoon the florist's boy brought a box of red roses, with a card, "To my dear wife, from your loving Hubert." It looked a lot like Miss Lilah's handwriting. In a few days I got the bill.

All that excitement was over the first two-week black eye I ever had. It sure was not the last one. Any little frustration, like being out of fresh towels or good port, could work Foots into a "fevah." When he would have an "attact," as his mother would say, he would be all elbows, knees and fists and heels. When I got tired of looking like a spotted dog, I took to sleeping in the room with Louise.

All that is surely of no consequence now; it's just a blur, all the years I lived with him I remember very little, in this stage of my existence. Only a few incidents come back; they are like sharp rocks sticking out of a peaceful fog. I guess predictably the worst were over money, and the children.

Pet, our little girl, was born right after Christmas that first year. We named her Natalie Pettigrew; we had such a time with that birthing that we were pretty sure there would be no little boys to be named Pettigrew later. She was a pretty little baby, as newborn babies go; right from birth she was the image of my mother, except her eyes were muddy, and we figured they'd be dark. Her father was real proud of her, when we first brought her home. While I still stayed mostly in the bed he would trot her out and show her off to all the people that came calling. It really pleased me to the heart; it was like we really were a family.

And then one night when the baby was about three weeks old she had the colic, I guess; anyway she cried. And cried. We had all walked the floor, even Miss Lilah had held her and patted, and put her down, thinking she was asleep. We had no sooner all dozed off than she set up a howl again. And Foots jumped up and grabbed her, out of her basket, and threw her at me. Threw her like a football, halfway across the room. "Get this brat out of here," he yelled. "I've got to have my sleep."

Well, by God's grace I caught her. I was too astonished not to. One thing I will say, it shut her up; her eyes were big as saucers. And I sure did get her out. We fled to Louise's room and finished out the night, and in the morning I gathered up some necessities and moved us over to Mama's. In that instant I had learned to be afraid of him, in a way I'd never dreamed of.

Oh, yes, I told my mother. And we considered all kinds of things. But to make my options clear (and her attitudes), you have to know that the state had no divorce law. If you wanted a divorce you just endured. If you had to have a divorce you went to Georgia and set up residence. And if you came back home you took the consequences. In Charleston society there was hardly a divorce that was not scarlet. You simply didn't tell that your husband beat you black and blue and nearly killed your baby. You found some way to go along and keep the surface smooth.

The prudent thing to do was simply stay away. We stayed with my mother most of the time until Pet was walking. Of course Mit and Camp had gone with us, and things were rough back at the house in town. Inevitably, one day when the spring gardens were all blooming here comes Foots, driving up to take his "precious little family" home. He was taking some new medicine, he said. And had I not promised to love him in sickness and in health? How wretched a man was he, he lamented, to have such an illness that had so turned his loved ones against him.

I packed up all my misgivings and took them back with me, to the mainland. But things went on fairly calm for a while; we had Denby with us for several weeks after lightning came down the chimney of his house and set the place on fire. Denby was a pacifying influence; he was a good audience to Foots' bitchy observations, a bland companion who de-fused his boredom. Besides Denby was good help around the house. He was a fussy cook and splendid with cut flowers. I felt real let down when his house was fixed and he left us.

The buffer was gone. I felt worse when I had to go to the doctor again. That time I told nobody until the fact was obvious. Miss Lilah was incensed. She glared at my waist one day and rammed out her jaw and said, "Don' tell me you ah goin' to burden my boy wid anothah baby. I-o-wa can tell you he don' need mo' responsibility in his condition."

It was the night of Valentine's Day when that baby came. It was real chilly; Mit was sick in the bed and Louise and I had gone out to her house with some supper and were coming back through the yard when I had the first hard pain. Foots had been mad at me for something, I don't remember what. When we got to the house he had locked all the doors. We hollered and banged; we could hear Pet trying to turn the knob, inside, but she was too little, and she started crying. Finally Louise went to a neighbor's and lied that our phone was out of order, and called the doctor, and then we got Camp to take me to the hospital. "If Hubert doesn't let me in to take care of that child I shall call the police," Louise said.

The baby was a little boy. I named him Hugh McAllister. His hair would always be black as ink and his eyes a bright, deep blue.

Most of their young lives, even after they went to school, the children lived with my mother. I might have to keep up appearances. But I wouldn't have them suffer for the error I had made. Mama was a goodnatured, off-hand kind of granny; actually she had money and help and wasn't too much bothered except when she chose.

On our side of the inlet, we had problems. We were not rich people, at all, but that was never understood by some. I found myself going to the lawyer's for advances from Mackey's money until there was hardly anything to advance. I also found myself extremely grateful that our house was still in Mama's name, so Foots couldn't go and borrow on it. Foots was a gentleman, you see, and gentlemen were due their funds, from some celestial source. He never hit a lick at a snake.

In time I found we were in straits. There were not many things a lady could do in Charleston that made money. I didn't know how to run a tea room or a millinery. I wasn't equipped to teach school.

Louise had her piano students; that helped to buy the groceries. And then something occurred to me: I thought about Madame Alexandra's creaky limbs and fakey French and hennaed corkscrew curls. "Old lady," I thought, "I'm about to beat your time." Genteelly as I could I put out the word that I was taking dancing pupils.

Afternoons and Saturdays they came to the sun room, swinging their little bandboxes. They came from miles around. Some came from out of town. We got along; it blessed my mind more than my pocketbook. It embarrassed the life out of me at first to take their money, but I got used to it. Nothing was going to keep us out of debt, as long as Foots could sign his name. But at least I was doing something active to help.

Aunt Mit and Uncle Camp worked mostly at my mother's since she had the children. I couldn't pay them. Camp insisted still on keeping up the yard. Mit would march her bulk right in and take over, anyway, if I needed her badly and she knew it. But mostly Louise and I kept house. You know, ladies never washed, in Charleston. So we rubbed out our wash at night and dried it in the attic.

The winter Pet was ten years old, Dr. Rehnwissel's sister wrote from Germany that she was very frail and poorly and begged him to come home. Mama was all for it; they had not seen Europe since before the war. They made haste to get themselves together and shortly they were gone. Then Pet and Hugh were with us all the time.

All things began to close in on me, right then. I could not make enough money. My mother had been paying the dentist and the shoe store and the tuition at the Latin School. She had no concept of my plight; I hadn't quite told her. I had held onto stock that was paying dividends. I would have to sell it.

I was coming back from the broker's with the money, when Foots came driving up in a nearly new Auburn Phaeton, 1928. "Is this not the most gorgeous thing you ever saw?" he hollered, as he rolled it into the garage. He had talked a comrade at the Bon Homme Club into selling it; the comrade would not miss it since he had just bought a '29 Duesenberg on a trip north. Foots had only had to sign a note. I was aghast. I was furious. I was just killed. "Take it back this instant," I said. "We can't afford it."

"Quit screaming like a yahoo," he said. His eyes were flashing.

He was getting very pale. "But then," he added, "blood will tell . . ."

There was a scythe hanging on a nail right by me. I snatched it down and raised it over my head. "No, no, my girl, you'd better not," he said. "How dis-GRACE-ful it would be, to hang." He turned and strutted into the house, pocketing, as he went, the key to the most gorgeous mechanical thing, indeed, I almost ever saw.

I stood there shaking. I was so mad. So hopeless. Louise had heard the commotion; she came out and when she saw what it was over she started to cry. "Don't let him get by with it, Sister," she said. "Put your foot down."

I had meant to go and pay off the grocer and get something for supper but I was too spent. The little girls were coming in, with their little round boxes. Louise said she would find something to cook and I went on and got ready for class.

The first bunch I got through all right. The second class, I heard Foots swearing in the kitchen. I put a record on the Victrola; over the Chopin I could hear him. "I am Goddamn tired of living like trash. Where is that niggra? Why can't we have some decent food in this house?" And then the dishes started to crash. The girls looked at me, alarmed. I went right on, facing them, going through the class, not missing a beat. Oh, the serenity. Oh, the perfect order. When we had done our hour, I bowed to them, and they to me. And when they were gone I went to face the chaos.

Foots had thrown a bowl of butterbeans at my mother's red velvet portiers. The soup was dribbling down them, onto the carpet. He had broken up all the china Louise had set out for supper. Louise was sitting on a kitchen stool, with her head in her hands, sobbing. Pet and Hugh were hiding somewhere.

Foots had taken his wrath upstairs and slammed the door. His mother was up there knocking, begging him to let her in.

I kissed Louise on the top of her bent-down head and went to the sun room and got my shoes, and I put on a hat and the light spring coat I had worn downtown that day, over my dancing class clothes, and went out the front door, and out the gate, and down the street to the sea wall. I walked slowly, watching the light fade. I walked on in the dark. I stood a while and watched the ripple of the lights on the blackness of the water. With no feeling, at all, I wondered who would find me, floating. I closed my eyes and I could see that pink silk billowing modestly over stiff, pink-stockinged legs and my hair loose and floating, just a wash below the surface. The picture pleased me. No more pain, no more humiliation. How might it be an accident? A decent way to die? There was no decent way to live. I am not afraid, I thought. I will be with my father. Mackey.

I sat down on the concrete ledge and started to cry. I cried till I choked and rasped for breath. I could see my father crying under the wisteria, helpless and lost in the wilderness. We were both lost and he had left me. I would never forgive him. I stretched my toe down but the water would not reach it. Cold and indifferent. You are nothing to me, I said to it, and yet here I am ready to give my life to you. I reached into the pocket of my coat for a handkerchief, and felt that envelope with the stock money. Good heavens, I thought. My whole estate, here in my pocket. If I leave it here on the sea wall, the wrong person will surely find it and the children will be left penniless. The only thing to do was to go home and leave it, and put some things in order, and then come back.

My ears were ringing, all the way home. My feet went like a wind-up toy. My head was not in control. I slipped in quietly as I could and went upstairs to the old room where my parents had slept, so as not to be disturbed, and sat down on the bed, to compose a proper note. First I addressed the money to Louise. "I am sorry to leave you with no more," I said. "It is the best I can do." And then I licked the end of the pencil and wrote on a note-pad, "Dear Pet and Hugh . . ." What should I say? "I am about to have an accident?" I lay back on the bed to think about it. I was so very, very tired. I closed my eyes and saw the water shimmering, and lapping, and soon was sound asleep.

Now some people would say I dreamed this, except I still heard it when I woke up. I woke up and sat up in the bed, and I still heard it. My skin crept up my collar bones and temples. My hair stood straight up on my head. Somebody in that house was fiddling. It must have been three o'clock in the morning and somebody was playing, like I hadn't heard in my grown-up life. It was like it was there in the room—what was the tune? I listened in the dark, with my heart pounding and my eyes bulging. Then it was like it was moving away; I jumped up and ran to the window, making the words then with my mouth: "Shady Grove, my pretty little pink, shady grove my love, Shady Grove my blue eyed gal, I'm bound for the Shady Grove. . . ."

It was gone. I stood there stood clinging to the windowsill till my fingers were numb. And then like something led, I turned around and tipped out, and into my own room, past Foots, who was sound asleep, to the closet and took down a few clothes, in the dark. I went to the attic in the dark and got an old suitcase and slipped into Pet's room. I closed the door gently and turned on the light. Hugh was curled up under the coverlet, at the foot of her bed. I knew then how worried they must have been.

"Get up," I said, "we're going on a trip."

"Good," Pet said. "Where?"

"We're going to Grandpa's," I said.

Hugh yawned and rubbed his eyes. "How long will it take to get to Germany?" he said.

"We're going to another grandpa's," I said. "We're going to my father's." Hugh really was alarmed, then. He pulled the cover tight around him. "I thought that grandpa was dead," he said.

"We are going to his house," I said. I opened my mouth to promise we would find somebody there alive, and knew I could not. "It's not as far as Germany," I said.

"Are we going on a ship?"

"No, no, we're going on the train."

"Why didn't you tell us before?" Pet said.

"I didn't know, before," I said. "We have only just now been invited." That sounded matter-of-fact, but they both looked warily at me, and then one another. I'm sure I did look glassy in the eyes.

"Get on up," I said. "Be very, very quiet. We don't want to say any long goodbyes. Just pick out a few clothes and get on something you're not ashamed to travel in."

As I started out, Pet called behind me, in a tentative little voice, "Are we ever coming back?"

"Oh yes," I said. "I'm sure. Sometime." I hurried out and started to get dressed. I wondered how we'd best go to the train station. Camp and Mit were staying a week at Mama's doing spring cleaning. I could call a cab. But the driver would know we'd gone, like this. All Foots would need to do would be to find out from the ticket agent where we had gone. In that case we might see him coming any time.

I remember I put on a green voile dress, with a lace bertha, and some silk stockings, and black patent shoes with a strap across the foot. All the while I was thinking. I knew it wasn't wise to take the train. I took my shoes back off and tipped into the room where Foots still slept, hoping he wouldn't snore and alarm his mother. I felt around for his pants, on the back of a chair, and inched my hand into his pocket, trying not to jiggle the change. Finally my fingers closed around the key to that Auburn Phaeton, that most beautiful thing. I stole $33 back from the envelope I'd leave for Louise, and left her not quite five thousand.

Once ten years ago or so Camp had tried to teach me how to drive the Buick. I had killed nobody that day; everybody we had charged was quick and nimble. "Get your pillows and your blankets," I said to the kids. As casually as I could, I said, "I think we'll take the car."

They were horrified but I dared 'em to cheep. I prayed nobody would hear the engine crank and probably they didn't; it was soft as a whisper. They might have heard the gears grinding, while I learned again about the clutch. They might have heard the gentle bump, on the garage wall, while I looked for the gear that went backwards. But then I found it. We were off. The first two blocks in reverse.

It was an hour before daylight, on the first day of May; der Winter was aus. Over. I had one moment of guilt, as I got us going forward, again, and passed by our sleeping house. I was committing a grave offense against the society of Charleston. I was going out without my hat.

∽3∽

THE FUGITIVES

WE WENT FIRST TO JAMES ISLAND, TO MY MOTHER'S. I HAD TO TELL Mit and Camp we were gone. There was a light on in the old carriage house. Camp always got up before day; he had the coffee pot on, already, and Mit came rolling out in her flour-sack gown. She thought somebody must have died, us being there so soon.

It was worse than that, in Camp's eyes, when he understood how we had got there. "De Savior he be ridin' the runnin' board," he said, lifting his grateful arms toward heaven. "I be drivin' you home."

Oh no, I said, we had gone along very well. The car had bucked and hopped a time or two, I said. ("All the way," Pet said, "like riding on a frog.") Only once or twice it had sputtered and died, I said. ("On the drawbridge," Hugh said darkly. "And it nearly wouldn't start.")

But had we not arrived? I said. And anyway, this was the point: we were not going home. Not home to Charleston. We were leaving. "Do hush!" Mit said. We were on our way to look up my father's folks, I said. We would be all right. And Camp asked, did they know that we were coming?

Well, no. I didn't want to say in front of the children that these people didn't even know we existed. Or that maybe there were none of them left. Nobody then would have thought this adventure was all right, except me. Camp stood there studying the linoleum. He knew.

"One time one of 'em come fuh see Mr. Mack. You an' yo' mama be gone," he said. "Young man he come knock at d' do', wants to know,

do Mr. Steele be in? He big tall man, like Mr. Mack. I see he face an'
I call 'pun Jesus; I see de very spirit of yo' daddy standin' at de do'."
Mackey had been buried then a week or so, Camp said. Mama and I
were gone all that summer. We heard no more, that I knew of, from
that visitor. That had been twenty years.

Mit fixed the children some cocoa; we had a cup of coffee and a
hurried conference. I wrote down for their eyes, alone, where I
hoped we'd be, and kissed them goodbye. When we walked out of
there, I would have cried, but the morning star was shining, and the
air was fresh and cool right off the sea, like it was full of new spirits
and new secrets. I took a good deep breath and felt re-born.

We crossed the bridges again and headed back through town.
Geography was not my strong point. Nor navigation. Ahead was all
new ground. Except that some people went to the mountains in the
summer, Charleston largely ignored the heathen lands that lay to
the west, beyond the alligators and the jungle. I knew we would be
going roughly northwest; somewhere we would have to get a map.
We took the one road I knew that went inland. It was getting light
when we cleared the town and faced the open spaces. Shreds of mist
drifted off the swamps on either side and hung among the cypresses.
We crossed rickety bridges, over slow black streams, and scared
long-legged birds eating their breakfast in the ditches by the road.
The sun came up behind us; we were going right, more or less, so
far. And I remember this: it didn't matter. Wherever we are, I decided, swelling up with joy, we were gone from Back There. Run
clean away and Gone.

We stopped at a store with a gas pump and an afflicted boy came
out and filled the tank. He shook his head about a map. He just
looked blank when I asked the way to Caney Forks. We went inside
and bought peanuts and crackers and were distressed to see there
was nobody home but him.

So we went on, into the pines, and the day got bright and warm,
and we stopped at a cafe and got some tea and sandwiches, and we
asked the waitress, and she hollered back to the cook, but they did-
n't know their geography either. So we went on into the cotton
land. The sun was to our back and left, and that seemed as it should
be. Along in the afternoon we got more gas, and got a map. We had

to ask the man then where we were, before we could figure where
we were going. He drew an *X* with his pencil, and we stopped later,
under a tree, and I looked for Caney Forks, and didn't find it. Red
Bank, though, was there, right over the North Carolina state line. It
looked a real long way.

I was getting very tired; I had a cramp in my foot from pushing
the gas pedal with the toe of my shoe. But we had to move on.

We had to find a place to spend the night. We would never make
it in one day. I guessed we were fifty miles or so farther along, and
the kids were thirsty, and worn out, when we came to a little sign,
pointing up another road, that said, "Tourist Camp." We stopped
to debate about it, and this old truck full of junk came by, and
turned up that way, and we turned and went behind it. Well, we
passed this one terrible looking old house, with junk cars and even
an old bus in the yard, and woebegone younguns and dogs sitting
on the steps, and there was a grove of trees close by, with a couple of
tents and a picnic table or so, and an outhouse, and we went on up
the road looking for the tourist camp.

And we were looking left and right—and not ahead—when a
tangle of barbed wire fell off that old truck. And we were on it, before I could stop. What a racket. It got both front tires, like they
were shot out with a gun. We were all struck dumb. We didn't say a
word—if we had we'd have ended up killing one another. I moved
the wire and drove off the road, *bump-bump-bump*, as best I could,
and we got out and started walking, back to the only sign of people
we had seen.

The kids on the porch ran around the house and the dogs slunk
off, looking back over their shoulders. A man with a week's worth of
whiskers and a red nose came out, when we knocked. He had on a
dirty undershirt and some britches with no top button, and no shoes.
"You want spend the night at the tourist camp, little lady?" he said.

"We were looking for it," I said.

"We seen you when yins passed it," he said. "It's right down yonder. Wha' did ye do with that fine autoMObile?"

"It's up the road," I said, about to cry. "It's got two flat tires."

"Hmmp," he said. "Leroy! Cebo! Come hep this lady change some
tahrs."

Two boys, might have been eighteen or twenty, came out from the gloom with an old dog slinking along between them. "She got spars?" one said.

"You got a spar?" said the elder. I reckon I looked real blank at him, and then it came to me. "There ought to be one in that round thing on the fender," I said.

Leroy and Cebo got in a jalopy and sped off up the road. There were some old cane chairs on the porch. Our host wiped one kindly, with his hand, and invited me to sit. My kids sat on the edge of the porch, forlornly watching up the sandy road for a sign of hope. The elder busied himself picking ticks off the dog and squashing them between his fingers.

When the boys came back they'd changed one tire, they said. They were rolling the two injured ones. The innertubes looked like they'd been in a sword fight. "Is there somewhere we can buy a tire?" I said.

The elder stroked his whiskers. "Not close," he said. "Yins'll not get one today. Good thing it happened where you can stay the night."

I was suddenly desperate. "Do you think one of 'em could be fixed?" I said. Cebo and Leroy looked at one another and said to the elder, "Yeah, we c'n fix 'em. Take a while."

The sun was getting low. Late into the evening, Cebo and Leroy stuck patches on those tubes, and pumped in air, and watched them go down. They brought in a tub of water from the pitcher pump, out back, and submerged each one and watched the bubbles rise, and put on more glue and more patches.

"You ain't got no tent," the elder said. "How was you goin' to sleep?"

"In the car," I said. I hadn't known exactly how a tourist camp worked.

"Where's your eats?" he said. "You leave 'em in the car?"

Oh my, I thought. "Yessir," I said.

"Well, no cause to worry about nothin'. We got plenty of place to stay right here. Plenty t'eat, if the ol' womern'll jist get movin'."

We had not seen the ol' womern, to that point. Directly she appeared, silent and gray as a spook. She had no teeth, but she was tying on a clean apron, and she had on some bright blue carpet slippers, and she looked at us and nodded, and said to the elder that supper was nearly ready. By then it was getting quite dark.

Weakly, I said, "We can make it further up the road if the tires are ready."

Leroy/Cebo dunked a tube back in the tub and the bubbles spewed and popped. "It ain't gon' be safe to put t'em tahrs back on till we see do they hold ahr overnight," the elder said. "Come on in an' mek yin's seffs to home."

The kids had been mercifully silent the whole afternoon. They had said not half a dozen words between them. Now, by the light of a lantern the Samaritans had hung on a nail on the porch, they looked at me beseechingly. I asked if we could go wash our hands, and the host handed us the lantern and pointed us delicately to the outhouse and the pump. "There's nothing we can do," I said, when we were alone. "Tomorrow's going to be a better day. I promise you."

That speechless lady sat us at the table, first, and brought us plates of grits and white gravy and biscuits and slab meat. She had piled up the plates, and it was not as bad as I had imagined. I felt bad about letting a bite go back, I thought it would hurt her feelings, except that dog-eyes looked longingly around the door jamb at every speck we tried to eat. I took the plates to the kitchen when we had done the best we could, and asked if I could help her wash dishes. "No, main," she said.

She wiped her hands on her apron and led us back to a room at the back of the house. There was no furniture but a slop jar and a tick stuffed with straw in a corner of the room, with a little light blanket spread over it. She went out and brought another little blanket, and when she left with the light, we were in the pitch black. The tick was ripe with the memory of other bodies I knew had been displaced so we could sleep. We sat down on it and took off our shoes, and held to one another, and soon fell back exhausted.

Dogs howled and whined. Once the chickens roused and started squawking, and then there was a shot and an exuberant cry, "You sonnabitch, I got che!" And peace was restored. We squirmed a good bit; something made us itch. The night went on forever. We would be here forever, I decided. We would be part of the family, sitting on the porch picking ticks off the dog (or off each other) waiting for our *tahrs* to heal themselves.

I watched the window for the faintest hint of light. The front of the house came to life first, though; I heard talking and moving around, and the front door bump. And a car went off, and directly two came back. I got into my shoes and went and looked out, and there was the car, on all four tires, and Leroy and Cebo and the elder looking over it, talking and grinning. One of the boys polished a place on the hood with his shirt and admired himself in the finish. I said thank-you prayers right then, I'll tell you. And I went and got the kids up, and we went forth to the landlord, all smiles and gratitude.

"What do we owe for everything?" I said. He cleared his throat and spat and considered the dirt. "If three dollar don't sound like too much," he said.

"Oh no," I said. "And how much for our room and board?"

"That's all of it," he said. "Three dollar. But you ain't had no breakfast."

That was quite all right, I said. We would hurry on up the road and get some later. I paid and went back in to the kitchen and told his wife goodbye, and thanked her. "Come again," she said.

We drove off, into the morning, and when we came to a patch of woods, with a little clear stream running through, we stopped and got out and straightened up and began to feel human again.

~4~

WE ARE SCARED

WE CAME THROUGH A HUNDRED MILES OF COTTON FIELDS THAT day, I know. There would be people out in them, hoeing, with big hats on, and they would be like ants so far away, little dots among the stripes of green cotton and red earth. And there would be houses perched on little hills, with trees to shade them, watching over their acres and the people working them.

There would be no hiding in that land. I knew how it must have felt to be a runaway slave, with only those slim thickets that grow along where branches run, where you could duck in and squat and wait for the dogs to come. I had my eye out all the time for bushes that would swallow a car, if need be.

I could just see Foots in full gray fury, ringing up the law. He would be good and mad by this time. By now police from Mexico to Maine would be on the lookout for a stolen car, two kidnaped children and a piece of thieving, thankless chattel. I wondered whether he had given them a picture for the post office. Would it be a wedding picture? No—I bet he would pick one from the coming-out ball. Any yegg could get married. Foots would want it known he dealt only with the crème.

Anyway, every vehicle that came in sight looked like the Black Maria. The kids looked out the back and sounded the alarm over hog trucks, ice trucks, mailmen and one-mule wagons.

We had the jitters, of course. We had slept so little in so long that we imagined things. I kept feeling something crawling on me; it got under my corselet, where I couldn't reach, and bit. It occurred to me that maybe those people we bedded down with last night had shared more with us than their straw tick. And that was not imagining.

Sure enough as we were going through a town a policeman got behind us. I saw him in the mirror as I was neatening my hair. I thought, Lord, show us the way. We went on, like we were unconcerned, through the downtown. It was too late to tell the kids to get down and hide; they had been looking at him too. We crossed several streets where the menace might have turned. But he did not.

Well, there comes a time when a run-down rabbit may just flop over and wait for the fox. I just stopped. True, I did not put out my hand like you are supposed to when you stop in the road, and he nearly hit us. And he drove around beside us then and looked at me very hard.

I leaned out and waved at him and said, "Excuse me, sir, but can you tell me the way to Hampton Street?" To be convincing I had to pick a number. "We need to find 400 Hampton Street, I always do get lost downtown," I said.

He was a stolid-looking kind of fellow. "You just crossed Hampton Street," he said. (Of course we had.) "Go on to the next street and turn left and go back around." Then he gave me a broad smile. There was something behind that smile I thought besides a broken tooth. I knew we better go to Hampton Street.

So we did, and we looked for the proper number and parked and got out, very business-like. "What are we DOING?" Pet groaned, exasperated. "I am NOT going in there."

"Oh, yes you are," I said through gritted teeth, "or you will be the greatest challenge these people ever had."

There was a sign on the green scalloped awning over the sidewalk that said B.V. STOKES AND SON FUNERAL PARLOR. We went inside to play our part.

There was a waiting room with musty green plush draperies and dark horsehair chairs and a table with a Bible on it, and there was a picture of Jesus on one wall, and a much bigger portrait of B.V. Stokes, Sr. on another. We were, for the moment, alone. I had this flash of hope that we could just sit quiet for a dutiful time and then depart, undetected, wiping our eyes. But nothing doing. The bell on the front door was a sign to the unseen. Somewhere back in the labyrinth a needle scraped down on a record, and a man began to sing, somewhat warpedly, "Safe in the arms of Jee-E-susss, safe on his genn-tull breast. . . ."

Our hostess pattered out like a trapdoor spider. She was really a sweet-looking little old lady with bobbed and curled white hair. She was gotten up in proper gray for mourning. I wasn't sure how well I could lie to her, or what the lie was going to be. But she came to my rescue.

"Bless my soul, Bertha honey, they've just this minute gone," she said.

"They have?" I said.

"Oh, law, child, they've been so worried about you drivin' all that way with just the chirrun. Your Aunt Zula's been a-standin' on her head, she said she'd not let your uncle be laid away till you got to see 'im, though. Mercy, it's been so many years since you was home and I don't believe you've growed an inch since your mama took you away . . ."

"Where did they go?" I was sort of groping in the dark.

"They went over't the house to eat some dinner, Lord child, I never saw the like of what them neighbor women and the Ladies Aids has brought t' the house to eat, hams and cakes and mackyroney pie. Now they're a-looking for you to come on. But 'fore you go, do come in here and look at Mr. Hopp, I think he looks so nice."

I felt Hugh's shoulder shudder under my hand. I grasped Pet firmly by the back of the neck and we proceeded through the arch of green curtains.

There was Mr. Hopp, under a fly-net. In the candle-light, he was a little bit green himself. His fingers were like wax, clasped over the stiff snowy bosom of his shirt. Urns of tuberoses at each end of the casket added a lot of weight to the atmosphere.

"Oh, Uncle . . . Hopp . . .!" I said. There was nothing to do then but cry. Pet stared, open-mouthed. Hugh spun around and buried his face in my dress, just sobbing.

"Your letters had meant so much to him, while he was sick so long," the undertakeress said.

I thanked her then and said I guessed we'd better run on over to the folks', since they were worried. And she said she'd see us, then, at the services. "Three o'clock," she said.

We were at the door when she had a thought. "Say, darlin', please come back and sign the book before you go. Folks'll be takin' on so this evenin' you might forget it."

I went back and my hand was shaking like the palsy, but I wrote, "Bertha Hopp (Scribble), Tootie and Bubba." I reckon I really looked wan, because she said as an afterthought, "I hope you never had no trouble on your trip."

I dabbed my nose with my hanky and told her, "No'm. So far so good."

She put her arm around me as a parting gesture, and squeezed my shoulders and said, "Honey, I'm so sorry about this."

"I am too," I said. And I meant it.

As we came out into the light, Pet was still pale as death and Hugh was wiping his eyes on his sleeve. A coarse-looking, hefty woman with two kids brushed by us, going in, as we passed under the awning. I made a last blubbering display of grief as we high-tailed it for the car and jumped in. Down the block, a police car moved away from the curb and slowly departed.

We made a rapid exit from that town. Hugh was still sniffling. "Darling," I told him, "People die every day. It may not be so bad that the first dead person you had to see was somebody we never knew. Like Uncle Hopp."

His voice quavered. The truth came out. "Mama, I was afraid you'd gone crazy. And I didn't know what we were going to DO." Poor little wise child, he was more on target than he knew.

Pet just sighed and said, "Well I only wish we'd gone on and got some of that dinner. I'm about to starve."

We would get something in Red Bank, I said. We would go into a restaurant and sit down and order real food no matter what it cost. Of course it was in my mind that Red Bank was going to be at least pretty near the end of our line; either we would have someplace to go or we would not. The moment of truth was now a couple of hours away and I was not sure I wanted to hear it.

We went through a couple of little towns, past their cotton mills and through their mill villages, where it seemed like everybody must have had a pot of cabbage or turnips simmering on the back of the stove (I envied them, oh my) and a line of clean wash flapping. Mackey used to say that the saddest thing that could happen to a farmer was to have to give up his land and go to spinning cotton for somebody else. When you worked your own land, he said, nobody stood over you but the Lord. I wondered how these people felt about that. I wondered what really made Mackey walk off his own land. And never go back.

We stopped at a crossroads filling station for gas and we blew ourselves to a nickel each for a dope. The filling station man had a little monkey in a cage and it kept putting its little arms through the bars and looking so pitiful, its eyes following every sip we took. I admit I wouldn't give it any of mine till I had all I wanted, but of course the children did and it was polite the way it drank.

The country was really rising, now. We were up and down hills and over clear streams, and I wished we could have gotten a good view, from the high places, but there was a heavy haze. It was clouding up ahead. A way off we saw a water tank. As we got closer, the kids made out what it said on it. It said RED BANK.

What I knew about Red Bank I had heard on a Lowcountry porch at night, and on long walks by still black waters, in stories told over a background of creaking rockers, and crickets and seabreezes rustling palmetto fronds. In Mackey's stories it was a town of breakdown dances, where young men danced each other down and fought with knives, sometimes about some girl. It was a town of chicken fights and horse trading and fiddling and feuds. It was three hundred miles away, and it was pure romance. The Blue Fairy could not have dispensed a more fantastic place.

Now, on this day, in this upcountry, it was a quiet little town, with its own cotton mill, and ranks of nice old two-story houses lined up along Main Street — they had porches, too, and roses grew on their fences, where ladies cut bouquets and talked, and a couple of church spires rose against the shadow of foggy hills.

We rode on down to the courthouse square. The street went around the courthouse block; there was a place to park in front, and we pulled up beside a Model A Ford that said SHERIFF on the door, above a gold star. A chicken was pecking something out of the treads on the right rear tire. Here, for some reason, I felt lots more at ease beside the law than anyplace we'd been.

There were a couple of dogwood trees blooming on what passed for the courthouse lawn. The grass was pretty sparse but narcissus blooms seemed to have come of their own accord, among the sprigs. The courthouse itself was gray stone, with two flights of stone steps leading up to a rounded porch.

Inside there would be the records of Tusquittee County. The births, the deaths, the weddings, the homesteads. Mackey's folks would be in those files, somewhere.

I sat very still, thinking and looking. The children of course didn't understand. There was fussing and grumbling in the back seat. I could not tell them that I was looking at this place through Mackey's eyes, seeing the things he knew and I know he had longed for. Here were the names of people he knew and cared for and remembered and talked about in his exile. Now they named the stores and the doctor and the lawyer: Tatum, Hambright, Spivey and Garner and Brock. . . .

"When are we going to EAT?" Pet said.

It had started to drizzle. Two men in overalls came out and stood on the courthouse porch, talking. I wondered who they were. I wondered if I ran up and told them who I was, would they remember? Maybe they were my people. They were looking at us. The younger one lifted his hat a half an inch, and smiled. The old one —he would be the one who would know—looked on with no expression at all. Just curious. Tears were dribbling on the front of my frock. My stomach growled. Everything I wondered about, all we needed so desperately to know, the answers were right there, in that building, for the asking.

I cranked up and backed out and drove away.

We had passed a decent-looking cafe as we came in, but it was getting late so we would try our luck at the next place. When we came to it, it said EAT in flaky red letters on the side. We opened the screen and stepped over a sleeping dog and went in. The waitress was languidly swatting at flies that were buzzing the windows, trying to get out.

"Whatchall want?" she said.

"What have you got?" I said.

"Soup. And sandridges."

"What kind of soup?"

"Vegeble and 'mater."

"What kind of sandridges?"

"Egg."

We decided on "vegeble" soup and tea and soon went on our way again, cheered somewhat. As I was starting up the car, Hugh leaned over the seat and asked me earnestly what neither of them had dared to ask before.

"Do you know where we're going, Mama?"

"No," I said. We listened a minute to that steadfast engine purr. I had no doubt it was tired, like us. I hoped we were near some pleasant sanctuary, for all of us. It was such a trusting machine, and so forgiving. Whatever, the game would soon be over. We were broke, friendless fugitives, homeless in the rain.

"I mean, I don't know precisely," I said. "But I've got to find out."

We crossed the railroad between the depot—I bet it was exactly the same as the day Mackey caught the train and left—and some old railroad houses. I always wondered why they painted railroad houses that dreary gray.

And then we came to a sprawling old ramshackle store, right at the end of town: OLLIE M. TROTTER, GENERAL MERCHANDISE. I told the children to sit still, I was going to get directions.

Ollie M. Trotter was slicing sowbelly on a piece of brown paper. He looked up over his little round glasses and nodded howd-do. I looked around and said I would like a few bananas, please. And, um, a can of Vienna sausages. And a box of Uneeda Biscuits. And a nickel's worth a chocolate drops. They had white specks on them where the paraffin had come through but they would do to keep peace.

There was a woman sitting in a straight chair, behind the cloth shelf, knitting. She didn't say anything, but she was looking. I didn't want to stare back but I noticed she was so interested her hands were frozen in mid-stitch. I told the man to put in some sardines, too, I knew the kids would say *peww* but we had to have supplies in case of disaster.

"Y'picked a turrable day for a joy-ride," Ollie said. Which of course meant what in the world were we doing here. "The sky looks to me like they's a-comin' a cloud-bust."

My heart was in a spasm. My knees shook. "We're on our way to see my folks," I said.

"Well, I hope they're here close by," he said. There was a lapse while he bagged the stuff and took the money and made change. And then he could stand it no longer. "Who are they?"

The woman leaned forward, not to miss it.

"The Steeles," I said.

The woman drew a little jab of breath.

"The Steeles?" Ollie asked. He was leaning across the counter, now, with his eyebrows puckered together in a frown, studying my pores. "Ben Steele?"

"Do you know him?" I said. I was squeezing those bananas to a mush against my chest.

The rain was drumming now on the store's tin roof, while he considered. It was a silly thing I had asked. I knew Ben Ivan Steele was so old he was probably dead. I didn't know how I could have hoped otherwise.

"I know him," Ollie said. And he turned to the side, and spit a great long brown *pttuuii* into some vessel behind the counter. "'Course I know him."

"What's the quickest way to his place from here?" I asked, putting on like I knew where his place was supposed to be.

"Well," he said, "ain't no good way from here. This road rightchere'll take ye up to the Forks, of course . . ."

"Caney Forks?" I said.

"That's right. But now, hit ain't much of a road, for a little ways up close to the river. They've got it all tore up, a-workin on a new bridge. But don't mind, just go slow, and keep a-goin' straight. They's some bad little old roads cuts off up-pair, and you don't want none o' them, eh, law, and it a-fixin to get dark early. . . ."

"How far you reckon it is?"

Ollie said, "Oh, abody could WALK it in half a day's time. But the way you've got to drive, why, hmmm, it's twenty-five mile, I guess. You'll get there by good dark, just mind, keep 'er straight."

I thanked him. I wanted to hug him. I was already outside the screen, in the rain, when he hollered at me, "What did ye say you was to Ben Steele?"

I hollered back, "His granddaughter." But I doubted he heard me.

So we were off again, and before the children could ask, I said, "We're nearly there." They were into the chocolate drops. Directly I looked back in the mirror and they were both asleep.

I didn't quite know why, but I was ecstatically happy. We were just humming along, and I was singing very soft, just for myself, "The squire he come a-ridin' home, inquirin' for his lay-a-dee, And the an-swer that they made to him was, 'She's gone with the Black Jack Day-vee, That rag-tag Gypsy, Day-veee. . . .'"

I don't know where that came from, it sure wasn't one of my mother's songs. Maybe Camp's, but it seemed like one of Mackey's. You know, things from very long ago sometimes just bubble to the surface like that.

Ollie was right. A mile or so out, the road began to get bad. It was getting real steep, for one thing, climbing and twisting. And it was wet, and just gravel, no tar. In the woods it was gloomy and I fumbled around again to find the lights. I guessed in time I would learn this car. I learned right fast that when you climb you shift gears; a couple of times it died and rolled back. I could hear Uncle Camp groaning, "Th'ow in de clutch, missy, th'ow in de clutch."

One thing, though, the threat of the law, or anything that Foots might do, I felt was safely left behind. To tell the truth I hadn't thought about what Foots was doing or any old troubles all evening. By the map, we had not more than crossed the state. But in my mind I had crossed continents and seas; I could not go back. It did weigh on me now that I better be thinking ahead. I better be thinking what in the world I was going to tell my people when I just popped in on them after thirty years. I wished I'd had the nerve to come out and ask Ollie about them, who was still alive and all. I guess he'd have thought I was plain crazy—who ignores her family her very whole life? Good grief, that ugly Bertha Hopp had more concern for her people than I did. Here Lord knows how many of mine had died when I didn't even know that they had lived.

Ben Ivan Steele, my grandpa, I still had him. I didn't know about my grandma. Her name was Daisy McAllister. Mackey was named for her folks. But whoever of them lived, I would make it up to them. I didn't know how I would get around the truth that I had made no attempt to find them. I could hardly say, "Well, I'm sorry but my mother was sure you all lived on bootleg whiskey and never wore shoes. She was afraid if she had anything to do with you at all you might come down and be tacky, and spoil her reputation and my chances."

Somehow I knew they wouldn't care. They were old; maybe I could look after them. We would be an unexpected gift to each other. I hoped the shock would not kill them in the hour of our reunion.

I don't know why it didn't strike me strange that they had made no effort to contact me. I just never thought about it then.

There were terrible ruts and mudholes in the road, where culverts were being laid and machinery had traveled. Then we came around a bend, and into a clearing. I never forgot that eerie yellow-gray light, it was so scary. And then there was the river. It was huge, just rolling, yellow with silt. There was a makeshift plank bridge across it, so low the water was licking at the boards, washing across. Oh, Father, I said. Not me! Not these children!

I could see well enough not to try to turn around there. It was a tormented quagmire of tracks and thrown-up mud and puddles. The prudent thing, it seemed, was to back up a way and turn around in a better spot and try to find the road. Somehow I had got off wrong. This was not the road to Caney Forks.

I backed up the hill and of course the wheels spun and the thing wouldn't go but so far before it would just dig in and slide and go nowhere but sideways. I was really panicky. Something told me *rock it!*—and I did—low and reverse, low and reverse. And finally it backed a few more feet and spun sideways and turned halfway around.

In that pose, the headlights picked up another road. Or, I thought, that IS the road. I had just missed this curve. We were on our way again. That bumping and grinding had jostled the sleepers around and Hugh raised up and said, "Where are we?"

"We're doing fine," I said, "this is just a bumpy old road. You can go back to sleep." And he did.

The road of course was still awful. It was running now beside the river, and the river sent up a mist that joined the rain to make it just impossible to see anything more than the ruts ahead, twisting around muddy banks and out of sight. I wondered how far we'd come, it seemed like a thousand miles, and how long we'd be to Caney Forks, at two miles an hour.

And then we came to a kind of level place, clear with pasture on one side, and up the road, in the fog, there was an old man leading a cow. Oh, praise God, a human. We bumped on up beside him. "Mister," I said, "You don't know how glad I am to see you. Can you tell me how far we are from the Steeles'?" I figured this must be real close to Caney Forks.

He turned around and looked at us. He had a long white beard and a long bony face; he was chewing tobacco and the juice made a channel in his whiskers. He came over to the car and peered in at me, with his chin working up and down, like he couldn't quite take in what it was he saw. And then whatever it was, I guess he believed it. His head jerked backwards, sort of sidewise, and his mouth fell open, and he had this look of horror in his eyes. And he took off running like a turkey up the field, dragging his poor old cow. And he never had answered me one word.

Now, I'll tell you, I had the creeps. Here we were, in this weather, out in nowhere with nothing but crazy people, and night was really closing in. There was nothing to do but drive on.

We were climbing again, back into the woods. And it seemed like the road was getting much worse. It was just old ruts with saplings growing between them that scraped the bottom of the car. There were rocks in the road as big as a goods box.

A couple of times we got stuck in mud and had to rock out. My ears were popping. I thought about all those patches on that tire and couldn't believe how it was taking all this, when sometimes the whole car would shudder.

The wind began to shriek. The sky fairly sizzled with lightning, and the thunder rumbled over us as though we were in a deep dark cave. For a while the rain was so hard I couldn't see a thing so I just stopped, and waited an hour or two, I was so tired but too terrified to sleep.

And then the rain eased up, and I felt encouraged, and started up again. It was some kind of miracle, I knew, that the car had not drowned out or shaken to pieces.

We crept along, still climbing. Once a boulder as big as a bushel bounced down the bank in front of us and rolled across the road and out of the lights, into some deep unknown. I was shaking worse than the car, clinging to the wheel like grim death.

And then we started coming down. By leaps and bounds. I guess something had happened to the brakes, they didn't help at all. The laurels whizzed by. I prayed for a good mudhole to slow us down. I would have settled for a good tree to run into but there was nothing in the headlights but mud bank and black chasm. Dangling briers and switches slapped at us. Something raked the top of the car and tore a big hole and rain splattered in on my head. There was a fearful roaring now, somewhere close beside us. Oh, I wished I could stop and wait it out till day. But we were moving on, for good or ill.

There did come a sort of leveling off, and we slowed down. All was not lost—there was a bridge ahead of us, another human sign. When the front wheels hit the planks, there was a hair-raising crunch and splintering, and we were falling and crashing and splashing, and the lights bounced, and died, and over that awful roar the children screamed. I could hear somebody real far away, screaming, "Oh God! Oh God!" And it was me.

It was blacker than a pit. The water rushed over my feet; I could hear the children vaguely, they were screeching "Mama! Mama! You drove us in the water!" But I couldn't see them, couldn't see anything at all, and it took me forever to get from under the steering wheel and over into the back seat. And I felt their panicky arms and legs wiggling and knew they were alive.

The front end had got the worst. The car was nose down; water came in the back but the seat was dry. I got my arms around the kids and we crouched there in a huddle while the water pounded on the wreck, jiggling it like a bobber in a pond. We were moving sideways, shifting, flamming, being battered. It was like we were in a flimsy casket being bumped along in a reckless hearse. There was nothing but blackness. We could see nothing, and hear nothing but that hideous roar. We could barely hear each other pray.

It was the end, we knew it. I had done an unpardonable wrong. And this was the price we all would pay.

∼5∼

REUNION

IT WAS MORNING OF THE THIRD DAY.

I knew it because the hole in the top of the car was our observatory. I remember telling the children sometime in the night to look up—out there in the hopelessness there were stars.

Once I know I whined out loud, "Foots, turn out that light—it's in my face." It was the moon; I was immobile, with an arm around each child and my feet against the back of the front seat to keep us from sliding off. Water seemed to come in from everywhere. It was way up in the floor, rippling in the moonlight like some dark channel.

The children had been very quiet. They were resigned, poor little things. I would drift away and groan and wake up. It was gruesome; it was real.

And then the blackness faded, and the stars faded. The sky was getting gray. I felt the children's warm breath with my cheek. They were alive, and more's the wonder, cold and wet as we were, they were sound asleep. I eased myself up and worked up my nerve, and I rubbed the breath-fog from the window, and looked out.

Gray water was swirling around us, gurgling over rocks. It didn't look very deep; I thought it might be below the bottom of the doors. The ocean at our feet was mostly drained away. I let loose of the kids as gently as I could and climbed over the seat, stiff as a board and aching like a rotten tooth from head to toe. The dregs of the flood were trickling out a hole in the front floorboard. If we'd had a watermelon on the floor we would have lost it. Under the hole dark gray water swept bubbles and leaves along, spinning them in little whirlpool dimples.

I tried the door on the right side; that was downstream. But there was something against it. So I tried the driver's side. It was bashed in, and jammed. The window was jammed. Dull light was coming through the roof; that raggedy hole in the top was going to be it. So out I climbed, bellying over the windshield and onto the hood. There was a silty torrent lapping at the running board. It made me dizzy. I perched out there like a kingfisher till I made myself quit looking down. The hood was sprung, but it was a good vantage point.

We were in a fairly level little place in the stream bed, but the course upstream was steep enough, I could see, to create a regular horror in a hard rain. There had been tremendous wind in that storm, for there were tangles of broken limbs along the bank. Pieces of the bridge had jumbled with brush to make a little dam beside the car.

We were butted into the bank. Nearly as high as the top of the fenders, the weeds were flattened like arrows in the mud, pointing downstream. I couldn't see how we didn't swamp. A few feet below us, the stream disappeared over a little ledge, and fell oh, maybe fifteen or twenty feet and ran a few yards further to the river. We might have been halfway back to the Atlantic Ocean by now, traveling by river bottom; we might have been well on our way back to Charleston, except that a fallen tree had caught us, and held us fast.

I needed to find out where we were. There were willows drooping from the top of the bank, so I grabbed onto one and it showered my misery with cold water while I climbed up, digging my bare toes in the mud. It was like rising from the dead.

I crawled over the edge, grabbing onto the sod, and stood up in a sea of meadow grass. To the left, between two hills, the moon looked like half a pearl in a pewter bowl of sky. The meadow rolled downhill to the right, to woods and the river. Beyond that, over the ridges that sheltered the cove to the east, little clouds drifted up wispy and pink.

There was no sound but the river humming and the branch where we nearly drowned chattering sweetly. It was the stillest place I had ever seen. And then all of a sudden right at the hem of my dress, a speckled little bird fluttered up from the grass and flew in spirals, higher and higher, and when it was a tiny fleck in the sky it began to sing, "See you—see heeeere . . ." The lark was waking the world.

I thought right then that I must have been wrong. I must be dead, really. This must be Heaven. I must have been forgiven. Except that I never had thought Heaven would be cold. Or that you would hurt when you got there. My legs were about to kill me.

I climbed back down to the car, reversed the acrobatic stunt to get in, and woke up the children. "Arise, shine, for our light is come!" I said. They stared at me like damp little owls, not knowing whether they would ever take my word again. But they clambered out.

"Is this Grandpa's?" Hugh said, rubbing his eyes.

And Pet said in a flat, defeated voice, "I wouldn't be surprised."

We stood in the grass and tried to get our bearings. There was no road in sight. "Was there a road last night?" Pet said. Indeed there was, I said, but I wondered too. We headed up the branch, and after a while we came to some splintered stubs of old timbers that used to be the bridge. Now we must decide which way we would walk for help.

"Which way did we come?" Pet said. I wasn't sure, till I saw that the bushes in the ruts across the branch were broken.

"We came that way," I said.

"Then I want to go back that way," she said.

"You want to try to go back to town?"

"I want to go home," she said.

I thought about that old man we saw with his cow. That was halfway back to Red Bank. But I wondered, did he have a house back there somewhere? Was he real? I thought, if he was real and he had a house, I bet he had a fire, too. And a pot of coffee. He wasn't friendly but he was a bird in the hand. I kind of sided with Pet.

Hugh was shuffling around in the mud. He had a problem of his own. "I've got to use the bush," he said.

"Well don't be so prissy, go on!" I said. "Find you a bush, nobody's looking."

"Don't leave me," he said. He went off up the road, crow-hopping, while we took care of ourselves the same way. I really was scared to pull my skirt above my knees. I didn't want to look at my legs. I didn't want to know how black they were. Black as ink. If I wasn't walking on 'em I would have declared they were broken. I guessed the steering wheel had done it, when the car went down.

But Hugh came back looking smug. "I want to go this way," he said, pointing the way he had just come.

"Why? We don't know where it goes," I said.

"We can ask somebody," he said. "There's a house up there."

I could have cried. "Well for pity's sake," I said. "Go! Shoo! Move!"

They ran. I hobbled along behind them, praying these people would help us.

As we topped that little slope I could see the house, up on a rise to the right. A big house, catching the rising sun in its face, shielding its eyes with great porches, upstairs and down. It was not painted; it was weathered to the shade of the bluffs behind it. The shingles of its roof were curled and rumpled like the feathers of some big gray wind-ruffled bird, and five tall chimneys towered over them. Oh, what a house!

I imagined that a regal old lady lived there, with her servants. No— a happy family lived there. Ladies rocked on those porches, in the heat of the day, making tatting. Children bounced and wallowed over those unbounded acres and soared in swings under that big tree.

Pet and Hugh were out of sight, the road was bending, but I could hear them hollering back and forth, excited, and a flock of partridges rose whistling as they passed. The people of this house, I was sure, loved larks and partridges. That was why they didn't cut their grass.

In between the children's tracks I spotted some dainty, pointed hoofprints I figured must be deer. They were fresh, certainly since the rain. Somewhere in this meadow, deer were watching us. Were the people in the house looking at us, too? I felt like they were and it made me feel sort of warm. Certainly they saw us. And people came this way so rarely, they'd be glad. And we'd be glad.

They were not up yet. There was no smoke from their chimneys. Maybe they didn't mind the cool. But I was sure they'd make a fire for us.

The road cut around right close to the porch, and there were steps going up the bank. The children got nearly there, and stopped, looking up, and I caught up with them.

Creeper climbed thick on the chimneys. Seedlings pushed up between the boards of the front steps and lilacs drooped in great clumps along the banisters. Upstairs, there was a broken window, and while we looked in awe, an owl swooped into the hole.

We took each other's hands and went ahead.

The steps were solid enough. Our feet rang on the porch floor. I knocked on the door and waited, and knocked again. The echo bounced through the house but there was no answer, and we waited, and there was no other sound except our breathing, and all around us the waking of birds.

We looked in the windows, then. There was a big room, with sunshine streaming in the side windows, but no furniture at all. We went to the other side of the porch and looked in, and in that room, it was very big, there was a huge stone fireplace. But no furniture.

What we all knew, and nobody wanted to say, was that there was nobody, nobody at home.

Bees were beginning to work the lilacs. The air was sharp and light and full of new sweetnesses, of clean wetness and field grass and ancient timbers warming in the sun.

"I guess we should walk on," Hugh said. He was trying pitifully hard not to cry. I didn't want to tell him that I couldn't walk far enough to find anybody more than a city block away.

"We haven't looked around back," I said. "We haven't looked down at the barn. Maybe down there, maybe at the sheds there'll be some sign of life."

We went around on the sunshine side. A monstrous fig bush huddled close to the chimney. It was knotty with buds of figs that one day the birds would enjoy. There was a long kitchen wing on the back, with its own chimney at the end and a porch all around. At its angle with the main house lilacs sprawled all over, tall as the eaves and bowed to the ground, some branches, bent by the weight of their flowers.

No one answered at the kitchen door, either.

Our mouths were like cotton. There didn't seem to be any well, but there was a trough that came almost to the back porch, and it looked like it was meant to carry water. Now it was dry, a cradle for drifted leaves, and the moss that had grown in it was black and curling. Weeds grew in the spillway that had carried the runoff. Leaning up against the sluice there was an old black iron wash pot, the kind with legs. A spider was living in it, working on her web. We followed the sluice uphill a way and found where one of its supports had rotted and left a joint gaping. Spring water was streaming through the hole; it had made itself a new little channel where it hit the ground. It was like ice and clear as diamonds, and we caught it in our hands and drank.

"What are we going to do?" Pet said.

I said I thought that for the time being, we ought to stay right where we were.

"Here?" Her poor little tired face said I was crazy, but she talked matter-of-factly, as always. "What will we eat . . . ?"

"There ought to be something we can salvage, in the car," I said. Part of what we had I knew would be ruined, but maybe some was not. So the children ran ahead, and when I got back down to the branch, they were already mining the back seat. Pet was handing stuff out the hole in the top to Hugh, on the hood, and he handed it up to me, on the bank. They took great pride in their finds:

"Two cans of (pew) sardines! A can of Vienna sausage! A can of tea! A box of wet crackers! Six chocolate drops." (All that paraffin made 'em waterproof.) "Three brown bananas . . . !" We would not starve that day.

We had no matches; we couldn't make a fire, and anyway we had no pots. I could only yearn for that tea. But we sat down on the bank, with little wild things blooming all around us, asked the blessing, and had our breakfast. I knew the kids were wondering the same as I was about where the next would come from, when this was gone. But they said nothing, and we delighted in what we had, and the sun shined on us and warmed us and we began to feel alive.

"I tell you what," I said. "That is such a pretty old house I know it belongs to somebody, and maybe they come sometimes to see about it. I know they wouldn't mind if we took our stuff up there and dried it, and rested awhile, where we could get out of the rain if it started again. Then when we feel better we can walk out."

We were warming to adventure; we went about this squatting with conviction. The kids climbed down again and began handing out blankets and pillows and loose clothes. The suitcase was full of water and it weighed a ton. Just as I thought we'd never get it up, a hole came in one end and the water squirted out, along with underpants and socks and things I decided we'd not miss.

"What else do we get out?" they said.

I knew now there was no hope for the car. "Everything," I said.

The spokes on the left front wheel grated on the rocks as the unloading party moved back and forth. The other angled under, pigeon-toed. The grill was smashed back into I didn't know what; the lights were broken, and some part of its entrails lay under the running board, with the water rippling over it. Had I been able I would have wept for this noble friend and servant. But I was not.

We divided up our plunder and started for the house. We left the suitcase for another trip; we needed the food, and Pet stripped a pillow case to hold it, and we needed to dry the blankets. We noticed much more, carrying that wet stuff, that we were climbing. Several times we stopped and dropped our burdens in the grass and rested. The day had gotten very bright and clear. On our left, the field went only a little way before it turned to woods, climbing greening slopes that rolled on into shadowy waves of mountains, like clouds against the sky. Ahead of us, the ridge rose sharply, at one point, almost straight up. It was bald on its crown, and sloped green and more gently toward the east. A natural lookout. You could see anywhere, I thought, from up there. But I would never make it, not that day. And I sure was not going to send the children by themselves. We would simply wait and see.

We walked along gawking like tourists from the grand hotel. Blue-eyed grass twinkled in the ruts. Wild strawberries lifted their three-fingered hands to catch the sun and now and then there would be clumps of thrift that must have run away from a lady's garden.

It was, I said, the most beautiful place that I had ever seen.

We came again to the house, and it was our duty to knock three times again, but nothing happened. Nobody came. Snatches of rail fence that one time must have kept in cows would do fine for a clothesline, we decided, and we draped them with our worldly goods. We spread the edibles out on the porch with a feeble hope the crackers would dry, and the bees commenced to swarm on the bananas.

Pet and Hugh flopped on the steps, exhausted. I stretched myself out on the warm planks of the porch, in the sun, and squinted out across the landscape, listening to the bees humming, and humming . . . And they were a woman, singing some quiet, happy, work-a-day-song, in the lightest, floating voice, softly, sweetly. . . .

When I sat up the sun had moved across the cove. The gum tree cast its shadow now toward the river. "Children?" I said. They were curled up at the far end of the porch, still asleep. I don't know what came over me, ladies never went into somebody's house when nobody was at home. But I tried the doorknob, just lightly, you know, to see if it was locked. And the door opened slowly, for it was big and heavy, and I had to go inside.

"Mama!" Pet said. I know my hair stood straight up. She was standing in the door, behind me.

"Come on in," I said. "I know there's nobody lived here in an awfully long time."

She didn't think much of such trespassing, but she woke up Hugh, so he wouldn't wake up alone and be scared, and we went on a tour.

There was a wide hallway, down the middle, with a staircase going up about halfway back, and at the end there was a door that went into the kitchen. On either side, the walls of the two big front rooms were paneled with some kind of pretty wood, but kind of dark. There were two rooms behind those that had the feel of ladies' rooms; they were papered with fine old silky wallpaper, with roses that had faded and paled, trailing lilies turned yellow with age and smoke. Every room had its fireplace and each was different; the big rooms had wide hearths and mantels of stone and the smaller ones were made of brick, framed in wood that somebody had spent a long time carving with reeds and running vines. We didn't go upstairs. Somehow that was presumptuous, even in here. But we went back through the hall to the kitchen.

The kitchen was as big as a lot of people's houses. It had its own fireplace, at the end, with a crane in it. There was a big, long, rough kitchen table, and benches, and a wood range, and wash pans hanging up, and a few pots. By the door that went out to the back porch

and the spout, there was an old bonnet hanging on a nail. By instinct I reached and took it down. When I did a mouse squealed
like it was murdered and jumped out and ran up my arm. And I
squealed and danced, and the poor little thing hit the floor running.
We looked inside the bonnet, and there was its nest of nibbled straw
and cloth, and its little pink babies, and we lifted it out, carefully,
and laid it in the corner where the mama cowered under a molding,
with nothing showing but her tail, and I went out and shook the
bonnet and clapped it on my head, ignoring the mouse perfume.

We walked up the lot and into the barn, and of course the first
thing Hugh saw was a blacksnake dozing in some hay as old as time,
and he grabbed it and flung it at Pet and ran. And when she got her
voice back she took after him, across the field, cussing like a sailor.

There was at least, then, other life, of sorts, on this place.

The smell got the best of me; I went to the run where the spring
came down and washed the bonnet, and hung it on a post in the afternoon sun. I would need it, tomorrow, when we went abroad ex-
ploring.

We went down to the car and got the suitcase, then, and carried it
by turns one on either side. And we hung our clothes on the fence,
and took down our blankets, for by mercy they were dry, and we sat
down on the porch and ate our supper. It never occurred to us to
look in the kitchen for a cup; we washed the sausage can and drank
from it. We did go look for matches, while it was light enough to see,
but we found none and decided to go to bed at dark.

We debated sleeping inside against sleeping out.

"I'm cold," Pet said.

"I would hear feet coming down those stairs all night," said the
man of our expedition.

We decided to sleep out, so we laid one blanket on the planks and
put the other two over us, and we locked arms, so if a bear or
boogerman got one of us, he would have to take us all. And the light
faded, over the west ridge, and the stars twinkled, and the peepers
took their pitch from their director, and sang. Down in the meadow
a whippoorwill called, and a screech owl answered from the gum
tree. Charleston crossed my mind, ever so lightly. And we slept.

The sun woke us, shining in our eyes. We went up and washed

our faces and drank our water and had our half a banana and limp crackers, and talked about what we should do. One thing, I said, before we might meet somebody we must get our dry clothes and go down to the river and really get clean. I admit we had avoided meeting the river up close. Pet and Hugh had looked the day before, from a safe distance, and declared it ugly. We had all had enough of ugly water.

But it might be better that morning. We needed to brave it. We got us a change of clothes from the fence and went down. Three or four hundred feet above the river there were woods, open more like a grove that sloped down to the water. The floor of those woods was a garden of ferns and flowers like some make-believe place in a picture book. Some of the trees we knew; we had dogwoods and Judas trees in our garden in Charleston that had already bloomed and dropped. But there were mysterious huge trees, we did not know chestnuts, and I suppose no one will ever know them again, but there was one hollow hulk so big we all stood in it and said if all else failed, here we could keep house.

Mostly, though, this grove was birches, thick as hops. They had to be old, they were so big. Their raggedy bark was shiny, like pale gold, and the new little leaves whispered and sighed when the wind played in their crowns.

It was the kind of place, I thought, where things might go on that literal folks would never be able to see.

The river bed was wide, where we came down, and what had sent me into panic (and a wrong turn) a few miles down, and what I dreaded so to see again was as innocent as dew. It was so clear it was almost invisible, pattering over its bed of little brown rocks, glittering in the sun.

What looked like an old road came down on the other side, through woods and a narrow strip of meadow. There seemed to be a break on this side too, where a road might have crossed the shallow and come over. This was a likely fording place. But there was nobody across the river, that we could see, and nobody here but us. So we took our separate places, and we washed.

We intruded on the pools of little fishes. Nothing would do, then, but that Hugh make a line out of something and fish to keep us from starving. "We don't have any way to cook fish," I said. But that was foolish, there was no danger of us having to try, and I told him all right, to go up to the house and dig through my pocketbook and he might find a pin or two, and a little sewing bag with a spool of thread in it, and I was sure that would hold what he would catch.

I walked with them back up through the woods, and left them, then, and went along up the field, upriver. The grass was tall and the stalks of last year's weeds came to my waist and the burrs of things stuck in my dress. I didn't think anything of snakes; I did watch the ground, I parted the grass and watched where I stepped because there were so many flowers.

It came to my mind, walking along, that maybe Ollie Trotter had seen my grandfather and had told him we had been to his store. And maybe he would send somebody to look. Maybe, right now, somebody was trying all the wrong roads we might have taken, maybe even the one we took. Maybe they would find the bridge out, and the car, and think we drowned. Nevermind, I thought, we will walk out today, and find our way to Caney Forks; very soon we will be hugged to the bosom of our family.

It was getting steep. I thought from so high a hill I might get a wide view and some ideas. And I did. The first thing I noticed was a wisp of smoke, way up the ridge across the river. The next thing was an old wrought-iron fence, at the very top of the hill. The briers had grown over it; there was some kind of yellow-flowered vine blooming on it, and as I got up to it I saw it had a gate at the upper side, and it was sagging open. There was a rusting lamb cast in the top of it, and under it it said in iron-work letters, SWEETLY THEY REST WHO REST IN THE LORD.

It was like the air itself was tingling. I pushed the weeds aside and went in. There were these rows and rows of stones. Moss grew on them. Brambles grew on them. Some were too old and dim to read. One had a clump of bluets growing at its base; I looked at it a long, long time. It said, SAVANNAH MCALLISTER STEELE OUR DAISY, OCTOBER 7, 1846–MAY 4, 1909. WEEPING MAY ENDURE THE NIGHT BUT JOY COMETH IN THE MORNING. On the one next to it was BENJAMIN IVAN STEELE, APRIL 12, 1840–APRIL 29, 1909 LOVE ENDURETH.

There was a little breeze rustling the grass. I could hear the children, like they were awfully far away, and they were anxious, and afraid; they were out here all alone, and they could not find their mother. I started to them, down the ridge. I was just sobbing. Out of control. The ground rolled under my feet like waves and I went tottering like a drunk. I could see Pet, running toward me, hollering.

"Mama! Where have you been? Hurry—brush off your dress and straighten up your hair. There's a horse coming! And there's an old man on it."

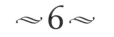

6

BEN AARON

THE KIDS CAME RUNNING UP TO MEET ME, AND HELD MY HANDS, and we went down the back lot fast as we could go. They had made it up between them, they said, that they'd go up the road and find town by themselves and run back and surprise me. What they did find was this man coming riding around a bend way above them. Coming slow, they said. I wished they had gone to meet him— what if he disappeared?

Pet snatched burrs off of me as we went. I looked down at myself and there were green streaks where the suitcase lining had run on that white muslin frock. My hair was flying forty ways for Sunday. I grabbed that old bonnet off the post as we went by and clapped it on my head. And I trotted in the back door and through the house.

There was, at the side of the front porch, what looked like a great stone statue. It was a big gray man on the biggest old gray horse I ever saw. I leaned over the railing to look close—I wanted to see that they were real. I was going to say thank you for coming. Well I could do no more than open my mouth. Nothing moved. Nothing breathed. I knew that face. Oh my God, I thought, we are all dead. This is where we go when we die. Oh, Mackey Steele, you have come to meet me! I stared at the spirit's hair, fluttering silvery around his ears in the breeze. Mackey did not die gray. Did death do this? I clung to the banister, about to wither over. Whatever he was, he stared back. I don't think he blinked.

"Sweet Jesus!" he said, very low. No, he was alive. The horse nodded and pawed and snorted; the white showed of his good eye (the other was blind white anyway). He was feeling his rider's uneasiness. Both, I thought, would have loved to turn and flee. From me? What had I done? This person was as scared as that old man down the road. But braver. And more polite.

He reached up a trembly hand and tipped his old gray hat. "Ah'hmmmm," he said, "Is there some way I can help you?" He knew we didn't belong here.

"You can help us get to Caney Forks," I said.

"Have you got people there?" he said.

When I thought about it, I said, sort of feebly, "None living, I guess. Do you know any Steeles?"

"My name is Steele," he said.

There was this ringing silence. Then he said, "Who are you?"

"Mary Seneca Steele," I said.

The next thing I remember was the smell of sweaty hat. He was fanning me with his hat, with my head on his knee. He had sent the kids up the hill for a sausage can of cold water, and he dipped his handkerchief in it and wiped my face. Gently, like I was a little child.

"Mackey's child," he said. "Yes you are. How on this earth did you find this place?"

I told him that I didn't. That somehow it had found me. I raised up and he sat me on the step, and kept his arm around me, and I told him some about what had happened. 'Course not all the truth. I said my dear husband was all involved with his business, and I had always been so interested in seeing my daddy's side of the family, and the children and I had planned this little trip. Pet and Hugh were standing there all the time, shifting their feet, rolling their eyes at one another. But I was lying only in the part about leaving, and all. The part about the road and the old man running from us and the rain and the wreck and all that, that part was all true.

And this was a great gentleman sitting beside me; he took every word, and he nodded sometimes, and narrowed his eyes and frowned at the account of our perils, and raised his eyebrows and smiled around his pipe over intimations of heroism and deliverance. It was Mackey, again, listening, listening to me go on about a big ugly worm that chased me out of the garden clacking its teeth.

"Which Steele are you?" I said finally. It had only been important to know that there was one.

"Ben Aaron," he said. "You know—no, you probably don't know—but your daddy and me, our fathers were brothers and our mothers were sisters, and they were cousins, besides."

"I got all mixed up on that, up there with the tombstones," I said.

"You found 'em," he said, not much surprised by now.

"Just a little bit ago," I said. "Till then I had no idea . . ."

"I'll swan," he said. "I'll swan."

"Plenty of us dead," I said. "How many of us living?"

"Three, now!" he said. He was plainly delighted. "Till today there wadn' but two. Punnammer and me."

"Punnammer?"

"Yeah. My mother's sister. Punnammer McAllister. Married Daddy's oldest brother Garland. Widdered sixty-somethin' years. She's a-holdin' court up at the Forks. Ain't but eighty-seven."

I closed my eyes and saw that letter again, crumpled in my daddy's hand, that running scrawl that ended up, "Devotedly Aaron. Panama sends her love. . . ."

"Eh, law," he said, "wait'll she sees what I found here this mornin'."

"Do you have a family?" I said.

"Yes," he said. "Hey, captain, what you doin'—diggin' a well?" He had turned around to watch Hugh tormenting the dirt with a stick.

"I got to get some worms to go fishin'," Hugh said. "We 'bout to starve."

"How many days since you eat?" our cousin said, getting himself up. "I ought to thought of that, first thing. Here wait a minute," he said, "it's awful to fish on a empty stomach. Fish can tell it. Makes 'em nervous."

He went and got a sack out of his saddlebag and handed it over. It had biscuits in it big as saucers, stuffed with slabs of ham, and must have been a whole fried chicken, and two baked sweet potatoes, split and filled with hunks of butter.

"Sawmill cook won't let abody go hungry," he said, grinning over the joy of the receivers.

"I told him I was scoutin' today so he fixed me a poke," he said.

"You work for a sawmill?" I said.

"Yeah," he said blandly, "I cut timber."

Pet gave me a biscuit. "Don't you want some of your own dinner?" I said. I felt bad about starving our savior.

"I' 'spect I'll live to get back," he said. "Now I'm going to send down and get you up to Nam's before night."

Suddenly, now everything was all right, and I was exhausted. Somehow I wanted to save this next reunion, until these others had sunk in.

"You know something?" I said, "If it's all right with you, could we just stay still tonight, and go up in a day or so? Maybe I can just walk to the store and get us some milk and bread," I said. "How far is it?"

"Oh, 'bout seven miles," he said, smiling. He sat on the step, considering, sucking little puffs on his pipe.

"Sure," he said. "You going to stay, though, we're going to see you don't sleep cold another night on the boards."

He got up, and handed me up. "Did you climb the stairs?" he said. I reckoned I could have, I said. But I didn't have the nerve. Took all I had just to walk inside that door, the first time. He leaned on the door frame and rubbed his chin, studying.

"Tell me somethin'," he said. "You say you just walked in. Was the door open when you got here?"

No, I said, and I told him how it was, that it was shut but opened very easy. He stepped back and closed the door softly.

It locked.

There was a look came over his face, the slightest smile. I would have loved to know what he was thinking. But he fished in his pocket and pulled out some big iron keys and turned one in the lock, it took a little force, for it was old and stiff, and he pushed the door open, and we went inside. "You'll see why I keep it locked," he said. He led me past the big staircase and back into the kitchen. Then he moved a big old cupboard, turned it aside, and poked a finger through a knot hole in the wall behind it, and undid a latch, and a door of perfectly matched boards creaked open. We went inside a dark little pantry kind of room. He took a candle down off a shelf, and lit it, and there was another door, and he unlocked it with another key, and there was a staircase, going up into pitch black. He held my hand and we went up.

We came out in an enormous room at the top. "Did you not wonder what was over the kitchen?" he said. There were some shreds of daylight from a vent at the far end. Little birds were cheeping in their nests in the eaves, and other small life that had long gone undisturbed flittered across the candlelight into the shadows.

There were rows of trunks and banks of humps draped in quilts and sheeting. Shelves held musty books stacked to the rafters. He lifted covers and the candle shined on polished wood and glittered in prisms and bounded back on us from mirrors dark so many years. For an instant we looked at ourselves reflected in one, mesmerized. And then he held the candle close to his chin and made an awful face, and we laughed, and moved on. He found some featherbeds, just feather ticks, you know, and laid out three, and some quilts.

Then, deliberately, he pulled a cloth down off the wall and held up the candle. Another mirror. No—but so odd. Just the clothes, mostly, were different. It was a painting. A portrait of two people. Square-jawed man, silvery hair, wise-looking eyes, kind of regal. And a little blue-eyed wife with dark curls caught up with some pearly combs. She kind of twinkled down on us. What an incredible likeness, of my cousin Ben Aaron and me. I started to shiver, I was cold from the inside out. My teeth chattered.

"My aunt and uncle, my cousins. Your cousins, too. Your grandparents," he introduced this portrait of just two.

"Daisy and Ive . . ."

I began to understand something about my family in that instant. This was more than family, in any usual sense. This was family you couldn't plot back on a tree; we were more like a vine, grown 'round and 'round ourselves, tangled and knotted never to come undone.

"I can't believe what I see," I said.

Ben Aaron laughed softly. "You see now how you give pore ol' Cud'n Barzilai Peek such a jolt, when you met him in the road," he said. "Lord, you raised the hair on my head, a-standin' down there on her porch, in her old bonnet. . . ."

"Yes, I see," I said. I thought I did. But I saw only partly. The whole picture had a good long way to come.

He took me down and made me sit on the steps and he carried down things he thought we'd need. The kids had gone to fish, and I sat there looking out, too dazed to really think. He shook out the ticks and spread them in the east front room, by the window where there was still a little sun. "It's nice to listen to the river in the night," he said. He carted down rocking chairs and lined 'em on the porch.

Then he came and sat by me. He picked up his damp handkerchief and began polishing his fingers, one by one. I noticed he had perfectly beautiful hands. I wondered how you kept hands like that when you cut timber for a living but guessed there was lots I didn't know about just everything.

He got up, then, and stretched, and said he'd be going 'long. "I'll get t'at window-light fixed upstairs right shortly, got to fix the shingles, too. Anyway I'll be back in a day or two to take you up to the Forks."

"Do you live in the Forks?" I said.

He stooped down and kissed the top of my head. "I'll take you to Nam's," he said. "I'll not tell her a word till the very minute. And I can't wait."

He started down the steps and a thought suddenly struck me. "Who owns this place now?" I said.

He stood still, looking a long way off. And then he turned to me and he said, "It'll always belong to the family."

∾7∾

NEIGHBORS

I REMEMBER HOW THE HOOFBEATS SOUNDED, GETTING DIMMER and dimmer, going up the road. Finally, the hum of the bees and the river and the birds were all there was, again. There is a sharp little ache you feel for human company, sometimes when you're all alone. Many's the time. . . . But anyway I sat there rocking; I got this eerie feeling, watching the wind rock the other chairs. And I thought of a dozen things I should have asked our cousin, but had not. Like, exactly when would he be back? He hadn't even told me where he lived. Tell the truth, I was not all that sure if he was real.

But it was the loveliest afternoon, so bright and green and blue. I got up and walked down to the river, found the kids hanging over a rock, jiggling a bent pin with the remains of a poor worm into a little green pool, entertaining a bunch of teeny fish the size of tadpoles. Readily they gave it up. "Till an hour," Hugh said, laying down his stick on the rock. (When he came back, oddly enough it was gone. He was sure some huge fish had bit it and towed it away. Maybe so, I didn't know.) But we went roaming around again; we walked downstream and found that boggy dark place down there, where the frogs are singing. It's a suckhole, there's a spring branch that comes out of the orchard and then goes underground down there, again, in this little bitty hole. Not our favorite place. Then on up toward the road we got into the orchard, all those old trees with so many dead limbs, all woolly green with moss. But some had bloomed; the petals had dropped not long ago and there would be a little fruit.

And we walked up again to the cemetery, and we counted forty-two headstones, some McAllisters but mostly Steeles, and then a few names like Shuman, and Gillespie, that showed up maybe only once or twice. And so many were babies. On some of the sunken places there were no stones at all. How many, I wondered to myself, had been born here in this house? How many died here?

We picked some flowers on the hillside, we found an old bottle in the barn and filled it at the spout and had us an arrangement for the mantel. A lived-in touch. The sun was getting low, it was getting gloomy in the house. Ben Aaron had set out a couple of lamps and some matches but we had no oil.

It was suppertime. The ants had carried off the last crumbs on the place. Of course we would not perish overnight; we might make it seven miles to town in the morning. But I was not going to enjoy explaining why I didn't want to go to town this afternoon, when we were invited. And I had eleven dollars to last Lord knows how long. Well, I would sit out on the porch and watch the evening, I decided, and wait for a revelation. And I had just commenced to rock when here it came, up through the field from the river.

It was a girl, this time. She was sitting astraddle of a mule, on a croaker sack, with her bare feet dangling down. We all went out to meet her. And it wasn't just because I was lonely, but when I looked at that girl I thought at once, "This is the prettiest child I ever saw." She had really gold hair, done up in plaits wound round her head, and her skin was a pale gold too, healthy, like she might spend time outdoors, but not burned brown. Even her eyes were sort of tiger-eye gold. She had on an old printed cotton dress, I guess made out of feed sacks, and it was gathered up around her knees. She sat up very tall and straight, like a lady; I figured she might be about sixteen.

She was not one to waste words. "Mr. Steele come by and told me to bring you some supper," she said. She handed down a bundle wrapped in a flour sack. "Be keerful of it," she said, "they's a jar of coal oil wropped up separate." And she tugged the rein and the mule turned around to go.

I hollered after her, "Where do you live?" I hoped it was close.

"Up yonder," she said. She pointed up the river over to the ridge, where the smoke I forgot to ask Ben Aaron about was still rising.

"How far is it?" I said.

"Three mile by the road. Not so far by the woods," she said. All the time she was moving on. Then she stopped the mule and turned around and said, "I never got your name."

"Seneca Steele," I said. She stared at me, and then slowly, it seemed like she looked pleased; it was hard to say.

"Seneca Steele," she said. "Mr. Steele never told me. What might you be to him?"

"His cousin," I said. "My father was born on this place, too."

"Y'ns better eat your supper," she said. "Hit'll be stone cold." And she goosed the mule with her heels and was gone, leaving a wake in the weeds. I had been too rattled to ask her name, or thank her as earnestly as I meant it.

We took the sack up on the porch, mystified, and pulled out a rag-wrapped quart of strong coffee, still real warm, a lard bucket of cooked white beans, with an onion sliced on top, and a thin flat cake of cornbread, covered with another clean dishrag. The jar of oil she had bundled in corn shucks, tied round and round with string, so it would not taint the supper.

We found a few old dishes in the cupboard, and spoons in a drawer. We wiped them with a dishrag and poured beans into bowls. The children had never had coffee; Miss Lilah had been against it. This coffee would have stood alone. It had a good bit of sugar in it, that helped some, and we drank it out of cracked dusty cups, every drop.

We filled the lamps with oil, and when we had watched the light fade behind the mountains and the stars come on, we lit one. It was like when the hurricane blew, Pet said, going to bed by an oil lamp. We lay in our glorious makeshift beds, making shadow figures on the wall with our fingers, and when the children slept, I blew out the light and lay there listening to the night, thinking about all that had passed that day.

I was dreaming there was a terrible thunderstorm when I woke up, all turned around like you get in a strange place. The elements (or something) were really pounding on the house. It felt like the place was shaking down. I got up and went to the window. It was just getting light outside. You could still see a star or so; where I was looking the sky was perfectly clear. And there was this creaking and thumping again, and *pound-pound-pound.* Whatever was happening I figured it best to meet it with more clothes on. So I got myself together and went outside to see.

I got out front just in time to see a figure disappear over the comb of the roof. And the pounding commenced again. I went around back, and there was a ladder up to the kitchen roof, and way up on the main house there was a man, nailing down shingles. I waved and hollered at him; he threw up his hand but he didn't answer. Later I could see he had a mouth full of nails.

I watched him work the width of the roof, smoothing all the ruffles, and then he hopped down on the kitchen like a monkey and loped along the ridge pole and down the ladder he came, with his hammer hooked in his belt.

He was hardly any taller than I, on the ground. He had sandy red hair that stuck up like a rooster tail at the crown. He walked with a bowlegged, cock-banty swagger.

"Where did you come from?" I said.

"I come from up on the roof. Now I ax you the same question!" he said.

"I come from out of the road," I said. "Purely by accident."

"Yeah, I heared somethin' about that," he said.

I guessed my cousin had told him, I said.

"Oh, yeah, he come up-pair, t' the house, gon' get Rose to bring somethin' t'eat down here last evenin'. Said he wanted me to come get t'is ol' house in shape for you to stay. You gon' stay?" he said.

There was a little waking sigh in the trees, bending the new grass, rustling the dead. The rim of the sun topped the ridge.

"A little while," I said. "Yes. A while."

I asked him, was that Rose that came up last night? I could not get over that kindness.

"Yeah, she got up a poke quick as she could," he said. "Hadn't milked yet. Felt bad about t'at, there being younguns. Brought y'ns some today."

"Is she your child?" I said.

"The oldest," he said.

"She's beautiful," I said.

"Image of her maw," he said. "Near smart as any man to work, I druther have Rosanner work wi'me as most men I know. 'Tween us we can really turn it out." That seemed to be the important part.

"I reck'n she's a big help to her mother, too," I said.

"Her mother's dead four year gone," he said. The look in his eyes near burned me.

"Left me and Rose four boys t'raise, oldest 'un seven," he said.

Then he cocked his head, and coolly looked me up and down, and his face brightened, and he said, "Have you got ar' man?"

"Yessir," I said, real enthusiastic. "I've got one back in Charleston."

He grinned and looked right through me. I felt this little flutter of panic. And then I thought, well, shoot. And I hugged him and said thank you, for what he and Rose had done. And I asked him in the manner of his daughter, "And what might your name be?"

"Coy Ray Wilcox," he said, swelling up taller. "Wilcoxes on 'is river 'fore ever a Steele come up here. Why, we was here when Ive McAllister was still wearing dresses an' a-blowin' on his wind-bag, over the water. Wilcoxes was here to fight the war. Hell, Wilcoxes set up-pair on 'at ridge, where you're alookin', and watched God make 'ese ol' mountains."

I was impressed. There was the security of neighborhood in that little breath of smoke up there, melting into the morning haze.

"By the way," Coy Ray said, "Rose sent you down some bread and coffee, too. I disremembered it till I reckon it's cold."

Well, I would just gather up some sticks and make a fire in the stove and warm it, I said. So I went about that, there was plenty of deadfall on the ground, and I broke up some sticks and took 'em and crammed 'em into the stove and stuck a match to 'em. And I ran to the spout and rinsed out a pot and came back and poured the coffee in it and set it on to heat.

Coy Ray was back up on the kitchen hammering away when this clattering came down the road. Here came Cousin Ben Aaron, with a wagon and two big red mules. Coy Ray got down and ambled out to meet him. I watched; I thought just then to comb my hair.

Ben Aaron got down and reached out a piece of window glass he had brought wrapped up in a quilt.

"Any fool could see that's too damn big," said Coy Ray.

"Any fool could cut it to fit," said my cousin Ben Aaron.

"Anybody but the damnedest asshole fool would've measured the goddam winder-hole first," said Coy Ray.

I opened the back door quietly as I could and slipped out on the porch. My cousin swept off his hat and raised his eyebrows and smiled his little smile around his pipe. He gave a sidewise look down at Coy Ray, it was like this great bird, here, studying whether it was worth its while to peck a little bug. "Mind yer damn fool mouth before the lady," he said. He reached a glass cutter out of his pocket and threw it to Coy Ray. Coy Ray glared and stalked back up the ladder and disappeared over the overhang of the porch.

My cousin leaned down and kissed my forehead, and we went into the kitchen.

"Kids up yet?" he said.

No, I said, even all the commotion hadn't waked them.

"Get 'em up," he said. "I'm fixin to take you all to Nam's."

"Did you not have to work today?" I said. I was not sure about lumberjacks' business hours.

"Oh, yeah," he said, "I've got to ride up beyond the Forks and do some figuring. I'll leave you with Nam and you can spend the night. Or I'll bring you back down here this evenin', if it makes any difference."

I went and hollered the kids up from the beds, and sent them out to the spout to wash their faces.

"Rosannah send you any coffee this mornin'?" he said.

Mercy, I said, I bet I had burnt it up. 'Course I hadn't, my twig fire had gone out at once. Ben Aaron laughed and went out and down into the cellar, and he came in with an armload of corncobs nearly gone to dust. He put them in the stove and lit 'em and took off the eye of the burner, and opened the damper, and the fire shot up around the pot.

"That was the most beautiful girl I ever saw," I said.

"Rose? Yeah, she is right pretty," he said. "Good girl, too."

"Must work like a dog," I said.

He got some cups and poured us coffee. "I would wish a lot better for her than she's gettin'," he said quietly.

"I take it you don't much care for Coy Ray," I said.

"What?" he said. "Whatever gives you a notion like that? Why we LOVE one another. The best of friends. He's got on a case of the pouts at me right now, thinks I got the best of him on somethin'. But if we'da been meant to kill one another, Cousin, we'da done it long years before now."

He took a swallow of coffee and chewed on one of Rose's biscuits, thinking. "I tell you one thing," he said finally. "Whatever abody can say about Coy Ray Wilcox, there's one more thing the truth. That sorry little bastard has got class."

~8~

FAMILY

IT WAS NOT AS THOUGH THERE WAS NOTHING TO PUZZLE ABOUT then, starting out on another journey. But a perfect May morning in the Blue Ridge is something to celebrate, whatever else. I was too happy almost to endure it, I didn't know quite why; the anticipation of that day, and beyond that day, was part of it. There were feelings I couldn't put my finger on. We were destitute and on the brink of disgrace, but I had never felt so rich in my life as I did sitting up on the seat of that wagon, rattling off up that twisty road.

There were all of those things I had wanted to ask my good cousin. But I had an idea that the things I wanted most to know would pleasure him most not to answer; somehow he was charmingly perverse. And at that moment nothing mattered.

We had not seen these mountains yet except from the cove. Now, climbing, we looked out on them as far as we could see. Pretty soon we would look down on a lot of them, they would look like great wrinkles on the face of the earth. We were looking down on those little clouds of morning that cling to the streams and bottoms until the sun melts them away.

We were climbing that wall that we had figured stood between us and the secrets of the universe. It was called the Hogback, Ben Aaron said; it had a razorback's sharp spine, bristled dark with some kind of pines. The Hogback stood between the place he called "The

Birches" and the north wind, he said; between that old house and the worst of snows, as well as commerce and traffic, good and ill.

The road, such as it was, did not climb it straight up, of course. It crept up sideways, one switchback after another, up one hump, level off a few feet, and up again. There were places in it so narrow you looked over the side of the wagon and down on the tops of trees way below. The kids rode in the wagon bed. They were fascinated, not saying a word. I clung on to the end of the seat-board, un-obviously as I could, till my fingers turned white and went to sleep. I kept my eye on the rhythm of those big red rumps; they were not troubled by anything but horseflies that they swatted with their tails. My cousin held the reins sort of absently in one hand. He reached his other arm around my shoulders, and I tucked my head under his arm, and relaxed.

The road had left the river, not far up from the house. There was no sound but hooves and wheels. And then around a bend there was a roaring, a booming, like an explosion that wouldn't quit. We came to a wide place and Ben Aaron pulled up the mules and we looked down on the narrows. The ridge came to a short-off a hundred or so feet above the river. Another bluff, not so high, faced us on the other side. Between them at the bottom there might have been a gap of fifteen feet. And the river passed through it.

"Did you hear the nar'rs in the night?" Ben Aaron asked. "Y'know, it's not far from the house—just over the hill, beyond the graveyard, you go around a good wide bend and there it is."

You could come this way faster on horseback, or even on foot, he said; there was a ledge down there covered over with laurels, just above the river. An old game trail ran along there, but not wide enough to make a road.

Well, I thought, HE might come that way. But as far as I was concerned, he could have it all to himself.

We came down then into a dip, close to a calm place in the river, and there was a road going off to the right, over an old plank bridge and up the mountain. I asked him where did that go.

"Up to the Wilcoxes'," he said.

"What do they live like up there?" I said.

"Like Wilcoxes," he said. He flicked the reins right sharply and the mules picked up speed.

We had yet to cross that rocky backbone. The curves got tighter till the mules would be heading east while the rest of us were still going west. The sweat bees hovered around their slick damp hides. And then for just a few feet, we were on top. Or almost. There was a bald place to the left of us, and a little pedestal of rock that we had seen from down in the cove as the perfect outlook. We stopped here, among the laurel clumps and huckleberry bushes, I guess to listen at the wind. Ben Aaron took out his tobacco and re-packed his pipe.

"All this you see. . . ." he said. And I waited. And the wind blew. And the mules blew. But whatever he started to tell me he thought better of it. And finally he clucked to the mules and we moved on, going down.

"I'll bring you back up here another day," he said. It was a much gentler slope we were going down than the way we had come up. Every now and then we could see the river below us, a streak of silver in a widening valley.

I don't know what made me think of it, but I asked him, "Where is Boney Creek?"

"Down here, just a little way," he said. "What you know about Boney Creek?"

Well, I said, I remembered Mackey telling me this story one time, about how some little boy in the family went out in the night, in his long white nightgown, and bridled his daddy's dish-faced mare and rode her "clean to Boney Creek Bridge."

"Oh, way beyond!" said Ben Aaron. "Boney Creek was where I run into a bunch of ol' boys comin' down from Wilcoxes', they'd had 'em a little dram or two and they were amblin' along, goin' home, and here we come, a-cloppity-cloppin' right through the middle of 'em, mind this was inside a dark bridge, that ol' mean mare an' me. She had her a bad name already, she was so bad to buck and r'ar and kick. She'd done bit the finger off a hired man when he tried to bridle 'er.

"Anyway, my folks would never have known a thing about that, except the next day one of them boys come up to my daddy at the mill with his eyes still this big, and he says, 'I never knowed how mean that ol' horse o' yourn really was till I seed her last night with a demon on 'er back.'"

"How old you reckon you were then?" I said.

"Oh, five, maybe six," he said. "I remember it. It was a pretty moonlight night. I'd been a-lyin, studyin' about something, lookin' out the window. All of a sudden I just couldn't stand it. It was two or three o'-clock, I guess, ever'body else dead to the world. And no reason not to go, nothin' in the world out here to hurt anybody, day or night."

We crossed Boney Creek through the old covered bridge and descended into the valley, and the town of Caney Forks.

The first sign of life we passed was an old church hugging the foot of the mountain on the left of the road. It needed paint; its old double doors sagged open and leaves had blown inside. Doves flew out of the steeple as we went past. The ravellings of a broken bell-rope fluttered in the breeze. Behind it there was a graveyard, all gone to wild things now; wild azaleas bloomed among the stones. The ground was fairly rose with crane's bill. I made out only one name as we passed. It was McAllister.

A chiseled marker in front said PISGAH PRESBYTERIAN CHURCH FOUNDED 1794.

"How sad that is!" I said to Ben Aaron. "What happened?"

"New church," he said.

The new church was maybe half a mile ahead, at the beginning of the one paved street in Caney Forks. It was all stone and stained glass and it had a copper spire. Its lawn was walled up with carefully mortared stone and the grass was neat and all one shade of green. Nobody seemed to have been buried there; maybe it was too new. Maybe they did not want it cluttered up. There was one of those glassed-in arch-shaped signs out front. This was All Saints Episcopal Church.

Across the street a few yards down, there was the Caney Forks Drug and Sundry Store, with the name of Ansel Shuman, M.D. lettered in black-rimmed gilt in an upstairs window. Ben Aaron stopped there and gave me the reins to hold while he went in to get some tobacco. That gave me a nice chance to study the landscape. And I must tell you what there was, back across the street, next to the church yard.

There was a house over there, on about a city block of land. It was a terribly large house, painted white, with more columns than the Parthenon. I guess as a nod to other cultures, it had a turret at either end, each capped with a sort of onion dome, and there was an imposing summer house in the yard built in the manner, somewhat, of a pagoda.

My eye was captured by the entry to the place, it was an arch of wrought iron grapevines that sprang from behind two granite pillars. Stone peacocks perched on the pillars; little painted stone darkies, in red jackets and caps, held lanterns faithfully at their bases.

There were more, let's say, engaging features about the lawn. A decorative windmill turned its arms by a spring-branch Zuyder Zee. Nearer the street, there was a pool, fed by a pipe only partly hidden by the concrete body of a cherub, who held up a tilted pitcher, spilling water into the gaping mouth of a concrete dolphin frozen in midleap. A pink plaster flamingo stood on one bent iron leg, admiring itself in the water. A family of fake deer, with wide enameled eyes, paraded across the grounds as silently as only stone can do.

I was all wrapped up in this vision when Ben Aaron came out of the drugstore carrying a bunch of ice cream cones.

"You want to go on a tour of the city before we go to Nam's?" he said.

"Exciting!" I said. Something mean was burning the tip of my tongue. "How about if we start with that tacky-palace over there?"

Ben Aaron threw back his head and hollered and howled and whooped and laughed. He rocked and roared. We took those ice cream cones before he spilled 'em.

"Don't laugh," I said, "it's grand. It's superb. Who lives there?"

"Beats me," said Ben Aaron. He climbed up and took the reins and we proceeded on through town.

The air was clear and soft and full of the smell of sawdust. We surveyed the commercial district: "Tatum's General Merchandise, Founded 1792," said our tour guide. "Original stock of fly-specked candy, yellow birthday cards and dried-up purgatives now on sale at full price." There were a couple of benches in front of the store and a half a dozen town elders in overalls sat on them, keeping careful watch on the street. Ben Aaron waved his ice cream at them. They were plainly interested in us.

We waved at Tom Joe Brock, standing in the doorway of his barbershop. "Cut your throat in a card game," said my cousin, under his breath, about Tom Joe Brock.

He tipped his hat at some ladies coming out of the Caney Forks Cafe. Their response was to study us intently, moving a corner of their mouths in quiet, shared remarks.

"The Bank of Caney Forks," said Ben Aaron. That and the drugstore were the only brick buildings on the street; everything else was frame and sort of propped-up looking. We clopped by Hambright's Feed and Seed, and the blacksmith shop, and the Caney Forks Coal Yard-Ice Plant and Filling Station. The pavement ended.

But the road went on, dirt, lined now on either side with little houses, more like cabins, all lots alike, some out of logs, some frame. There were dozens of them. Little kids played in the yards in the sun. Women hung their wash on lines front and back and visited on porches. Ben Aaron waved at them as we went by; they waved and hollered back as though they were all friends. I started to ask him was this where he lived but did not.

And then we came to a ramshackle sprawl of boards and corrugated tin; it might have been a warehouse, a big one. It seemed to cover acres. Plumes of smoke and steam rose from its stacks and chimneys. Flickers of light and thumps and whines of machinery came through the cracks. It smelled delicious.

"You want to see where I work?" said Ben Aaron.

"Don't you work in the woods?" I said.

"Sometimes do, sometimes not," he said. "Have to come in here, when the flour gets low, and pick up m'pay."

We went through a gate, into a compound of sheds and ponds full of floating logs and mountains of sawdust and piles of slabs and stack after stack of lumber. A young man coming out in a shiny yellow roadster pulled over to let us pass. He leaned out to speak very nicely to Ben Aaron and smile nicely at me.

"Slick lawyer," Ben Aaron said. "Slick and dirty. Best kind."

A locomotive sat puffing, going *chunk . . . chunk . . . chunk* while a bunch of men loaded lumber on a string of stake-sided flatcars. We bumped over the track in front of it. I felt a shudder start at the back of my neck and go down to my fingers and toes; it was peculiar. We went on and stopped in front of a bad-looking old building.

There was a sign by the front door that said, CANEY FORKS LUMBER CO. I. AND D. STEELE AND SONS LOGGING LUMBER MILLWORK.

"Mackey was one of the sons, you know," said Ben Aaron. "Worked here till he was twenty-three."

"And you were the other one," I said.

"I was eight years old when your daddy left. Looks like a eight-year-old's piece o' management, don't it?" he said.

Way up the track, in a long tunnel of pines, another engine blew. I linked my arm through his and held his fingers very tight. We watched it come laboring in, ringing its bell, pulling half a dozen cars of logs onto a siding.

"No," he said, "our daddies were both alive back then. They were great gentlemen, both of 'em. Knew about as much about business as a tumblebug knows about grand opera. Never figured they had to know; they owned timber. Mack was the one had the gift. He made the wheels turn here; it was a long dark time after he was gone."

I was about speechless. "You've kept it," I said finally.

He sighed and squinted straight ahead and sucked his pipe. "I did what I thought I had to do," he said.

He sat up straight then and clucked at the mules. "Let's us get on over to Nam's," he said, "it's a-gettin' dinner time."

He took a road that turned up through the mill village and cut back south, skirting the town. It seemed to be the residential street, the street of old white houses and gray houses and a brick house or two, with wide cool porches that looked out across the valley, with willow trees and quinces and snowball bushes in their yards, and latticed well-houses, and their clotheslines all politely in the back.

We came to one on a corner, back near downtown, that was dazzling, fresh-paint white, like a three-layer wedding cake. We stopped in front of its picket fence and Ben Aaron got down and draped the reins over a post and we alighted. Golden bells poked through the fence. Budding roses trailed over it. Ben Aaron hesitated a minute with his hand on the latch of the gate. This was the old McAllister house, he said. Not the real old one—that one was burned during the War Between the States by Union-serving neighbors whose names (even their descendants') were never since mentioned in this house, not even today. "We don't even th'ow up a hand when we meet 'em in the road," he said. He was smiling but I felt like he meant it.

This was a house of the age of gingerbread. It had a frilly porch around three sides, every banister and post turned and joined to look like lace on a petticoat. It had high steps going up, with spirea bushes drooping white by the railings. The ceiling of the porch was painted sky blue. There was a fan light over the front door, and an oval glass panel in the door itself. Ben Aaron opened the screen door and knocked and hollered, "PunNAMMER . . . hey, PunNAMMER! Come looky here!"

We could feel the light approach of feet, very fast for someone eighty-seven. A face appeared then in that oval glass, it was a person not nearly as tall as I, a tiny, blue-eyed person with black hair skinned back in a bun and little gold spectacles on her nose. Ben Aaron stood back as she flung open the door, and we were face to face.

It was another frozen moment. She clapped her bony hand over her mouth and stared. "In the name of the Lord, Aaron, what stunt are you pullin' on me?" she said. Her chin was trembling.

He answered her in a high, cracking voice. "Mack's girl," he said. And he turned away, then, I guess he could not bear the sight of women just boo-hooing.

Finally, when I turned loose of her, she stepped back and pulled down her upper lip and wiped her eyes on her apron, and flipped up her frock and blew her nose on the hem of her petticoat.

She looked at me again, more calmly. "They law," she said, "she does so favor Daisy . . ."

"She does that," said Ben Aaron.

~9~

REVELATIONS

"WOMERNSES, WOMERNSES, A-KISSIN' AND A-CRYIN'," BEN AARON said. He took out his handkerchief and blew his nose quite loud. "I reckon I'm a-gonna have to cook my own dinner. These younguns and me's eat nothing but biscuit bread all day."

"G'won, then, go to it," Aunt Nam said. "Sass will get you nothin' in this house but a whippin'.

"Come on in the house," she said, for we were still clustered on the porch. She smothered up the children and made over them; "What a pretty child, Lordamercy. And such a big fine boy. Handsome! Favors us some, don't he?" I saw that he certainly did.

She tripped off through the parlor, it was a regular Auntie parlor, all that dark wood and faded rose damask and shelves full of gimcracks. We followed her through the dining room and into the kitchen. The kitchen smelled of woodsmoke and strong soap and coffee and green things boiling with fat meat. She chunked another piece of wood in the stove and took up the lid off an old black pot, and the steam rose off about a gallon of pole beans, simmering on the back of the stove.

"Were you looking for somebody to come to dinner?" I said.

"Nobody but Aaron, he generally comes ever' day or two when he's not gone someplace," she said. She put on slabs of ham to fry, and made up cornbread, scoops of meal and pinches of salt and soda and unmeasured calculations of buttermilk and grease and dumped it in a hot black pan to bake, talking all the time.

"You come up to So-Fier's last night?" she said.

"Hmm?" I said.

"She come in down at The Birches," Ben Aaron said, answering for me.

Nam stopped in mid-stir and peered at me, frowning. "How in the world?" she said. I told her the highlights of our coming, and Ben Aaron told her how he had found us. He told her he had gone down there to see what the storm had done, and found something had blown in, instead of blown away.

We touched lightly on the odd things about it, and there was a thoughtful little silence while she poured hot water from the kettle into the coffee pot and dumped in a scoop of coffee and set it on to boil. It was, right then, one of few things, as I would find, upon which Aunt Nam ever reserved comment.

"You stopped by So-Fier's on the way up then this mornin'," she said, throwing that puzzle out again.

"No . . . I don't know," I said. Ben Aaron opened his mouth to say something but didn't, and went back to studying the toes of his boots. "We stopped a couple of places," I said. "Where is it?"

"Darlin', if you ever went there you'd of knowed it," she said, with the merriest glint of malice. "It's the showplace of the town."

"Captain, do you and Sis like horses?" Ben Aaron said, plainly uncomfortable. Hugh gave him a sort of tired smile and a nod, but I don't think it would have mattered if the child had said, No, they petrify us both. Ben Aaron was going to say, "Well, come on, let's go over to the stable," anyway.

"No, you don't!" Nam said. "Don't you leave this house. This dinner is ready to put on the table."

She went to the pie safe and got out a platter of fried apple pies and some cold biscuits. She got jars of chowchow and molasses and jam and peach pickles from the pantry and went out on the back porch, to the ice box, for a jar of milk. She poured coffee in the pan with the ham to make gravy, and dished up the dinner, and we went to the dining room and sat down in state.

She squinched her eyes and dropped her chin and began to pray, "Lord make us thankful for these and all thy blessings we ask it in

Jesus' name Amen. And Lord I thank you for my children." Then she made us eat. And we did.

I sat there chewing on a piece of cornbread dipped in molasses, thinking this outdid all the Thanksgivings and Christmases of my life rolled into one. We talked about our lives as though we had lived them together and had parted only days ago. We told things we remembered about Mackey; I felt real warm and good that I remembered so much, and that they were so anxious to hear it.

We got up for more coffee and went through the whole plate of pies. The children slipped out and went to sit in the porch swing, and we talked on.

A worrisome thing was preying on my mind, even while we laughed and dwelled on pleasant subjects. Plaster deer and flamingoes marched across my conscience. I knew I shouldn't but finally I asked, timidly, "Who is So-Fier? Is she some of our kin?"

Aunt Nam looked at Ben Aaron sidewise, frowning. Ben Aaron looked down at his plate. Very quietly, he said, "She is my wife."

It was clear, right then, the insult I had handed him, back in front of the drugstore. I was mortified. "Oh, I am so sorry!" I said. "I mean. . . ." I knew the more I said the worse it was going to get.

But he was smiling at me, a smile I never forgot. It was a tight little flat-mouthed smile; his eyes were smiling, really sparkling. And then he told Nam what I had said about the house he had built for Sophia, his wife, and he started to laugh and the dishes rattled. Nam clapped her hands together and then held in her teeth and laughed. I never thought it was funny in the first place, but being sure I was forgiven, I laughed too, knowing full well I should be ashamed.

He got up from the table then, still grinning, and hitched up his britches and said he'd better go. "I've got to ride up on Wolfcreek and look about a boundary somebody wants to sell," he said.

"How big a boundary?" Aunt Nam said.

"Oh, 'bout six hundred acres."

"Timber or land?"

"Both. Said it's a right smart of walnut and red maple," he said. He emptied his pipe and stuck it in his pocket and lit up a cigarette. He was talking business.

"What they want for it?" Nam said.

"Said they want fifty dollars an acre. It's heirs, wantin' all they can get."

"What'll ye give?"

He raised his eyebrows and studied his fingernails. "I'll not give that, for danged sure. I may give thirty-five, I don't know. Don't know if I'd have it atall. That's long-time Harkins land. I never lost nothin' up there . . ."

He sauntered toward the parlor and turned back, in the doorway. "Y'uns need to go back down for anything this evenin'?"

"No, they don't," Nam said. "They're here till I talk 'em to death. G'won about your bidness. Stay the night up there, why don't you?"

"I'll take my blanket then," he said. He came back and kissed us both on the face and took his leave. I heard him holler goodbye to the kids as the wagon rattled away.

We cleared off the table and covered up what food was left and put it in the safe. The icebox at Nam's, I learned, was for ice. And milk and butter, in warm weather. She poured a kettle of scalding water in the dishpan and rubbed a rag on a block of homemade soap and commenced to wash the dishes. "Tell me," she said, "how did Mack die?"

I had always wondered, I said, did anybody really tell them he was gone. She said, "Well, the way it was, the day when Ive took sick, Ben Aaron sent your daddy a telegram and told him please to come. Ive was groanin' ever' breath, 'Mack . . . Mack . . .' We got no answer, got no answer. And Ive died. And Aaron sent again, said, 'Your daddy's gone. Come home.' Mack never came, and we never heard. In just a few days then, Daisy, she passed on. . . ." Big tears were dripping in the dishwater.

"Ben Aaron said that mornin', 'Don't you lay Daisy in the ground till I get back here with Mack Steele.' He went to Red Bank and got on the train and went to Charleston. Didn't nobody hardly have an automobile then, you know.

"He got down there and he found the place where you all lived, said they wadn' nobody in Mack's family home but an old nigger man come to the door. Good ol' man. Said tears come in his eyes when he said, 'Why Mr. Steele's done been buried now two weeks.' Said your ma had took you and gone to Paris France, to get it off her mind. And in the meantime, I think it was that very day that Ben Aaron went, a letter come from your ma, said only that Mack had died, said she was in such a state she had to get away. I wrote her after that, asked her to come and let us see you both. But I never did hear from her again. Aaron did, I know; they had some business back and forth.

"But tell me," she said, switching back, "tell me how it was he died?"

I told her, all of it, as I have told you; it was pain, for I had carried it all those years, for there'd been no one to tell it to before.

We were sitting in the kitchen, wiping our noses, when the clock in the parlor bonged four. "Mercy!" Nam said. She trotted off and got some paper and a pencil and sat down and began making some kind of list. Then she went and called the children, they had found the way into the cellar, under the back steps, and they came forth musty as the grave, and she folded the note and put it in Hugh's shirt pocket and pointed them off toward the store. As soon as they were out the gate, she cranked the telephone.

"Pearly, ring Jasper," she said. "Jasper, I reck'n you've put up Ben Aaron's mules? Well hitch up a buggy directly and go down to Tatum's and pick up my childern. Little boy and little girl. They've got a load they'll never carry."

She hung up and cranked again. "Pearly, now I want Grover . . . Grover, that's my childern comin' yonder, I forgot to write give 'em a cold Co-coler. No, one apiece. And now you make sure they's lean in that meat, wadn' none atall on them hog breasties you sent over here last time. If I want lard, I'll say lard . . . Yeah, put it all on my book. . . ."

Come to find out, some while later, the store belonged to Ben Aaron, too; it had first been McAllister's, and Tatum had bought it. And Ben Aaron had bought it back. It served as the commissary for the sawmill, as the house of haute couture and haberdashery and the larder for the town of Caney Forks.

"Do you know I've not been down to The Birches in years?" Nam said. "I used to go right often and look after the graves. But it got to be so sad, that ol' house just a-standin' there like it was a-waitin' for the wind to take it down.

"Honey," she said, "it's such a blessin' you've come home. No Steele knows what to do with itself away from here."

"Why did Mackey leave?" I asked. That, right then, was the second most pressing question on my mind. The first I had no heart to bring up again.

"That must have been one thing you were too little for him to talk to you about," she said. "Did Aaron tell you anything about his sister Lucy?"

"Ben Aaron has told me as little as he could get by with about anything," I said.

Nam rocked and swung her foot. "Aaron's kind of flummoxed right now I 'spect," she said. "He'll come around. I tell you, the thing about this tribe that makes us a little quare to other folks is how we have generally married with our cousins. You see, Garland and Ive and Dave Steele, they were cousins of ours, they were brothers and married us McAllister sisters, we were Ariana, Savannah and Panama but never got called anything other than Arie, Daisy and Nam. This has gone on always, far back as I know anything about us. I don't know why that is, it just suited us to marry who we married. 'Course along the line some went outside, there was a few. . . .

"But all Mack's life, from the time they were tee-tiny, he had his eye on Lucy Steele, Arie and Dave's little girl. Oh, you should've seen her, you'd know why. She was the prettiest one ever was of us. Hair like light honey, the biggest eyes. Had eyes the color of Aaron's; you know I don't know what you call that. Have you looked at his eyes?"

I thought about it. Hmm. What would you call the color of fallen leaves, under little shallow water, in the sun? Or river pebbles. Several colors; they changed with the light. I had noticed. An eagle's eyes were the same color; I saw that when Bird here came to live with me.

"I reckon brown," I said.

"Lucy was tall too and long in her bones," Nam said. "Looked a lot like Aaron, 'course she was way many years, twenty-three years, I guess, the oldest. The two little middle babies died, then long after they'd quit looking for another one, Aaron come along.

"It just seemed like to ever'body that Lucy and Mack would marry. He thought so. Till he put the notion to her." Nam got up and went to the window. "Thought I heard the buggy," she said.

"What did Lucy say?"

"Said no." Nam was not believing it, to that day.

"Did she give him any reason why?"

"Said, 'Look at this family. Look at the feebleminded ones, poor old Uncle Pink a-settin' out on the back porch day in, day out, fishin' in a bucket. The women would set him out there in his chair ever' decent mornin', fetch him his pole and string, and ever' now and then they'd look out and say, "Pink, darlin', are ye ketchin' anything today?"

"'Think about Aunt Liza, settin' astraddle of the comb of the roof in the middle of the night, a-screechin' like a peacock. Think about Cud'n Vick, down there tryin' to poke her youngun through a chink in the bridge. And all the little babies that live just long enough to cry.'

"About then, Lucy started to wail and cry," Nam said. "She screamed at him, 'I love you, Mack Steele, but before God I won't marry you, for this has got to stop.' They were settin' out here on the porch, I remember it like yesterday," Nam said. "She flung down the steps and leaned on the gate and sobbed. Mack went out there and put his arms around her but she shrugged him off. He just stood there a little bit and watched her cry, and then he sort of sagged and went out by her, and got on his horse. We never saw him again."

I cried into my sleeve till it was soaked. "What happened to her?" I said.

Nam blew and sniffed. "Oh, a couple of years after he was gone, she married a Gillespie boy. Nice fellow, not our kin. She tried to have a baby; it was real big, and she was made too slim. Just couldn't. She's a-lying down at The Birches, with that baby in her arms. They took it after she was gone. But it was dead.

"And then," Nam said, sighing, "Ben Aaron done what it was he done. Went way up the branch to find him that woman. Lord, I don't know what for; we had cluckin' old hens aplenty here close around home. And I'll swannie, I don't know how anything could of come of Lucy and Mack that would of touched that match, for pure disaster."

∼10∼

SETTLING IN

"I HEAR JASPER A-COMIN'," NAM SAID, LEAVING ME SUSPENDED ON the edge of my chair. She went out on the porch and hollered at him. "Leave it all in there," she said. "Drive on down in the lot and put the buggy in the shed. You can turn the horse out, I'm a-gonna need it in the mornin' early.

"What we'll do," she said to me, "we'll get up soon in the mornin' and we'll go down and get you set up to keep house. I reck'n the mice won't spile our meat and meal and stuff over just one night in the shed."

The kids straggled in with a bag of peppermint sticks and chocolate drops from the free hand of Grover Tatum (Aunt Nam said wryly not to worry, that it would show up on the ledger), and as the day wore out they clung around our skirts, tired and a little bit bewildered.

We washed that night in hot water, for the first time in nearly a week. And we slept in beds up off the floor, with clean smooth old sheets that smelled like those little bags of herbs old ladies put in their closets. A couple of times in the night Nam tipped in, in her old pink flannel gown and sleeping cap, and tucked the covers up around our chins.

In the morning, we went down to The Birches.

The buggy was piled up with sacks of meal and flour and sugar and cans of lard and coffee and packages of cured meat and soap, and the four of us sitting on them, and on one another. I was sorry for the horse. But Nam let him go pretty slow, and we talked about who used to live where, and what went with them.

She had kept going to the Presbyterian Church, she said as we passed it, even when she would be the only one there. And the preacher got to coming only once a month, then, and finally not at all. And even then, she said, she would go sit in her pew on Sunday morning, "Only me and the Lord." And she kept the church house swept out, and everything in order.

"But I am done got old now," she said. "I am too old to do it anymore. Things have to pass; it'll tumble down someday. And I will, too.

"Oh, I go to church sometimes," Nam said. "Sometimes I'll go down on Beaverdam with the Baptists, they worry I'm not saved, but they're as good to me as they can be. Sometimes I sit in with the Episcopals but most times not."

Well, I had been raised in the Episcopal church, I said. But that didn't come from the Steeles. Who had brought it here?

"So-FIER!" Nam said.

We rode along a little way. "Tell me somethin' about Sofier," I said, finally.

"What you want me to tell you about 'er?" Nam said.

"Well, whatever," I said.

She screwed up her mouth and cocked her head and considered.

"You won't like 'er," she said.

I sat there waiting for more, I felt sort of sorry for the woman, like the jury had convicted her before I got a chance to hear her case.

"Why won't I like her?" I said, deciding I was going to like her, if it killed me.

"She's pure outlandish," Nam said. "Look at the daisies, a-startin' to bud up. Bless their little hearts, you know they'll be daisies of some description all summer long." The subject of Sophia was hereby closed and bolted. "I remember when your granny was born, it was gettin' on into cool weather. I was about five, didn't know a thing about how babies come or any of that; Mama had six, 'course three of 'em died. I didn't even know when Arie come, I was up then about eight years old, and I didn't know where they come from.

"Mama went down to The Birches to have her babies, she'd go down when one was time to come and we'd not see her, then, till it was born. There was a good ol' granny woman down on Long Branch that brought 'em all, ol' Aunt Lillie Brock, and she'd come bring the baby and then stay a week or so. I guess that was one reason the babies would all come there.

"Lucy, one time, when she was in a brood and talkin' dark, said our babies had to come there because it was so handy to the cemetery. I wonder now if she just always somehow knew. But when Poppa took me down after Daisy was born, he just said we were goin' down to see Mama. He was all smiles, as happy as could be. We got there and he took me in the room where Mama was—I remember there was a big flowerpot of little purple-lookin' flowers, they grow all over in the fall of the year—and he took this little bundle from Mama, and handed to to me to hold. I never will forget it, he said, 'Look what we found down in the daisies!'

"I'll not forget that little face, it looked for all the world like a little bud. She had the bluest eyes —blue from the day she was born. She looked at me like she knew the funniest thing there was, and she stayed happy like that, all of her life. They had 'er baptized Savannah. But she was always Daisy."

"Did you never have any babies of your own?" I said.

"I had one," she said.

After a little bit I said, "It died, didn't it."

And after a little bit, she said, "It died."

And that, of course, was the prelude to a story.

"The last time Garland came home from the War Between the States I made him marry me," she said. "He didn't want to then; said, 'Let's wait till this ol' war is over, and start out better. You know I might not get through this.'

"And I said, 'I know, that is why I want us married.' Daisy and Ive was havin' a fit to get married, but Poppa said no, indeed. Daisy was just seventeen. But Garland and me, we went ahead. In less than a week, he had to leave again.

"Well, it was about five months, and we got word that Garland was in a hospital up in Petersburg, with his arm shot off. I said right then I was a-goin' after him. There wadn't an able-bodied man left in this part of the country to go with me. But Daisy said well, she was goin' too. Ive was in the same company and she'd not had a word from him in months. She'd wore a regular trench in the front porch, a-walkin' up and down.

"Now we were all down at The Birches, then, our house had burned and Poppa was somewhere in Virginia, fightin' in a different company. Uncle Ham was old and crippled with a stroke and all the women had their hands full, just to keep the place goin'. There was nobody to help us. And nobody to stop us. We had nothin' left but the poorest ol' horses, the good 'uns was all gone to the war, you know.

"We left out one night, with two of them old bone-piles hitched to a wagon. Sneaked off. We left word sayin' where we were goin' and not to worry. We'd a been scared to death if we'd had a lick of sense, but we didn't. We were goin' by a map out of a geography book. Nowhere on it did it say 400 miles. And half that again, for the times we got lost. It didn't say nothin' about rain, either. Or there bein' days without a store or a house or a clean spring of water. Somebody did tell us along the way that we'd better watch out for people that'd take our horses, there were lots of desperate folks in that time.

"So we went as much as we could at night, hid and slept days in the canebrakes and woods. We had a sack of corn dodgers and some apples. We had a gun but squirrels and rabbits had got mighty scarce. If a house looked friendly we'd stop sometimes and ask to be sure we were goin' right. Sometimes people'd offer us a little somethin' to eat; 'course we'd not ever ask.

"We'd tell 'em where we were a-goin', and people were nice to us. Even one place a woman said well, her boy was in the Union Army and had been killed. She made us take some biscuits with us. I thought I couldn't cry any more, I'd done run out of tears. But I cried ten miles after that place.

"Well, we wouldn't have stopped at all except we had to be so careful not to kill the horses. We had been gone two weeks or more, and we commenced to see lots of soldiers. We'd ask 'em if they knew Garland and Ive, or even where the company was, and they would point us on toward Petersburg. Then one mornin' we met Ike Tatum, from right here, walkin' down the road with a bunch of men leadin' some mules. He said, 'Ive and Garland's both in a little old church that's been made a hospital.' He pointed us exactly the way to go."

By then we had come to the narrows. It was a noisy place, and it was one of those times, anyway, that Nam would have to gather up a voice to say what she was trying to say. Directly, then, she said, "I knew when I saw Garland he'd not make it. He was shot all to pieces. One arm gone was about the least of it. He kept tryin' to talk to me, I put my ear right down on his mouth, and he said, 'I kep' on livin' 'cause I knew you'd come. . . .'

"Ive was shot through the chest. When we got there the doctor was runnin' a silk handkerchief clean through him, to get the maggots out. We never asked a soul, we just got some men to help us load 'em both in the wagon, and we started for home. We went by what we remembered, and by the sun, and the stars.

"Daisy was drivin'. I was holdin' Garland's head on my lap when he died. It was early one mornin'; I held him on all that day, I took off my bonnet and covered his face. And we started out the same way, the next day. I meant to bring him home. But it got warm, and Ive was so sick. We stopped on a little hill, lookin' down on a river, it put me more in mind of The Birches than any place I saw. There was an old house down in the bottom. Daisy went down, and an old man came out. She told him about us, and he brought a shovel and helped us. He made us stay that night, I know he gave us some boiled potatoes but he had no salt; 'course we didn't care.

"The next day then we left out again. Goin' out of sight, I thanked God so much that Garland would lie on high ground. I was so thankful I'd made him marry me, and that he'd lived till I could get to 'im.

"We got home with Ive. He was a sorry lookin' somethin', Lord weren't we all. Soon as he could stand alone, and Mama and Aunt Bet had got the lice off him, they let him marry Daisy . . ."

"You mean you had a baby, in the middle of all that?" I said.

"No, I had it about six weeks after we got back, I reck'n. What it was, we all took the dysentery, had nothin' to doctor it with but blackberry wine. The rest of 'em got all right but me. And finally, that poor little baby came. It was an eight-months baby—you know they don't live, lots of times. It was a tiny little girl. It never even breathed."

It was one of those up on the hill, with a lamb on the stone, she said. "We named it Elizabeth, for Aunt Bet, even though it was dead. Bet, you know, was Garland's mother. And I knew I'd never have any more."

Always, on that road, I would think of her. I would think, she went through that, and she lived to be old. There would be times I would have to think of it.

We could look down now on the back lot, and the back side of the house. It made me catch a quick breath. I don't know what it was, just a feeling. The grass had been cut around the house. We went around to the back, in the buggy, and got down and carted that stuff into the kitchen. When we went through into the house we saw that somebody had brought down furniture. We had chairs and a table in the parlor, and a couple of bedsteads up in the sitting room, where we'd slept on the floor. The beds were made up, with counterpanes on them. There was a big old clock on the mantel, going *tock-tock-tock*.

We had a dining table, now. There was, as Nam would say, a flowerpot in the middle of it, a vase of flowers picked out of the field, sitting on a plate so as not to make a ring. There were doilies put about sort of at random, and pictures, sort of at random, here and there on the walls. It looked like somebody was playing house.

"Well, I see Rose was here," Nam said. "Coy Ray's goin' to say, 'Rose holp me,' when the fact is Coy Ray help Rose, a little bit."

"I can't believe that child," I said.

"She puts me in mind a lot of Lucy, so independent," Nam said. "You know Cleone, her mother, was kin to us. Cleone's grandma, Aunt Sallie McAllister, was Poppa's sister. Cleone's daddy, old Jake Shuman, owned a good bit of land over on the far side of the Wilcoxes'. Pretty high-type people. Died, her mama and daddy, right together in the typhoid epidemic. Ansel was off in medical school. Cleone was there with 'em by herself. Her hard times didn't begin with Coy Ray Wilcox. But it didn't take 'em many years to end there."

We were washing the dishes out of the cupboard when somebody came pecking at the back door. I looked out and it was old Cud'n Barzilai Peek, that old man that ran from us on the road. He still had tobacco juice running down his beard.

I opened the door and said, "Cud'n Barz?" He looked like he was meeting a spook. "Miss Cud'n," he said, taking a step back, "I wonder if I might could talk a little bidness wif ye?"

"Come in! Come in!" I said, all bright and chirpy. "Aunt Nam!" I said, "Look who's here!"

"I done seen 'im," she said, cutting her eye at the door. "You watch 'im."

"Uh, could we talk private?" he said. He would not come in, so I went out. Very low and confidential, he said, "Miss Cud'n, I've got a trade to make ye for that machine down yander."

I felt dumb. "Machine?" I said.

"At'n down yander in 'na branch. All tore up. Ain't t'at the one you come here a-drivin'?"

"Oh, yeah," I said. "But honey, it's wrecked. It'll never run."

"Hit will when I hitch me some steers on the front of it," he said. His eyes were gleaming.

Nam came out, drying her hands on her apron. "What you offerin' to trade her?" she said.

Barz put a thumb to the side of his nose and blew; he did a little shuffle on the product and Nam glared at the nasty place it made on the porch floor. He was plainly discomforted by this extra presence. "Uh," he said, "I got a fine animal at'll get this young lady anywhere she wants to go."

"Let's see it!" said Nam.

We followed him around the porch. There was an old dark relic of a mule standing in the sun, with its bridle draped over its neck. It would not have had the strength to wander away. It stood there resigned, with its ears laid back and its sticky eyes closed against the gnats. Its neck was stretched, low and funny; it made a raspy grunt with every breath. One of its knees was very large.

"Nice of you to stop on yer way to the glue-works," Nam said.

"Good worker. Best I got," Barz said at me, ignoring her.

"Well, you got my sympathy," Nam said.

"Peaceable, too. Womernses don't gen'rally like to work a mule that acts too vygrous," said Cud'n Barz.

"I don't know what her car is worth but that mule ain't worth thirty cents," Nam said, flattening her mouth.

"Car ain't wuth a copper brownie in 'na branch," Barz said.

The mule lifted its tail and did its business. It swung its head around and showed me its poor old nubs of teeth, and looked embarrassed. I couldn't help but rub its head. I said then to Barz, "I'll trade you."

"The Lordamercy!" Nam said. "Darlin' girl, you'll have to keep that thing in the house and chew for it. That's the sorriest swap that ever come down the pike!"

"It'll be a way to get around," I said. It heaved a rattling cough as Barz led it off to the barn. "We'll have to fix the fence around the lot."

Nam said, "Looks to me before this day is out you'll have a great big hole to dig."

What was a wonder to my mind was that without thinking or planning any such thing I had made a commitment, flimsy though it might appear. It was a borderline thing to let Nam stock us with staples for a month. Neither she nor Ben Aaron seemed to have a solitary doubt that we had come to stay; that matter had been a question only to me. But it was like I had no control—or wanted none—over the answer.

We did around all day, putting things in order. In the afternoon Ben Aaron came by. He was on his way to Red Bank to record the purchase of six hundred acres in Wolfcreek Township from the family Harkins, at thirty dollars an acre. "All the timber worth a damn is down in an auger hole," he grumbled. "Never get it out."

I didn't have the nerve to say, What did you buy it for? I had to show him the mule.

We went down to the barn and it was standing there slobbering over a pile of hay I had raked up from the grass-cutting. Ben Aaron looked at it and started to laugh. "Oh shit!" he whooped. "OH SHIT!" And it did.

When he came back from the courthouse we had supper. Afterward, he knotted his horse's reins and climbed in the buggy with Nam, and they headed home, with Cy, that was what he called that one-eyed horse, trailing along. They had settled us in.

Early next day I took a bucket of gruel down to the mule and then let it out to gum a little grass. It eased my mind that at least it had lived out the night. I was back up at the spout coaxing the spider out of the washpot when here came Barz around the house.

He was leading the ugliest cow I ever saw. I reckon it was the only genuine ugly cow I ever saw; I didn't know many cows. This one had long-hair places and short-hair places and no-hair places; it was red-spotted, and mud where it was supposed to be white. It had a sharp backbone and a slatternly expression and it was big as a barrel, right ready to calf.

I shamed myself. Before I even said good morning, I said, "Hold on, now—I've got nothing left to trade."

"You don't need no trade," Barz said sorrowfully. "Ben Aaron Steele said I owed it to ye. He come down yestiddy a-pitchin' and a-rarin', said I done you wrong about your car. Said the mule wad'n wuth it, said I played wrong wif you cause you never knowed no better. That never set right wif me, I must say. But since it's in the fambly. . . ."

"Why, I had thought nothin' of it," I said. "I liked that mule just a whole lot." Then I had to ask him, "Did Ben Aaron pick out this cow?" It was one of those things you just have to know.

"No'm, he never keered about that, he dist left that up to me. I went out early and kotched this'n. Two for one! Pretty soon you'll see." He laughed at last, a toothless, gaping laugh, rusty as an old hinge.

I stroked the side of her face and she licked me. I thought to myself, She would have bit me, but she has no teeth. And I laughed with Barz, I was so relieved that he had quit being scared of me.

We strolled the old cow to the barn and put her in a stall. However homely she was, there was a good feeling about her being there, and I couldn't help but put my arm around her neck and lay my face on her and feel her good motherly warmth, sensible and solid.

As we started back to the house Barz asked me, "How do ye fare, Miss Cud'n? Are ye lonesome? Does this old place trouble you any?" He sounded tentative, like it had somehow troubled him.

"It is the happiest place I have ever been," I said. I would have liked to say, I don't understand everything about it. Sometimes it makes me a little nervous.

But then he said, "Well, it is—it was—the happiest kind of place. They done ever'thing good here. They worked hard. They loved one another. They birthed, and they died, I hope ready to go. 'Course, they done ever'thing bad here sometime too. Drunkered. Fiddled. Danced." Barz had early joined the Baptists.

"Now they never made no whiskey, as I've heared of." He spit a squirt of rusty juice and went on, "Never had to. Wilcoxes done that for 'em. A Steele never had no use for a Wilcox except for one thing: to make his whiskey. That was what a Wilcox allus done the best. It was no use to try to out-shine a Wilcox—their way with shine was somethin' give to them by Nature.

"I've heared it said too that Wilcoxes used to be right smart of fiddle-players," Barz said, wistful for the good old days of sin. "But they was so triflin' they had done fell to banjer-pickin', long afore my time. . . ."

~11~

SECOND THOUGHTS

THE WAY THINGS GOT DONE AROUND THE PLACE, I WOULD HAVE put it all down for magic if I had not seen Coy Ray Wilcox at work. The fences got put back where we needed them. He fixed the spout so we had water to the back porch again, and into the spring box by the back door, and back out into the run-off branch. He cleared the weeds way down into the barn lot. And he built us a privy. I didn't think to ask what had happened to the old one, but it had been a delicate matter, doing without.

I hated to see the meadow mowed before the spring flowers were gone. But it did look nice; we could see down into the birch grove then, nearly to the river. The kids had enjoyed being able to get lost a few feet from the house, but I had not enjoyed that at all.

Then early one morning, it was Coy Ray's habit to get moving before daylight, and we heard this cussing and carrying-on down in the bottoms. "Whup, thar, lazy ol' bitch. Get on, nair, goddam ye." Coy Ray was plowing with Ben Aaron's red mules.

Other days he had done his bit and got away while it was still soon. He went up to the sawmill and worked, it seemed, when it pleased him. And it was like Barz said, Coy Ray had a business venture of his own—that was simply understood—and sometimes it required his attention night and day.

But this day he worked on into the morning. He worked with a vengeance until nearly noon, and I went down and saw he had turned up a great brown patch already, and the birds were hopping along behind him, pecking in the dirt, and his clothes were drenched with sweat even in the cool. I made him come on up to the house and eat his dinner.

He washed on the back porch and came in mopping his face with his handkerchief, and we sat down at the kitchen table, just Coy Ray and me. The kids had eaten and gone about their business.

I liked him fine. He was a curiosity, he could do so many things— if, as Ben Aaron said, he was of a mind. It made me a little bit uneasy not knowing how all this work was going to be paid for; it was sure beyond the call of neighborliness. I still had that 'leven dollars, but I doubted it would cover what was going on here.

"Might as well be new ground down-nair," Coy said, slicking back his hair. "Ain't been worked in twenty-odd y'ar."

"What we fixing to do?" I said.

"Plant corn," he said. "You got all 'at fine livestock now, you got to feed it."

"I don't know how to thank you enough for what you're doing," I said. "I could never have asked anybody to do all this."

"Thank the good Mister Steele," Coy Ray said. "I don't do nothin' only what he tells me." It was impudent as could be, how he said it.

"What all do you do for him?" He had put me off balance.

"Anything dirty, anything'll make a body sweat," he said. "Mister Steele ain't one to strain hisself."

I had hit a sore spot there so I went in another direction.

"Have you got your garden in yet?" I said.

"Corn 'nis high," he said, measuring a couple of inches above the table with his little freckled hand. "Come up right atter the rain. Up any sooner, storm would of rurnt it."

Safe subject. "How many acres you own up there?" I said making talk.

He sat there with half a potato suspended on his fork, looking at me. He looked at me so hard I was forced to look back, clear to the back of his eyes. Back behind that cool pale blue there was something fierce. I can still see it.

"Lady, I don't own a goddam inch," he said.

Well, I pressed another biscuit on him. I knew it wasn't any of my business. But it was too. I said, "I thought you owned Wilcox Ridge. Some of your folks own it, don't they?"

He jabbed his fork into the butter and mashed up a blob with his honey.

"Some of YOUR folks owns it, Missy. Ben Aaron Steele owns it. Owns it to the last tomb-rock and privy pit."

"Why did you sell it to him?" I said. It was the dumbest thing I could think of to say.

"Did I say I sold it to 'im? For God's sake, woman, since when do you have to sell Ben Aaron Steele anything for him to get it?" Coy Ray leaned across the table, glowering. "He gets what he damn well wants. Now you mark I said that."

A couple of days later, I got up before the sun and went down and fed the mule and the cow—in good weather, at least, it was right pleasant to go down to the barn when the birds were just waking up. It was good to be welcomed by living things. And I came back up and went upstairs and dragged myself a chair out onto the porch, up there, and was watching the morning when Ben Aaron drove up, with Rose on the seat beside him, and the wagon bed full of freckled little boys. Coy Ray was somewhere about his own devices.

I leaned over the banister and waved.

"Hey-o Cud'n Sen," Ben Aaron said, "You ready to go to town?"

"You going to Nam's?" I said.

"Red Bank," he said.

"Let me get the kids," I said.

"No, Rose will stay with 'em, she's brought hers here. They all just as well get acquainted," he said. Rose sat straight as a poker and silent. She looked up at me, expressionless. The little boys, all of them toy versions of Coy Ray, sat still as mice until I said, "All right," and Rose turned to them and told them they could get down.

Mine had just waked up and wandered into the kitchen. We had no milk yet; our miraculous pitcher in the barn was still dry, so Rose had brought a gallon jug. I had cooked a pan of sticky biscuits, rolled with cinnamon and sugar. I told Pet and Hugh I was going off for a little bit and they did not seem distressed. They stood on one side of the kitchen table looking at Coy's kids lined up on the other side looking at them. Rose poured them all some milk and put the jug out in the spring box.

I left them and went and changed my dress and combed my hair, and pinched a little color in my face.

And we started out, Ben Aaron and me, alone, going south. Ahead the road sort of faded into the river mist. We went around the bend and headed directly into the morning; the sun was still behind the mountain, but the fog glowed. There were flowers along the road, and in the road. I had this eerie zingy feeling in my head. I put my hand on Ben Aaron's arm to be sure this time it was real.

"Hmm?" he said.

"How are we going to get across the branch?" I said. "You know what I did to the bridge. . . ."

"Some bridges we cross when we get to 'em," he said.

And we came to one, some raw, sappy logs staked down and planks nailed across them. "You hadn't seen this?" he said. "Coy put it back, oh, several days ago."

"Coy's been plowin' lately," I said. "He's got half the world plowed up, down in the meadow."

"Hope so," Ben Aaron said. "We're going after seed today. I've got us some tobacco plants coming, I hope they've got 'em. Tobacco'll bring you in a little money. You can make money on just a little ground. It's some work but it beats being a slave to a hoe."

There had been a light drizzle of rain along in the night, and the woods were washed and tender and new. I had seen none of this territory in the light; my memories of it were nightmares. I was surprised to see it not murderous at all. Except, as we climbed around that mountain that shut us in on the south, the passage got narrower and there was only a steep clay bank on the right and a jump-off place on the other side.

"Ain't you glad you couldn't see where you were?" Ben Aaron said, reading my mind.

The river was green and frothy down below us. There were springs trickling over the bank above us, little waterfalls down into the ditch.

The ditch was full of flowers. The mules would stop and drink and snort. There were ox and tire tracks in the road.

"You want to cut around by Barz's and see what he's done with your car?" Ben Aaron said.

The idea made me cringe. No, I said, I was not ready for that. It would be like seeing a mummy of a member of the family, or something. That business reminded me that I was going to have to write Foots that we were with Mackey's folks and doing fine. To not tell him where the kids were would be wrong, whether he cared or not. I didn't know what to say about the car. I decided I wouldn't mention it. As far as Foots needed to know I had just misplaced it. But the thought put a damper on the perfect pleasure of the morning. I was annoyed.

We came down past a pasture fence and then a tended field. It looked awfully different in the sun than it had in that horrendous gray-yellow light, that day Barz ran away.

"Barz is got his corn up good," Ben Aaron said.

"Has," I said. "Real pretty. We got to catch up. Coy Ray says his is THIS high," I said, holding up my hand.

"Hmp," Ben Aaron said.

I knew better than to go on, but I did. "Ben Aaron," I said, "You didn't tell me you owned Coy Ray's place, too."

He kind of hunched over, looking straight ahead. "Was I s'posed to?" he said.

"S'posed to what?" I said.

"S'posed to tell everything, for Christ's sake," he said in a tone I had never heard before. It poured over me like hot water. I shrunk up real small. I felt like a wart on the wagon seat.

"I really don't care," I said. "I was just makin' talk."

"What's Coy been a-tellin' you?"

"Nothin' only he doesn't own a damned inch. That's what he said."

"I bet. Listen, don't be so free talkin' with the help," Ben Aaron said.

I made up my mind right that instant that I would go to the telegraph office at Red Bank and wire Louise to send me some money to come home. I would buy three train tickets and go get the children and we would not let another sun set on us in this strange place at the mercy of this awful man. In fact I would not ride with him to Red Bank, I would tell him to let me off and I would walk.

But I was too mad to speak. If I opened my mouth I would cry. We rode on.

And directly, he sighed a big sigh, and said, "He's right. I own it. If you ever own something by holding the deed."

"I don't care. It's none of my business," I said. I might as well have been a fly buzzing.

"I bought it from him, just right recently," he said, clearing his throat.

We went on a little way, very quiet. Then he turned around to me and said, "No. That's a bald-faced lie. I never bought it, atall. I won it off of him in a card game."

"You didn't," I said.

"Fair and square, oh, yes I did," he said. "All the cards on the table. I laid him my note for four thousand dollars against it. Right there on a board across two sawhorses in his own barn."

"What in the Lord's name did you want with it? Don't you have enough?" I said.

"Didn't want it, in p'tickler," he said, blowing a puff of smoke from his pipe. "Thought I might as well. It was up for grabs. Coy'd done lost every cent he had. Tom Joe Brock walked off with his black game rooster. He lost a fine old bedstead, the one Cleone died in; ol' Perley Ramsay won that off of 'im, but never took it. He was the only one so tender-hearted. Rest of us took."

"Ben Aaron!" I said. I was thoroughly appalled.

But he puffed his pipe and narrowed his eyes and looked straight ahead. "Yeah, pore ol' Coy," he said, "the best he could do was a pair o' jacks. I had me three aces and a joker, and a deuce 'at was wild. Hotdam, what a hand. . . ."

So folks really did each other such a way. "You were lucky not to get shot," I said. I was stunned nearly hoarse.

"Aww, Coy was mad," he said. "He flung cards and whiskey all over, ever' stick that wadn't nailed down he flung it against the wall. Rest of 'em left— some folks is scared of him when he gets hot, but I just set him out.

"Finally he wore down. Said, 'Well, I reck'n I better get out in somebody's woods and put my younguns up a brush arbor. I guess even as lowdown a bastard as you are you'd not turn us out before mornin'.'"

The corner of Ben Aaron's mouth crinkled around his pipe, smug, you know. It galled me that he was really proud of himself.

"Well, did you turn 'em out before day?" I said. I know I sounded sanctimonious.

"Where'd you get the idea I was so low-down?" he said. "Coy tell you that too? I never did turn 'em out, not to this day, nor tomorrow, and not fifty years from now. I told Coy, I said, 'See that you go down to the courthouse in the morning and make me a deed. Beyond that,' I said, 'you can forget this ever passed. Let your younguns be. Say nothing. Do nothing. You're at home as you ever was.' And, by noon the next day, I had the deed in my hand. Coy didn't exactly love my soul. But that was nothing new."

"How much of it is there?" I said.

"Oh, a little better than a hundred acres."

"And a house? For a hand of cards?"

"Listen, Mary Sen," Ben Aaron said, "there used to be five times that much land, oh, more than that. Reck'n where it went? It was sold, piecemeal, to pay some Wilcox out of a scrape. My daddy bought a lot of it. Coy's awful bad to gamble. Thing is, he can't stand to lose. He'll just keep on.

"Think about this," he said, being very earnest. "I wadn' the only one playing cards with him that night. What if Os Hambright had drawn that hand that I had? His WIFE—that Baptist, card-hatin', church-goin', rump-sprung old heifer—would've had Coy out by morning. And his younguns in the road."

"What did your wife say about it?" I said.

"My wife? Why would I tell her?"

There is a place where, as you go around the last bend coming down to meet the river, you can look out over the whole countryside, Red Bank and everywhere. We could hear steam shovels working down on the highway. We could see the low water bridge.

"This is where you made your bad mistake, my dear," Ben Aaron said.

"That's so," I said. I was feeling wretched and confused.

We came to the turn and I looked back on the road we had come down. It was not much more than a trail. Bushes grew between the ruts, undisturbed. I wondered how I had ever taken that for the way I was supposed to go.

We passed a bunch of oxen dragging in ties for the new bridge. Ben Aaron stopped and talked with the man who was driving them. Business. Ben Aaron's timbers. Ben Aaron's steers. Ben Aaron's man. I sat with my hands folded in my lap. The sun was cooking my nose. I was miserable.

He clucked at the mules and we went on toward town. "Anything special you want from the city?" he said.

"No sir. Nothing but I want to send a telegram," I said.

I could feel him looking at me but I looked over the mules' heads, making my neck long and stiff.

"Anything you need to buy?" he said, sort of plaintively.

"No. You certainly shouldn't have made this trip if it was just for me."

"Oh," he said, "I come down every few days anyway. Always got business here, you know. It only crossed my mind that you might want to come along. Might want to get away little bit."

He pulled in at Ollie Trotter's, and we got down and went in. Ben Aaron sauntered back to the feed department where Ollie was weighing out seed for somebody.

"Well, glory be. Twic't in one week, when I ain't seen you once a y'ar," Ollie declared, upon seeing Ben Aaron. He raised up and squinted at me, then. "Thank the Lord y'uns got together," he said. He said he'd not slept a wink the night of our first encounter. The river had come way up over the bridge that night, he said. But in a couple of days, the word had drifted down that we had landed at The Birches.

"You know what I thought she said?" said Ollie to Ben Aaron. "Thought she said she was your granddaughter."

Ben Aaron reached a long arm and pulled me to him and sank his fingers firmly in my shoulder. He was grinning, showing teeth clenched around that eternal nasty pipe.

"She could pass for my daughter, I'll own 'er that," he said.

He bought seed corn and tobacco plants. He bought at least five pounds of candy, divided in two sacks, and two big bags of those awful, stamped vanilla cookies.

"Where is the telegraph office from here?" I said.

"Do me a favor," he whispered. "Pick out Rose a pretty dress, and tell her it come from you."

I went and looked over what was on the rack. Not just for one that would do, but for something better. I must say Ollie had no eye for fashion. What was there was pretty ugly. I went back and said that quietly, and coolly, to Ben Aaron.

He rubbed his chin and looked down. "Would you know how to make her one?" he said. "The child's near nekkid as a jaybird." It sounded humble, like he was asking something very big.

"I'll see what they've got for goods," I said. I went and looked among the bolts of calico and sheeting and linty widow-black. And there was a bolt of thin white cotton, printed with blue forget-me-nots. I wasn't sure of the size for a pattern. The truth was I couldn't sew worth a doodle; all I knew I learned from Mit and she wasn't exactly a Parisian dressmaker. But I would make this up for Rose, if I had to make it on her. I got some new thread and needles, but I knew full well somewhere in that house Daisy had a sewing box and I would find it.

While Mistress Ollie measured out the cloth, still as chatty as a pine stump, Ben Aaron shopped further. He came up with a straw hat with an enormous brim and a pink ribbon around the crown. When we carried the stuff out to the wagon he planted that hat on my head.

"You dang near blistered in that sun," he said.

He drove us up the street to the cafe for a sandwich. And then he turned the mules toward the mountain and popped the reins. "We got to get these plants home to the shade," he said.

On the way back, and I know he remembered it, there were some old wild rose bushes trailing down the bank. There was one open bloom; he stopped and picked it, and stuck it in the ribbon of that hat.

"I'm sorry," he said.

"Sorry for what?" I said.

"Sorry you think I'm a common sonofabitch," he said.

I had not let him see me look at him since he made me mad. I right then considered the bushes and the rocks. Actually, I thought, he was a splendid, ruthless, enigmatic sonofabitch.

"I could never think you common," I said. "You are my cousin."

~ 12 ~

THE FIDDLER

BY THE TIME THAT WE HAD GOT ALL THAT STUFF IN THE GROUND, the corn sowed and all those rows and rows of tobacco planted, I had kind of worked off my mad.

I sat down by the lamp one night and wrote a letter to Louise. The more I wrote, the more fanciful it got; I told her where we were, that we were having a wonderful visit and it was doing us a lot of good. I said the children were outdoors a lot, enjoying this big farm, and the people were so good to us, and all was bliss in the Elysian fields (I was not sure what that meant but it sounded good) and not to worry. I told her to give Foots my regards.

Coy Ray was down here working more every morning, a lot of times with Rose and the little boys helping, and I got him to take the letter up to Tatum's store; that was where the post office was. I felt like a load of guilt had been lifted. I had declared our whereabouts.

When I would think back on that journey to Red Bank, though, that dreary day with Ben Aaron, it would make me a little uneasy. I could not feel completely justified in being here; there was something wrong with it. And it had nothing to do with being a runaway wife.

After he had left that day I had not seen Ben Aaron, and that began to bother me too. I had acted righteous. I had pried into his business. I had hurt him. And he had been so good to us. Oh, I was sorry. It lay on my mind like a wet rug, every night. I felt sorrier every day.

Coy Ray came one morning, then, and plowed another place, one that would be separate from the cornfield and the tobacco. He fixed me this nice little garden out close to the barn, where I could plant what we wanted to eat, and it would be easy to run back and forth from the house.

He had gone home with the mules and I was out there planting seeds. I couldn't find a hoe anyplace, I had forgot to ask if Coy Ray could leave me one, so I had me a stick and I went along and gouged little trenches, and I was barefooted, and I was poking the beans down in that cool brown dirt with my toes. The children were at the river with Coy Ray's crowd. I had the happy thought that I would run down there too, directly, and wade till my feet came clean.

But I heard an old truck straining, coming over the mountain. So I ran up to the spout, combing my hair with my fingers, and I kicked around in the runoff and splashed my face and dried it on the hem of my dress, and ran around the house to meet Ben Aaron. I had an idea it was him. He.

Well, he pulled up by the porch and hollered, "Am I supposed to know somebody named M.S. Steele?"

I could have danced a jig. "You got it!" I yelled. "Uncle Camp sent the box!"

"Somebody sure sent you a mess of somethin'," he said. "What in God's creation is it? The missionary barrel? A house and lot?"

"It's clothes and stuff I didn't have time to get together when we, uh, decided to leave," I said.

He could give out the warmest, softest looks sometimes. Almost under his breath he said, "On the run, were you Cousin?"

I looked down at my toes and he just went on, "Hey, you ain't been here two weeks and here you are pore and barefooted like us — mind, you'll get the hookworms. Did you not read about that in school? We've all got 'em, you know, we dist lie up in the shucks and drink whiskey for it, 'course never get well."

"That's why you don't weigh but two hundred pounds," I said.

"Maybe a little more," he said. "I ain't THAT wormy."

He hauled out the crate like it was a match box and put it up on the porch. "Now I reckon you want me to open it," he said.

"You just want to see what's in it," I said. And I really did too. I told him I didn't have the vaguest notion—really—what it might be. I told him how I had gone to Aunt Mit and Uncle Camp in the middle of the night and asked them to, uh, collect some things without being seen, stuff they thought we would need, and how Aunt Mit had blazed her eyes and said, "What you mean, us steal, you bad girl—what if Ol' Miss ketch us?" But I knew Camp understood, he was grinning, and I knew they would help us. And I told how I had left them a shipping tag, made out to me, at Red Bank.

"Lord, Ben Aaron," I said, "What blind faith! What if we'd never found this place?"

He cut his eye at me and laughed, "Hmp, Hmp," around his pipe.

He went off and got the hammer and came back and pried up the slats. When he got the top loose there was a layer of newspaper, first, and I folded it up to look at later. I wanted to see who had got married and who had died and what was happening to Maggie and Jiggs in the funny papers.

There was a lot of tissue paper, then, and a sheet, and then a layer of hats. Oh, my. Hats with crowns stuffed with paper, some of them with their big flowers wrapped in old silk stockings. I put on one I had loved. It was a pale green straw, with silk leaves around the brim. "Now this costume Madame Serrec recommends for the spring cow-patty promenade," I said. I showed him how one should tip among the cow-patties, holding up the hem of one's skirt.

And Ben Aaron got tickled. And I couldn't get him away from that stuff, then, and he kept pulling things out. There were a couple of evening dresses, and a pair of silk evening slippers, and when he brought up some frilly teddies, he laughed so big the racket bounced across the cove and back.

"I do declare, Cousin, I am going to have to red up the hog lot and get you some real fine pigs so you'll have someplace nice to go in the evenin's," he said.

"You are a coarse, mean person," I said. "Aunt Mittie thought I was coming to stay with quality folks."

Thank goodness they had sent nearly all the wearable clothes the children had. I had not even thought of their coats, when we left, but

we sure needed them before we even got here. And here they were.
And then, here was Mama's family Bible, and Grandma Twyning's
crocheted bedspread. And some old silver goblets that had been put
away for Pet. There was no doubt that Aunt Mit had given us up for
gone.

Under all this, wrapped up in a blanket, there was this peculiar box.

"What is that?" I said. It looked for the world like a little long
coffin. But somehow it was familiar.

Ben Aaron turned awfully somber. He lifted up that box like it
was crystal and ran his hand along the top. He squatted down and
set it on the floor of the porch, and undid the little brass latches and
raised the lid. There was something wrapped in an old red rag. I
knew that rag, and that box. Mackey's fiddle.

There was a piece of brown paper stuck in one of its holes. Ben
Aaron handed it over to me, it had some laborious printing on it:

"This blong to Mr. Steele. Miss Nat she give it to me wen he die
but I never plays it. Aunt Mit say love. Camp."

I handed him the note back. It was one of those times when I
could say nothing; I would have choked. There was a bird singing
in the lilacs, and we could hear the children laughing and playing
down on the river. I swallowed, and said, "It was Mackey's."

There was no way to put into words what I was thinking. I was
thinking, here is the precious thing, the tangible link that I can hold
in my hand. It left this house with my father. It was his comfort in
that foreign country; it was his tie with his people. Now it had
come home again. I blessed Camp in my heart; it had come home,
through me. It was like Ivan McAllister Steele, himself, had been
able to come and say, yes, this is my child—this is her home. It is
right to take her in.

Ben Aaron picked up the fiddle by its neck and blew on it, and
fine dust flew out into the sun. He smoothed his fingers over it and
he took out his handkerchief and gently rubbed its back till the
whorls of the maple wood picked up the light and glowed.

The strings were slack. One was gone, along with its peg. I wondered if maybe Mackey had been working on it, before he died. The
bridge was loose in the case; Ben Aaron set it back under the strings,
and turned a peg slowly, and whanged the string with his finger,

and went to the next, turning and plucking, and the next, then back to the first, a little at a time, listening, coaxing, pressing, praying, it looked like, and cocking his ear for a decent pitch.

One of the pegs kept slipping back and its string would whang down. It was too old and dry to hold. So he took it out and undid it from its string, and he laid down his pipe and popped the peg into his mouth.

There was a nub of old rosin in the case, as dry and hard as stone. He reached in his pants pocket and fished out his knife, and scraped that rosin to a powder in the palm of his hand, and went to work on the bow. He tightened the frog, and trimmed the straggly hairs, and ran the bow across his palm and worked in the rosin. And then he took that spitty peg, and rosined it, and stuck it back and tightened the string, and it held.

All this went on in silence; this was a religious rite. He tuned the thing again, G—(no D)—A—E, G-A-E, till it suited him, and he stuck his pipe back in the corner of his mouth, and re-lit it, and took up the bow and drew a lick across the strings. Awful. The thing screeched and howled and squalled like something alive, like something dragged screaming back into the light, after twenty years of dark and peaceful sleep.

Ben Aaron took off his hat, then, and settled himself back, with a satisfied look, against a porch pillar, and he dangled one long leg down the steps and fastened his eyes upon the hill, and he began to play. I would see him later on playing with the chin-rest down under his collar-bone, sort of unconcerned, while people danced. But not now. He rested his cheek on this fiddle's own face. And he played.

He played with no visible effort, with the smallest motion. I had wondered about those strong polished fingers; now I knew what they were for.

"Do you know this?" he said.

I felt small and humble. "Yessir," I said. "Mackey used to play it."

It was "Fisher's Reel," and it was sublime. Paganini could have squeezed no more flying notes into a measure than my cousin Ben Aaron on only three strings.

One tune slid into another, he would stop and tune and pick up in another direction. He bowed and plucked and the fiddle danced and

barked and cackled and crooned; it had a hundred voices and sometimes they talked two at a time. "You know 'Paddy on the Turnpike?'"
he said, and I guess I did, but never like this.

It raised my hair. I got goosebumps. I squatted there by him, afraid
if I drew a long breath it would go away. Lord, he could play. There
was a quality about it that was beyond this nice man sitting here; it
was more than just loose and running and rejoicing, it was cocky, and
powerful, and tireless, merciless, I thought. It would wear you out
and lift you up and make you move, until you died of joy. It was se-
ductive.

All this on those old rotten strings. When he was down to two, he
laid the fiddle on his lap and took his handkerchief to it again. I was
mesmerized. "Mercy on us, Ben Aaron," I said, sort of squeaky. My
mouth was dry.

"Aww, this thing needs some new pegs, bad," he said. "See—
(plunk-plunk)—it won't hold its key. When I get a chance I'll make
some pegs and I'll bring down some strings and we'll get the thing to
play."

"Oh, no!" I said. "You take that fiddle right with you. Lord
knows you ought to have it."

"Oh, I'd not do that," he said. "I've got one, o' course, not a bad
'un, we all had one, you know. All of 'em homemade, like this, and
pretty good."

He got up with it and held it out into the sunlight, so that the
sun shined in one of the holes, and he squinted into its in insides.

"Lookahere, Cousin Sen," he said, "you need to know what this is."

He held it for me to look inside. There were some dark letters on
the bottom, it looked like they might have been burned: I. MCA.
1797.

"I'll bet you this was a present that old man Ivan McAllister made
for his son-in-law—Hamilton Steele, the one that built this place.
It's kind of passed down with the house. You've got the children," he
said. "It belongs with you."

He wrapped it up in its rag. "I remember," he said, "when they used
to have dances here, and your granddaddy Ive would play it. Now, he
could PLAY. And Aunt Daisy, she would dance. People would stop

and stand back and watch 'er. She could out-dance anybody that ever I saw. Out-buck a man. That was the dancinest woman alive."

He closed up the little coffin and got himself up and stretched. "I've got to go," he said. "Tell me where you want this stuff to go and I'll carry it."

No, I said, the kids would help me get it.

He took me by the shoulder and kissed the top of my head. I just hid my face in the front of his old checked shirt. I know I left it wet. But I didn't want him to see me cry.

~13~

THE LOVE OBJECT

IT WASN'T BUT A COUPLE OF DAYS THEN TILL HE CAME BACK. BEN Aaron, I mean. He brought Aunt Nam that time; she said she thought it ought to be time for the wild strawberries to come in. I hadn't known to look.

We took a little pot apiece and went out in the field. Once she showed me, there they were, a sea of them, with their little heads bowed to the grass. It passed through my mind that back in Charleston the vegetable man had strawberries on his wagon nearly two months ago. Sometimes I missed him so; I missed sending up the street to town, for this thing or that. There was nothing fresh here, yet, but turnip greens and a few green onions. Nam kept the pantry loaded with canned pole beans and soup mix; she would hand out apples from her cellar, she had a few still, all wrapped up in brown paper, way back in the cool.

But to find strawberries wild—well, I was so happy just to sit in the grass up there on the hill with Nam and smell them, and lick that sweet juice from my fingers. "Mind the slugs," Nam said. We'd pick all we could reach, sitting on our spread-out skirts, and then move to another spot. When we had enough for a couple of pies we went back to the house and commenced to cook dinner.

Ben Aaron was out on the porch with that old fiddle across his lap, whittling pegs. The kids were sitting on the floor beside him, bent over a jigsaw puzzle he had brought them. It was a sailing ship, in a gaudy sunset. It gave me a little sharp pang.

When we called them all to come to dinner, Ben Aaron stood out there a minute holding the fiddle, turning it one way and another, thinking whatever he thought. The kids went on in. I just stood there in the door, looking at him. It was like I had never seen him before.

"You get it fixed to suit you?" I said.

He told me what all he had done, and I don't remember, it was like I didn't hear him. I guess it was the way the light hit him. I don't know. It was the way his hair curled around behind his ear, like a swirl in a silver sculpture. His nose was too long, of course. All our noses were too long. It was a family mark. But his had a firm nobility about it.

There was a quality in the way he moved. And in his speech—which could go all sorts of ways, depending on the mood of things, and who he was talking to. He was bilingual even in English, and that was just the beginning of it.

Grace. I guess that is the best I could call it. Creature of the earth that he was, there was something exquisite about my cousin. There was one word that meant it all, ever after when I thought of him. It was beauty.

He looked at me funny, a little hurt. He had asked me something and I had not answered. "Hmm?" I said.

"Would you care for me to take it home a night or so?" he said again, turning the love object in his hands. "I need to make a little glue."

"Lord, honey, do anything you please with it," I said. "Far as I'm concerned, it's yours."

"No, but I would like to borry it one time," he said. "Some people's made up a little old dance down in Red Bank, tomorrow night. Asked me to play," he said. "I'd like to see how it sounds."

"Help yourself," I said. I thought, I'd like to see how it sounds too; I'd like to see the bright lights of Red Bank, for a little change. But he didn't mention it. I guessed it was a private party or something; I guessed he would take Sophia. I guessed he should.

We went on in and ate dinner and talked about our progress with the place, and then he got up and ceremoniously wrapped the fiddle in its rag and packed it in its case, and carried it out. Then he unhitched Cy from behind the buggy and rode off about his business.

When we had cleaned up the table Nam and I went upstairs to look for Daisy's sewing box. There was a sewing machine, Nam said. We took lamps up and rummaged around until we came on an old machine with a comforter over it. It was an old treadle with fancy wrought-iron legs and lots of gilt. In its lap drawer, just as she had left it, there were a couple of pairs of scissors, and the littlest thimbles, and a pack of needles rusted to the paper, and spools and skeins of thread, and a flat tin candy box of buttons. We decided we could drag that machine downstairs. As we pulled it out of its corner, we turned over a carton and spilled things all over. "How you fixed for clothes?" Nam said.

"I don't need evening dresses," I said.

She cackled and set her lamp on the machine, so she could see what we had found. "Looks like Daisy's stuff, law yes," she said, "I remember this, we made us a dress apiece out of these goods. . . ."

She took up a stiff blue dress that had been folded with paper so it wouldn't crease. "Now this here, Ivan brought her this whole bolt of brocade one time from Savannah. Said it come in on a ship from China. She never wore this but to buryin's and weddin's."

There was a black calico dress in the pile that caught my eye, I guess because it was out of that same stuff as that old sunbonnet that hung in the kitchen. I held the dress up to the light. Packed up in there, it had fared better than the bonnet; the mice had not cut it.

It was made by a pattern we found later in another box. It had a high neck and a low, pointed waist, with little fine pearl buttons down the front. It had long slim sleeves, and a ruffle around the bottom; on Daisy it probably was long, down past her ankles. But it looked like a dress for a child.

"Now that went to many a dance," Nam said. "Boys, even when she had some age on 'er, that gal could dance. Had the best-lookin' legs ever anybody saw, 'course she wadn't supposed to show 'em but that never stopped her, she'd yank up 'er skirt and fling 'er heels.

And she'd not get tired. She'd go all night. Most times her man Ive would be fiddlin', and she'd dance with anything that would ask 'er till she wore the men clean out. And flop down just a laughin', fannin' 'er skirt. It was like a game between her and Ive. She could dance as long as he could play."

I unfolded that dress all the way, and shook it. Twigs and the dust of leaves, or flowers, flew out of it in the lamplight. "Sweet bubby," Nam said. "I'd say she packed that up herself. If there was a sweet bubby bloomin' she picked it and put it in her clothes."

Sweet bubby?

"You know where the bubby bush is? It's still there, out there right by the window. By Daisy's old sittin' room, there. It's that bush with the brown flowers on it, I bet it's got some right now."

Sweet shrub. I imagined I could smell it. I laid the dress over my arm and we started again, we put a lamp at the top of the stairs and thumped down the steps with that machine. We put it in Daisy's room, by the window with the bubby bush. And then we went back up and looked some more, and straightened up behind ourselves.

Coy Ray came down along in the afternoon, from wherever he had been. We wouldn't have known he was there except we heard him hammering on something down in the lot. He didn't come up to the house; he did that way sometimes, come and do what he meant to do and go, without letting on. That evening, after Nam went home, I went to the barn and there was a little pen down there that had just appeared, during the day. I wondered about it but nothing much surprised me; so far there was nothing in it.

And then the next morning here came Rose, riding up from the river with a box in her arms. She hollered out by the barn. She couldn't get down off the mule without dropping the box and I ran out there and took it from her. It rustled and cheeped. She opened up the little pen and took the box and began to fish out biddies, "dibs," she called 'em, a dozen little yellow chickabiddies and dark biddies and a couple of tiny brown-and-gold ones, guinea chicks, she said, and then a buff-colored mother hen. The babies pitted round and round in the pen, making biddie noises, picking at the wire.

We went to the house and got some corn meal and put it in a pie pan for them and of course they got in it and scratched. They walked in the pan of water we put in for them.

"Pap'll put up a good chicken yard," Rose said. "You just got to keep 'em up tight till they get a little size. A snake'll help hisself to one or two; a fox or a weasel'll rurn ye."

We squatted and watched them. We watched a hawk circling over the birch grove and we hollered threats at him. Rose had saved the eggs and set the hen; the biddies were another of her gifts to our welfare. Her mouth turned up at the corners, just so slightly, and her eyes sparkled when she watched them.

I brought her up to the house, then, and I got out that pattern of Daisy's, the one with the pointed waist, and held it up to her. Rose was much taller. I would have to cut it longer, and wider, in proportion, too, although she was real slim. But I liked it. I imagined that blue-flowered goods made into a dress like that. Only for summer, I thought, I would just cut a fichu collar to drape over the shoulders and not make sleeves. I didn't know how to put sleeves in. I was studying all that when she said she had to go home and fix some dinner for the little boys.

Well, after she was gone I laid out the cloth on the kitchen table and bit the tip of my tongue while I cut out that dress. I made the kids take their dinner and go out on the porch. And I ran the seams up on that machine; it worked real good when I finally got it threaded right, and got some rhythm into pedaling.

A few hours later, when the pieces were together, it looked like a passable garment. There was some tatting in the machine drawer, wrapped around a spool; I decided to wash that, it was kind of yellowed, and to put it around the fichu because I was not real good at pretty hems either. And not being much on buttonholes I made some loops out of the cloth. And by suppertime, it was ready for the buttons and the hem.

I had not done much else that day. Things were sort of lying around. I had needed bad to do a washing but let it go; the kids had some clean clothes and I figured I could go sort of soiled until tomorrow; then I would wash.

Well, lo and behold, just as I got the stove going to put some supper on, here came Ben Aaron, trotting up in the buggy. He got down and came striding up on the porch, hat in hand.

"You ready to go?" he said. He looked sort of dubious when he said it; I was barefooted and not much fixed up.

"Go where?" I said.

"To that dance," he said. "I told you I was goin'.'"

"You never told me I was goin'," I said.

He sighed a weary sigh. "I thought you'd want to hear the band," he said.

"I've got to get the kids home," I said, half panicked. "They went off over the hill to pick strawberries."

"I'll go get 'em," he said. "You go on and do what you got to do."

He drove off around the house, and I splashed around in the wash pan and doused rosewater on myself and ran about in my petticoat, looking for something to put on when I knew there wasn't anything. I didn't much think an evening dress would go over in Red Bank. I looked at Rose's dress—no, I couldn't do that. Anyway it would drag the floor. I knew I couldn't button that dress of Daisy's, to save my life. But I put it on over my head and squirmed my arms into the sleeves. And was trapped.

Oh, Lord. I couldn't get it off. It was tight as a drum. It was a straitjacket. Well, I ran to the mirror, like that would help. I saw it didn't look so bad at the bottom, it hit me right at the ankles and that wasn't so bad. And I started at the bottom of the waist, where it was not so tight, and buttoned; I sucked in, and buttoned it to right under the bosom. I heard Ben Aaron and the kids come in the house. They hollered, and I hollered back sort of feebly, I had been a while without a breath. Pet came back looking for me.

"Help!" I said weakly, "I can't get out of this thing and I can't get in it."

'Course she started to laugh. And I couldn't. It was a miracle to me how that old cloth and thread held together. No, it was a torment. If I could have torn it I could have escaped.

And then I looked in the mirror and there stood dear Ben Aaron, leaning on the door frame, just laid back laughing.

"Where's all them dauncy dresses?" he said.

"You get out of here!" I said. I threw an old pomander at him, an old mummied orange I had found in a drawer. It hit the wall and shattered into brown dust.

"I got to," he said, undisturbed. "I'm going to be late." And he turned around and started ambling off.

"You come back here!" I screeched. I was going to that dance. Well, he stood and smirked at me, and then he went on back to the kitchen and disappeared. I heard him tell the kids to fix some jelly biscuits to take along. Then I heard his feet going up the attic stairs. And directly he came back down, and he threw me a red checked folded something.

I held it up; it was a ruffled pinafore apron. I shook it out and put it on, looking in the glass. I reached under and undid the cruelest buttons. Then I tied the apron strings right snugly behind. And I brushed down the frizzes in my hair, smooth as I could. The effect was right cunning. I looked at myself and smiled, like it was someone else. In the mirror, there was Ben Aaron, standing behind me grinning.

"Vanity of vanities, all is vanity, saith the preacher."

"Stop that!" I said. "How did you know where all that stuff is? How can you remember everything?"

"Packed a lot of it up m'self," he said. "It's got some order to it. There's a box of stuff that was packed right off the kitchen table, just as Daisy left it. She'd done a big ironin' the day she died . . ."

That stopped me cold, for a second. I put my hands in the apron's pockets, then, and followed him and the kids out to the buggy. But before he put me in, I begged for another minute so I could run and pick a bubby for the neck of that dress.

We all squeezed in on the seat and he laid the fiddle case across my lap. The sun was getting low and the little frogs were singing. I figured I had probably made him late.

"Where is your wife tonight?" I said. "Did she not want to come?"

"Gone to Baltimore," he said.

When we had gone on a way, with only the little evening noises from the woods, I knew he was going to volunteer no more. "Does she have people in Baltimore?" I said.

"You and me go to Red Bank to the store. Sophier goes to Baltimore," he said.

We had got across the bridge and started up the mountain when Coy Ray passed us on a mule. He tipped his straw hat grandly as he went around. He was sort of squatting up on a croaker sack, hugging for dear life with his knees. He had a banjo case strapped on his back.

"Is he going to play too?" I said. As often happened, I got no straight answer.

"Rides like a cow tick," Ben Aaron said.

It was still light when we got down to town. We went to an old dance hall, an old barn kind of place. After he hitched the horse and helped us out, Ben Aaron left us to our own devices while he got together with who all else was going to play. There were a lot of people coming in; I found myself looking at them sort of anxiously, a little wistfully, maybe. I felt somehow like I ought to know them. And that some of them maybe should know me. A few times I noticed people, mostly the older ones, looking long at me. Some of the younger ones looked too, but that was very different. It made me feel better to see that the get-up I had on was not so strange; a couple of other aprons turned up. Fashion seemed to be pretty slow to change in this part of the world.

The band set up on a little stage. There were a half dozen or so, a couple of guitar pickers and a mandolin player and a bass fiddle. Then there was Ben Aaron. And Coy Ray. They all chewed and smoked and plunked and cocked their ears to one another and tuned. Ben Aaron looked around the hall, then, and got down and went off in a corner and found an old barrel and toted it up to the stage and sat down on it. Coy Ray moved close and stood beside him. They were, in that posture, nearly eye to eye.

It was warm-up time; somebody in the crowd hollered, "Billy in the Lowground," and they began to play. It was a spectacle, just the way they played together. I mean, Ben Aaron and Coy Ray. There has never been such fiddling or such picking, not to my ears. They played over and under and around each other, they would back each other up, one would stop and let the other shine. It was like they would hop the fences of harmony and time; they would lag and rush and go off two ways up the branch and come out like clockwork. They were like one mind.

Somebody hollered "Blackberry Blossom." It was something you'd remember. I remember watching. I was wondering about two people who hated each other being side by side like that—in that little space—without elbowing each other, or biting each other to death. There they were, sawing and picking and sweating and every little bit Coy Ray would look Ben Aaron full in the face. I didn't know Coy Ray had a look like that in him.

In a little bit Ben Aaron just laid down his bow and let Coy Ray go it a while alone. He just sat there and watched Coy Ray, with this funny little mesmerized smile. They looked like they had a case of the raptures. Of course there was thunderous yelling and clapping and stomping out on the floor; it was some kind of mass hysteria.

They started to play some old tune, and the caller hollered, and there was a big rush to get in the circle. We didn't know what was going on so the kids and I leaned against the wall and watched. I watched the dancing. It gave me a queer restless feeling in the bottoms of my feet. It gave me what was almost pain in my neck and collar bones. I could feel my rib cage lift; my breath got funny. I watched Ben Aaron. He was sitting on that barrel, fiddling; he might as well have been alone, against those old knotty boards, in that red checked shirt. My mouth got dry. There was a zinging in my ears. If I had not been leaning on the wall I might have fallen.

I closed my eyes; I remember the drumming of the feet, shuffling and stomping, louder and louder. And all of a sudden a man—I never did know who he was—ran up and grabbed me around the waist, I remember him hollering to Pet and Hugh, "I'll buy you a lemonade if you let me dance with Sis."

And the next thing, we were in that circle. I didn't know what we were doing, but whatever it was, it sure felt right. Before we got back to the wall an old man grabbed me. I didn't have time to breathe. I know he looked at me peculiarly the whole time. He was puzzled; he didn't even know what it was he wanted to know. I patted his arm and thanked him when I went to the next one.

Somebody, I saw, had bought the kids a lemonade. Somebody later got them in the circle. Though not with one another.

I was not sure what Ben Aaron saw, or whether he would think I was acting scandalous and wish he'd left me home. It was his fault; the more I listened at him the worse it got. Such an odd feeling. I felt so giddy. I got this strange pain in my nose. My eyes went bleary, and when I could see again, I saw no one but him. Only he looked a little different, too. And he called out to me, in a different sort of voice. "Jig!" he said. And I stood there, with my feet tight together and my back and legs so straight I ached. I nodded him a solemn little bow. And he began to play. And as though we were one creature, he and I, I clutched up the sides of that skirt and apron, and I danced.

Did you ever dream of flying? This was like that. It was freedom. I could feel my feet beating the floor, I could feel the speed. But it was no effort. There was no sweat, no breathlessness, no one but the two of us, nothing but the joy.

When it stopped, I was in the middle of the floor alone. He was sitting on his barrel, staring, in the midst of the band. The walls were lined with people who had moved out of the way. There was this eerie silence. Instinctively, I did a little reverence to him and moved fast to the sidelines. While I was thinking if I ought to be embarrassed or what, the band started up loud and fast, "The Forky-Horned Deer." And the crowd just sort of exploded, glassy-eyed, like people driven.

They danced that way, one set and then another, and another. Until in the frenzy somebody got carried away and swatted somebody, back in a dark corner, and the next thing there was a fight all over creation, women hollering with children clinging to their skirts. An old man that had to be past eighty grabbed me by the shoulders and glared in my face. I could smell the homemade likker on his breath when he growled at me, "Yurr HER, I knowed it. What kinda hoodoo ARE ye, in the name o' Godamighty?"

The sheriff came between us. He had been there a good while anyway; he got a few sober people to help him knock some heads. The dance ended, Ben Aaron said later, as the dance always ended—in a rumpus. He ran us all to the buggy with that fiddle case hugged to his chest, gleefully dodging the melee. He cracked the reins and the horse did a little dance of its own and took off up the road. And he roared and laughed then, and said he had thought the fun would never begin. "A dance ain't no good till the law has to come," he said.

Neither of us mentioned the other thing that happened there that night. To us. I really couldn't remember. I doubted he could, either. There was lightning flashing over the mountain, as we went along; it began to drizzle on us halfway home. The kids went to sleep, exhausted, between us. Pet lay over on Ben Aaron's arm and Hugh's head sagged onto my lap. Ben Aaron smoked his pipe. I just thought.

Finally I said, "I was sure glad to see you and Coy Ray get on so well for a change."

Afterwhile he cleared his throat and said, "Well, he's a triflin' sonofabitch, but he can sure flam hell out of a banjer."

I had forgot to leave a lamp burning. We had never come into that house in the pitch dark before, so Ben Aaron got down and went in first and made us a light, and then he helped the children in. I asked him please to stay, I said he could have my bed and I would crawl in with Pet. Or I would make him a pallet. But he said no, he would have to go on. And he didn't tarry.

Coy Ray had stayed behind to have a drink. I heard him coming up the road as I told Ben Aaron good night. I heard Coy Ray holler, sort of low, that he had a jug—somebody had traded him; somebody else's likker was a novelty, like restaurant cooking.

Coy Ray tied his mule behind the buggy and got in beside my Cousin Ben Aaron. As it seemed somehow like I should, I closed the door gently and left them to go on. Wherever they went from here, they were sheltered from the rain. I saw then that he had left the fiddle on my dresser; I don't remember that he ever would play it again.

After a little bit of a futile struggle I blew out the light and lay down in that dress. Pet would help me get loose of it in the morning. I closed my eyes but I listened to the rain a long time before I went to sleep. Even then I must have had lots of thoughts; I woke up in the morning with two ditches between my eyebrows that I tried to rub out with some butter on my fingers.

~14~

SOPHIA

IT RAINED ON THROUGH THE NEXT DAY, AND THE NEXT. WE STAYED shut up inside, except that we would go out a couple of times a day to see what was coming up in the garden, and we had to feed the cow and mule and chickens. The kids loved to turn the biddies out; they would follow us every step we took, going *chee-chee-chee*, running between our feet. The notion that we would be expected to murder them one day got to be repulsive.

We swept out the house and scoured pots and it felt good to keep the stove hot so we made strawberry jam by Nam's directions she had written down. For a change it was good to be in the house; we had spent so much time working in the field that we had missed the quiet, unbroken days when you could just sort of sink in and be at home.

Pet took the scraps from Rose's dress and settled down to make herself an apron. Hugh found a shelf of Mackey's books in the attic. He sat down in a little old cane chair by the fire and read *The Water-Babies*, oblivious to anything else going on. I sat across from him to do the mending and the fire shined in big tears rolling down his cheeks, he was so caught up in the plight of the poor little boy that swept chimneys.

Rose came down one afternoon, in the drizzly fog, just to see how we were. Her chickens had got a bump or two of the pox on their combs, she said, and she brought us some sulphur and lard to doctor ours before that should get started bad. Chicken pox was a mess in the wet, she said.

We showed her the dress. I don't know when I was so proud of anything. She bit her lip and clenched her hands. "You mean you made that for ME?" she said.

"I made that for you," I said, not believing it either. She had to put it on so I could hem it. Her long legs and undershirt and flour sack bloomers showed through, of course. We would have to make a petticoat. I was grateful we had plenty of sheets in the attic. I would have to take in a couple of seams a little bit too, but it was all I could do not to cry, looking at her. It was like she shimmered. I wished Ben Aaron could be there to see, he was so really fond of her. I made up my mind to make more. I would get patterns. I would experiment. I had done something right.

That bad weather was the first time I'd had, since we came up here, to sit and do handwork and think about things. I wondered about things I didn't know. I wondered about Ben Aaron, how he managed for himself, alone up there in that side-show of a house, while that flashy vain woman was gone to Baltimore to spend money. The more I didn't see her, the more I wondered about her. However tacky her taste might be, she must be beautiful, I thought. She must have some wondrous quality in her head, or under her skirt. Or somewhere. Ben Aaron had married her.

I confess I dwelled on it. I bit a needle in two that I was holding in my teeth and had my funeral all planned by the time I caught the point end with my tongue and spit it out.

We had decided we were in for forty days and nights, but it was only three or four, and there was one of those bright, hazy mornings that will restore your soul. I went out and gathered up sticks to put under the washpot. Stovewood cut to fit was too precious; there was plenty of deadfall up in the hemlocks and I dragged that down and broke it up. 'Course it was damp. Coy Ray had said you could burn anything if you started it with pine with lots of sap, so I broke off some boughs and shook 'em fairly dry, sacrificed a stick of light-wood and to make sure it all went I poured a good slosh of coal oil on the pile, and set the wash pot over it, and filled the pot with a bucket, from the spout. And then I struck a match to that handiwork.

Well, Dear Lord, there has never been such smoke under the sun. That mess sputtered and popped and black night enveloped the earth. I went coughing into the house to round up the clothes. When I passed a mirror nothing looked back but the whites of my eyes, with pale tear-streaks under them. The only thing good about it was that my cousin Ben Aaron was not there to laugh. And just as I was yanking the sheets off the beds, I heard the horses coming.

I wiped my face and hands desperately on my apron and ran to look out. Oh, it was a buggy coming. Saved. Aunt Nam.

I went out on the porch. It was not Aunt Nam's buggy, it was a carriage I didn't know. There was a young boy in overalls sitting up front, driving, and two big ladies with parasols sitting in the back, dressed fit to kill. Mercy—who in the world?

They pulled up, and I went down to meet them. The boy got down and gave his hand to one of the women, and she hiked her frock and stepped out. And in spite of the boy's help she landed right heavily— *Plunk*—for she was pretty stout, though much constricted by her corset, one could tell.

She was wearing a picture hat with a maline brim and pink silk flowers around the crown. Her hair was cut and frizzied in dark corkscrews around a face like a plate of dough. She had squinty eyes, and a little owl's bill of a nose, and a tiny, thin mouth that she had transformed into a cupid's bow with right much bright rose paint.

Her dress was brown silk printed with pink roses. The rhinestone buckle of her belt was most prominent, for her stomach could not be restrained. That dress had a low neck, I remember, and her bosom looked like clabbered milk, spilling over.

We greeted each other. Ordinarily I would have kissed anybody that came, but I was so dirty. I started to put out my hand, and then I saw that it was dirty. She made no move to touch me—I thought at first because I was dirty.

"How do you do?" I said.

She nodded politely. "I am Mrs. Steele," she said. I thought, Which Mrs. Steele? Where did this one come from? I know I looked dumb standing there trying to figure. Then she went on, "I assume you are Mr. Steele's cousin. But I don't recall that he ever told me your name."

"Seneca Steele," I said, not thinking.

Her penciled little eyebrows shot up. "I had assumed you were married. My husband said you had children."

Her husband. Oh, this was not real. "Oh yes, I am married," I said. "My husband's name is Lamb. It is just sort of a Southern way," I said shakily. "A Steele is a Steele . . ."

"That is the way it was with the Orpingtons," she said, with a flourish of her parasol. "I was an Orpington, when I married Mr. Steele."

I took a breath and said, "So-fie-a."

She tilted her head so as to look somewhat down her nose. "SOPH-ya," she said, correcting me. "I see you have made yourself at home at The Birches," she said.

"Oh, quite," I said.

"For such a homely place it has so much romance behind it, you know," she said, squinching her eyes and puckering her mouth to make a smile. "Mr. Steele and I spent the first two years of our marriage here—our honeymoon. You can understand why this is one of my favorite properties. . . ."

There was that other woman still in the carriage, a large person, in a dress with many pink organdie frills. She kept dipping and doodling her parasol and grunting distracting noises while we talked. I nodded at her, and I said to Mrs. Steele, "Won't you ladies please come in? I shall put us on a pot and we'll have tea."

"Oh, no," said Mrs. Steele, "we are only out riding, on such a lovely day. We had not intended a long visit. I DID want you to meet our daughter—did Mr. Steele tell you we have a daughter? I expect not. Mrs. Lamb, this is our daughter Celestine."

I had not fully noticed Celestine, this other apparition had so devoured my attention. Celestine scooted across the seat, working her mouth sideways, trying to speak. Her eyelids drooped. Her face twitched as she reached out her big fair arms to me. My eyes were fastened on the pale, perfect skin and those gold eyes. I heard myself make an involuntary groan. I jumped on the step of the carriage and caught her in my arms, and kissed her face, and held her gold head to my neck. Oh, God, I thought, what next?

"Celestine," I said, "I am your cousin Sen. I am so glad to know I have you." I held her by the shoulders and looked into her face. It was, spastic or not, a very pretty face. Her eyes were wet with tears. "How old are you, Cousin?" I said. Her jaw worked, but the words could not quite form.

"Celestine is seventeen," said Mrs. Steele. And then she proceeded to enlighten me. "You can see that she is an unfortunate child. She suffered a terrible accident at birth. She was born, in fact, right here in this house, Mrs. Lamb, during Mr. Steele's absence. Mr. Steele was at that time given to long absences. And under those circumstances Celestine was born to me with no physician attending. . . ." She rolled her eyes around toward the driver; he had sucked in his cheeks and was studying the heavens. Then she proceeded in a coarse whisper, "and I was alone here with only an ignorant servant girl who nearly let Celestine DROWN . . ."

Hmm? I thought, clapping my hand to my mouth in sympathetic horror. I was really truly stunned. I was overcome. My heart nearly broke, right then, for Ben Aaron. Oh, Father, this would have to be only the tip of the iceberg.

Having scored, Mrs. Steele moved on to other things. "I am surprised at your traveling without your husband," she said. "I travel without Mr. Steele only when his work will not let him go."

"My husband is very involved with business right now," I said. "That is why I wanted to get away for a while."

"Oh?" said Mrs. Steele, "What is his business?"

"He is very busy disposing of an estate," I said. And I didn't add that it was mine.

She called for the boy to get down and hand her back in. They both puffed a little from the exertion.

"How many days do you suppose you will be able to stay, then?" said Mrs. Steele, playing her last card. She had a splendid talent for making herself clear.

"Several," I said. This was, after all, my grandmother's house. The family's house. Ben Aaron had said so. And I was beginning to love it.

~15~

PERSPECTIVE

I'LL TELL YOU, ABSOLUTE FURY RUBBED OUT ONE WHOPPER OF a washing that morning. Righteous indignation cleaned out the chicken coop. Conviction went down to the field and chopped weeds.

The kids had gone off with Coy Ray's boys to set some rabbit gums. When I wound down a little bit I went back up to the house and made some tea and put some of those big old store-bought cookies in the warmer. They had lasted till they got limp because they were so awful.

I had sat down in the rocking chair in the kitchen to consider recent events when Ben Aaron hollered at the door and came on in. I had not heard him coming down the road, nor seen him out the window. He had come in from the south, from a trail down by the branch, he said. He had taken a logging team down into Shiloh, that was the next big cove over west. He had started a lumber camp over there, he said; there were a few old houses over there already, and they would have to throw up a few more.

He would be working maybe thirty men in Shiloh in the fall, he said. It was funny, but I hadn't really wondered what was over there at all. All the world these days was The Birches, suspended on a strand of web anchored to Red Bank at one end, and the Forks at the other.

He sat down at the kitchen table and I fixed him some tea. I could feel him looking at me while I busied around.

"What you so red in the face about?" he said finally.

I was about to bust. I opened my mouth to let it all roll off my tongue. I wanted to say, All right, now I understand ONE tragic thing, but there is something worse I will never understand. I wanted to say, Why?

But I stood there and looked at him, slouched out like he was, relaxed as an old cat, with his face so concerned and trusting. And I said, "I have worked real hard all day. I put out a big wash, and I worked a while in the field."

He looked relieved. "It did turn off a pretty day," he said, "the clearest I b'lieve it's been since you were here."

We sipped politely on our tea. Directly, he said, "You got anything more you really have to do today?" He sounded like a little boy who knew where the Easter baskets were hid.

"No, not a solitary thing," I said.

"Then you can go someplace with me," he said.

I said I would have to get cleaned up; I had streaks of sweat running down my neck, and chicken-doo on the hem of my dress.

"No—not a soul will see us," he said, "you don't even need to put on shoes."

So we went out; he had been leading an extra horse behind Cy, and he put me up on it, and we went off across the scrub field, going west, and picked up a little trail that headed nearly straight up Hogback, west of the bluffs.

"Grab you up a good handful of mane and hang on," he said. I grabbed me two arms full of neck and clung for dear life. He let me go ahead and he followed. I dared to look back at him once; he had the reins sort of draped over one wrist and the other hand on Cy's shoulder, patting him along. My horse just picked its way along, with no direction from me.

When we got to the ridge we were in a grove of hemlocks and the trail was soft and quiet under the horses' feet. Ben Aaron went ahead, to the right, across the comb of the ridge. The sun came through the trees in slanting stripes of light and made light splotches on the ferns and the floor of the woods. We were climbing still, but gently.

And then we came out onto the bald, into the sun. He stopped and stared way off, saying nothing, like he was counting the hills to be sure nobody'd taken one. There was not a shred of fog, a breath of haze; the air sparkled. He moved on, then, still quiet. The trail was a worn, one-horse track over the moss and through the grasses on the rock.

We came to that stone pedestal that was the high point of the mountain, and from that side it sloped enough so that the track could go up it. Ben Aaron waited at the base till I came up beside him. "Lean over here and put your arms around my neck," he said. And I did, and he lifted me over on Cy, in front of him, and looped my horse's reins over a stob, and we rode on up. The top of the rock was not much more than one horse wide.

We were up there above the bushes, above the treetops. A hawk circled over the valley of the Caney Forks; we were looking down at him. We could plainly see the "forks," where Big Caney and its west prong joined. Spirals of smoke and white steam rose just in front of the silver streak of river; the sawmill gave us perspective for the rest of the valley. Overhead the sky was deep blue, and the world was that green of new summer, rising and falling every way we looked.

We sat there absolutely silent, motionless. That was not deliberate, it was the effect (at least on me) of awe. I knew that this little trail he'd made alone. This rock was his. He was sharing the most precious thing he knew.

"All this you see," he said, finally, starting over from the first time we were on this mountain, "all this . . ." and he stalled again.

"I thought you might like to see what I have gotten back," he started over.

"Gotten back?"

"It was nearly all gone," he said.

"Gone where?"

"To anybody that had a little money, or a little likker, or a good hand of cards," he said. "To the tax collector, part of it. The horse trader, whoever come along. Just not much to you and me . . . not without a fight. . . ."

"Who did it belong to?" I said.

"Hmmp," he said, amused and a little pleased I didn't know.

"From the top of this ridge north over Wolf Den—that's the mountain there beyond the forks—that belonged to old Ivan

McAllister. That was your great-great-granddaddy. He came in here in the 1780s and started a trading post.

"He found out then he could get a land grant of three thousand acres if he started an iron forge. He did that. He traded horses and furs and he built a store and bought up a few thousand acres more. Guess it didn't cost anything hardly then. Sometime around 1790 or so he wrote his cousin Hamilton Steele in Philadelphia, and told him things were pretty good, to come on. Said he'd found just the right piece of land across the ridge from his own place, called it 'a bonnie grove o' birken' or somethin' like that. The letter's still in the attic, I expect. Ought to be there in a little tin box."

Well, Ben Aaron said, Ham Steele was a young man then. His folks had been shipbuilders, they had a boatworks on the River Clyde, somewhere near Glasgow in Scotland. Ham had sailed his own ship to America, brought a bunch of passengers, and all his belongings, and soon as he dropped anchor and unloaded he sold the ship. Then he waited in Philadelphia to hear from old Ive.

So he came south into the mountains with a little money. He came also with an extra wagon for his books and tools, and a "blue-black body servant, from Barbados," Ben Aaron said, and a taste for things of the spirit, but not too much for work.

He bought about nine hundred acres, from this ridge south, east along the river and west to Shiloh, Ben Aaron said, He put him up a cabin, and went up to the forks and married Ive's daughter Ariana. By the time they had a couple of children he had started his real house in The Birches.

"He and Ive had their fingers in all kinds of pies. They knew lumber, and began to cut timber. They ran the forge. They made brick. They had a tanyard, and dealt in hides. 'Course hired somebody else to do most all of the work. Ive built the town of Caney Forks and Ham went after land."

They owned everything from the head of the valley down the river—on this side—to Red Bank. They bought west, across Shiloh, and north to Wolf Creek. They didn't move east. Not at least in any big lumps. Over there the Wilcoxes grew like cuckleburrs, Ben Aaron said. And next to Wilcoxes' an old German named Henry Shuman owned a thousand acres and couldn't be moved with a crowbar.

There had been other families who had held to little pockets, against the avalanche of McAllister and Steele.

"Can you see that steeple, back over there, shinin' in the sun?" Ben Aaron said, pointing over in the northwest corner of the valley. "That's Beaverdam Baptist. That's in what we call Harmon Field, over there. Ol' Ive had one son, named Aaron, married Mallie Harmon. They turned out McAllisters for Ham and Arie's children to marry. Now, Ive had one other girl besides Arie, she was a kind of a weak-minded gal, had to be looked after. It was always told that she was sittin' out on the porch one day, crochetin' a long chain of thread, and ol' Lije Peek come along, stopped to talk to her. He wadn't what you'd call right bright, either. And the next thing her people knew, she was gone. Lije had took her off to get married. It was a terrible disgrace. 'Course they found her and got her home but she come up with a baby, Simmy Peek. That was Barzilai Peek's granddaddy, case you wondered how he was kin to us."

I had.

"There, over that way," Ben Aaron said, pointing at some humpy hills that lay south and west of Harmon's, "that's the Tater Hill mountains. The gap between them is Gillespie Field."

We sat very still. A little breeze rushed around us, cool, so sweet on us rooted to that rock in the sun. "My sister married a Gillespie," Ben Aaron said.

"Nam told me," I said. "The minute I knew where I was, here, I had to know why Mackey left. Nam told me."

For the longest time, then, again, nothing passed. There was plenty more to say, but it had to come in its own time. "Down there on the Boney Creek they hanged a bushwhacker one time," Ben Aaron volunteered cheerily.

"Oh, awful!" I said.

"Meant to leave 'im for the buzzards. . . ."

"Hush!"

". . . but Granddaddy Mack, Nam's daddy, he was a Confederate captain you know, he went out and made 'em cut him down. Made 'em bury him, in a decent way. Said he'd not have such as that to blight this place."

"Oh, don't!"

"Don't what?" he said.

"Don't blight this place."

I shivered, and I remember the comfort of leaning back on his chest, with his arms around my waist. I remember he rested his chin on the crown of my head, and I couldn't see him, but I imagined he was smiling.

"So it was all gone and you got it back," I said.

"I don't know if you know," he said, "but we don't come from the most provident line of people. My pa did love his likker. That was a common trait among 'em. The men. Your granddaddy Ive, he was a fine, gracious gentleman. Read Latin and Greek. Whittle and fiddle and read a little bit, that was a day's work for him. Ol' Ham Steele warmed over. Except Ben Ivan wasn't near as sharp as Ham was, with money."

He sucked his pipe and shuffled his thoughts. A few little white puffy clouds drifted over; we watched their shadows move across the valley.

"I worked in that sawmill from the time I was little. Before I ever went to school. When your daddy left, business started on the down-go in earnest. I knew about the debts that were run up and not paid, the land being sold off to strangers. The year I finished college my daddy died. I came home for the funeral and Ive just plain handed the mill over to me. The whole works. We were about to go under. The land at the Forks was down to about a thousand acres, with money owing. Ivan still held the birch cove intact, but that was Daisy's doing. It was hers by birth as much as his—Ham Steele was HER granddaddy, too.

"Daisy would have died before . . ." he stopped for a long sigh, "Daisy was never going to give up The Birches. But everything else just dribbled away."

"What did you do?" I said. I couldn't imagine. Or wouldn't let myself.

"It took a little time, and all kinds of ways, I'm not real proud to say," he said benignly. "Nature and bad fortune helped me, time to time. The tax collector helped me a time or two. A heart of granite helped me. Sometimes the good Lord helped me, odd to say. And in the nastiest times, I simply helped myself. . . ."

"You got it all?"

"And a little extra. . . ."

I wanted to ask him how much of it there was. But I didn't. "All this you see . . ." was all my mind could handle.

But then, like a cockroach swimming in the punchbowl, one of Sophier's great lines of the morning came across that euphoric scene: "One of my favorite properties."

I started to say something. I was about to say, "Oh, by the way, I had company this morning." But I didn't want to blight this place.

"I guess the younguns'll wonder where you are," Ben Aaron said, straightening up in the saddle.

"I guess we better go," I said, with no heart in it. When we came down off the rock, he reached and took my horse's reins off the limb, and knotted them, and threw them over its head, and clucked to it and it followed us along. "Steep goin' down," he said, "it's as well you stay with me."

It was another strange rite of kinship we had passed up there. I had been fascinated by Ben Aaron; I had admired him. I had been furious with him, and I had loved him. Somehow now I was kin to him, comfortably, intimately, in a way you can only feel and not describe. I felt more from him than the tenderness of something big for something little; I guess it was the joy of something that had been lost and given up now being found, and dark and lonely corners opened to the light.

He had lifted me off Cy and was about to go when I finally said it. "Oh, by the way, I had company this morning."

"Did," he said, biting down on his pipe. "I guess it was about time."

I was afraid of what I could say. I couldn't think of anything right.

"Why didn't you tell me?" I said.

"About what?" he said, mild and innocent.

And I was damned, whatever I was about to say. But then he went on. "About Celestine? Hmmp. Soph gets so much pleasure out of tellin' that, would I rob her of it?"

I was right on the brink of tears. "Ben Aaron, how . . .?" I started out. But he gave me one of those firm, unblinking, Presbyterian elder looks, and moved down the steps, just out of reach.

"I meant to tell you when we were up on the ridge," he said. "I meant to show you Shiloh Cove. When we get that camp goin' we're goin' to have families in there. We'll have to have a school. It's goin' to be a lot easier for your kids to go there than to try to go up to the Forks."

"Oh, by the time school starts we'll be gone back, I 'spect," I said, with no conviction at all.

"Next time I'm by here, I'll show you what's over there. Ol' Shiloh Church, been deserted, it'll do all right for a school. I'll show you how the kids'll have to go," he said.

It was like he hadn't heard a word. Or just knew better.

~16~

THE WAGES OF SIN

ONE OF THE THINGS THE KIDS DID EACH DAY, THEY WOULD TAKE the mule and the cow down to the grassy bottoms and let 'em graze. We didn't have any serious fences, except around the barn lot. So the livestock had to be led out and tied and tended. After a fashion.

The mule had picked up some; it looked better and was holding up its head. Aunt Nam said the eats were none too good at Cud'n Barz's place, for man or beast. Said she watched him feed the mules one time; "He give 'em each two ears o' corn and a hand o' fodder and said, 'Now, eat till ye bust.'" The mule was improved; the cow I couldn't tell much about, I mean what was fat and what was calf.

We had gotten up the nerve to ride the mule sometimes; we would bridle it and put a croaker sack on it and ride it, oh, as far as the river, maybe. We had saddles but that poor old thing could not have stood the extra weight. Pet and Hugh could ride it down to the pasture and lead the cow, and as long as the kids didn't go out of sight they could stake 'em out, tie 'em to something, and go do as they pleased.

So I didn't worry, that afternoon, when I got home and the children were nowhere to be seen. I made the fire in the stove to cook supper, and went out and brought in the wash. It wasn't till the sun went down that I got uneasy and went out to call them.

I hollered and they didn't answer. I went down to the barn and the mule and the cow were still gone so I figured they were still down on the branch. But I couldn't figure how they'd gone too far to hear. The

light was going. I called and called. Nothing answered but the absolute still—that is the scariest sound you will ever hear, if you've
lost your children in the woods.

I thought then that maybe they'd gone up to Coy Ray's. I walked
up as far as the burying ground and called. Not that they could hear
me, with the narrows between us. But I could see the smoke from
Rose's supper fire, rising in the dim. I knew that she would have realized how late it was, and would have sent them home.

The stars were coming out. The last birds were straggling in and
making their little goodnight noises. Bats flitted and dipped over
the field. No Pet and Hugh. I thought about Ben Aaron already
home, sitting at the supper table with a big stuffed hen. Seven miles
I would have to walk to get him to come and help me—if the
Mistress Steele would let him come. I thought of Coy Ray and
Rose, of course I would have gone for them first. I could wade the
river and get up to their house, steep going though it was, in less
than an hour. But it would be pitch black.

I was thinking whether to take time to get a lantern. I was seeing
little bodies tumbling down the narrows, in the foam. Floating in
the dark of the suck hole. Limp and crumpled at the bottom of
some old well or mine-hole. It came to mind that I would have to
tell Foots. The car was one thing. But the children? I called out in
panic, one more time.

Way down the cove, a little voice came back. I ran down to the road,
it was now just a lighter streak in the dark of night. Way off, I could
make out a dark something coming. Two kids on the mule. I ran to
meet them, being thankful every step, and kissed their dusty knees.

"Mama, we don't know what to do," Pet said. "Hugh has lost Miss
Murchie." (They had named the cow Miss Murchie for the head-
mistress at the Latin School. She was a right bovine lady, thick as a
pudding, stolid and immovable, it was true.)

"We've been miles and we can't find her." Hugh was suffering as
only Hugh could suffer, the sins of the world a dead weight on his
tousled black crown.

"We'll find her in the morning," I said. "All I care about right now is
here." Miss Murchie had never been my great mottled hope, to begin
with.

But a wrong had been done, and the righteous would not rest until the whole thing was reported.

"He tied her to a willow limb, it wasn't hardly more than a leaf. And he went off to fish," Pet said. Hugh sat convicted and condemned.

"If you saw that why didn't you tie her better?" I said.

Pet was in all things a logical child. "It was his day to take care of the cow," she said. "I had the cow yesterday."

Well, I assured them, Miss Murchie would turn up. She had not come up on high living; she had camped out on many a less pleasant night than this one. And when it got light, when we had all rested from our crises, we would find her.

Later on, when we had blown out the light, I didn't think about Miss Murchie. I did think of the terror that had just passed, and of the debt of piety that I owed because I had promised, and my children had come home. And that out of the way, I thought about Sophier. Soph-ya. And other things.

Uncle Camp used to practice his sermons in the kitchen, when I was little. He preached one Sunday a month at the Second Beulah Land Baptist Church. One that stuck in my mind (I guess because so often it applied), was about thinking bad thoughts.

I could see his face, the veins in his temples, the dark brown satin skin tight over the jaw and cheekbones. I could hear the rise and fall of the message as he embraced the imaginary flock with a grand gesture of the dishrag. "We all thinks wicked thoughts sometime . . . Bad thoughts be like duh buzzahd. He fly over yo' head, an' my head. I can' mek 'im stop. But I don' need fo' ox 'im to make a nest in my hair!"

If I had dreamed at all that night, it would have been of buzzards circling and roosting in my hair. I lay there with my eyes closed, trying to put things together in my mind. There was a picture of Ben Aaron on my eyelids. It was as he would sit up there on that rock, on that old horse, looking out over all this that he loved. And then there was Sophia, preening and poking out of her Baltimore dress, lording it over us.

I could not put that pair together. I couldn't believe that Heaven had done that, either. It made me shudder. I thought about things I had no right to think of, and I couldn't help it. I thought about those butter-churn legs with the flat black hairs, next to him in bed. Oh God—did he TOUCH her? Did she flop those pasty bumpers over him at night? Certainly they had Done It, at least once. That child was the image of her father. I said to myself, now, that's none of your business. But hot water welled up in my gullet and I had to get up and spit.

Finally, I was so tired, and it seemed like I had just dozed off. And I heard this racket. I thought first I was dreaming it. Maybe somebody was snoring. It did it again, and then I was awake. It was terrifying.

I lay there listening, too scared to move. Thank the Lord it was outside. I thought, Are the doors locked? Of course they were not—who would ever bother us? And it did it again—it went *MaaaooooooOOOOO . . . MaaaaoooooOOOOOoo.*

We had heard some awful screams in the woods one night, just a few days after we got here. We had huddled together wondering if we should go help whoever was being killed. But Coy Ray came, before good daylight, and he laughed when I told him. Said, "Awww, it's dist a ol' panther a-yowlin'. No harm to it. Dist keep your younguns in, of a night. . . ."

This was nothing like that at all. This was a BIG something. I had never doubted for a minute that spirits had this place, but I'd never thought of them as anything but good. The thing hollered again, louder. It had a deep, fog horn kind of voice.

Miss Murchie. I had never heard a cow trying to calve before. I leaned over and turned up the lamp wick and felt around for a match. All the shadows that light made didn't do my feelings a lot of good. I crept out of bed and went to the window and listened. It was Miss Murchie, somewhere down in the bottom. And she was in terrible distress.

I woke Pet and Hugh and told them to get their shoes on quick, and I went to the kitchen to get the lantern, and we went trailing off into the night. Every time that moan would roll across the field, all our feet would want to turn around. But we followed the sound. I didn't know whatever we would do, when we found her.

We were going down into the birch grove. An awful likelihood occurred to me. "Did you all look in that thicket around the suck hole?" I said.

"No," Hugh said. "We didn't want to. . . ."

"I don't blame you one particle," I said.

The nearer we got, going through the vines and spider webs and dew, the weaker the wailing got. We got into the bog, over our ankles. The lantern shined on water that was coffee black by day. You could hear the hole that drained it going *slooop . . . slooop. . . .*

The light went almost nowhere. I thought for a second I was back in bed, having a nightmare. There was a long lull between groans and we stood still, not knowing which way to slop. And then there was just panting, the whistling of breath from somewhere in the tangle of laurels and dog-hobble bushes. And finally, the lantern light glinted back from an eye.

Miss Murchie was down on her knees in the thicket. Her eyes were rolled back from suffering. Her bony sides heaved with her struggles for wind. Her back legs were spraddled out in the muck. She had slipped away, going deeper in the thicket as they hunted her. She had found a private place to have her calf, all right, but then she couldn't do it.

I gave Pet the lantern and got Hugh to help me try to push her over on her side. It probably was wrong to do that but I knew her front legs had to be aching. We counted and shoved and our feet slipped in the mud. We couldn't budge her. Her tongue lolled, she gave a feeble grunt and lifted her tail. A dainty hoof showed in the mess. Then the joint of a leg. It was a little hind leg. She was calving backwards. My insides ached for her.

Then of her own, she rolled over on her side. "We've got to get some help," I said. That meant somebody was going to have to stay, and somebody would go. Somebody would have a light, and somebody none. I thought we might break some bows and make a fire. But we were too much in the wet. And so inept. If we let the lantern go out, we'd be in a mess.

"Who's going to get Coy Ray?" I said.

"I will," Hugh said, in a quavery little voice. "It's my fault."

But while I tried to make him know that this was by nature the way things sometimes go, Miss Murchie heaved, and gurgled up a mass of bloody bubbles. A great shudder went over her, and she lay still.

Hugh squatted and rubbed her head, with tears falling on her. "She was just too old," I said.

But there was that little leg, sticking out of the cooling corpse. I never wanted less to put my hands anywhere, but I had Pet hold the lantern down close, and I ran my fingers up along that leg, and found the back, and the other leg, and clutched and pulled. I could feel the poor little joints giving. Then we had two bloody legs free, and a tail. Half a dead cow lay relaxing on that little body trapped inside.

The legs were limp. I could feel no life in them. I was lying on my belly, at the cow's behind. I tugged but I had no leverage. I couldn't bring the body.

"Let me try," Hugh said. He needed to feel like he'd done the best he could. I moved and let him, but his hands kept slipping.

"It's dead," I said. "It may have been dead for a while." And at that point of despair, the lantern died, and nothing but the orange sparks on the wick glowed in the dark. We were in complete blackness.

We stayed still until our eyes got a little more adjusted to it. Things went plop in the water, now and then. The night bugs droned, and the river talked, as if to reassure us. Finally I told the kids to take hold of my gown and when they thought they could, to lead me out. And they did. When we came out of the woods we could see the dark shape of the house, up the hill, and the glow of lamplight from the front room window.

We stopped at the runoff and washed and washed. I told the kids to leave everything but their underwear on the back porch. I had Pet throw me out a big apron and I stripped off my nightgown and washed again at the spout, before I wrapped myself up and came inside. But all night I knew I could smell cow, and dying, on my hands.

When we slept it was the sleep of the dead. As soon as they woke up the next day I sent the children after Coy Ray. The buzzards were circling, for a fact, and I didn't know what to do. Coy Ray was gone, of course, but the kids left word with Rose, and she said not to worry, she would keep us in milk as long as we needed.

And afterwhile, Coy Ray came with the two biggest boys and a pair of mules. I don't know what they did. I never asked. It was just that they knew how to do it, and for that I felt humble and blessed.

∼17∼

THROUGH THE GLASS DARKLY

THERE WERE NOT MANY FOLKS UP HERE HAD TELEPHONES, IN THAT time. I think they didn't need 'em. The wires could not have carried the word to Aunt Nam that Sophier had been here a bit faster than the mountain news service.

I cannot tell you what it did for my spirit, as the undertakers were down there disposing of Miss Murchie, to hear Nam's buggy coming like the wind. I ran out to meet her and fell on her neck.

"If you didn't come I was coming to you, as soon as I could get up and creep," I said. And I told her about our adventures of the night before.

"I would of been here at day this mornin' but pore ol' Miss Nannie Brock was taken right about four o'clock and they wanted me to stay and dress 'er," Nam said. It had been a cheerful morning for us both.

That news disposed of, we proceeded to vital matters.

"Sophier was here," she said.

"How'd you know? Ben Aaron tell you?"

"I smelt the singed feathers all the way to the Forks," she said.

"What you mean?"

"I hear you give 'er as good as you got," she said.

"Did Ben Aaron tell you that?" I said. "I never said a word to him, except that she was here."

She smirked and rocked and swung her foot. "I've got other con-
nections," she said.

"Well I never said anything unkind to her, I don't think I did," I
said. "Except—I didn't let her run me off."

Aunt Nam popped her hands, "And that's exactly what she meant
to do. Billy Shuman, Ansel's boy, he's the one drives for 'er, if he can't
get out of it. 'Course he got ever' word, comin' and goin'. Said she
come down here fully intendin' to put y'uns on the road. And you
never paid 'er a bit of attention in the world. Said you never even
acted upset. Said she rared and carried on to that pore afflicted girl,
all the way home, about Aaron's deadbeat relations."

I could still see Billy Shuman, Ansel's boy, sitting up behind those
horses, hardly able to contain himself. "Wha'd you have to give him
to make him tell you all that?" I said.

She turned around and faced me, holding on to the arms of her
rocker like she couldn't believe her ears. "Why, he's our KIN," she
said.

"You and Ben Aaron are my kin," I said, a little bit puzzled, "and
there's a whole sight you've not told me."

She laughed and raised her eyebrows, looking wise. "All dead men
will float up sometime," she said. "Now tell ME something. Are you
still tryin' to like Miss Sophier?"

"No, I am not," I said. "I don't think I can stand her."

"Why, what in the world?"

"She talked ugly to me about Ben Aaron."

"I can hear it—don't tell me. He went off and left her and that
youngun was born in that plight and it was all his fault."

"Does she tell that all over?" I said.

"Wherever one or more are gathered together," Nam said.

"How in the world does Ben Aaron tolerate that?"

"Humph," she said. "Humph. I reck'n he just considers the source."

"Said it happened right here in this house."

Nam sat there rocking, picking at a thread in the front of her
skirt. "Lots of things happened to Sophier right here in this house,"
she said, a little bit subdued.

"Yes, it did," she went on, directly. "Things went wrong for Sophier
right from the start. Right from the day Ben Aaron brought 'er here.

First thing, she wanted 'im to carry 'er over the threshold. Lord do! Well he was goin' to do the best he could. Unlocked the door, opened it, heisted 'er up . . ." Nam went through the motions of Ben Aaron raising Sophier, down to his straining neck, and strutted jaw, and red face, "and just as he got 'er all gathered up the door shut in 'is face and he couldn't get it open to save his life. Put 'er down finally and pushed and rattled and shoved. Wouldn't open. Gave up on it and went around to the back, come through and opened it from inside, and let Sophier in . . ."

I couldn't help but think it was not much romantic of Ben Aaron to tell that kind of thing about his lovely bride. But then Nam said, "She quarreled about these old fireplaces too, all the time. Said they were filthy. Said no matter where she sat the smoke came in her face. Ben Aaron was listenin' at 'er go on about that one time. I'll never forget the devilish look on his face, nor how she clucked and preened, when he said, 'Well, my love, smoke follers beauty.'

"She worried him so about the floors bein' humpy till he had new joists put under these two rooms, here, on the river side. Old ones was whole dressed logs this big, solid as the day they were laid. But her chair kep' a-turnin' over even with that done.

"She claimed the mice had plain took over, even made nesties in 'er shoes. Her last go-round though was with the privy."

"They did have a privy?" I said. I had wondered why there wasn't one, with all the niceties around.

"Haw, they had one. Matter of fact they had two, a men's and a ladies'. Men's was up in the hemlocks, 'course way below the spring. Tree fell on it, after nobody was here. Sophier burned the ladies'."

"What?"

"She burnt it. She allus used a chamber pot, 'course, in the house. Or did when they was somebody here to wait on 'er and empty it. Well, but one day she was down in the garden, must of been a-lookin' for Ben Aaron, for she never worked out there, as anybody knew of. And she had to go to the toilet. Set down on the seat and a yeller-jacket popped 'er. Well, maybe it was several. You know they like to nest in the hole.

"She yowled for Ben Aaron to come a-runnin' but he was a good ways off, somewhere. 'Fore he could get there she had gone in the house and got coal oil and a rag, goin' to burn out the yellerjackets. 'Course she set the outhouse on fire, burnt it to the ground."

Right after that, Nam said, they moved up to the Forks, anyway.

"But she really had a baby here? What did she mean, it 'nearly drowned?'"

Aunt Nam drew up a good breath. "Oh, law, she had it here," she said. "And, it nearly drowned. She had it in the slop jar."

"No!"

"She had it in the slop jar. Cleone was here then, doin' all the work. Sophier went on about how she craved some kraut. And Cleone fixed it. A pot of pork chops and kraut. Sophier eat about the whole thing. Cleone had made a couple of green apple pies, it was that time, and Sophier eat one of them, too. She took a fearsome case o' the trots, and here that baby came."

"Was that Rose's mother that was here?" I said. "Was that the 'ignorant servant girl?'"

"Did she really say that? Did that heifer say that about Cleone? Lord have mercy," Nam said. She rocked and puffed and then she said, "Servant girl my foot. Cleone was our cousin. Her mama and daddy had one of the nicest places around here. Old Jake Shuman place, over across the river there. House is since burned down, but they lived nice. Back about 1912, there come a typhoid epidemic through here. People died with it, ones that didn't die laid helpless for months sometimes, fell away to just weak bones, hair fell out; whole houses would smell like rats. Where typhoid was, you could smell it.

"Cleone's mama and daddy died of it. She was eighteen or so, not married yet. So she was there to wait on 'em. Cleone never got the typhoid herself, but by the time they died she was down to a rag. Ans was off in medical school; by the time she got word to him and he got home, it was nearly over. Ben Aaron'd go up there and he'p 'er when he could, they'd always been close. Finally when her folks were gone he brought 'er here. He didn't want 'er stayin' in that old house alone.

"Well, 'course you can imagine what happened. . . ."

I could imagine all kinds of things. So many I just kept rocking and said nothing.

"Cleone was here not even a week when Sophier made a house-maid out of 'er. Soon as Ben Aaron had to go somewhere and leave the two of 'em alone. Sophier's always had to have a maid you know; never could keep one. Had a woman here from the start, to clean and cook. Then she brought in this poor little French woman, don't know where she got 'er. Always wanted a French maid to dress 'er up and rat up 'er hair, the like of that.

"That'n didn't last long though I tell you. That gal and Aaron'd sit at the kitchen table, a-talkin' French."

"What?" I said.

"Oh yes," she said, sort of cool. "Did you think he went off to school to learn saw-millin'? He spent six months in France, in the big war, talkin' French to people for some high-muckety officer, some friend of his at school. Was sent for, just to do it."

I thought about the worn little books of French poetry on the attic shelves. They were so old they surely belonged to someone be-fore Ben Aaron's time. Someone, I figured, had read them to him, and planted yet another wild, unlikely seed.

"Anyway," Nam went on, "you know it never worked, that woman bein' here. Sophier couldn't understand what they were a-sayin'. Next thing anybody knew that French gal was off to the depot with 'er suitcase in 'er hand. By the time Ben Aaron brought Cleone home, the housekeeper had walked off too. Wouldn't anybody stay, the life was so hateful. And on top of her meanness, Sophier was beginnin' to get big. So it fell to Cleone."

"Even delivering the baby?"

"Oh, it brought itself. Cleone got the blame. No, Ben Aaron got the blame. Of course, he was off scoutin' timber somewhere, gone two or three days. They weren't lookin' for the baby for five or six weeks; he was goin' to bring Sophier up to the Forks and move 'er in with me. We could get the doctor in a few minutes, there. He'd have been glad for 'er to go home to her own folks to have it; that's what she planned, at first, to go home at about six months. But then for some reason she changed 'er mind. . . .

"Well, it came the way it did. And when we looked at it, we all knew somethin' was wrong. I tell you, I don't think it had a thing to do with where that baby was born, or anything else that happened.

Except she was born too hard and too early. Makes me sick right now the way that nastiness gets talked about, right in front of that sweet youngun. Like she's some kind o' show-freak. When the truth is she's got a way yonder better brain than her ol' mammy."

"Did they never get a doctor?"

"Oh, law, we got ol' Doctor Bryson from up at the Forks to sit by Sophier, her a-moanin' and a-groanin' about her own self. I stayed with her while Ben Aaron and Cleone took the baby to a specialist in Asheville. He told 'em about somebody else in Atlanta and they took her there a couple of times. Finally Ben Aaron hired a nurse to come stay, I b'lieve she was from Asheville. Worked in the hospital. She was here a week or two, next thing Ben Aaron come home and found 'er all packed up waitin' for a ride to town.

"The only soul that would stay was Cleone. I don't know what on earth they'd a done without her. I don't know what 'twas, but Sophier couldn't get 'er goat. Cleone just ignored 'er and went about 'er business. Did the cookin', cleaned up, washed, waited on that wench and tended that little baby. Just doin' the way she figured kin-people ought to do, I guess."

It was, I thought maybe, just like Rose looking after us. "How long did that go on?" I said.

"Till Cleone married Coy Ray," Nam said.

She got up and reached into a sack she had brought. The smell of roasted coffee beans made me wince with the memory of that first morning I stood on that porch. Oh, how I had hoped that there would be somebody with a pot of coffee, in the house. Or even just somebody. . . . It seemed like so many years ago.

"I ground this before breakfast," she said. "I'll go put on the pot."

No, I said, I would in a minute. "Tell me about that wedding first," I said.

"Well, you could've knocked me over," she said. "Now, Coy Ray had been a-courtin' her all his life. If he shot four doves he brought her two. If he had pretty apples he took her the best of 'em. She was always good to him, she was that kind of lady. But nobody ever in this world thought she'd marry Coy Ray Wilcox. Other things aside she was a full head taller!"

"And not a bit of kin," I said. I didn't mean it to be ugly—just an observation. But Nam flattened her mouth and was quiet till I begged her to go on.

"When Celestine was a few months old," she said, "Sophier decided she wanted to go home to 'er people and get away from the baby; if Cleone put it down it hollered like somethin' wild in the woods. Sophier wanted Ben Aaron to go with 'er, leave the baby with Cleone. First he said he would. But he was strugglin' with the mill, about to get it on its feet. At the last he sent her on and stayed.

"I guess she was gone six weeks or so," Nam said. "Cleone kept the house and looked after the baby. I 'spect they were right happy. Peaceful. Sophier hadn't been back but a week or two, then, when Cleone packed up and left, one night, and married Coy Ray . . ."

A breeze came up, it made that little shivery sigh down in the birches. We watched a wasp butting the ceiling, falling back, butting again.

"Why did he do it?" I said. It was due time.

"Who do what?" Nam said.

"I tried to ask him and he put me off like I had a pox," I said.

She rocked and frowned and studied.

"If I was to tell you what I think. . . ." she said. "No, I can only say what I know. You know, this whole place was in straits."

"He told me," I said. She looked a little bit surprised.

"Did he tell you what a time he was havin', how he went from shipyard to shipyard, all along the coast, tryin' to sell lumber? They had been our biggest market and they weren't buyin'. And finally, somebody he knew told 'im about Sophier's daddy, wantin' to move a furniture plant south from Massachusetts. Did he tell you that?"

No, I said, but I was getting a picture.

"Well he went up to see the ol' man. Right then the ol' man had a big contract for a lot of school furniture. And hadn't bought the lumber. Aaron of course had on all 'is charm you know. Ol' man Orpington took 'im home to supper. Had two daughters. I don't know this for a fact, but I've seen the other'n once. And I'd say, since Ben Aaron had to take one, he took the sweetest and the most beautiful."

I guess I had been waiting for somebody to drop that. But still I marveled at it. It was just like he had said. He had done some things he wasn't real proud of.

"He'd do anything," I said out loud.

After a while, Nam said quietly, "Yes, I think he would. In fact I think he's done it."

I was not surprised; I don't know what I was. Except weak. I staggered up, directly, and went and put on the coffee. I would have loved a drink of likker at that point but there was not a dram in the place.

Even without it, I let it slip what I was thinking. "How could he?" I said. "It's not how she LOOKS . . ."

"But you can't figger out what 'e does in the bed with 'er," Nam said. She was always subtle. "I had bad dreams, m'self, about that quare match o' legs all tangled up."

We laughed out loud. Mainly, with me, it was from the mouth out. But a big dark issue was at last in the open.

"Shoo, I don' know," Nam said. "Some men they say'll do it with a cow. Or a sheep. I reck'n a GO-rilla'd do all right for some. I reck'n this ain't much worse than that.

"On the other hand," she said, warming to the subject, "it's been told around that ol' Chick Aleywine, ol' slutty woman up at the Forks, it was told she had a litter o' pups. Now mind, I never saw 'em. Or anything. . . ."

I got up laughing to see about the pot. As I started in the door I got an awesome feeling. I stood and felt the door jamb, thinking about that house.

"I am sorry for Sophier," I said. "She really had such awful troubles here."

"She despised this place," Nam said. "And the feeling was mutual. This house plain turned her out. She thought she was comin' to white columns and I bet she hoped for slaves, and what she found— she liked to say it, was 'a tumble-down old barn.'

"'Course, I will say, it was in a way the truth. It had stood empty three years since Daisy died. Ben Aaron hadn' had a chance to fix it up since he bought it from your ma . . ."

Well, I stood and stared down at her. My head swam. "What did you say?" I said, finally.

She turned and looked at me, wide-eyed. Then she frowned, and said, "Did you not know that either—that he bought it from your ma?"

"No," I said. The word came out very small.

"Did you not know it was left to you . . . ?"

~18~

COMING TO TERMS

MY MOTHER WAS IN EUROPE. IT DIDN'T MATTER, WHAT WAS THERE
to ask her? What was there to be done? We are all ignorant until we
learn better; I came up here as ignorant as she. Almost. I thought
about the summers in Europe, the opera houses, what I had gotten
from that. Magic. Most of it. Now I knew what it had cost. I
thought about it while I chopped weeds with the hoe. And while I
mended our clothes, and rubbed out wash, and pulled the tall grass
off the cemetery fence.

It was well enough that this was Ben Aaron's place. I would as soon
it be his place as mine. But I felt like he should have told me. Exactly.
If it was his, it was Sophier's too. "The family's," he said. And that
meant her, not me.

He came by one day very soon after Nam's visit; he was over in
Shiloh a lot, that summer, and it was only a couple of miles through
the gap. He came out to where I was working, that morning; he
stopped at the spout and got a drink and came down in the garden,
wiping his face on his sleeve.

"I hear you and Nam had a nice talk," he said, overpolitely.

"I know things now I ought to have known before," I said. I kept
on hoeing. I didn't know what more to say.

He stood there watching me a little while. Directly he came up
and took the hoe out of my hands and leaned on it, looking at me.

"You didn't know anything about it, ever, did you?" he said. I looked at the ground and shook my head.

"Your ma never told you?"

"No."

"Did you never wonder? Did it not occur to you, even since you got here, how it must have been? Did it not cross your mind that you were Daisy's only heir?"

"Yes it did," I said finally, and that was the truth; it had, many times. "But I couldn't ask you anything about it. When I ask you anything it makes you mad."

His face wilted. He looked down at his feet. "You never mentioned it to Nam," he said. I could tell they had fully discussed it.

"No," I said. "I figured if it was any of my business somebody would tell me, sometime." What I wanted to imply was I had trusted him.

"Oh God, if that ain't us," he said. He got out a cigarette. His hand was trembling when he put it to his mouth and struck the match on the sole of his boot.

"Well. I'll have to tell you how it was," he said. "I guess Nam told you how little we ever heard from your ma. We just couldn't find out anything down there at all. It was a bad time, with Ive and Daisy going as close together as they did. And us not even knowing about Mack."

I said yes, we had talked about it, Nam and I. I was sorry about how Mama did, I said. She was not a bad person, I said, only flighty. I meant shallow. She was pretty, I said; she had a pretty voice. I did not want Ben Aaron to despise Mama. Even if there were moments when I had hated her, these last few days.

He nodded and said of course.

"You understand, now, that your granddaddy Ive being three years older than my daddy, and their brother Garland being dead, Ive got this place when their father died. Mack was Ive and Daisy's only child. Had he outlived them, and then died, your mother would have probably gotten it. But Daisy outlived him. You were her heir. And as soon as I got Ive and Daisy's business straightened up, I wrote your mother and laid it out to her. You were also due Ive and Daisy's interest in the sawmill. Or I would buy you out—if that was what she thought the best. She wrote back that 'you' would rather have the money. I wrote her then that I would raise that money. I sent her a pitiful little check from the money Daisy had on hand. And I sent her the deed to The Birches . . ."

He stopped talking and turned away from me, and looked off across the field. I heard him draw a deep sigh, with a quaver in it.

"It was years, I'll have to tell you, before I could send her the money for your part of the mill, what it was worth when Daisy died. It amounted to mighty little, I admit. We were so low at that point nobody would've paid a nickel for us. We owed too much."

He scuffled the dirt with the hoe, with one hand, while both of us stood speechless. Then he said, "I don't want you to think, 'course, I couldn' blame you, the way you've been done all the way through . . . I wouldn't want you ever to think that I set out to cheat you, Sen," he said. "I can't say I always did so pure, with other folks. But in this case . . ."

Such a thing would never have entered my mind. I didn't know how to say to him what did hang over me so heavy. What could be more heavy than the spectre of Sophier? He seemed at that moment right on the brink of tears and I didn't know what to say.

All of a sudden my stomach growled the biggest growl, it went *YOWWWwwwrrr!* It snarled like a lion. I started to laugh. I laughed and ran and threw my arms around his waist and hugged him to me, liked to squeezed him in two. And we stood there clinging and rocking back and forth in the bean rows, laughing to tears that were not from laughing at all.

"Ben Aaron, Ben Aaron," I said, "I am starving to death. I have not swallowed a bite since Nam was here yesterday. Come in the house with me, and let's get something, before I fall over." We went up toward the house arm in arm.

"I've got to finish telling how I came to buy you out," he said. "You'll understand things better."

I said all right. But at that point I didn't care a lot.

"I never thought of this place being sold," he said. "I thought your mother would know you ought to keep it. That's how ignorant

I am about the world. First I knew of what she had in mind, I just happened to be in the courthouse one day, oh, a couple of years after your daddy died. Man I never saw was in there talkin' to Philo Spivey, Philo's the tax collector. Wanted to know about the taxes on a piece of property, had a legal description on a piece of paper. Wanted to know if the taxes had been kept up, what it was worth on the books and all.

"Well, you know, I ah . . ." he stopped and cleared his throat and went through a noseblowing ceremony. "I know a little bit about these things . . . so I was listenin'. When he gave the owner's name, 'Natalie T. Steele, trustee for Mary Seneca Steele,' my innards went into spasms. Philo looked around the man at me but I shook my head no, don't say anything. I just leaned back agin the wall, like the ol' dumb mountain boy I am, y'know.

"Finally I said, 'Hit's a cryin' shame what thur a-askin' for that ol' snake-den, up yander.'

"That flatlander turned around to me like he'd found 'im a good friend. 'Sir do you know anything about that piece of property?' he said.

"'Tell me which it is, let me be sartin,' I said. He showed me the paper. Lord, girl, there it was. 'Nine hundred and thirty-three acres, more or less, bounded on the east by Big Caney River . . .' I shook till I could hardly read the thing.

"I stood there sizin' that old boy up. He was a soft-lookin' son of a bitch, hair greased and parted down the middle, little moustache turned up with wax. 'Yeah, I know OF it,' I said. 'Know whur it's at, been by thar sevral time. Hunt bear, wild hogs, they use about that place a lot. Ol' Steele place, ain't it?' I said.

"'That's it!' he said.

"'I reck'n you must be a-wantin' a huntin' persarve, 'at's all hit'd be good fer,' I said.

"'Well, actually no,' he said. 'I want a nice summer home for my wife. We have a lovely home in Charleston but she is too delicately disposed to take the heat of the summers.'

"'She like snakes?' I said. I could tell by his looks that did not go over good. 'Lot o' land for a summer home.'

"'My plan is to renovate the home to live in, and subdivide the acreage,' he said. 'I can see a hundred cottages — a summer colony! — along that river.'

"I thought, well, buddy, I'll be damned if you ever will. 'I guess the old house could be made nice with a hell of a lot o' work,' I said. 'You been in it yet?'

"'No, I am supposed to find the man up here who has the key,' he said.

"'Ben Aaron Steele? He's in the penitentiary,' I said. 'If he ain't broke out agin. Near killed a furriner, flung rocks at 'er 'cause he kotched 'er pickin' flahrs on his land . . .'

"I saw he was gettin' impressed," Ben Aaron said. "I said, 'But if ye want to look, you don't need no key. They's holes you can crawl thu, head and shoulders. 'At's the way they say them snakes come in 'at killed them last people.'

"His eyes got this big. He started to open his mouth but I had to keep on him. 'I guess t'd be all right though if ever ye could get the stench out of it,' I said.

"I waited for him to say, 'What stench?'

"'Why, from the dead people,' I said. 'Road's bad, river comes up when it rains you know. Big rain driv them snakes in the house. River was over the road. Nobody got to them people for about six weeks. And it was a long hot spell, about that time . . .'

"I was watchin' Philo nearly split his gut, behind that sucker's back. That ol' snake tale had a long white beard, I'd even read it in two books. . . ."

We had got up to the back porch and I stopped to get a mason jar of milk out of the spring box.

"That dunce believed you?" I said. "Why did he believe that junk?"

"I've got an honest face," said Ben Aaron, his honest face full of smile. "Besides, I'm too stupid to make up a lie."

"And that man was never seen again?"

"No, and in the evenin' mail I sent your ma a letter, made her an offer I could no way afford and she could no way refuse. I overbid that guy by two thousand dollars."

I dried the jar on my apron and looked at him squarely. What I said was as mean as a snake. "Where'd you get the money?" I said. It was mean because he knew I knew.

"I got it," he said, raising his eyebrows and studying his hands. I knew he'd gone as far as he was about to go. But he helped me fire up the stove and set the table, and I cooked dinner, and we called the children in and we all sat down and somehow a sweeter peace descended.

We lingered of course. Always, we lingered, over the crumbs and dishes. Every half hour maybe we'd spoon another bite, butter another biscuit, pour another hot cup. Ben Aaron sat playing with his tea cup, thinking, studying the dregs.

"I see two people in here just a-grinnin', on their way to Shiloh School," he said.

"Not in summer!" Hugh said, absolutely stricken. Pet turned her cup round, slowly, and reported, "I don't see but one goin'; there's another one in short pants walkin' backwards, goin' 'BooHoo! BooHoo!'"

Hugh was furious. He couldn't bear her to tell that he cried about going to school sometimes. She loved to tell it.

"We've got a new teacher comin' and she looks like this," Ben Aaron said. He ran out his tongue and lifted his nose with his finger and pulled down the corners of his eyes, looking walleyed. Pet laughed and reached and rapped his hand with her spoon. Hugh half-believed it, and shuddered. "Brrr," he said, with his mouth full of grits.

"Oh, it's not till August," Ben Aaron said, to comfort him. "I bet they'd never let you out of school to hang tobacker in Charleston. Will, here."

"They wouldn't admit there IS such a thing as tobacker at the Latin School," I said.

It interested me how he pursued the school business. I turned it over in my mind. If these children were in school here it meant we lived here. And still, especially in this new light on things, we were only guests. And in a precarious state of welcome.

"Coy Ray's kids'll go," he said to Hugh. "Uh, sometimes they go . . ."

He reached across the table then and got me by the wrist. "Do somethin' for me, will you?" he said. "Somehow get Rose to go to school. She's not been one day since her mother died."

I was appalled. "That's frightful!" I said.

"It's just the way it is," he said. "That oldest boy Ned had just started school when Cleone died. Herman, the littlest one, was a babe in arms. It was a case of have-to, with Rose; she's sent the boys, off and on, the ones big enough to go. But she had too much to do at home. Get her to go any way you can. I believe she could finish in a year or so. She's smart, you know."

Heaven help that child, I thought. I could see her studying to catch up, into the night, getting up by moonlight in the morning to do all the work and sitting in a schoolhouse all day long.

"Yes, she's got to go," I said. "And Coy Ray Wilcox will have to hire a housekeeper."

"Well, you tell 'im that, I can't," Ben Aaron said.

So as our cousin took his leave that day, questions never spoken of had been decided.

We were tenant farmers, going into the wild hare race of summer, and there would not be one hour to look back. The field would be our lot by day, the kettle and stove by night. The beans came in in the middle of July. We picked beans every day. Many a day Nam came and helped us. We canned beans plain and we canned beans pickled. We let beans grow big in the pod and let 'em dry and shelled 'em, into our laps, by the light of a lamp. We went to bed feeling fuzzy every night into September.

Corn came in right along with the beans, field corn, not the sweet stuff everybody planted later. We pulled corn every day. We cut it off and salted it down and put it up in jars. We roasted it and ate it every day; we ate like horses because we worked like mules. When corn got hard enough we took our first load to the mill and watched it ground, and brought home sacks of meal that would bread us, as Ben Aaron put it, through the winter.

We dug potatoes and pulled onions as big as baseballs and strung 'em from the rafters of the porch to dry. There were two red plum trees out on the side of the road that were heaven for the kids and the yellowjackets. The grape arbor had fallen in and the vines had nearly strangled themselves but we had a few straggly bunches of grapes; all the fox grapes ever we would want in our lives made arches over the branch, on the way up to Shiloh Cove.

There were some old peach trees on the place; they were so forlorn of old age I didn't know what they were, until the peaches showed and colored. They are full of worms, I said to myself. But when we cut into them I was surprised. We dried peaches on sheets of roofing tin, out in the sun, and nearly bankrupted ourselves of sugar on preserves.

And we had figs. Nam marveled at the figs. "That tree was nothin' but a snag, dead as a doornail," she said. "It gets too cold here for figs. That one lived because it was on the sunny side and by the chimney. Daisy petted it along. There was allus a fire in her fireplace there, where it grows on that chimney. Kep' it warm. It hadn't had a fig I know in more than fifteen years . . ."

Coy Ray made a little grape wine for us. And when the apples came he made a little brandy. I thanked him very much.

We picked blackberries. Blackberries were something else the Lord just gave us. We did not have to grub for blackberries, we only had to endure the bad temper of their canes, and pick 'em. The kids detested it, but I didn't. There was a first-class patch over around a little spring in the scrub field, and another, down along the branch, at the bottom of the orchard. There were plenty all over but some were bitter and weechie and hard; you wanted a patch where they were big as thimbles and sweet. That kind nearly always grew with their feet close to the water.

I liked to go down on the branch in the mornings by the earliest light. Before the kids woke up. I would take my bucket down there, in the foggy dew; I would feel the deer looking at me but they wouldn't let me see them. I would only see their tracks, in the soft places.

One morning I very well remember, I was thinking to myself I had never felt so happy. All the sound there was, was the branch trickling, and the birds waking. But in my head, it was so strange, I heard a woman singing. She was singing a song I had never heard. And yet I knew what the next words, and the next verse would be. I wondered who had sung down there, picking blackberries, a hundred years before I came. I wondered who had left that song.

When I went home up the field, feeling a little bit lighter than air, there was another woman singing that song—do you know it?—it started out, "Well met, well met, my own true love; well met, well met cried she . . ." It was the same, unruffled, placid kind of voice. And that time it was me.

⁓ 19 ⁓

A SHORT CHAPTER

NOW, WHEN THE CROPS WERE LAID BY, COY RAY WENT UNDER the house and dragged up the two old swings and put 'em up, one at each end of the porch. I think he had himself in mind; he took to coming up from whatever he was doing around the place to "set and blow," he called it. He liked for me to sit with him. It was so far from one swing to the other you had to fairly holler. So we would sit in just one, and talk about the vital matters of the day, like the feeblemindedness of the Revenue agents, and the whelping of pups.

I loved to listen to him, but that enthusiasm was not shared by certain others. One day Ben Aaron rode up on us while we were swinging and kicking our feet, and Coy Ray was telling this big tale about the time he planted some slop in a leaky old still, back up here on a branch, 'course on Ben Aaron's land, and he "borried" Ben Aaron's old hat and hung it on the mash paddle and then slipped the word to the Revenue. Ben Aaron walked right up on him telling that, and Coy Ray never broke off the tale, till he had told it all, and laughed *hee hee hee*. And Ben Aaron cut his eye at me, and glared at Coy Ray and said to him, "Coy, I b'lieve I heered the hogs a-callin' you."

Well, Coy Ray yawned, and got up and made a show of stretching, like a peacock strutting its tail and sashayed off about his business, but very slowly.

Now Ben Aaron had just left, going over to the lumber camp,

and Coy Ray had been watching his chance to come back, and here came that little lawyer from up at the Forks, in his yellow roadster, on his way down to Red Bank. That was where his real office was; he just visited up at the Forks to take care of the sawmill's legal business.

His name was Harmon Garrison. I call him little; what I mean is he was at least some younger than I was, and he was sort of boyish-looking, he had inky black hair and big dark eyes and dimples. Ben Aaron swore by him as wonderful at law, "slick and dirty." If that was really so, I thought, his great weapon was surprise. He looked so innocent.

Harmon was our cousin. Not real near, but his grandmother was a Harmon, half Cherokee, and we were kin to the white Harmons way back and so we had this natural link, you see. So that time when he stopped by we sat out in the swing and drank lemonade and talked about the family and things.

And every few days then he would come by. I don't know how on earth that car took the torment of that road. He took to coming in the early evening, along in the summer. Ben Aaron would nearly always be gone home by that time; Sophia put out the hook for him at six o'clock by the church chime every evening. And Harmon would come, sometimes he would take supper, and we would sit and listen to the bugs and the nightbirds. I would beg him to go before pitch dark so he'd get down the mountain more safely, but he'd not always do it.

Sometime along, then, he took to acting strange. He would slip his hand over and hold mine, just keep on talking like he wasn't noticing what he was doing. And finally one evening we were sitting out there watching the lightning bugs and the little bats, and all of a sudden he turned around and kissed me. And no sweet nanny-peck, either.

I didn't know what to say. The truth is, what startled me the most was that I liked it. It stirred up some strange feelings, though; it was kind of distressing.

"Now!" he said, "I am going to get you a divorce and I am going to marry you."

I was too addled to think with anything but my mouth. "I can't get a divorce," I said. "You can't get a divorce in Charleston. You can't get one anywhere in the state. Nobody can get a divorce. . . ."

"You are not there, Love, you are here," Harmon said. "You can get one here. I am going to do it for you."

Well, while I sat there swinging, not saying yea nor nay, my mind was running up and down the porch wringing its hands. "No no," I said, finally, when I was able. "No no, it just won't do."

But when he was gone that night I thought the matter over. All night I thought it over. The notion made me restless; I squirmed the sheet off the bed. The next day I thought of it. Harmon was good enough to stay away and let me think.

A couple of days later Ben Aaron came by with the wagon, going over to Shiloh. He stopped and hollered did I want to go and certainly I did. I hopped up beside him, and he told me he was wanting to show me the stump of an old dead tree that they had cut and it had so many thousand feet of lumber in it, he said. And I was turning it over in my head what I would say to him about what had been on my mind; whether I should say anything at all, or how I should put it, not to sound shocking, or maybe I wanted it to sound shocking, I don't know. But finally I put my hand on his knee, and he looked down at me, and I said, "Ben Aaron, Harmon Garrison wants to marry me."

I didn't say it very loud I guess. I said it more into the neck of my dress.

"Said what?" he said.

"Harmon said he wants to get me a divorce so I can marry him," I said.

His ear was down close to me. I could see the muscle tighten in his jaw; he was biting the stem of his pipe. But he raised his eyebrows to make a calm bland face.

"Did," he said. I nodded.

He broke the quiet, after a little with a studied snort into his handkerchief. "And what did you say to that?" he said.

"I said I would have to think about it," I said.

He raised his chin and looked amused. "The Noble Red Man, eh? Well," he said. "Harmon's fine as he can be. It's something to think about, all right."

If he thought of it anymore it certainly didn't show. "You know," he said in about the next breath, "you could about build a house on that ol' stump up yonder. The lumber was sorry though, riddled clear through with worms. Good for nothin' but acid wood. Wadn't hardly worth haulin' out, for what the paper mill will pay . . . ."

~20~

CHICKENS WILL ROOST

MAYBE THE ODDEST THING ABOUT THOSE CONVERSATIONS I JUST mentioned was that the subject didn't come up again. Well, not soon, anyway. Harmon said nothing more about it; next time I saw him, up at the Forks, he was pleasant and nice and that was that. I'm not sure it ever registered at all with Ben Aaron. Who knows? The truth was I didn't think about it either. Much. Life was good and fine and smooth, just so right the way it was.

It was so right, in fact, that a little voice would nag me, sometimes. It would say, "For all this dancing, the piper will be paid." That was usually in the night. In the day there was too much to do.

For one thing, Coy Ray was putting up a tobacco shed. The barn lay too low he said. Too near the river; too close and damp. "Hit'll mold afore it cures," he said. "Hit's obliged to have good circa-lation." Ben Aaron said put it up behind the house. "Smothered 'tween a bluff and a spruce pine grove," Coy Ray said, disgusted. After the inevitable knock-down-drag-out, he hauled the timbers down just above the or-chard, close to the road, in a wide-open spot and commenced to build.

I thought well, now, this is my chance to get next to him. To get my word in. He had his two oldest boys there working with him, and I pranced down there and said to them, "I'll help your pa if you all will go burn that ol' wasp nest out of the crib. I'm just petrified to go in there." It was only partly a lie. And they went off, and I took over holding timbers while Coy Ray nailed. Directly I said,

"Coy Ray, what are you goin' to do for help this fall when the youn-guns are all gone to school?"

"Herman ain't goin'. He ain't old enough," he said, pounding away.

Well well, I thought, I have surely made a strong presentation. I must continue firm. "Who's gon' stay with Herman while Rose is at school?" I said. I was braced for the blast.

He never even looked at me. "I got me a hahr'd womern a-comin' t' keep house."

I nearly fell backwards off the plank I was straddling. "You mean you got somebody already?" I said.

"What you wantin' a job?" he said, not quite really nastily. "I got Chick Aleywine, movin' in Sunday week. You know Chick Aleywine?"

No, I did not. Hey—yes, maybe I did. I was astounded. It almost came out of my mouth, You mean that woman Nam said had pups?

It didn't. But the next time Ben Aaron came by I had something to tell and something to ask. What he came for, that time, he came to see if we wanted to walk over to Shiloh, to the schoolhouse. "You ought to walk it a time or two with 'em, to satisfy yourself the bears ain't lined up a-waiting for their dinner, or anything," he said.

Of course the kids had already been over there time and again, with Coy Ray's bunch; this was just a formality, but I put on my sun hat, and Pet and Hugh loped on ahead, and Ben Aaron and I set out into this beautiful afternoon, walking along slow. And we came to the path, down next to the branch, and turned up into the woods. The way was worn good and wide and clear, already, by his comings and goings over the summer. It had the feel of a very old trail, like maybe Indians had used it.

"Wild hogs mostly use it," Ben Aaron said. But with the corner of his mouth all curled up, on my side of his pipe. He draped his arm around me, and pulled me close to him, and we walked along in that close confortable rhythm of inside legs, outside legs, and I could feel the strength of him, from the hipbone to the ground and I basked in that security and forgot what all I had stored up to tell him.

The kids popped in and out of sight, far ahead. "Oh," I said, when it came to me, "did I say that Coy Ray had a housekeeper?"

"Hmmm?" he said, "Did you sure enough get him to do that?"

Well, ahem, I said, errah, it was in a way his own idea.

"Y'don't say," he said. "You say he's got somebody already? Who'd he get?"

"You know Chick Aleywine?" I said.

He stopped cold and turned and looked at me. "Don't tell me," he said. "Sonofabitch."

"You know 'er," I said, assuming.

"Not as well as some folks do, I'll tell you," he said. "I 'spect Coy Ray knows her inside and out. Shit fire, Sen—he called THAT a housekeeper? Why she's so nasty you can't hardly be in the room with 'er, closed up."

"Thought you didn't know her that good," I said.

He glared at me and then he laughed in spite of himself. "Housekeeper my ass," he said.

"Does she not work for other people?" I said.

"Depends on how you mean," he said. "You take somethin' with big dinners and the scruples of a tick, it'll make its way in a sawmill town. Plenty of takers like Coy Ray around, pantin' to hop anything atall."

When that filtered through I was mortified. "Ben Aaron!" I said. "Mercy goodness!" I had never known a man who could be so courtly, in one breath, and so coarse in the next as my cousin.

"A nanny goat could make it," he went on, unrepenting. "A nanny'd make a sweeter screw than ol' Chick Aleywine. Lord God Almighty, Sen, he's bringin' that into the house with Rose?"

Well, I said, really Rose wouldn't be there all that much and when she was she'd be too busy to get corrupted. Besides she had too much sense. Maybe it was the best that Coy Ray could do. "Does this woman know anything about children?" I said. "Has she ever had children of her own?" I thought it best to not bring up the pups.

"Grass don't grow in the middle of the road," he said. Dejectedly, he put his arm around me again, and we walked on.

We came down the rise and crossed a new footlog over Shiloh Branch and came out into the clearing. The kids were coming back to meet us, up through the sparse little graveyard of Shiloh Church, which stood gray and weathered as its own tombstone. "We didn't go in," Pet said. "We could hear somethin' moving around in there."

"Oh, yeah?" Ben Aaron said. "I think it's apt to be the boogerman himself." He grinned and got her by one pigtail and took Hugh by the hand, and we went to face the worst. And as we came down through the graves the bell in the steeple gave a mighty *Bong* and even our cousin Ben Aaron near left the ground.

"Cole! For the Lord's sake!" he hollered, when he found his breath.

A head of wavy pale red hair appeared at the opening of the belfry. A young man with spectacles leaned out. "I'm tying a new rope," he said. "I guess rats chewed the old one, it broke off in my hand."

As we went up the steps we could hear him descending. "Cole Sutherland," Ben Aaron said. "He's come to teach for us this year. You're goin' to like him, that I can tell you." Out of the narrow little stairwell came this tall thin scholarly-looking boy; well, he had started a mustache to make him look more formidable, I guess. The cut of his clothes, the softness of his hand, even the look about his eyes said "Money." Never worked. But he had studied. He had finished college that past May. There were few urgent cries for majors in Greek literature, at the opening of the school year in 1929.

"His daddy was a friend of mine at school," Ben Aaron said. "Lives in Richmond. We never did lose touch."

So Cole had come here, to teach school. A whole new thing, for him. A whole new people. He would cut the wood for the stove, and enforce respect for the privies; he would have the water bucket filled at the spring and passed down the rows, with the dipper, twice a day. He would school eight grades and then some, row by row; he would tend as best he could to toothaches, and weep behind the scenes, with understanding, for those little ones who simply could not see. He would resort a time or two to a great long hickory, and cast it, broken, into the stove, in his own pain. Cole Sutherland was wonderful; that first time I ever saw him, I just knew it.

He had brought in a wagon-load of books that day, most of them his own, and had set about turning the choir into a library. Desks already took the place of pews; "I've got to wash the windows," Cole said. "The better we can see outside, the less like jail." We would help, we said. We would get rags and vinegar and come back the next day.

We asked if he'd come home with us to eat, and he said, well, he'd settled in to board with Ans and Myrtle Shuman. But when we went over the next day and helped clean, he did come back with us, and it was sort of like a whiff of jasmine, on a dark warm night, to hear about the outside world again.

Rose went with us, on that day, and stayed and ate with us that night. That was something she almost never did, and it was so good right then because the business of going back to school, and her so near grown, was weighing on her, I could tell. She said almost nothing, the whole time, but only worked and listened. I could almost feel her getting easier, though, as the day went on.

I wondered when something like this was going to happen: while we were eating supper I noticed Hugh looking at Cole, and looking at him. Finally he aid, just so innocent, "Cole, why did Ben Aaron say you were going to look like this?" And he pulled the corners of his eyes down with his fingers, and made his nose turn up. Well, we all hollered. Rose laughed till she almost cried.

"He just wanted you to be prepared," Cole said. "If you expect the worst you can't be disappointed."

It was getting near dark when we realized how late it was. When Rose jumped up to go, Cole asked if he couldn't take her, on his horse. I was surprised when she said yes; it wasn't really like her.

So the start of the school year was peaceful and secure and uneventful. Rose came by with her brood earlier than need be, on that first day, and off they all went. They came back with tales of who was old enough to have a beard, and who had wet the floor; as it turned out, Rose said she was not the oldest kid, at all. Two were already seventeen. One brought her little sister and brother who were not more than three and four. It was not the Latin School. The novelty would keep mine interested, until the love of Cole took over.

The advent of Chick Aleywine on Wilcox Ridge was not as eventful as was expected, either. Rose said little about it unless asked. She did volunteer that she had given Chick her bed in a little makeshift alcove off the kitchen; and had moved herself into the loft, with the boys. Chick would never have made it to the loft, Rose noted. And if she had the boys would have thrown her out. If anything unseemly did go on, at least it did so out of sight of those it would have offended.

A more material nastiness began to bother Rose. She was as exasperated as I had ever seen her, talking about the chicken doo in the butter. "The flies is bad enough," she said. "She'll let the doors hang open till the flies is so thick you'd think the walls is a-wigglin'. And course the chickens'll come in. Come in and just he'p theirselves to everwhat they want off of the stove, or the table.

"Whew!" she said, screwing up her face, "I don't like t' tell this, it makes us sound so cyarny." (Rose's word for really stinking rotten.) "But I wisht you'd seen Pap's face the other night, when he set down at the table an' the chickens'd done been there. Put his fork in the butter, an' spread it on 'is bread an' took a good-size chew. 'This butter is gone bad,' he says. And then he looked and seen what it was." She broke down laughing. "Pore ol' Pap, he liked to died," she said.

Whatever the attraction had been, it began to cool. I can only guess the high life of Caney Forks began to look real good to Chick, again. Cold wind whistling through the cracks of that pole cabin would have helped along with that. One morning that fall, Rose would come by on her way to school with all the boys, including Herman, and report Chick had taken her bosoms back to the Forks, unmourned and unlamented. Herman went along to school sometimes; he thought it was big. When it was very cold some days he would stay with me. Sometimes Coy Ray would take him off with him. At any rate life and learning both would go on.

But in the meantime, the summer left us in the tobacco patch. Cole turned out school a week in September and Coy Ray and his kids came down and we cut poles and then we cut down the tobacco and skewered the stems, sort of, on cross poles all along the rows. It hung upside down that way a couple of days or so, till it had wilted and begun to fade.

And then we gathered it into the wagon, and took it to the shed and hung it there, for it to cure. We had a real good crop. Coy Ray named us, all the while, the things that could go wrong between the field and the auction barn. A bad damp fall could make it mold. Or it could get too dry and brittle, or the color could go bad. I never took those things too much to mind. The ironweed and the joe pye were blooming along the fencerows, the richest purple, and a dusty pink. The little purple daisy things were blooming, and the black-eyed Susans, and Queen Anne's lace. There was nothing on this part of the earth to bode anybody ill.

Anything ill would come from somewhere else.

We went to a couple of old raucous dances, that September, at Red Bank. I don't know why I liked them; they tended to end up bloody. Nothing as overwhelming happened to me those times as did at the first one. But there was something odd about it; some sensation long forgot, like the smell when we were cleaning out the springs. It made a current from my toes to the roots of my hair. Part of it, I know, was that every one we went to, Ben Aaron would have to play.

I would go about the work at the house, hearing that in my head, one old rant or reel and then another, as if the very walls were full of them. Sometimes there by myself I would be moved by some un-heard tune to dance, to go from room to room with that peculiar buck-dance gait of snapped-back knees and heels. The ring of it on those old boards was just about intoxicating.

I had a kettle of applesauce on, one day, when that came over me. The house was full of the smell, which was provident, for I had not cleaned it up in quite some time. But I was just so happy. If the chickens of my deplorable deed were coming home to roost, I thought, they're still way down the road.

Well, I was clicking my heels from the stove to the kitchen table, and somewhere in the house another rapping echoed. My hair stood straight on end. I have courted the Devil, I thought, or I have fetched a haint.

While I stood there frozen, it rapped again. And then it had a voice. "Miss Steele?" it said. "Miss Cousin?"

I went trembling to the door, with my legs made out of water, and lifted the latch. There stood Cud'n Barz, hat in hand. "Them womernses wouldn' get out o' my rig till they knowed if you was to home," he said, apologetically. I looked beyond him, to the road. Hitched to two oxen was the back end of an Auburn Phaeton, with TAXICAB, in sort of casual red letters, painted on the door.

Ensconced in the back seat were two ladies. One gray-haired and at that point real pale, holding down her little black hat with one wan hand. The other had her head tied in a dew rag. In spite of her ordeal she had remained quite dark.

"Oh, God have mercy, Barz," I said. "Where did you get 'em?"

"They come in last night on the train," he said. "Nobody there to bring 'em up hyar, till I come down this mornin'."

I was absolutely mute. "You'd ruther me t' take 'em back?" he said.

"Only one of 'em," I said.

"Well some folks does feel quare about colored people in thur house," he said, understandingly.

"That's the one I want with me," I said. "It's the other'n I could spare." But I didn't know how to tell Mit that I was home, and Miss Lilah that I wasn't. So I gathered my skirt around me and went forth to do my duty.

Tell the truth I don't know what shocked me most to see, the "womernses" or the car. Miss Lilah's suitcase was strapped on the running board. Mit clutched her carpet bag in her lap. Miss Lilah's head lay back against the seat, her eyes rolled back like in a faint. She was too far gone to see me coming. "D' Lawd done shown us mussy, Mary Sen!" Mit cried, holding out her arms. I opened the door and leaned into that embrace and kissed her over and over.

"I-o-wa, how could you do dis to us, Mary Seneca?" Miss Lilah croaked feebly, half reviving.

"It wadn' all that bad," I lied, "it's just a little hard and strange, the first time you come up." I went around the car and kissed her, over the door, and Barz undid her baggage and gallantly helped her out, and got her up the steps. When we got to the door he showed me his palm. "That's eighty cent, please mam," he said.

Miss Lilah fumbled in her pocketbook, half-heartedly. "That sounds like way too much to me," she said, regaining her sense of values. "I wish dey'd been anothah way." I made speed back into the house and brought out the better part of our family fortune, and settled the account. As Barz tipped his hat and turned to go, I said, "This is my cousin, Mr. Peek. He's the first friend we met when we came up here."

"Yes, mam. Howd-do. Well. Goodbye," said Barz, making his retreat.

"Where are de chirrun?" Miss Lilah said.

"Dey—they're at school," I said.

"Yo' little visit sounds mo' like an abandonment to me," she said. Like the frozen viper the man warmed in his shirt, Miss Lilah was beginning to thaw.

"I think we need some dinner," I said. "I know you probably haven't had a thing since last night." I meant to keep the conversation to no consequence, till I could get my balance. I showed Mit the pantry, with all the stuff we'd put up, and got out stuff to heat up, and made a pan of bread. They ate like they were starved to death, and then thank God exhaustion took over. I fixed them two beds and tucked them in for a nice long afternoon nap so I could finish going crazy.

This was something I had known was going to happen. I could not keep this place unsullied. It was sure as the rising sun that Foots or his mother would come and put a mark on it. There never would be peace.

Despairing, I flew around and straightened up. Cleaned the lamp chimneys and swept and filled the reservoir on the stove with water to warm, and put out clean towels on the wash stand and picked flowers for the table.

Things were in such order that when the kids came in the first thing they wanted to know was who was coming.

"Better ask who's here," I said, I guess right unhappily.

They stopped in their tracks. "Daddy," Pet said.

"No, his mother," I said, "And Aunt Mit."

"She made Aunt Mit come so you'd let her in," Pet said. "She's goin' to try to make us all go home. Granny Lamb don't want to take care of Daddy."

"Just be nice," I said. "Remember who you are and behave that way."

When she heard them Mit came in, all stiff from sleep on top of that journey, and they perked up a little bit then. They wanted to show her around. And she said to me, "Go now ketch yo'seff a nap. I'll fix de suppah. Dese sweet chirruns, heah, dey'll hep me."

The offer was too sweet. I went and collapsed on Pet's bed, for Miss Lilah was in mine. And the sweet chirruns, what they did, they took Mit on a tour that got sidetracked at one point. I don't know where they went, but I know they left Mit, and were out of sight. They had showed her, though, the pen with the biddies that had grown mostly into strutting young roosters, who passed most of their time in combat. They were sacred roosters, raised by Pet and Hugh. I jumped up when I heard 'em squawking and I looked out just in time to see two of 'em twirling by their necks in the able hands of Mit, while the others cocked their heads and clucked, astonished.

We'd not sat down to such a table since we'd left Mit behind. When he had eaten a peck Hugh sighed over the litter of bones on his plate and said, "Aunt Mit, did you bring this chicken on the train?"

"No, sweet baby darlin'. These be yo' own you raise. Be so fat an' good, ain' you proud?"

Well, the chicken parents looked at one another. "Herman and Arvey," Hugh said, in a cracking little voice. "Fidel and Ned," Pet whispered, not believing. Through four, the chickens were named for Coy Ray's boys. And there on from the Bible. "Nahum and Hackable, they were the fattest," Hugh said. Tears were dropping on the ruins. Pet got up very quickly and took the plates away.

"I 'clare, you chirrun cry about a ol' chicken, do you ever cry fo' yo' ol' Granma Lamb, an' yo' Daddy, an' yo' po' sick Aunt Louise?" Miss Lilah said, with her typical sympathy.

Hugh sniffed. "I cried about Aunt Louise one night," he said. "I dreamed she had an ice cream cone and Daddy took it."

"You say Louise is sick?" I said.

"You know she's sick," Miss Lilah said. "You know about huh heart. An' dese chirrun bein' stolen off like dis has broke huh po' cripple heart in two."

Mit got up and went to cleaning up. I said nothing. I just fumed.

"By d' way, I don' see Hubert's new car. Where is it?" said the inquisitor.

"It needed some work," I said.

"He sho' had his feelin's hurt about his car," she said.

Somehow, we passed that evening without blows. By the grace of God the old woman went to bed early and slept late. Mit rose with the larks so we could have some time to talk.

"Don' you pay no mind to dis one minute," Mit said. "Miss Louise, she tell me that ol' woman fixin' to try to git you back. She out o' money, that's why. Miss Louise she say, 'Tell 'er pay no mind.' Say, 'Stay where you is at.' Ol' Foots, he gettin' worse an' worse. T'row tings. Sass peoples.'

"It maybe be two year, yo' mama say, befo' she gon' be home," Mit continued. "Don' you come back home, Mary Sen, befo' she home to hep you. That be my rupinion . . ."

I had lived the most of my life by Mit's rupinions. Never had one suited me so well.

Miss Lilah woke up while Coy Ray was throwing off a wagon load of sawmill slabs. 'Course he talked to his mules in words they understood, and when she came downstairs, she said to me, "The servants roun' here shu'ly are profane."

"Ain't no servants up here," I said. "Coy Ray's my friend."

To entertain for long I needed to go to the store. I didn't think to tell Coy Ray.

"Maybe Ben Aaron will come by," I said, as an afterthought. I wished he would, somehow. I needed his moral support.

There was a glimmer of recognition in Miss Lilah's eyes, over her coffee cup. She frowned and thought. "Is he d' one. . . .?" she finally said.

"Which one?" I said. I guessed I'd mentioned things he'd done for us, in letters to Louise.

She looked sort of pale. "D' one dat was in prison."

"In prison?" I said taken back.

"Somebody tol' me dey'd come to see about some land up heah, an' d' man was one of yo' kinpeople, an' he was in prison. Fo' killin' a po' woman wid a rock."

"Oh!" I said. I was feeling much brighter. "Yes that's the one I think, but that happened before we came. He wadn' in jail real long I guess. It wadn' very serious."

While I was doing about I noticed she was having a hushed conference with Mit. Then she called Hugh, and he came to me and said, "Mama, can I have the mule to go see Cousin Barz?" He had not been all that thick with Barz, as I knew of, but I said, why certainly. "Granny wants to go home," he whispered in my ear.

So early in the afternoon, in time to catch the evening train, our guests got ready to depart. As her parting soliloquy, Miss Lilah stood on the porch, watching the approach of the "taxicab" and recited on a scene I well remembered.

"I can' fo'get I stood there, in d' room where I remembered yo' daddy's casket, an' I heard you say to my son, 'In sickness an' in health, till death do us part.' I can't hep wonderin', Mary Sen, what yo' po' daddy would think of d' way you honored yo' obligation."

No lightnin' on this porch, dear God, I thought. Wait'll the old buzzard gets out to the road.

Mit came out with all their belongings and helped Barz load up. He lifted his hat and looked expectantly at me. I was embarrassed. "Can I settle up the fare when the crops come in?" I said.

"Yes, mam," he said gravely. "'Course hit'll be a dollar, then."

I promised to put it on my book, in case I died. It was all I could do to say a cordial goodbye, to half of the departing. But then I thought how I'd miss Mit. "Give my love to Uncle Camp. Tell Louise I love her," I said. "Tell her maybe we'll see her Christmas, if we do real well."

Mit puckered her mouth and shook her head, as the oxen started off. I couldn't watch them down the road.

It was not far behind them that Ben Aaron came. When I told him that his lie was now a legend in the Lowcountry, he stomped and hollered and whooped. What was more, I said, it had probably helped to keep me from murdering somebody, myself.

I felt better then. Only that night I couldn't help but think, why here? Will it follow every place I go?

But then in the morning it had turned off bright and cool. When I looked out the window, it was October.

~21~

BAT DUNG AND HIS DAUGHTER

I HAVE CARRIED IN MY MIND A KIND OF MYSTICAL IMAGE OF THAT first October here on Big Caney, the way the color started in the sugar trees on the ridge tops and trickled down the mountains, and the air turned sharp and cool, full of strange rustlings, sweet with pinesap and curing tobacco and woodsmoke and fruit gone to wine.

Even the wind in dry leaves still reminds me of how happy Hugh was, running wild in the woods with Coy Ray's boys. You wouldn't hear a peep out of that bunch of little cigar-store Indians when they came around the house. But they chased behind a litter of baying pups up and down the valley, flushing rabbits and great flocks of birds, being chased themselves by hoop-snakes and boogers and howling with joy.

Pet clung to Rose, they brought in walnuts and hickory nuts and made apple butter and mothered flocks of half-feathered chicks. They liked to sing quietly together, learning songs from each other as though it was a personal thing, their fair heads close over the work Rose always had at hand.

That October made me drunk. I felt something new I could not give a name to. Or maybe it was something old and always hidden. It was one of those times you knew right then, this is too fine and perfect ever to forget.

But beauty was not all of it.

The dirtiest old man on Big Caney lived up beyond where the river forks, up at the head of the valley. His name was Bat Dung Aleywine. Well, his name was really Luther; people took care to call him Luther to his face because he was awful quick to get mad and fight.

And he was not all that old either; truth is, I don't suppose he was as old as Ben Aaron. But Bat Dung was peculiar. Quick to take offense at the smallest little thing. Like if somebody called him Bat Dung.

How he came to be called that, Bat Dung had a big high bluff at the back of his land and way up in the face of it there were caves. You could see 'em from the river. Looked like the eyes and nose in a skull, way, way up in the cliff. Looked like wildcats and panthers and things probably lived in there. Except you wondered how anything that didn't fly could get to 'em.

One thing that went in there did fly. Bats. Of an evening the bats would roll out like a black cloud, darkening the sky. They must have lived in that cliff for a million years. Doing their business, dying, falling down, making dust. It was a regular guano factory back in there, and guano was about the most valuable fertilizer in the country.

Bat Dung did not fly. He used ropes. He had it fixed so he could let himself down from the clifftop on some kind of a rope contraption and he would go back in the caves and bring out guano. Bring it out by the bucket full, and let it down to the base of cliff on a pulley, where he could pick it up in his truck. He had himself a real good business, bagging that stuff and selling it.

The first time I saw him he brought a truckload of guano down to The Birches when we were working our first crops. Coy Ray did the trading with him. I would probably not have seen Bat Dung that day except that he came up to the spout to get a drink while I was out there filling the wash pot. And I thought to myself, now that is the dirtiest man I ever did see.

'Course, I never let on. I just put out my hand to him, I said, "How-d'y'do-sir, I am Seneca Steele."

He glared and backed off. Left me with my hand out in space. For a minute I thought maybe it was me that smelt so bad. He did bob his head and lift his hat, but he was annoyed that I was there. I somehow got the feeling, as he drank with his dirty hand and got out his dirty handkerchief and dabbed his dirty mouth, that Bat Dung was no ladies' man. He probably had faults, I said to myself, but womanizing would never be among 'em.

Which was a kind of a paradox. Come to find out, he was a brother to that awful Chick Aleywine that was supposed to be keeping house for Coy Ray. It looked like the only thing that pair had in common was a fear of soap.

But Bat Dung was a worker. Some people thought he was probably one of the richest men in the valley. He was not known to spend. "Parsimonious," Aunt Nam declared, "is Bat Dung's middle name." I knew it wasn't Charm.

Chick's life was much more "loose," so to speak. Chick worked mostly lying down, Ben Aaron said. Plenty of that kind of work in a sawmill town, he said. It didn't sound too good. But anyway she was a jollier sort than Bat Dung.

The next time Ben Aaron came down I made it a point to find out some things. "I think I'm in love," I said.

"Don't get your heart broke," Ben Aaron said. "Coy Ray ain't about to throw Chick over. Have you seen the dinners on that woman?"

"No, and I surely hope you've not," I said. I made my neck long so I could look down my nose and he turned a little bit red, which rarely ever happened. Then I told him about my meeting with the other Aleywine.

I acted us out, how it passed between Bat Dung and me at the spout. I thought Ben Aaron would laugh. But he did not.

"Mind how you deal with Mr. Aleywine," he said. "I'd about as soon you never dealt with him atall."

"Why?" I said.

He was puffing on his pipe, squinting off across the cove. Finally, Ben Aaron said, "He ain't got no sense of humor."

To make that point he told me how one time somebody painted "Bat Dung Express" on the passenger side of Bat Dung's old truck. Said they did a real nice job. Big arty letters; the *T* was made like a bat dropping doo-doo. And Bat Dung drove all around the country with it there, and the more folks snickered the more puzzled and aggravated he got. Till he stopped at a filling station and went around to put some air in his tire. And saw it.

"He flung a fit," Ben Aaron said. "Two boys standing there, he went at 'em with the dung shovel, broke one's arm, made the other'n get a rag and kerosene and scrub off the paint while he held the shovel on him. And they hadn't done a solitary thing but laugh."

That wasn't really all, Ben Aaron finally admitted. Bat Dung had a serious history of righteous indignation.

He was shell-shocked and in an Army hospital in France when the armistice was signed. He'd been gone from home over a year when he finally got back, and he walked in his own front door one day, so happy, thinking he would surprise his wife. Well, it was some surprise to both of them. There his wife was, big.

"He never said hello, yay, nay nor kiss my foot," Ben Aaron said. "He just went right on past her to the wood box and took him up a pine knot and brained her. Just like that. There stood their little girl, looking. I guess she was, oh, four or five years old. And Bat Dung took that little kid by the hand, then, and walked off to town, and told the sheriff what he'd done.

"Of course they had to arrest him. Had to have a trial. But they couldn't help but find that he was crazy. He had to go to the asylum for a little while; they couldn't just let him come right back home."

I wanted to know whatever became of that little girl. I wondered if she could be right in her mind, after she'd seen such a thing.

"Oh," Ben Aaron said, "what really set Bat Dung to raving was sweet sister Chick getting that child to look after while he was locked up. You know he had to be thinking about what that heifer might be doing right before her or even teaching her to do. But it wadn't but a few months till he got out, and first thing, he went and got the kid, and they went home."

My cousin was looking down at his long, fine fingers which he was polishing with his handkerchief, studying about something. "Bat Dung keeps a sharp eye on that youngun to this day," he said. "What little bit I have seen of her, she is a very nice young lady. But I am sorry for her, I'll tell you, if ever she makes one step out of line."

The fall of 1929 was not for celebrating in the world we had left behind, but Wall Street seemed like as far away as Jupiter from this place. Hardscrabble was nothing new along Big Caney. We had some sleepless nights but ours were full of coon dog songs and

brandy and persimmon beer, and of fiddling and dancing and acting the fool. It was, as we were reminded often by our Baptist Cud'n
Barzelai, a time set aside for the Devil and all his filthy works.

One afternoon the kids and I were down at the edge of the field
loading pumpkins on the wagon when Rose came riding up from the
ford on a mule. She was coming at a pretty good clip.

"Mr. Steele sent word by Pap, he's comin' down to get you directly,"
she said.

"I can't think whatever for," I said. I had begun to notice that Ben
Aaron liked to use Rose as an emissary, or diplomat, or buffer in his
dealings. At least with me.

"It's some kind of a farmers' social thing up at the Forks," she said.
"What it is, there's going to be this big dance. After the speaking.
Mr. Steele thought you would like it 'cause him and Pap has prom-
ised to make the music."

Oh well, then.

"I couldn't think of leaving the children," I said. I was wondering
what I was going to wear and how long I had to get myself washed and
get into it.

"Well if Pet and Hugh don't care to come home with me I'd be
glad they'd just stay the night with us," she said. That meant, I figured
out, that if they didn't mind staying with her, she'd keep 'em.

"Are you not going to the dance?" I said.

"No mam. Chick and me, we got a bushel of fruit that needs to be
done up. I think I'll just stay home and make them apples into sass,"
she said.

That didn't sound quite right for a sixteen-year-old. Even one as
old at heart as Rose. Anyway my conscience was rapping on me. I
said, "Look here—you go to that dance. I'll take care of all the kids."

She looked down at the mule's neck and screwed her mouth kind
of sideways. Rose was a total flop as a liar. "It's just as well I don't go,"
she said. "I go most every time. I go aplenty. But you see, if Pap is
going to play, it ain't all that much fun. I mean, not for me. When
he's up there playin' he's got nowhere to look but square at me. Last
time I went to one of them dances, one of them outlandish boys,
one of them black Frenchmen brothers—you know the ones I
mean? That work for Mr. Steele?"

Yes, I did know. The Boulangers were Canadian lumberjacks, good musicians, too, with great dark soulful eyes and rosy cheeks and hair as black and shiny as a crow. Now THEY had charm.

"Well it was one of them took a shine to me and danced me all over that place," Rose said. "Pap thought he was trying to get wise with me. But he wadn't. He was real nice. Told me I was good looking, such stuff as that. And no more come of it than that. But Pap was mad for a week. He was swole up like a toad. He was almost as mad as Bat Dung."

"Oh, Lord," I said. "What did somebody do to make Bat Dung mad?"

Well, Rose said, that other outlandish brother had tried to dance with Sue Annie, Bat Dung's daughter. "And Bat Dung come after him like a rooster. Scared the liver out of 'im.

"But even so," Rose said, "that Frenchman he went to Bat Dung's HOUSE to try to see Sue Annie. And he run into HIM instead. Come off with a big flat nose and a pump-knot the size of a horse apple on his head. But at least he come out. . . ."

Rose leaned down, talking much lower, letting the mule graze. "The worst is—I got this at the mill while I waited for the meal yesterday—well, Bat Dung has got Sue Annie locked up. She can't get out, can't nobody else get in. Pap and me, we have our fusses. But Pap ain't that kind o' mean. Bat Dung will kill a man."

I believed that was so. Now, what to do?

Rose studied the ground. "We can pray, I reck'n," she said. "I tell you, folks don't like to mess in another family's business."

As it was, Rose said, with her friend Sue Annie imprisoned, and no partner to dance with that Coy Ray would approve, she believed she'd sit this one out at home. "Mr. Sutherland, he said he might come help me catch up with my arithmetic tonight," she said, pretending it was an afterthought. That young teacher, I had seen the tender way he watched this gilded creature who sat at the head of the "high school" row in his schoolroom. All wisdom and innocence, she thought she had a secret.

"Long as nobody comes to court me, long as it has to do with work, it's all right with Pap," Rose said, sighing. "Long as that old sow cat is there to watch me. Eh, law." Ben Aaron's assessment of the Chick matter crossed my mind. I could see her keeping watch with her green cat eyes, and her two-tooth grin.

One thing still did not jibe. "I've got no business to go to any dance, for I've got nobody to dance with either," I said.

"I don't know what Mr. Steele has got on his mind," Rose said. "All I know is he never asked ME." The implication was that for some reason — and I suspected that Rose knew exactly what it was — he had asked ME. And I had every right to be suspicious.

Rose hollered for my kids. "If y'uns want, we'll all take our quilts and go sleep up in the loft, in the hay," she said. That sounded good to me. Cole Sutherland taught them all, in school. Pet had a ten-year-old's crush on him; wild mules could not keep her away from the Wilcox domicile since there was no doubt in any of our minds that he would be there. Hugh would joyfully have lived on Wilcox Ridge with all those red-haired, freckled little boys and their dogs; it was his escape from a female-dominated world.

So Rose handed them up behind her, onto the mule, and off they went, happy as larks. And I ran to the barn and fed the stock.

I washed, then, and put on a blue gingham dress I had made, after my Grandma Daisy's pattern. I thought of Daisy, "the dancin'est woman alive," as I fastened the straps on those black shoes with the clicky little heels.

Here I was, a runaway married woman hiding out in my granny's house, getting ready to go to a dance, doing up my hair, powdering. It troubled me as I put a little grease on my eyelashes and stood in front of the old dresser mirror to study the effect. In the mirror there were two of us. I can only tell you. Two so alike they both were surely me, but one had on something white and her long black hair was loose and sort of floating. "Pinch a little color in your cheeks," she said, in a voice that was not exactly mine. I pinched. And then I heard hoofbeats on the road, and Ben Aaron's footsteps on the porch, and I was back alone.

It was the strangest feeling. So warm and loving. I was standing there dazzled, with Daisy's black-fringed woolen shawl over my arm, when I heard Ben Aaron rap at the front door.

I never knew how my cousin might arrive. In a rickety wagon? A logging truck? This time he was on his big old gray horse, and he was leading a slick, dark little mare with a funny-looking saddle.

"Here—swing your leg over thisaway," he said. "Did you not ever ride side-saddle before?"

"Mercy, no," I said.

"Well this is to suit Aunt Nam," he said. "She claims it's vulgar for a woman to straddle a horse."

It was a perch that would take some getting used to, but I smoothed down my skirt, and Ben Aaron rode around to the left of me, the better for us to talk. Which, for some curious reason we did not. No matter, I thought. The sundown behind the mountain was turning everything to gold. The hills below us looked like some grand jewel box had turned over on them, with rubies and emeralds thick all over. After we crossed the Hogback the river shined like a golden ribbon, in the deep dusk of the valley. We were part of the landscape; all around us was hushed and still.

And the moon came over the ridge, big and full, and it shined a chilly light. I pulled the shawl tight and studied my cousin Ben Aaron Steele. He was thinking. Something deep and troubling, he was thinking. Something grave. Whatever is going on, I thought, I will remember this night. If it is something bad I will remember the way this looks, the way we are, right now, and I will not regret it.

When we had passed through the Boney Creek Bridge I finally said to him, "I've got no business going to a dance. I've got no partner."

"Aw," he said, straightening up. "You know these ol' play-parties. Somebody will turn up. You know they's always some old widower or a foolish-witted boy or two around without a woman."

That did not sound reassuring, somehow. I thought about that first dance I went to, down at Red Bank, where my dear Cousin Ben was the fiddler in charge.

"Will there be a fight?" I said. It was only curiosity.

"I hope not. But if there is," he said, looking at me intently, "you light out of there for Nam's as fast as you can go. Don't even look back. You hear?"

I shivered. But I didn't ask any more.

We went to the sawmill; one of the big, closed-in ramshackle sheds was cleared out and there was a meeting already going on. Outside there was a little knot of figures huddled. We got down and one of the lurkers took the horses, and Ben Aaron took me by the hand and we went up to the door and looked inside.

I had been away from town long enough that it startled me to see electric lights. I blinked and looked around. Every farmer in three counties was in there, it looked like. Somebody was reading a copy of Senator Borah's speech about the plight of the farmer; it was about tariffs and stuff I knew nothing about. I mainly looked around to see who was there. I noticed my cousin was very soberly doing the same.

And then I saw Bat Dung, sitting over against the wall. There were a couple of empty chairs beside him, on one side. On the other sat a slim, dark-haired young girl.

Ben Aaron gave me a little shove inside and turned back to the dark and was gone like a shot. Before I could go after him old Vicie Hambright grabbed me and started a long account of her latest bowel complaint. My gut curdled while I stood there saying "Oh, how dreadful!" I was dying to know what was going on outside.

There was a bunch out there leaning around on the Frenchmen's old Model T. I could see the fire of their cigarettes. When I poked my head out into the dark I could make out Coy Ray, and the Boulangers, and Ben Aaron, and one other, Sheriff Wylie Brock. They were talking very low.

I caught somebody saying, "Kill 'er if he knew." Lord save!

"Sweet Jesus!" said Ben Aaron. The fiddling Boulanger—I never could recollect their names—he was hunched over with his elbows on the hood of the car, and his head in his hands. And they huddled closer, and talked lower, and then Ben Aaron laughed out loud and said real low, "We'll get 'er with a dollar."

"Oh, he dearly loves the dollar!" somebody said.

And then they moved and stood in the doorway, just the fiddlers and pickers, waiting their turn. And there were more people coming to the dance, laughing and gossiping, and when the meeting was over, the band set up and twanged and tuned, and people moved their chairs back against the walls.

Bat Dung was up and steering his daughter to the door. She was looking at him, pleading. I could see her mouth working. He had her by the arm, tugging.

Now, Jack Garner was going to do the calling. He was the head sawyer at the mill. Ben Aaron was up there on the make-shift stage, whispering in Jack's ear. And Jack clapped his hands to get attention. "Don't nobody leave that likes to have a good time," he hollered. "We're agoin' to have a GOOD TIME here tonight!"

'Course that just sailed by Bat Dung. I shuddered to think what he would call a good time. He was still making progress toward the door with his captive.

"Anybody leaves is gon' be sorry—we got all kind of PRIZES coming up," Jack yelled. "Gon' be MONEY change hands here tonight. The real SPONDULIX!" There was a sort of a panicky edge to this exhortation. Like a preacher who had seen the fires of Hell.

Folks hollered and cheered. I noticed even Bat Dung seemed to be quite moved. He hesitated, and then he steered his girl back to their chairs. I hoped nobody else saw the victorious look she shot that fiddling Boulanger.

The band was finding their key and one of the sawmill boys came sidling up and asked me would I dance and I said yes. And the revelry commenced with "Cotton Eye Joe" and the whole crowd, nearly, in the circle. As we promenaded by I saw Ben Aaron looking at me with that same look Coy Ray must have used when he wilted Rose. And I thought, well, Rats! What did he bring me up here for if I was not supposed to dance?

Not everybody was having fun. The Aleywines sat tight against the wall. Bat Dung glowered. The girl looked absolutely pasty. She was a pretty little thing, with a fluff of dark brown curls, but nobody was inviting her to dance. I couldn't imagine her daddy being a gallant dancing partner, even if a person could get near him. Whew! The bare idea of dancing with Bat Dung!

After a couple of tunes, the band just stopped, and Jack raised his hand and said, "All right now! The youngest married couple here, come up and get a prize!" There was mumbling and craning and a pair came forth, they were fifteen and sixteen, and their dewy faces shined when the boy pocketed a five-dollar bill.

Now I wasn't about to let my cousin's hard looks cow me, but I thanked my partner kindly and went and took a seat beside a stout lady who was gasping and fanning. And Ben Aaron sat down upon his barrel, where he always sat to play, and lit his pipe, and Coy Ray laid his banjo down and hunkered down beside him, to rest, and the Frenchmen took up their guitar and their fiddle and began one of those metronome reels—you know, where the guitar goes *ump-thunk, ump-thunk,* like the ticking of a clock, and the fiddle-dee-fiddle-dums are as precise as cross-stitch. They were so good and regular I knew if I danced to that I would fall down.

And then they were stopped. In mid-swing. Jack called up the couple with the most children and there was all that hoorah again, and a skinny little bald man and his big rosy wife called out, "Seventeen!" and trotted up to get their crisp five dollars.

I noticed that Bat Dung was getting more interested. Five dollars was a lot of trips back into those dark holes with a guano bucket. I also noticed some agitated whispering between Ben Aaron and Jack. Ben Aaron was rubbing his hands and frowning. Every little bit, they would glance down at certain ones but plainly did not want us to notice. Whatever it was he had been thinking about all night, Ben Aaron had not made it work, quite yet.

So he started the band off on a dreamy, draggy waltz, very slow. I stole a peep at Bat Dung and I had a mean idea, I wondered if they would think to give a prize for the dirtiest neck. But no. Jack called for the oldest mule that had made the trip that night, and that took some hollering and debate and finally an old man who looked to be a hundred yelled out in a quavery voice that he had ridden there on one that was thirty-one. And he hobbled off with another five dollar bill. I wondered who was handing out all those bucks behind the scenes.

Well, the band took a break, then. Jack said, "Now don't nobody go away—the BIG prize is yet to come!" I wondered what it was. I had an idea it wasn't going to be real free.

They brought out sawhorses and boards for tables, and the ladies set out sweet cider and tea cakes, and the men were ambling slyly out to their cars and wagons, and lingering, smoking, passing the demijohns and fruit jars around and coming back refreshed. I decided to go speak to that Aleywine girl, Bat Dung or no. I would offer to bring them some cider, and I had started over that way when Ben Aaron strode up and got me firmly by the elbow.

"I want you to go sit with Bat Dung Aleywine," he said. "And I want you to get him to dance. I don't care how you do it, you just get him to dancing and keep him dancing no matter what."

I opened my mouth to protest but he looked so deadly serious that I just nodded, and edged around the crowd. Somebody was yelling at Ben Aaron to get back up and play. There was a lot of whooping and clapping going on and he started to go up, but then he ran back and caught me again, and whispered desperately in my ear, "And for God's sake, remember his name ain't Bat Dung." Then my cousin loped back to the stage and pulled his barrel forward and sat on it, and somebody hollered, "The Devil's Dream," and he began to play.

I slipped through the crowd until I got to Bat Dung. Er, Luther. I took Sue Annie's hand, it was cold as a frog. She was such a slight thing, with her heart-shaped face and little pointed chin, her gray eyes full of suffering and her olive skin so pale. I told her I was Rose's neighbor, and how sad I was that Rose couldn't come tonight. I asked would she like some cider, since it was plain her daddy would not budge, nor let her, either.

She gave me a wan little smile and said yes, thank you, and I went and brought us all a drink. And then I took my seat by Bat Dung. He was listening raptly to the fiddling.

There were a few men that had been out to the wagons who came in frisky and commenced stomping and kicking around. Then lo and behold a hefty lady joined them, holding up her skirts. And one by one young girls came forward, wholly in the spirit, dancing up in front of a man and matching shuffles and flinging heels. I was entranced. My eyes were glued on them. There was a frantic quality to the fiddling; the dancers' heads bobbed like corks and their feet were a blur. And yet they looked in their faces so blissfully relaxed, their legs independent of the rest of their bones and brains, following the dictates of that mesmerizing tune. Nothing else in the universe mattered.

When they had run down Ben Aaron sat mopping his brow while Jack proclaimed the high point of the night.

"All right, neighbors, here's what you've been awaitin' for. I've got a twinny . . . dollar . . . BILL here in my hand." (He flourished the twinny . . . dollar . . . BILL.) "And it's agoin' to some lucky couple here tonight. Now. You boys out-tair that think you can dance. Catch you a good breath and a high-steppin' womern. 'Cause you're gonna need 'em both tonight!"

Well. There was a general stirring around, looking around and considering. Weighing chances. Jack's hollerin', "We gon' start this music, start the circle movin', keep it amovin'. Couple hangs in the longest, buck and squaw, gon' walk off with this TWINNY DOL-LAR BILL! These musicianers, Brother Wilcox, here, Brother Steele, the Brothers Boulanger, Brother Spivey, back 'air, they'll hep you keep ahoppin', they'll lead and inspire you, as long as you can stay in this circle and dance. Ain't that right, boys?"

"Eah. Yes-SIR. That's the truth!"

The musicianers were plunking and re-tuning. I could feel one's eye on me, sharp as a hawk's.

Strange matches were being made on the floor, for this strange game. There was a lot of laughing and horse-trading, One real big lady in front of us was trying to peddle off her man to a young, strong girl. "We'll split that pot!" she said. Old men were willing to trade off lively-dancing wives. Half a twenty-dollar loaf was, after all, ten dollars; it was hard times. Girls who could dance like that, or would show it, were a whole sight scarcer than men. It was the men who strutted their tail-feathers and danced like cocks. When a woman did it, she was remembered. I heard it again, in my head. "Daisy McAllister. The dancinest woman alive."

A couple of men cast looks over at me, but where I was sitting made them think better of it. The raggedy circle grew on high hopes. Out of the corner of my eye I saw Bat Dung make a motion to get Sue Annie up to dance. It was a half-hearted move; he knew it was futile. She was sitting with her eyes half-closed, with her head leaned back against the wall like she was about to puke. But he got up. And finally she got up, and shivered, and hugged her shoulders and sat back down. Her eyes got wide as something wild's. Her face was bluish, like skim milk. Either the girl was mortally sick, or she was petrified. She darted another quick look at the Frenchman. The sweat was rolling down his face. His shirt was stuck to him.

The caller looked out over the assembly. "I see some folks ain't even game to TRY," he said, incredulous. "Who's gon' let all this money go without a TRY?" Bat Dung puffed his cheeks and blew a dejected sigh. Ben Aaron was glaring slits through me. I turned to Bat Dung. And what do you think? Bat Dung was turning around to me. Why, it was the most natural thing in the world.

"What say, Missy—will we win it?"

"Why, thank you, B . . . Luther! We will try!" I said. And I rose and took Mr. Aleywine's arm, and asked the blessing of his daughter, whose eyes were sparkling with tears.

"I hope you good luck," she whispered.

I couldn't even answer. You too, I thought. You too.

Don't know why this stays with me but the start-off tune was "Bile Them Cabbage Down" and we were caught in it like leaves in a whirlpool. Shuffling, stomping, shuffling, stomping like some kind of drum. Fast. I wished it was not so fast. A couple of times I saw my partner look back to see how his girl was passing her time. And then he got so caught up, so oblivious, we were flying. It was like a stampede, the pounding feet, and the bystanders were clapping and stomping while the sea of denim and feed-sack prints rose and fell, rose and fell with that driving beat. For the first time in a dozen years, I bet, Bat Dung was grinning. He was having a good time.

There was no break in the rhythm, not one lost beat when Coy Ray moved up front with his banjo and slipped into his specialty, slick as grease. Tom Spivey plunked behind him on the bass and in that false-high, minor-keyed nasal whine, commenced to singing, "Run nigga run nigga run nigga run nigga pateroler gonna gitchee pateroler gonna gitchee, Run nigga run nigga run nigga run nigga pateroler gonna gitchee better git away. . . ."

It was hypnotic. I could feel the swamps and cotton fields under my feet. Out of pure terror I could have danced a hundred miles. Nobody would notice that there was only one fiddler now, a tall, gray-headed man, my cousin Ben Aaron. None of us could know the fearsome crisis going on outside, as the Frenchman cranked, jumped in, swore, jumped out, cranked again. A confederate cranked and the engine turned and died. Turned and balked. Turned and shimmied into life, sputtering, shuddering, backfiring like a gunfight.

On and on the circle went, panting, groaning, on went the red faces, bobbing by. Sweat streaked Bat Dung's face and made black puddles on his collar. He danced me up and down like I was a wood doll on a stick. He had this peculiar hopping hitch to his step, and he was energized a lot by the sight of others dropping out. He would not drop out. He was unbeatable. He was crazy. He encouraged me as best he could: "Git yer secont wind, Sissie." And that had its problems too.

But there is such a thing. It came in the oddest way. It was as though something jerked me up by the hair, straightened my back, lifted my ribs. I felt it in my nose, and my eyes. It was like I was somewhere else, and had just put down fifty pounds. I wonder now if it had something to do with the countenance of my cousin, who never took his eyes off us for an instant.

Tune after tune. Just to be sure. My legs were like jelly. "Old Joe Clark," they had no bones at all. "Soldier's Joy?" Whose joy? I was sinking. Why would my Ben Aaron, who loved me, try so hard to kill me? I retched. The lights went dim. We were turning, turning, like leaves in Seven Mile Branch. Turning like the skinny wheels of a T-Model Ford, spinning, leaping, rolling, whirring, joyously showing the town of Caney Forks their dust. Gone.

So was I gone. But not for long. Not so anybody noticed. I woke in a chair, panting, and they hadn't missed me at all. Ben Aaron was fanning me with his hat that smelled of sweat and sawdust. Sweet. He was all joy. "I think we ought to make that twenty dollars each," he said. "I'll match that twenty dollars!" (I would figure up later how much this escapade had cost him.)

Bat Dung was jubilant. People were pounding him on his soaking back, going on over him, and somebody gave us each a swig from a fruit jar, and it burnt like fire.

This might have been the happiest moment in Bat Dung's life. He looked around to share it with his daughter. But she was gone.

Ben Aaron slipped me out and deposited me in the sheriff's car, and the sheriff brought me to Aunt Nam's for the night. I had visions for a while that Bat Dung would figure the whole thing out and come looking for more of his style of vengeance.

Truth was, I didn't see him anymore till nearly spring. I was down at Ollie Trotter's, buying onion sets. And Bat Dung was there. Only I almost didn't know him. He was clean and shaved, had on nice clean clothes.

He showed me a little sailor suit he was fixing to buy, a tiny blue suit with a whistle on a cord tie at the neck. He was taking it to Canada, he said. Catching the train in Red Bank on that very day.

He pulled a wrinkled letter out of his breast pocket and unfolded it for me to read. "Dearest Daddy," it said. "We have a baby boy. His name is Jean-Paul Luther Boulanger. He will be christened the first Sunday in March. We would be real glad if you could come."

∼22∼

OLD TERRORS, NEW DREAMS

SLEEP ON, BIRD. THERE'S A HAIR-PULL FIGHT GOING ON BACK IN the hemlocks, but you needn't pay it any mind. Owls have got a nest back in there and they quarrel. Don't know if it's him and her going at it or if she's got a boyfriend that intrudes sometimes.

But it brings back that first fall; first time I heard that I thought for sure it was the boogerman about to get us. Still had the quilt up over my head when the kids woke up and said, Hey! Listen at the owl-fight! They'd heard 'em up at Coy Ray's and loved it. So have I, ever since. It brings back a happy time that makes me ache to remember it.

I guess partly it was so new, and free. I always think of it when the fog is full of the smell of late apples, or when the moon comes up big and orange, over the ridge. Oh, the most is the smell of persimmons all mushy on the ground. There are so many on this place. Nam knew where the best lady-trees were; only the ladies had fruit. She cautioned us to watch 'em, to let the 'simmons dangle like little Christmas balls on their bare limbs, till they were frosted the color of sunset and so heavy with sugar they'd fall. Anybody that robs a persimmon tree before it's ready to share gets a mouth full of repentance.

Clear nights when I would lie sometimes just too stirred up, I guess, to go to sleep I could hear Coy Ray's coon dogs, singing along the ridge. Oh I know I ought to have been sorry for the coon and all that but most times the dogs were more noise than threat. A half-witted coon is smarter than a dog. And I would lie back and listen, wrapped in the wild sweetness of the night.

I said that one day to Ben Aaron when we were out with Coy Ray, stacking stovewood. I said how much I loved it.

"Eh, law, 'simmons do bring the possums out. That possum music's mighty sweet I know," he said, making a big yawn. Coy Ray drew back a pine knot and glared and scrinched his teeth. The vilest insult you could pay a man was to hint that his coon dog might hunt possum.

We would keep a fire going, then, most all the time. The mornings would be sparkly with frost; I could hear the children's feet crunching a long way down the road, where the ground would freeze and spew up. The days were getting short. The kids would not be home from school before the long, cold shadows.

I made it my pleasure to spend a lot of time in the woods. I picked up great sacks of hazel nuts and hickory nuts and walnuts and chestnuts and at night we would sit by the fire and crack nuts and pick 'em with a hairpin. The kids were not enthusiastic except that Nam had offered five cents a cup for walnuts for her Christmas cakes. They were the very dickens to shell but the money talked. So they picked.

And we brought down hampers full of books from the attic, and lit the lamps and read by the fire. It made me feel close to our folks, sitting on their hearth, reading their dusty old dog-eared books. They had marked places with broomstraws and slivers of dressgoods. There was a pulverized brown thistle marking a page in the *Life of Burns;* it was at a poem that went, "Farewell, my friends! Farewell, my foes! My peace with these — my love with those — The bursting tears my heart declare, Farewell, the bonny banks of Ayr."

It would have been one of the old ones, I thought, a hundred years ago, that put that homesick flower there. And I wondered about another one, I remember; somebody had marked Gray's "Elegy," in another poetry book, with a yellow baby-curl tied with a faded blue ribbon.

Somebody had loved horses; there was a set of leather-bound horse-breeders' journals with the most beautiful pictures of race horses. And somebody read a lot in Latin; there were several Latin books. And somebody read in French.

One awfully pretty day at the end of October, Ben Aaron came by to get (he said) a bucket of persimmons. Nam wanted to make a pudding. I had made a couple of pies, and we heated up the soup-pot and had a little dinner, just Ben Aaron and me. He acted pre-occupied, somehow. He picked up a little book of French poetry that was lying on the kitchen table, and thumbed through it, and sort of absent-mindedly stuck it inside his jacket.

I said I'd go with him, down to the grove to pick up 'simmons, and we went along down the field, and he was so quiet, and I said, What was the matter? Well, he said, sighing, he had heard on the radio that the stock market was just in a terrible dive. Some rich people were ru-ined. People were jumping out of windows.

"What is that going to mean to you, you think?" I said, not seeing any way it would mean a thing to me. I took his arm and we walked along, through the warm dry grass.

"I expect no more than I'll let it," he said. "We'll weather it."

We found a lot of persimmon trees, along the edge of the birch grove. Most of the fruit was fallen and shrivelled but we filled the bucket, and ambled back up the field. Slowly. And we came to a big rock and he sat down in the grass and propped his back on it, and I sat down by him and spread my skirt down over my feet, and it was warm, there, in the sun, and the dead grass smelled so sweet. And he pulled that French book out of his jacket and read to himself, a little while, and then he read to me. He read beautifully.

"Where did you learn to do that?" I asked him. I remembered what Nam had said. I was thinking how Mama's face would look if she could see this.

"Learn a lot a' things in a lumber camp," he said, not looking up from his place. "Half the men I was raised with spoke nothin' but French. Best timber men. Canadians, Cajun or so. Younguns all play together and you learn to talk. Your daddy helped me learn to read."

I leaned back on the rock myself. Warmed to the heart, I closed my eyes and he read on, softly, "I shall be buried under the earth, a ghost in the shade of myrtle, while you sit by the fire, a gray grand-mother . . . My love, remember and regret."

I put my hand across his mouth. "Hush, hush!" I said. "It's grue-some! Don't read that anymore." He was so pleased I understood it, he kissed my fingers. And I turned my face and kissed him just so quickly, on the mouth.

It was the first time anything like that had happened. And it seemed like time and breath were just suspended, there, for an instant, like a hummingbird at a flower. "Well, I better go," he said, clearing his throat. And he got up, studiedly slow, and stretched, and reached down his hand to me. And we walked on up to the house, not saying anything, but thinking plenty, on both sides. When he went to get on his horse I said, "You better let me brush the straw off your back. It looks like you've been wallowin'."

He sort of flushed and grinned and brushed his tail himself, and swung up into the saddle, and I handed him the bucket, and he tipped his hat goodbye. I had never before seen the man embarrassed. But I felt very warm, and I smiled to myself about it after he was gone.

We didn't see him for a while, then; it didn't worry me, Coy Ray said he had gone off on a round of the furniture factories. If there was any money flowing he was cutting channels. And then Sophia hauled him off to Baltimore at Thanksgiving to go Christmas shopping. Ordinarily I think she wouldn't want him on those trips. And I can't imagine he would want to go.

But, now, Nam was going to have us all to Thanksgiving; with the children and me there, we had a family. Not, apparently, Soph's kind of jollies.

It snowed the first good snow a few days before Thanksgiving; we woke up and saw the world all white and all three of us were six years old. We played in it till our fingers hurt.

On Thanksgiving day we went to Nam's. We had something concrete to be thankful for; Coy Ray had taken the tobacco to the auction at Red Bank and it brought us a little over $400, and we divided with him, half and half; that was the way Ben Aaron had prescribed it to be. So we were not as broke as we had been.

And it was just after Thanksgiving that it came a snow, again. Really big, so soft and light we kicked our way through it, to the barn, but it was drifted against the privy door, and we were digging our way in when we heard something whooshing through the snow, down the road. The front steps were drifted over so the visitor came around to the back. It was Ben Aaron, with Cy hitched to an old sled.

His face was lit up like neon. He was tickled pink with something. "You warm enough? Come get on. I want to show you somethin'," he said. So we all got on with him, and he clucked at Cy and we went off, down the road, and turned up then toward Shiloh. Our noses were running and our mouths were too cold to talk so we asked no questions. All I could say was, "Oh, it's so beautiful." Our breath made a trail behind us.

We went past the camp and the school and across the tracks that had been laid for the logging trains, and the road narrowed till it looked like we were just out in the woods. Ben Aaron stopped, and listened, and got off and led us up the hill, a little way, through a bunch of hemlocks. He would stop and listen. And then we came to the top of the rise and I heard it. It was the chugging of a steam engine, out of sight in the woods. There wasn't any track up there. And then I saw the light, coming. It was coming right at us.

I threw my hand to my mouth and screamed. "It killed you! It killed you!" It was bloodcurdling. I couldn't stop, I flung myself on Ben Aaron and screamed and screamed. And the whistle blasted, right at us; the whole woods shuddered with the *chunk-chunk-chunking* of that horrid thing so close its hot breath hissed around us. Before it had passed us by I fainted. The next thing I knew Ben Aaron was holding me across his knees, looking down in my face. The kids were staring at me, petrified. I could hear the thing puffing, close by; it had stopped, and some men were coming to us.

Ben Aaron was looking me in the eyes, saying, "I am not dead. Look at me, I am not dead!" I raised up and said, "The man in the tree is dead. Get him down! Get him down!"

"We did get him down," he said. "It's all right, now. It's all right."

"She's all right," he said to the men that had got off the engine. "She's just scared of that thing. I ought to have known she would be."

"City gals," one of 'em said wisely. "Scared of their shadder." I kept my face hid in Ben Aaron's jacket until they went away. And I heard the thing going *chunk . . . chunk . . .* again.

"Let's look at it," said Ben Aaron.

"No!" I said.

"If you could put your hand on it . . . . it's nothing but a machine," he said.

And I screamed, "NO! NO! NO!" and buried my face again, sobbing, like a little girl. I was twelve years old, in the dark, among strangers, and I had just seen somebody die.

Ben Aaron got up then and picked me up like I really was a child. "Just keep your face to my neck," he said, "and I'll tote you out of here." So we went down the ridge that way; I could feel the heat when we passed the thing.

"I wish she didn't act that way," Hugh said wistfully. "I'd like to ride on it."

"We better not do that today I 'spect," Ben Aaron said. "But I think she might get over it. Don't give it up."

He set me down on the sled, then, and started us off for home. When we got inside, and got the fire stirred up he excused us from the children and took me to the kitchen and fired up the stove. "You were on the ground," I said.

"I was on the ground," he said, looking very serious. "How do you know all this?"

"You were burning," I said.

"I got some hot coals down my back," he said. "It didn't do much harm. Just a few little places. Could of rurned my looks," he said, trying to be light. "How do you know it?"

"It was in the winter. It was 1912."

"I had just got the thing. Belonged to Sophier's daddy. He'd quit the lumber business and sold me some equipment. That thing's made to go on snow or soggy ground you know. Called a Lombard."

"It was off the track."

"Don't need any. Skids on the front, treads on the back. You put half a dozen cars on skids behind it and you're haulin' timber."

He wasn't taking his eyes off me. "I think you better tell me," he said.

I told him. I told him about what I saw, in a dream, on a cold night in a boarding school in Paris, I told him I had sat all day in the kitchen with the cooks, and they had petted me a little bit, because I was "homesick."

He was not put off at all. He sat considering, a little bit, and then he told his side.

"We had cut a road through a big stand of white pine, up near the Forks," he said. "We'd come around the side of the mountain with it, blasted out some places, one place it was too narrow, I knew it, and real steep. Anyway we fired that thing up, I'd just got it down here and it was a real play-toy, you know, and we had it up there bringin' logs down to the railroad, havin' a big time with it. It'd warmed up that day and the snow was soft. The ground was soft. We were comin' around that narrow bend, I was sittin' up in the cab with the old boy we'd hired to run the thing. And the ground just gave out from under us. Over we went. I don't know if he jumped or was pitched out."

"He was in the tree," I said. "He was dead. I saw his eyes."

"He was in a tree with his neck broke."

"And you were on the ground."

"I stayed with the thing all the way down, till it hit bottom. Then I hit the snow, with a few hot coals on top of me." His voice was shaky. He got out a cigarette and tamped it in the palm of his hand and lit it, and looked at me very long and hard.

"I was knocked out for a little bit," he said. "While I was lyin' there I saw somebody—I thought it was Daisy, but it was much too young. It was a beau . . ." it was a child that looked just like me, he said. And she was screaming hysterically, and he couldn't figure why.

We digested that in silence, for a while. "Thought I'd never get that engine up from there," he said. "Didn't give a damn, either. Didn't go about it till spring. Finally took a bunch of oxen down in there, and righted it. Dug out a road around the base of the mountain and dragged it out of there. Boiler was busted. We hauled it back up to the mill and put it in a shed. Jack Garner got it fixed, used it a while, while I was gone, in '17-18. I never used it again myself, never went where it was runnin', till just now."

He frowned, studying his fingers. "Why did I do this to you?" he said, finally. "It just makes no sense."

I was finding it easier and easier to forgive my cousin anything. Anything in the world. But some things I did ponder.

It was just a few days after that that half the school at Shiloh came down with the measles. Pet had had 'em, when she was about two. Hugh never had, till then. Cole Sutherland brought him home early one afternoon, just burning up. Cole didn't feel too good either, it turned out. When he broke out himself the school closed down.

I had halfway agreed to take the kids home for Christmas; I really hadn't meant it but it was something to get those people down there out of my hair. I sort of sadly realized we had the money to go on, 'course if it fell into certain hands when we got down there we'd never get back here, or we'd come back broke as haints at best. Well I confess I seized upon Hugh's measles as a perfect excuse. I waited till he ought to have been nearly over it, it was along about the middle of December, and then wrote Louise that sad to say I guess we couldn't come.

Well, the penalty for that sin was that he didn't get over it. The littler Wilcoxes were sick too but they were up bright as pennies when Hugh was not able to even stand on his feet. He kept coughing this dry, wracking cough. I heard him groaning and talking in the night one night and I jumped up and lit the lamp and felt his forehead and it was like a coal.

It was sleeting out and black as pitch, and I didn't know what on God's green earth to do. He was making a queer noise when he breathed. I got Pet up, I didn't have the faintest idea what she'd do but I didn't want to be alone with him. He was taking spells of shivering; his teeth would chatter and his lips were right blue and cracked and dry. When he coughed and blood flew out on the comforter I started to cry in a panic.

"Hush, Mama, I'll go get Rose," Pet said.

"No no, I'll go," I said. "I can't have you out there in that dark."

"I'll not stay here alone with him while he dies," she said, pulling on her rubber boots.

Well, I got the lantern and went with her to the barn and bridled the mule, and started her off around the road, though it was farther; I wouldn't have her ford the river like that and go up that icy trail for anything. And I went back in, dreading it, but I could hear Hugh breathing before I got in the room and that was some relief.

It seemed like forever before I heard two sets of feet come on the porch. It was Rose and Coy Ray; they had left Pet at their place in front of their fire. She was drenched and freezing. Coy Ray looked down at Hugh and turned around and started out the door. "I'm a-goin' after

Ans," he said. And that was all there was to that. Off into the gray he went, for it was getting morning. When he and Ansel Shuman came back down in a buggy, it was day.

I remember Ans coming and standing by the bed; his hands were cold and he didn't want to touch Hugh so he stood there frowning down at him, counting the pulse in his neck. Then he went and warmed his stethoscope at the fire before he put it on Hugh's chest. Ans was like that; he was big and white-headed and heavy, not so fat as just big. And quiet; he never did say things just to be talking, it was funny how in his bigness and stolidness I could see some kinship to Rose's leanness and grace; a gentle, good soul.

Hugh's eyes were glassy from the fever. His mouth was all dry. Ans sent Rose to the kitchen to make tea and Coy Ray out to the woodpile to bring in lots of firewood. He kept leaning down and listening to Hugh's chest. Finally he straightened up and his face lightened a little bit. "I think it's just on one side," he said. "I think we might be lucky."

He went and raised the window some and said to keep a big fire all the time. He said to keep spooning tea and cider and grape juice into Hugh's mouth till he was able to drink. He made up a mustard plaster then and put it on one side of Hugh's chest, and told me to watch and not let it blister, and he said he would be back the next day. He seemed to be confident there would be a next day.

But pneumonia to me meant death. I was stunned, I felt condemned. I had brought this child up here to die. I was glad Ben Aaron had gone to Pennsylvania, or someplace. He was part of why I felt guilty.

Nam came trotting down that afternoon. Ans had called her. She came like she always came, with her bag of provisions. Coy Ray had chopped a bunch of wood and gone home. Pet came riding down on the mule when she was assured there was no dead body here. Rose was able to go home when Nam came.

"Lordamercy Ans Shuman's a-goin' to freeze this child to death," Nam said, slamming the window down. "You got to smother the pneumonie fever. He won't never learn. Wha'd he put on this baby's chest?" she said. "A mustard plaster? In the name of the Lord what ignorance." She went tearing off to the kitchen with her bag and I smelt the onions frying. Directly she came out with an onion poultice and yanked up Hugh's undershirt and plunked it on him. He stretched his lower lip and gave a little retch. But after a while we all got used to it.

Day by day, night by night it was the same. Ans would come in every morning and quietly go open the window and throw more wood on the fire. He would take off the onion poultice and listen to Hugh's chest and "forget" to put the onions back on.

As soon as he was in the road Nam would run heat her onions up, or fry a fresh batch.

Hugh held on, rattling and spitting and shivering and talking about things we could not see. It was like he was melting right in front of us. His cheeks got hollow and his skin was tight and blue-looking. I had the horrid dread that I was going to have to send Louise word that he was dying.

We would sit by him and rock. Our talking didn't seem to bother him; he was not with us. No comfort to me, Nam catalogued the children up on the hill. All the little stones with such sad stories. Some of them came with awful things wrong with them. Some never breathed. Several came frail in the mind; a few of those lived awhile, loving and trusting and all the more grieved over when they died. A couple lived on and were good children all their lives. The ones Nam didn't talk about were the ones that died coughing and burning and wasting. Like Hugh.

On the seventh night a screech owl settled in to gurgling, over the house. Hugh got real restless. He thrashed his arms about and fretted that his fishing line was tangled in a bush. I started to cry. I put my head down in Nam's lap and wailed till I was absolutely limp. She patted my back. I could hear her sniffing. We had given him up.

I don't know how in that posture we went to sleep. I guess we were exhausted. But sometime close to morning I heard Hugh holler, "No I won't drink anymore! It's bad!" I jumped up and turned up the lamp and looked at him. His hair was stuck to his head with sweat. His pillow was wet. He had kicked off his covers.

He opened his eyes and peered at me. "Take that stuff away, Mama," he said. "It tastes awful."

"What stuff?" I said. And it was like he had waked up, then, from a deep sleep.

"Where is your other dress?" he said.

That made no sense. "What dress?" I said.

"That white dress you had on," he said. "I liked it."

He just sort of faded out then; he lay back and smiled, and drifted off, and his breathing was easy, and he slept.

Nam had got up. "I smell pennyrile," she said. "Did somebody bring some pennyrile tea in here? I wish to the Lord we had some for this child. Your daddy liked to died one time and Daisy biled up pennyrile and boneset and made 'im drink the tea."

"He's asleep, Aunt Nam," I said. She looked close at him. His face was pink and calm.

"He's come through the crisis," she said. "Praise the Lord."

Hugh was sitting up in a chair for the first time the day Ben Aaron got back and heard about our near-miss. It was two days before Christmas and it had snowed a blizzard, when he came down. As it turned out he had been supposed to meet Sophia at her folks' in Massachusetts for Christmas but he had to come home to the mill for some reason, and had sworn to get back to her at least by Christmas Day. And here he was, down here at The Birches.

Hugh was sitting by the fire with a quilt around him looking at a catalogue, happy as a lark. "I think this place needs a Christmas tree," Ben Aaron said. "Come go up the line with me," he said to me, "I know where there's the very one."

We left Pet in charge and went off with the axe, up to the base of the ridge and into the woods, just this side of the river. The woods were mostly brown and bare; the snow was drifted against the laurels, and clumps of young hemlocks held snow in their arms. I thought one of them would be beautiful.

But there were some hollies scattered about, too. We came to a particular tree that was thick with leaves; that is rare, they usually are right sparse, in the deep woods like that, wild. It had a splendid shape, not so very tall, but full of so many berries it was like it was decorated. "I've watched this grow for years," he said. "I knew sometime there'd be some use for it." And he took the axe and started to take a swing at it.

"No, don't!" I said. "Don't cut it down. Don't kill it, I can't bear it."

"The kids'd love it," he said.

"They'd love a pine," I said. "I can't take that. It's perfect."

He stood there looking at it and sighed a drifting cloud of a sigh. When he answered me his voice was funny. "Most perfect things are doomed," he said.

There were some stumps around, I think he might have cleared out around that tree to give it room to grow. And all of a sudden he flung the axe down and turned around and yanked me up and stood me on one of those stobs. There I perched like a bird, leaning on him bosom to bosom, with my arms around his neck, looking him fatally in the eye.

When I kissed him, as I was obliged to do, he kissed back decidedly, and at length. And over, and over. He pushed back my hair and kissed me on the forehead and on down to my neck. Silent and slow-motion, like a dream, all foggy with our breath. Snowy woods had never been so warm. Anything he started then and there he could have finished, with all the help he needed.

The whole matter was in that moment made absolutely clear. I had never loved any creature like I loved Ben Aaron Steele.

"This is a mess, Ben Aaron," I said finally, feebly.

"I know it," he said, and sighed, and kissed me long and hard again. And then he just jerked around and left me to hop off that stump myself, and he grabbed up the axe and went to flailing away at the trunk of a little hemlock.

It didn't matter a whit at that point what we trailed home with. It could have as well been a bare gum, or a dog hobble. Nothing was said, all the way home. We just trudged along, pulling the tree between us. When we got to the house he took it around to the back porch and made it a cross-piece stand. I was in the kitchen fixing dinner and I heard him out there sawing and hammering, singing, like he was almost unaware, to himself, "Come, pretty maid, don't be afraid of the chill of the foggy dew . . ."

He didn't stay, he put the tree up in the sitting room and said he'd sworn to take dinner with Nam and would have to make swift tracks for the Forks. He went out, just hollering a casual goodbye, and rode off up the road.

So I thought well, that's it, till after Christmas. He will leave out for up north tonight. I had a sinking, let-down feeling, a little bit forsaken. The lights had gone out.

And I knew that was ungrateful and wrong; nobody had more to be thankful for that Christmas than I; nobody was ever so blessed. There sat my baby child that I had given up for dead, cutting out pictures of toys from a catalogue to hang on the Christmas tree. There was Pet, in the kitchen, rolling out gingerbread dough, with not one protest passing her lips. I had this home; I had a family; I was, to an end good or ill, so much in love.

We popped a lot of corn and made a lot of cookies and did up our tree, and if it looked odd, we thought it was still quite fine. That night we ate our supper by the fire, and read from a little Bible I had found in a dresser. The binding was all tattered; it had stamped on it in gilt, SAVANNAH MCALLISTER, CHRISTMAS 1860. I said I could imagine Daisy, and whatever other kids there were, getting a Bible apiece and an orange and a little box of ribbon candy at the Christmas program at Pisgah Presbyterian Church.

She had brought that Bible down to The Birches, to live out the war; otherwise it would have burned. I wondered, did it go with her and Nam in that wagon to Virginia? It had a yellowed crocheted marker in it, marking a place in the Psalms. I opened it and the first line that jumped out at my eye was, "My soul thirsteth for thee, my flesh longeth for thee in a dry and thirsty land. . . ."

I cringed at my depravity and turned as fast as I could to Luke and read firm and aloud about the Virgin Mary birthing in the shed. I put the kids to sleep, reading with such conviction as to purify my spirit. But when the firelight flickered on their eyelids, and their heads drooped, I laid the Bible aside and fell headlong into the sin of coveting.

When I crawled into the featherbed, and the quilts warmed around me, I looked out the window for so long a time at the patterns that bare limbs made against the sky. And in that spell between sleep and waking, those things I'd dare not do in the flesh danced a jig with my imagination. I felt that weight and warmth in my arms and traced that perfect mouth, in my mind, with the tip of my finger. I undid imaginary buttons and rested my face on that broad hard make-believe chest and pressed my ear against the heart. And I heard it racing; it startled me awake. It was my own, in my ear, against the pillow. And I closed my eyes again, and studied that face that would fade in and away, and that mouth, before I kissed him, and slipped into forbidden places in my sleep.

Ben Aaron, oh, Ben Aaron. It was only once to anyone, and surely not to everyone that such a thing was given. Who had been so much in love?

It was Christmas Eve, the next day. We fed the mule and chickens such a bait as to last while we were gone, and Nam came down with the buggy and bundled us off to her house to spend the night. "Aaron's supposed to have gone today," she volunteered on the way. "But when Jasper brought our goose this mornin' he said he saw smoke comin' out of Sophier's chimney. I don't know what's goin' on with Aaron. She'll cook HIS goose for a fact if he don't get gone."

Nam sounded a little bit troubled about it. I was glad she couldn't hear my pulse pick up. But when we passed by the palace, it looked cold and deserted. And then I felt the same. Till I saw Cy standing out in front of Tatum's, with his head down, forlorn. Waiting. There were a bunch of wagons and mules out there while people shopped for Christmas and no one noticed Cy there but me. I kept it to myself.

When we got in the house Nam put the wood to the stove and popped the goose back in, to get hot, and flew into the rest of the dinner. "Put some candles out," she said. I lit one in the bay window, and just as I looked out I saw an old gray horse coming up the road. Well, I lost what little reason I had left and ran like a wild colt through the house to the back door. "Here here—is the devil got you by the tail?" Nam said. It was too near the truth to answer. "Ben Aaron's come," I said.

He came on the back porch with an armload of bundles and I let him in the door. He was just beaming. I could feel the pink start at my collarbones and flow up to the roots of my hair. We stood there with our mouths open, looking at one another.

"I thought you were gone," I finally said, squeaking like a mouse. "I thought so too," Nam said flatly, not taking her eye off her pots.

"I'll go directly," he said.

"You don't get there and your name's hog shit," she said. She glanced at him sidewise, made a tight line of her mouth, and slammed her biscuit pan into the stove.

He slumped and laid his burdens in a chair. "Just plunder for the kids," he said. I went and put my arms around him. His jacket was cold. He still had snow on his boots. "There's a shay comin' in, in a little bit, over on the spur," he said. "I've done told 'em I need to go up to Miller's Creek Siding. Train'll come along on the mainline there about 8:30 tonight."

"You'll not make Boston by dinnertime," Nam said.

"I'll make it by evenin'," he said. "I'll make my peace." He bent down then and kissed me on the head. "Merry Christmas, sunshine," he said.

"It is the best I ever knew," I said. And it was. It was one shining hour of happiness that we spent that night, all of us around that table, even with Nam in a sull. I couldn't figure why she was worrying so about pleasing Sophia. That had not been, so I could tell, her usual priority. But in a little bit she brightened, "If I had just one Christmas left," she said, "I'd thank the Lord for makin' it like this." I looked at Ben Aaron across the candles. His eyes were brimming. He turned his head politely and blew his nose. Nam reached and took his hand and held it between hers, and bit her upper lip. Down by the sawmill, a long sad whistle blew.

"I've got to run," he said. He motioned with his head, so slightly, for me to come outside.

Out on the porch he hugged me to him just an instant. His arms were shaking. Then he reached into his jacket pocket and something glittered in his hand. It was a long gold chain with a sapphire on it the size of a plum.

"I found this rock in Wolf Creek," he said. "The minute I saw that star, I thought about your eyes."

Quickly, he slipped it into the pocket of my apron and loped down the steps and out the gate. I watched him go off into the dark. Did your heart ever feel so empty, and still so full it could explode? That was me, in the happiest sad moment of my life.

When he was out of sight I went back in to help Nam clear the table. She didn't look at me and that was kind. I felt flushed and breathless.

"Children, take all that stuff Ben Aaron brought you and go in yonder by the fire, why don't you, and look what's in it?" she said. I could tell she wanted them out of the way. And merrily they went.

"Sen," she said then, "stop it now. Stop it," she said real low, 'most under her breath.

"I can't Nam," I said. "I'd easier stop my breath. Or the blood in my veins. That man is more to me than life."

"Then in the Lord's name stop right now. Go back down yonder to where your mammy lives, if that's the only way. Only don't let this go on. The direction it's a-headin', none of us can afford the price we'll have to pay."

~23~

A QUARE THING HAPPENED TO DAISY

NAM BROUGHT THE MATTER UP NO MORE, I GUESS NOT WANTING TO put a damper on our Christmas. The "plunder" that so occupied the children turned out to be not only theirs, as they got around to telling us. There was a package of deep wine silk dress goods, marked for Nam.

"Aw, foot," she said, plainly tickled. "That rascal knows I don't wear nothing RED. The bare idee." She sat there smoothing it over her lap with her knobby little hand, thinking what pattern she would make it up by, while the kids undid bundles of wool socks and caps and mittens and cartons of hard candies with roses in the centers and a flashlight apiece, which of course they commenced to shine around till Nam got after them for wasting all the juice. There was a baby doll with eyes that closed, and a wind-up cowboy on a bucking horse and then there was a book. Pet opened it and handed it to me.

On the fly-leaf the giver had written, "Sen, when I saw this I thought at once of you—Your loving cousin B."

It was a book of fairy tales, with the most beautiful illustrations, pale-lit woods and translucent, fairy-creatures with drifts of scroll-like curls and filmy gauze dresses that floated on the wind. I had the excuse to sit and look down at it, for quite some while. I put my hand on the treasure in my pocket that I could never show to anyone.

I did not know how many country roads there were to cross, between the Forks and Miller's Creek Siding. But I imagined that I heard the whistle blow at every one, and on north, into the night.

We went back to The Birches on Christmas day and started to set ourselves in order. It had been weeks that very little got done besides tending the sick. Hugh was still frail but at least he could feed and dress himself. Pet and I raked out the house and did a huge washing and cleaned out the ashes and the chicken house and the stable. When the children fell asleep on New Year's Eve, waiting by the fire for the old clock to strike midnight, I sat and marveled at where that year had brought us, and where the next might lead.

Nam had said if we felt up to it to come on back to her house New Year's Day. My motives were not quite pure, of course; I was not drawn so much by the bright lights of Caney Forks, nor the ceremony of hopping john and greens, as I was by the reckoning that the traveler was likely to return. Though surely not alone.

So we did our chores and early New Year's afternoon, we borrowed a team from Coy Ray and went up for the night. I felt a sort of a splinter of wonder that Nam didn't come down for us, I expected all the way to meet her coming. It finally entered my mind that she might be sick, though that never happened I was sure. When we got within sight of her house a pall of doom seemed to hang over it, sure enough. I thought Oh, Lord, what if she's dead?

Well, we didn't even knock or holler, we just walked in. And lo and behold: What did we see but Ben Aaron and Sophia Steele and their daughter Celestine, sitting at the table while Nam fixed their supper. Now, talk about suspended animation, there it was. Six people in a room, and five of 'em with their eyes popped and their mouths open. Only Celestine did not freeze. At once she began bouncing on her chair, grunting, with her arms flung wide.

I went around the table to her, and returned that crushing hug. Her father was sitting next to her. He arose, solemn as an undertaker, in his fine gray worsted suit with a gold watch chain dangling on the vest, and nodded. "Good evening, Seneca," he said. "Happy New Year, sir," I said, over Celestine's head. She held me fast.

Hugh and Pet were still standing stiff as pokers in the door. Hugh's thin little face was all eyes. "Is that Sofa?" he said, into the void. I winced. I thought Pet would hit him, but he was too puny. She put her arm around him and pulled him to her.

"How do you do, Mrs. Lamb, was it?" said Sophia, ignoring them.

"How do you do, Mrs. Steele," I said.

"Well, well," said Nam, in the kitchen door. "I'd done give you up."

"We weren't sure you expected us," I said. "I didn't know you were expecting the, uh, travelers back."

"Seddown, seddown, I'm a-fixin' to bring our supper on right now," she said.

So we sat, though like the chairs were porcupines. I stationed myself beside Sophia, and politely introduced the children, and prompted them to thank our cousin for the Christmas packages, which they did, by some wiser instinct rather guardedly, for facing Sophia they could see the curious lift to her eyebrows more clearly than I. Ben Aaron nodded and studied the table cloth intently.

I hollered to Nam did she want some help and she said no, and Sophia proceeded to explain what brought them as supper guests. I never thought it was kinship.

"Mr. Steele neglected to leave instructions for Françoise to expect us home this evening and that she should prepare dinner," said Mistress Steele. "I assume he neglected also to tell her to come to work today." Françoise, I was figuring, was the latest cook-of-the-month. Tomorrow or next day she would pack up her duffle—if she hadn't already—and most gratefully go back to where she was Frances.

Well, Nam brought on the bowls and platters of peas and rice and ham in red gravy, and stewed cabbage and all the stuff abody must consume for good luck in the new year, and her version of a fruit-cake, it was layers and layers of thin cake with a filling of cooked dried apples. And then as an afterthought she wanted to know did anybody want some pea soup; she had saved back the soup from the peas before she put the rice with 'em, for hoppin' john. She always loved the soup, the pot-likker, of anything the best.

Sophia of course disdained the soup with a shake of her head. The sun came out on Ben Aaron's face, for just a second. And then he said inaudibly, to the tablecloth, he didn't care for any. So it was only Nam that had soup. Which she commenced to eat, *slip, slip,* from her spoon. Not slurp; more ladylike. *Slip, slip.*

Ben Aaron had helped Celestine's plate and was cutting her meat. Celestine was chewing on a piece of cornbread.

"Celestine," said Sophia earnestly, "please don't make that noise with your soup."

All eyes involuntarily focused on the cornbread in the poor girl's hand. Hugh opened his mouth and I glared at him. Nam took another spoon of soup. *Slip.*

Now, I must think back here on how Sophia was arrayed, not that it applies to anything, but just to share the picture. I remember that she had on a white petaled cloche, to go with her white wool shift and redingote, her traveling costume. A regular snowbank. Or as I could hear Nam thinking, a walking bale of cotton. Anyway, Soph cocked her head and puckered her mouth into a knowing smile, and she said, "You know, I am thankful for my wonderful parents, God rest them. My mother was a regular LIONESS about manners. My most cherished memory of her is of the way she ate soup. . . ."

"Ahem," said Ben Aaron. It was the most daring opinion he offered that evening.

"My most cherished memory of my mother," Nam said brightly, "was that she knew how to make a pot o' soup. Startin' with the hog, if she had to. And thank the Lord she made her gals all learn."

It was a conversation headed for the shoals. Ben Aaron looked positively pasty. "Did you have a nice visit with your people?" I said to Sophia, steering toward (I thought) calmer waters.

"Delightful!" Sophia said. "My sister and I are very devoted, you know. We have many common interests. . . ." Before she could detail them, alas, Celestine turned over her tea. Nam bobbed up to get a towel but Ben Aaron said no, no, he'd do it, and he quietly cleaned it up, most of it was down the front of him anyway. Celestine's eyes clouded; she was upset, but he squeezed her hand and calmed her and Sophia took up her recitation of holiday delights.

"I'm sure Mr. Steele enjoyed visiting with my Uncle Melrose," she said. "My uncle, you know, owns fifteen—is it fifteen, Mr. Steele?"

"Um," said Ben Aaron, surveying the wet splotches on his gray worsted belly.

"Fifteen of the businesses that our lumber company here serves. Uncle Melrose was a partner of my father's, you know. My father was quite big in furniture."

It's in the genes, I thought real unkindly. "That's fascinating!" I said, real sincerely. It certainly was. I was beginning to thoroughly enjoy our visit. But we had passed few more remarks when Ben Aaron got up and said, "Well, Madam, I don't know about you but I need to go on to the house."

"Yes, we must go," Sophia said. She heisted herself up and looked sidewise at me, and then coyly at him. "It's been so long since we've been alone together. Even with my family, we missed our privacy."

Oh, good God, I thought. I kissed Celestine goodnight and got a deep, grave nod from Ben Aaron. He had the saddest eyes I ever saw.

"'Enjoyed my Uncle Melrose' her old foot!" Nam said, when the door had closed behind 'em. "If Aaron didn't run up there ever' breath and tell that old poot what t'do, they'd be in the road, the whole mess of 'em. I couldn't abide her ol' daddy, but he did have business sense, that I'll say. He'd gyp the socks plumb off yer feet. 'My Uncle Melrose' can't use the chamberpot without he calls up Aaron to come tell 'im how. My God, that boy, yoked to that dratted heifer!"

But that was the end of the subject. The steam was vented and the lid came down.

When we left the next morning, Nam went with us. It was turning damp and drizzly, a good time to hole in for a good visit. Course it was a sin just to sit with idle hands and gossip about others, so we found all these quilt pieces in an old trunk in the attic and justified ourselves.

Daisy had been making this quilt, Nam remembered. Some squares had been pieced; it was a Dresden Plate. All the pieces were cut, and the blue squares that would join them. We decided we would finish it.

We sat rocking in front of the fire, sewing and talking, and it was a warm kind of pleasure, working with little pieces that were left from dresses and shirts made here so long ago by my grandma, who loved this place so much.

"She was hell-bent to stay on here," Aunt Nam said. "The day Ivan was buried we got her to go home with me to the Forks—for one night. And even at that I had to watch her. Bedang'd if way in the night I didn't hear her go out. By the time I got to 'er she was headed down the road. She was dazed, you know. In shock. I got her back in the house and made her lie down, but I kept my eye cracked, I'll tell you, till I knew for a fact she was asleep.

"And the next day bright and early she was up like a little bird, with her nightgown packed in her satchel. Arie and Aaron and all of us were sittin' around the breakfast table and Daisy got up and said, 'Well, Aaron, I am ready to go home.'

"I can't tell you why to save my life, but all of us were terribly uneasy. Her behavior was just so odd. She never seemed even sad. Aaron looked at his mama and me and we both shook our heads and give him the high-sign, no no.

"And he said to her, 'Aunt Daisy, I don't know. I don't think that's a good idee quite yet, do you?'

"'Well, I don't know why not,' she said. 'I've got to go sometime. And I think it's just like wearin' new teeth; if you wait till your mouth gets tough before you put 'em in, you just never do get used to 'em.'

"She acted as chipper as if nothin' had happened atall. 'You goin' to take me, or am I a-goin' to walk?' she said, finally.

"'Well I reckon if you're goin' in spite of us, I'll take you,' Aaron said. But we none of us liked it much.

"I got to thinkin' about her that evenin' out here with the owls, and that fresh grave. You know she was plain foolish about Ivan. He was about her, too. So I got the buggy and I lit out down here, and when I got here, things seemed pretty much all right. She had put out a little washin', 'course we had washed the bed clothes where Ive had laid, first thing, and aired the bed. But she had done up his clothes he'd wore, and she'd redded up the house, got ever'thing picked up, from so many people bein' in and out. And she had a pot of greens cooked on the back of the stove, and bread made, and a pot of coffee a-boilin'—it looked to me like things were too good.

"I stayed that night, and the next night. And by the third day gone, I don't know what it was, but a quare feeling hovered over this house like a buzzard. That night I couldn't keep my eyes closed. I was sleepin' in the bed with Daisy, and it came to me how quiet she was. I raised up to look at her and she was gone.

"Now I never was one to be scared, Lord do, child, I'da never got through this life bein' scared. But all at once a cold chill seized holt of me, I just got the shivers I was so panicky. I thought maybe she had got up to go to the toilet. You know that chimney closet up there, she kep' her chamber pot and her wash pan back in there, always kind of dainty about herself.

"Well, I called, and she never answered. It crossed my mind that she might have gone downstairs to the kitchen, she'd not eat anything to speak of all the while Ivan was sick, nothin' atall while he laid a corpse. I hoped maybe she'd got hungry. I got up an' put on my carpet slippers, I thought I'd go down and see if that was it.

"Now, the moonlight was just a-streamin' in the window. It was about light as day, outdoors, the prettiest I can remember. And I remember, because somethin' told me to look out.

"And there was Daisy. Not walkin', mind, but runnin' like a child. With her hair and her gown floatin' behind her. Out there barefooted, and it cool, too, a-runnin' in the dew. And her sixty-two years old.

"At least I thought, well, Praise God, she's not runnin' to the cemetery. She was runnin' down to the birch grove. I opened my mouth to call 'er, and all of a sudden, nothin' would come out.

"Now it wadn't anything I saw. Mercy—even now when I think of it, it wadn't anything I saw. But what I thought I heard. Even though I know good and well it couldn't be so. And I'm not even goin' to say—because you're a-livin' out here now and I shan't plant any scary notions in your head. I'll not say what it was. . . ."

I sewed on a few stitches. I was piecing something else together in my mind. Finally I said, "You don't have to say. That's all right. I'm not scared. I've heard it."

Nam's rocker stopped. "Since you been here?"

"Not here," I said. "If it's what I think, I heard it one night in Charleston. And that's how come me to be here."

She stared at me. It's the only time I ever saw her look afraid. "There are things about us I think we'll never understand," I said. Nothing horrible, I said, or anything of that sort.

"No," she said. "Just unspeakable."

We sat and sewed, quiet while fine rain fogged the windows.

"What did you do then?" I said finally. "What did you do with Daisy?"

"Well, I kept still, like my ear was glued to the air," Nam said. "And then I fetched a scream, I heard myself screechin', 'Daisy! Daisy!' She stopped stock still, I could see her white gown in the shadows sort of hovering. And then she turned around and come back up the hill, walking real slow, and tired, like a old widow-woman."

"Do you think she was walking in her sleep?" I said.

"Well! I sure wanted to think so. That's what I told her she was doing, she didn't act like she knew. I got 'er back in the house, and dried her feet, and put her back to bed with a hot water bottle. And then I laid there the rest of the night, a-studyin' what we must do.

"The next morning I talked straight to her. I had to get back up to the Forks. Arie was awful poorly, she'd had kidney trouble all her life and she was failin' right before our eyes. Ben Aaron was runnin' the mill all by himself, he couldn't afford help with the manage-ment, it was in such straits, and he was pushin' and sellin' hand over fist and havin' to oversee the whole works. I'd been a-cookin' for the hands, and keepin' the books. Anyway, I said to Daisy, 'Daisy, you've got to come home, now, you can't stay down here by yourself an-other minute.'

"And she looked at me, the gentlest, the sweetest, and she said, 'Panammer, I AM at home. And I never am goin' to be by myself.'

"Well, the hair of my head practically stood on end. I told her, 'I've got to go up to the Forks this morning, I've got to see about Arie and I want you with me; let's get up your stuff and go.'

"She said, then, well, would I mind if she stayed that day and sorted and put stuff away and strawed over her flowers and things she wanted to do if she was to stay gone awhile. I didn't like it, but I said, well, if it would make her better satisfied, some of us would be back by dark, then, to get her.

"She looked at me just as straight and sensible, and she said, 'You mustn't worry to get here till morning. I can come in the morning, ever' bit as well. It's you that's scared out here—not me.'

"I hitched up the buggy then and came home. When I got there, Arie was down. The doctor was there, he took me aside and said she was goin' to have to stay off salt and meat and stay in bed, and what's more, I was to watch 'er, for she would bait up on anything she wadn't supposed to have, and then she would swell. Daisy was always impish and devilish and stubborn; Arie was just stubborn.

"Along late in the afternoon Arie took a terrible headache and her eyes got puffy. Ben Aaron had promised to go to Red Bank that night, he didn't hardly get to go anywhere at all, but that little old Allie Tatum, I don't know what become of that child but she was wild crazy over Ben Aaron, and she'd hinted and wheedled him to take 'er to that dance, and finally he had said he would.

"When he saw how things were, he said well, he'd just back out. But I told him no, Arie would probably get better, it was Daisy giving me the jitters, and that I had said we'd get' 'er, sometime that evenin'. I never let on about her roamin' like she'd done. Well, then, he said he'd take the buggy, Allie would like that anyway, and goin' down he'd stop and see about Daisy, and pick 'er up on the way back, that night.

"He did stop, said she was just a-clickin' her heels all about, coverin' the furniture, packin' stuff she wanted him to send a wagon for, and he said she told him please not to try to get back early, that it would be morning, at the soonest, when she'd be ready to come. He told her then that he'd look for a light when he come by, coming back, to be sure she was all right."

Aunt Nam rocked on a little bit. She took off her glasses and wiped her eyes and snuffed into her apron.

"While they were in Red Bank, there come up a tremendous rain, and wind. When they come back up the road, Ben Aaron said there was a light, all right. The front of the house was afire. He jumped down, there was a horsetrough between the corner of the porch an' the road, and it was full, and he grabbed the bucket and commenced to run and fling water on the fire; it hadn't spread but around the front door. And he got it out."

The bushes were tapping on the window, in the wind. We

needed a lamp; it was most too dark to sew. Anyway I had quit.

"Where was Daisy?" I said.

Nam had to rock a little bit before she could say. "She was down in the river. It was the next day when they found 'er. And she looked just like a child."

~24~

THE BALLAD LADY

THE COLD OF THAT WINTER WAS SOMETHING I WAS NO WAY READY for. The wind howled up and down these ridges day and night. The laurels huddled their leaves tight and mourned. Now, this house was built as sheltered as a house could be, up here, but a trip to the barn, or lots worse, to the privy, was something to put off as long as we could.

When it would snow, that helped. Maybe it was insulation. Maybe it just covered up the bare and made the cold count for something. It was not just that it was terrible outdoors; going from room to room was awful, too. Everything we did had to be done within about three feet of the stove or the fireplace.

It seemed to bother the kids a lot less than it did me. Oh, Pet could fuss about it, but she got up in the mornings and went on to school with the Wilcoxes and survived very well. I think the worst of my misery was in being forsaken. I even felt deserted when Hugh insisted that he wanted to go back to school. He felt perfectly fine and got very tired of being wrapped up by the stove. Ans Shuman said he could do anything but go swimming in the river. Of course he was well; I just liked to have some other soul in the house that I could talk to.

At the heart of bad matters, Ben Aaron had not been here in several weeks. He had not been here since we went to cut the Christmas tree. I had not seen him at all since we all had dinner at Nam's on

New Year's Day. I knew very well what had transpired. Nam had put the fear of God in him. She was right, I couldn't deny that. And I loved her and needed her. But I had to watch to keep the bitter off my tongue when she and I would be with one another. I suffered. And I couldn't talk about it.

Coy Ray would come and bring anything from town that we needed. It was too cold to go to town on the mule, too much trouble, too; the poor old thing would follow the sun around the barn and that was as far as it would move. The weather never seemed to faze Coy Ray much though. He had a tattered old lumberjack he wore when it was a blizzard blowing or something but most times he went without a coat; he bragged that he slept on the ground many a time with no blanket, and thick frost on his clothes.

Well, along the end of January I guess, Coy Ray had this little good luck. He won a pen of late-spring pigs from some old man in a card game at the Forks. It was good luck on top of bad; his sow had run off with this old bandit of a wild hog that roamed the riverside. The wicked thing had collected itself a real harem over the years. Somebody was always pretending to hunt it but I think they hoped not to meet it, for it was quick to take offense. Coy Ray said he had heard folks say it was big as a bear but he said, "I've seed the thing and that ain't so, it may be MOST as long as a bear but half of that is its tushes."

Anyway, he brought his "winnings" home. And then he got to thinking about how he would feed three hogs through the winter. And he decided he would pen the two boar shoats and fatten them a few days, and he brought the pretty little gilt down to me. She was pinky-white with shadow spots, and she had a nice smile, and Coy Ray built a snug pen with a nice southern exposure. The day he butchered the other two I went up to his place, with a queasy stomach, to help Rose. Coy Ray killed 'em and put 'em in the scald barrel and Rose and I scraped 'em and cleaned the guts and the little boys got the bladders. Coy Ray tried to give me a bladder-balloon tied on a stick to take home to Pet and Hugh but I declined. It hurt my belly down low just to think about it.

We had started real early, just when it got light enough to work. I got the kids up for school, although Rose and hers were staying home to help with the pigs. It had turned off a really lovely day, sunny and calm, really nice, one of the "take hope" days of February. It was along in the afternoon when I went home, time for the kids to get home from school. I stopped at the spout and washed off what I could of the hog blood and smell on my hands and arms but it was too cold for much; I figured I would heat up a tub and scour myself. When I went in the back door the stove was going and the kettle was on. I thought how nice, the kids had thought of me. I took off my muddy shoes and went barefooted through the house looking for them.

There was somebody talking in the parlor. Not a familiar voice at all. A lady, plainly a Yankee, was saying, "While we are waiting for your mother, could you possibly sing a song for me? Could you perhaps sing a song your grandmother sang to you?" It stopped me in my tracks, out of sight. I wondered what they would do. I could hear them mumbling, consulting with one another. And then they started to sing. Or Pet "beed the piano," as they used to say, she improvised the piano part, mocking every turn and trickle of the "brook." And Hugh did the melody line: "Das Wandern ist des Müllers Lust, das Wannn-dern! Das Wandern ist des Müllers Lust, das Wann-dern!" Forgive me, for they were my children, but they had beautiful little voices.

I had to see that lady's face. And I don't know which was the biggest jolt, Schubert lieder back in this cove, or me with the hog blood all over me. I don't think I even registered, right at first. Her mouth fell open. She stared from behind her big glasses from them to me. She dropped her pencil. "Schöne Müllerin," she said, sort of breathless.

"Do you want to hear the next one?" Pet said. They were beaming. They were enjoying it. "Yes yes," the lady said, kind of weak. "Sing me the next one. No, wait!"

I will not forget how she looked. She had very blond hair, almost white, done up in a knot at the back of her head. She had on some riding pants and a fine sweater. She was tall and refined, a gentle-looking person, not terribly young. Or some older than I, I thought. Her hands were trembling. She groped around in her pack and brought out a flute case, and put the flute together. And she said no more, but started to play "the next one," she played the rushing brook part, very softly, and Pet commenced to sing, and Hugh picked up with her, and I stood there biting my lip. It was a kind of joy that can't be put in words. At the end she and I looked at one another and dissolved into tears.

Her name was Leonora Liebman. She was from New York. She had been teaching music at some little college in New England, and the school had met its last full payroll Christmas week. she did not want to go home and sit down on her family; they had pressed her to marry well and be secure. She had a friend, though, who had a little money and a dabbling interest in doing a book on ballads. And this friend had hired her to go about the country and pick up what she could, getting people to sing.

She had found her way, by some error, to Caney Forks, where she inquired at the store and met a tall and attractive fellow there (in her words), a Mr. Steele. He had offered her "a dope" and some crackers, and they had sat by the stove at the store, and they had talked. He was not much at the old ballads himself, he had told her modestly. But, down at the old home place, he had a cousin. "My cousin and her kids know the oldest songs you'll ever hear," he said, and she reported, when she was sure I would not take offense.

"Well, you just met the biggest liar you'll ever see," I said.

She smiled a wide smile. That illegitimate, I thought. Sending that poor woman on such a wild goose chase. When Pet brought in the tea I excused myself and washed as quickly as I could and got on clean clothes. When I got clean I felt more charitable. I saw things a little better. Cousin Ben Aaron had done something he thought was kind. He had sent me somebody I could talk with, about things I had not yet heard anybody talking about in Caney Forks. He saw that this lady was lonely and weary; he knew she had been out batting about in the cold, among strangers, for weeks and weeks. Good heavens, how nice and thoughtful of him. I wished I could hug him. Oh, I did.

We got us up some supper and sat down by the fire, she and I, after the kids went on to bed. She was naturally curious. "Where did your children learn . . . ?" she started out, and I laughed, and I said, "From their granny." They sang the stuff they did, as a matter of course, the same way a Baptist preacher's children would sing "Bringing In The Sheaves," I said. It was what they had grown up with; they were great little parrots, they didn't have an idea in the world what they were singing. Or I don't reckon they did. It was a sharp reminder to me, when I thought of it, how much they had stayed with my mother, and what a sparse little homelife they had had with me.

Of course that part I didn't go into, with Nora. Or not right away. She wanted to know what we were doing up here. Explaining that, I said, was a right big order. I said for the moment I would rather hear about the world outside and she told me things that were happening in New York, who was singing what and playing where, and dancing. Diaghilev had died that summer, she said; the ladies in white dresses, as I would always think of them, were fluttering about and lighting in other companies, for Diaghilev's Ballets Russes had died, too. We talked until she nodded off to sleep, in her chair. She was exhausted. She was a shy, sensible and sensitive creature, moving about in this foreign land lost and in the dark. I put her to bed with a warm brick at her feet and a feather bed for cover. And I went then and crawled in with Pet and I was up from the depths for the first time in weeks.

We talked three days. Nora would never quite be satisfied that we were staying here. She was awfully concerned about the children's future; she was pretty taken with them. And they were too, with her. She had not been a ballad collector long enough (and I thought never would be) to see the value in what this part of the universe had to teach. She showed me some notation she had taken, a couple of places where she had been. I read it as accurate to the last slide and whang but figured she had no more idea what the singing was about than the kids understood "Die Schöne Müllerin." No, much less; at least the kids had caught the spirit.

I wished with all my heart that Ben Aaron would come and play for her. That, I think, would have opened her ears. But he didn't show; he had done his social part by sending her. So there was no way, I supposed, that I could make it clear. You had to hear; it had to breathe on some special nerve. And this, I thought, may not be a universal nerve. Maybe it is peculiar to us, and our kind, in this place.

The last day she was here she said wistfully that she would so love to really earn her pay, small though it was. She wanted to bring back something that would thrill her mentor, even if it didn't do much for her. I said well, I didn't know much about these songs, for I had missed out on the whole lives of my ancestors who did know them. Or I guessed they did, who can be sure? "Have you heard this?" I said. And I sang to her about the unfaithful wife of the house carpenter, and the pitiful end she came to in her lover's leaky boat.

"Where did you learn that?" she said, going for her note-book.

"I learned it in the blackberry brambles, early, early of a morning, in the fog," I said. And I sang to her about the wife who ran off with Black Jack Davey, and the squire who came a-ridin' after her, trying to get her to come home. I sang her things I learned from the river; from somewhere many years away, the river brought them back. And songs the bees sang to me, in my sleep, and songs the wind would sing on the stove pipe, when I would doze off in the rocking chair, sometimes.

And it didn't surprise me that she looked at me real strangely, but with more understanding than I would ever have hoped, from someone from outside. For she had stayed in this house three days, and she took down her notes quite seriously, and accepted.

She left out for Red Bank; she needed to get to the post office to mail her notebook in before she started out again.

I cried after her, as her horse went off down the road and out of sight. I cried for everything I had known and been and for delicacy and silk and perfume and people who wore tailed coats and played the violin. I cried for Mit to hold me, and to hear my mother sing. The chill closed in. I was lonely to the core.

In just a few days though I had a note from Nora, written in Knoxville. She had heard from the man she worked for, she said. He had written as soon as he had got her notes. "He was positively elated with what I got from you," she said. "He said, 'This material is clearly very old, and uncorrupted.' I must never tell him that you learned it from the berries and the bees."

She said, too, that somehow she had begun to feel differently about "the culture" around here. Maybe there was much more here than met the casual eye and ear. I did not tell her, when I wrote her immediately back, that I had begun to see things differently myself. She had been right. The children were bright and deserving. It was not fair to isolate them here, however happy they might seem to be at times. Or how happy I might have been, one time or another. As for that part, it was all past. The times ahead, the way things were, looked as bleak as these icy hillsides in the wind. She had been right. As soon as I could work it out, we would be gone.

~ 25 ~

THE FOGGY DEW

THERE WAS A CERTAIN PLEASURE IN NURSING THAT RESOLUTION through the cold of early March, through the misery of ice and freeze and lonesomeness. And then there was a thaw. The sun shined warm and the spring beauty budded, down in the woods. The bulb things and the violets poked up to see if it meant it. Certainly it didn't; spring never means it, quite, before way into April up here.

But there was something about it. There was a wave of restlessness that rippled over everything. The bare trees sighed. The mule brayed. The pig ran up and down in her pen; she would put her little feet up on the boards of her fence, and put her nose through, and squeal to get attention.

One evening then a cloud swept down, on a gale of cold wind, and it rained in the night, and the next morning was clear and the rain had frozen on the bushes and brush and trees and the sun shined on it like it was millions of diamonds. It was magic. It made you feel like your eyes could not be big enough to see it all.

It was a feeling, too; I moved about real slow, that morning early. We had a fire of cobs and little sticks because we hadn't brought in wood. We needed to split some stove wood and everything was damp. We had just fire enough for breakfast. And I didn't care. I flopped around, sighing; I didn't go out to the barn until the kids were gone. And I dawdled around at that; I put on my camisole and step-ins and petticoat and cotton stockings, and looked at myself in the glass and fiddled with my hair. It was cold as Christmas in there but I had a sort of swelled feeling just below my ribs and it spread out warm, in both directions. I put on my dress and smiled. I thought I might ride into town.

Well, I went flouncing out to the lot, going *la-la-la,* and the chickens came clucking and the mule snorted. But there was no pig. There was a hole under the wire. Signs of furious digging on both sides. Tracks all around. Piggy had rooted out, with some help. She had not gone by herself.

There was a little stab of ice in the breeze. I went in the house and got on an old wrapper and a shawl to put over my head, and started up the river. I decided that was where I would go if I were a pig in a romantic condition. Oddly I was not mad at her at all. I smiled to myself; it takes a heifer, I thought, to take sides with a hot pig. The river was up and rolling. It was cold and cloudy with silt. I didn't like to look at it.

The narrows were roaring. Long before I could see them there was silty foam bobbing on the current. Patches of ice slicked the trail. As I went by the narrows on that little ledge of rock I pulled the wrapper around me and made myself tall and looked down at the river boiling and I said to it, I am not afraid of you. It was too extraordinary a day to be afraid of anything.

It was good I had to mind where I stepped; right there on the rock there was a pile of pig-doo, untidy and still very fresh. I was walking along, then, as happy as ever could be, and I came up at the bridge on the road to Coy Ray's.

There was a meadow on the far side of the river; it was a field of mossy rocks over there and clumps of laurel and huckleberry bushes. I was standing there thinking what a nice place for a pig tryst when I heard a horse behind me. I turned around and there was my cousin Ben Aaron. He pulled up, there, and just sat looking. And I stood there looking. And finally he said, not terribly kindly, "What are you doing up here?"

And I started to tell him. But I did not, right off. Instead I looked him long in the eye and said, "I am looking for you."

"Have you got nothing better to do?" he said.

"I ought to be looking for my pig," I said.

"Where is your pig?" he said.

"If I knew would I be looking?" I said. I stood my ground. He tapped Cy with the reins and rode on up on the bridge.

"Lookin' for a pig can be perilous business," he said, a little softened.

"Where are you going?" I said. He didn't answer.

"Here," he said, "come on and I'll help you if I can." He got down and swung me up on the back of the horse, and got on in front of me. It was not very comfortable back there; Cy's rump was as broad as a dinner table and there I sat behind the saddle with my legs sticking out. How odd. But I put my arms around Ben Aaron's waist politely.

"You looked on the other side, I guess," he said.

"Yes, and I saw sign," I said. He lit a cigarette and sat there blowing smoke. Finally he nudged Cy's ribs and started off down into that meadow. We went very slowly, and perfectly quiet, down the river, stopping to look through the bushes. We saw more sign. "It's several," he said, "or else that's one shittin' pig." We went along and directly we began to see rooted-up places. There was the head of a snake in one of 'em. There was a little dip ahead, a sheltered place warm in the morning sun. Very slowly we went to where we could look down. There were half a dozen grown hogs and some little ones, lying down there stretched out after breakfast. Mine wasn't there. Ben Aaron leaned back and whispered, "Ain't all of 'em. The old man ain't home."

It suddenly dawned on me that I was where the saddlebag and rifle ought to be. If we met the old man, we didn't have a thing to use to reason with him. I got bristles of my own, on top of my head. "Let's just go," I said. He eased Cy back up out of the pigs' sight, and started back up the river.

"I'll get Coy Ray to come down with me and we'll get 'er," he said.

We had gone just a few yards when Cy stopped and flung his head and snorted. There was this thrashing in the bushes and all of a sudden here came the ugliest creature I ever saw in my life. It did look big as a bear except it wasn't as fat, it was just a mean dark wedge of ugly, with little bitty eyes and elephant teeth that crossed.

"Woop!" Ben Aaron said, jerking straight up. Cy started jittering and dancing like I had never known him to have the energy to do.

The thing was coming full speed. "Hol' on, Sen," said Ben Aaron. He cracked Cy on the flank with the flat of his hand and headed into the river. Without any doubt it was the best thing to do; a spavined horse carrying over three hundred pounds was not going to outrun that thing. A scared horse would throw off three hundred pounds and head for cover. Cy was terrified. He plunged into the water, it was about up to his belly, and started across. And he had got out into the current, and his hind feet must have slipped on the rocks. Or else he had a cramp; the water was so cold it burned. And down he went, backwards. I don't know how I turned loose of Ben Aaron. I don't know a thing about what happened there. I hit the water and the shock of it took my wind. I remember being tumbled about like a rag and being snatched up.

The first thing I sort of knew was being held tight to Ben Aaron, in his arms, going by the narrows, going home. My teeth were chattering like a woodpecker. Ben Aaron was wet too, so he was not much warmth. Cy was so cold he moved in slow motion, shuddering: Every breath of the wind was misery. I remember getting warm and drowsy, as we passed the cemetery. I remember Ben Aaron shaking me, and rubbing my arms. I was vaguely aware of the barn, then, and coming up to the front porch.

He left Cy there, in the sun and out of the wind, and carried me in the front door and back to Daisy's sitting room; most times I had a little fire in there. There was not any, that morning. There was not any wood inside. He set me down in a chair and snatched up that quilt I had just taken off the frame, and wrapped me in it. He went to the kitchen and brought back the bucket of cobs, and lit them in the fireplace and plopped me on the hearth. He ran outside, then, and I heard him chopping like a mad man, and directly he came in with a great armload of wood and kindling, and he fed the fire and got it roaring.

I guess I must have looked blue. He got down with me and took off that wet wrapper. That dress I had on was buttoned with a dozen little buttons, up the front. My hands were shaking so I couldn't help myself at all. So he started under the chin and unbuttoned me like I was a child. And I held up my arms and he pulled off the dress, over my head, and he pulled off that sopping petticoat, and wrapped that quilt around me, and then he got down and took off my shoes. There

I sat, in my underwear and stockings. He turned around to the fire and said, "I won't look. You need to get 'em off."

Well, I managed to get rid of the stockings and he sat down there on the hearth and commenced to rub my feet. He was wet to the skin himself. The steam was rising off his jacket. "Did you swallow any water?" he said. "Get any up your nose?"

I was real surprised when I thought of it. "No," I said, "I think I must have quit breathing. But I got ice rattling in my ears."

"How do you feel?" he said. I remember how his face looked, with the firelight flickering on it. This was a different creature, all serious and intent. His hair was all rumpled. He had lost his hat. My own hair was stuck wet to my face. I pushed it back and pulled the quilt around me. I was about to quit shaking.

"I feel really good," I said. "I wish you would get that wet stuff off of you. You must be nearly dead."

He got up and took off his jacket; I remember he had on a red-checked wool shirt under it. And he took off his boots; they squished when he pulled 'em off. He sat back down, then, and took up rubbing my feet. He had the most marvelous hands of any human being I ever knew. There was a big vocabulary in those hands. He stopped and fished around in his jacket pocket for a cigarette. The pack leaked when he pulled it out. There was a little flat can of tobacco though, that had kept miraculously dry, and he got out his pipe and stuck a twig in the fire and lit it, and sat down, puffing away, and rubbed my feet some more.

It was very quiet. The wind was scratching the window with the sweet bubby bush. Ive's clock chimed ten. Finally, he said, "Are you sure you're all right?"

"Ask me a little bit later," I said.

"Will you be all right while I go get some wood?" he said. And he went out and chopped some, and came back very quickly. When he sat down again, I put the quilt around him, too, for his shirt was still wet and cold. We sat very still, there, and very quiet, in the perfume of wet wool and wet leather, looking into the fire. I put my hand on his arm, once, and he was rigid.

"Well," he said directly, "if you are going to be all right I will go on." He sounded hoarse. His voice was much too high and funny.

"You are too wet to go anywhere," I said. "You will be sick." But he put off the quilt, and he got up, and started to get on his boots. "Don't do that," I said. He looked down at me with this soft look. And I got up and put my arms around him. "Don't do that," I said. He stood there stiff as a poker, not hugging back. I laid my ear on his chest and listened to his heart. It was like a gourd rattle.

"I've got to go right now," he said. I did something that I never in all my life would have thought I would do. I slipped my hand down the front of his shirt, and down under his belt. It was like I had shot him. He shuddered and let out this little cry; it was like the dying wail of a rabbit in the jaws of the fox. I thought, oh, God, what have I done? But he didn't back off. He let his arms fall sort of limp around me, and laid his cheek down on my head. And I began to unbutton his shirt. Slowly, my hands were shaking so. And he did nothing but breathe, breathe, while I undid the buckle of his belt. I slipped up his undershirt and laid my face on that skin. I can't say what it was like to put my mouth on him; it wouldn't do. It was like moving in a dream; slowly and deliberately I undid the buttons and pulled away the wet clothes, and he let me. And when I had rid him of them all I could only look into his face; it was what I wanted, to look into his face, and I just held him like that, and looked up at him, and it was the tenderest face, it was like he would melt and run down.

The rest of it happened much too fast. I must not say too much about how it was, except that it was not easy. There was a minute or two that I wondered if I would live through it. And that didn't much matter, I decided, at the time. But when he had done what it was he had been so determined he would never do, he rolled over and held me on top of him, and smoothed my hair. And he said, "Well, that is the second time today I guess you thought I was try-ing to kill you." If it was so he was not very repentant; he lay there with his eyes half-closed, looking at me, half smiling. I traced his mouth with the tip of my finger and thought how perfect he was, and how gracious in defeat.

"If you were, you did not do very well. You will have to try again," I said. And, in a little while, he did. A lot more like somebody in love. There had never been (as far as I would know) anything quite like it. The thought flitted through my mind, like a mouse across the tea table, that he knew a great lot about women, somehow. I ran out my tongue wondering how much of it he learned from Sophier. And then I didn't care. I didn't care if he learned it from a monkey. My cousin, the prism, I thought, just drifting. Every way you turn him, some new light. Dazzling, mesmerizing, weightless, blinding. There was nothing in the world but his breathing, and that light. It seems like after that we must have slept a while. I know he raised up once and threw some wood on the fire.

The next thing, the clock was striking twelve. There was something doleful in its tone of voice. Ben Aaron sat up and felt around for his pipe. He stood up then and got his tobacco and stuffed it and lit it solemnly. I watched him, every move. I was thinking, what immortal hand or eye had shaped something so lovely. He stood there bare as the day he was born, one foot cocked over the other, studying the wallpaper.

Finally, without looking at me, he said, "Sen, you are the victim of a terrible fraud, my dear."

"You never told me you loved me," I said, teasing.

"I've not told you the truth about a lot of things," he said. He blew a long slow puff of smoke. "I've not told you the truth about this place," he said. "I didn't have the guts."

"Guts never appealed to me all that much," I said, "I kind of like legs."

He wouldn't be amused. "I made you think we own it. It's not so."

"Daisy owns it," I said, "You didn't have to tell me that. It don't bother me."

"Daisy owns it, all right," he said. "But she ain't got a deed that would ever hold up in court."

"What do you mean, then?" I said. He was beginning to make me real uneasy. "If it's not ours then whose is it?"

He heaved a deep sigh. "Sophier's," he said.

Sophier's. I could see old Sofa again, big as life, waving her pink-gloved hand over "one of my favorite properties." And all this time I thought she was just blowing. "Sophier's," I said.

He looked at the ceiling. "And her sister's. . . ."

"How? In the name of God will you tell me how?" I said.

The house creaked in the wind, like it was cringing. He sat down and draped a corner of the quilt across him, modestly. One by one he inspected his fingers. "I think I told you once . . ." he started out, and stopped to clear his throat. "I think I told you we were just a jump ahead of the wolves, up at the mill, when your ma put this place up for sale," he said.

"Yes, you did," I said. "And I asked you where you got the money. You never told me what magic trick you turned. I bet you never did this one with a deck of cards." I was getting loud. I felt hysterical. I was crushed.

"Did I ever tell you I was Pure-Peter John?" he yelled back. "You're absolutely right. I sold my ass. Now. You go look out that door yonder and come back and tell me how low I am. Go up on the hill and tell it to my mamma and daddy. Tell it to Daisy and Ive."

"Tell 'em what?" I said. "Tell 'em, 'Folks, your very bones now belong to Sophier Orpington, whom you so dearly loved when she lived on your place?'"

He flung a chunk on the fire and sparks flew out all over the hearth. We sat there sulking, not touching, not even looking at each other, like two lumps of pain. Directly he maybe got over wanting to hit me. He sighed, finally, and commenced again.

"As I said, I had not two nickels to rub together in my pocket. And nowhere to get 'em. And maybe a day or two, or a week, to make that offer good, if your mother decided to call my hand. I had a bid ready to go off to Orpington Industries, they owned several furniture and veneer plants up north and I had sold to 'em before and I was trying to sell 'em again. I was not real crazy about the old man Orpington; he was a braggy old bastard. But he seemed to like to do business with me. When I'd go up there he'd always take me home with him.

"He had these two big old overstuffed gals. They had sat looking out the bay winder for Prince Charming so long that their fannies had taken root in the davenport.

"But to make it short, nothing worked. The night I was to leave up there they invited me to supper. While the old man and I were talking in the library, and I was getting nowhere, and feeling like absolute shit, I could hear Sophier and Patience in the next room havin' a hair-pull fight. One of 'em screeched at the top of her voice, "You ugly toad, he's asking Papa for ME!'

"And I said then, to the old man, 'Before I leave I'd like to talk to you about a loan. There's a place for sale that I know about, big house and a boundary of virgin timber. It will make a nice home for your daughter. . . .'

"I never asked Sophier to marry me at all. I never even said which one. The old man called Sophier in, and congratulated us from the bottom of his heart, and Patience flammed the wall with her fists and wailed. Sophier, you see, was the oldest one; Sophier was older than God.

"I left there in a half an hour's time with a loan in my hand and a ring through my nose for the rest of my life." He hushed and put his head in his hands and sat still for a while. Finally he said, "Sen, can you believe I did that?"

I didn't know what to answer him. I moved over and put my arm around him and held him to me.

"Now, in a little while I brought Sophier on down here," he said. "She was insulted at this place right off and let me know it. But I put every waking hour nearly into that mill. We started shipping lumber out of here. We hustled like hell. I got out and went to the plants and we got lumber moving. The old man did bring one outfit to Virginia and we had a good contract from them. We moved day and night; I put on men that hadn't worked in years and we skinned the big stuff off the mountains with steers all day and we'd use some of the same help to run the mill at night.

"Soph's old daddy sold me some equipment, 'course on a credit; I bought a steam tractor for road work. And that big old thing that scared you so bad, we'd run it in the deep snow, Lord, nothin' kept us out of the woods. We made money. Sophie helped herself and had her a house built, you know, to her own tastes. I kept out of that except to hand out money. It kept her occupied. And I paid her daddy on the dot. Ever' three months I made a big payment on what I owed him.

"And then, come the summer of 1916, the river wiped us out. It came out all over the town. It got all the lumber we had sawed. Took the log piles. Took the sheds, and all the machinery it didn't take it buried in the mud. It took a locomotive and washed it way downstream. I stood up there on the hill, where Ans and Myrtle live now, and I watched it go. I thanked God we had enough money in the bank at Red Bank to meet the payroll a few more weeks at least. But there was not a stick of lumber much bigger than your thumb to meet the orders we already had.

"Well, we went to work on it. We cleaned dead fish and chickens out of the kiln house, that was most of what we had left. I set out to borrow what I could but ever'body in the mountains nearly was ruined and borrowing.

"It didn't make it any better," he said in a smaller voice, "that Sophier and I were at cross purposes lots of the time. She is . . . watchful, you might say. She had it in mind that I needed to be watched. I know good and well, because of that, she engineered the next that happened."

"Something bad," I said.

"Worse," he said. "The second payment I missed the old man sent me a notice of foreclosure. And there wasn't one damn thing I could do. Every cent that came in had to go for new machinery and the payrolls. I had borrowed every dime that Aunt Nam had. There wasn't a thing on earth I could do but let him have it."

"Oh my God," I said. "It's a wonder he didn't sell it to a stranger just for spite."

"Well, he didn't because he had a heart attack a few weeks after that, and he lay an invalid, with Sophier hoverin' over 'im, till finally he had another one and died. And Sophier came home fannin' a deed to The Birches. Now, he never left it just to her. He figured—she figured—I would switch around and get ahold of it, if it was just in her name. No. He left it to her and that raspin' old wall-eyed sister of hers—jointly. It give 'em somethin' to get along over, for a change."

"Would they sell it?" I said.

"Lord no. They'll not sell it to anybody. For they know I'll go right behind 'em and buy it back, even at twice the price. And they'll surely not sell it to me. You ought to know I've tried. Ever since we got out from under the flood we've made money here hand over fist. Most of what's in our bank here's mine. And of course Sophier's too, though. What would she gain to sell this place to me? She's got me like a snake in the fork of a stick."

He was the picture of resigned despair, sitting there looking into the fire. I wanted so bad to gather him up and somehow make it all right. Any notion I might have had about staying on here was dead and cold, but it was not my plight that broke my heart, it was his.

"What are we going to do?" I said. He seemed to be studying.

Finally he said, "About what?"

"About you and me," I said. I was a little bit astonished. He studied some more. "Oh, I don' know," he said. "I don' know. What is there to do?"

"We can leave here," I said. "We can just go away. We can go some-place far away and start all over."

"Leave here?" he said, like he hadn't heard right. "What would go with it?"

"Let Sophier have it. Let her worry about it," I said. "After all," I said, sort of mean, "it's HERS."

He didn't answer that, he just sat there blank and glum. "Look," I said, "Sophia has got one thing in the world that I can't live with-out. And that's you."

He gave me this older-and-wiser sweetbody look. "I think you are wrong, my dear. On one count and possibly two," he said. I was try-ing to figure that out when he went on. "Now, of course we could leave here. But you'll have to tell me where we will go, and what we will do. Oh, I could sign on as a logger somewhere. If I could find a camp besides my own that's working, anywhere in the country. For that matter we could find a place we liked and go on the county. You ready to go on the county and get some welfare?" He smirked and reached over and patted my leg. "You're already supportin' one sorry man right now, little sister. Don't tell me you're tryin' for two."

"I would give you anything I had on this earth," I said, "and I'd think I was lucky if you'd take it."

"I know it," he said. "But you've got the kids to think about, too. And I've got mine. . . ." The memory of him spooning food for that girl and wiping dribbles rose up and smote me. I remembered something Nam had told me, too. She said he dressed Celestine all the time, when she was little; that he had taught her to dress herself, somewhat, while her mother insisted she was hopelessly helpless. That he still read to her every night, at bedtime.

"There is something else," Ben Aaron said, considering his fingers. "There are about two hundred men up there at the Forks that are living off that mill. And most of 'em have families. The whole town lives off that mill. How long, my love, do you think that thing would run, this day and time, if I were gone?"

I felt terribly cold and forlorn. I pulled the quilt around me and talked down into it. "I don't care," I said in the smallest voice. I can see his face now. It was tender and loving and absolutely tragic. It has haunted me ever after.

"Oh, YES you care," he said. "You wait and see how much you care." He reached over then, and pulled away the quilt, and looked at me again, the longest time. His eyes were shimmering. And finally he said, "Beautiful," under his breath. And he reached for his shirt then, and started to put it on. And I could not bear it. I held out my arms to him, and brought him down again. And it was different, it was like a solemn ritual, of some kind, and I was not sure if the damp his face left on mine was sweat or tears. I thought how strange, for I was so happy; I would never get tired of him, there would never be enough of him, and if I could not have him rightly—which of course I could not—then I would simply have him wrongly. I had found it could be done. Lightning had not struck. By dang I would have him every day.

I could only guess, and I suppose be thankful, that at that tenderest moment he was not so carried away as I was. For all of a sudden he untangled himself. Vaguely, I think I heard Cy neigh a time or two, but it meant nothing to me. Ben Aaron hopped up like he was shot out of a gun. He practically jumped into his britches and crammed his underwear as an afterthought into the front of his shirt. The front door was creaking open when he threw my clothes down on me and bundled me like a package in the quilt. He was the picture of composure when the kids walked in the room.

"Your mother has been swimming in the river," he said, before Pet could open her mouth. "Go get some kindling and get a fire in the stove, and get the teapot on," he said. "I'm coming out to cut some wood." It was a firm and direct and purposeful speech. They put down their sweaters and their books and made speed to do as they were told. Rose had stopped by with them. She lingered, for a minute, in the doorway. Rose could put on a look like when you throw a coverlet over an unmade bed. Her face was totally blank. But there was plenty behind it.

"Florine Todd got sick at dinnertime today," she said, expressionless. "Mr. Sutherland turned school out. He had to take her home." I could feel her eyes seeing everything that had happened in that room. But then she was gone, back to the kitchen.

"Get on your clothes," Ben Aaron said, under his breath. He jerked on his boots, and he bent down and kissed me, quickly. And in the door he turned back and gave me one last soft look, and he was gone.

I could hear the axe flailing away at the woodpile. I heard him talking to Hugh; I heard him say goodbye to the kids at the side of the house, and the muffled clumping of hooves. I had my dress on. The rest I would hide in the quilt. We had made a pretty bad mess of that quilt. If I could wash it, privately, somehow, right now the stains would come out, I thought. If they dried they might never. I ran my hand over the splotches, and folded it up, and put it away. Hugh came in with a load of firewood and went back to get some pieces for the stove. I sat still, in front of the fire. It seemed like the prudent thing to do.

Shortly Pet and Rose came in with a cup of tea. Dutifully I started to tell them about chasing the pig, and meeting the boar, and getting in the river. And happily Pet, especially, was not near so impressed with my mishap as she was with Florine Todd's.

"Myrtle Mae said Florine was having a baby," she said, still in awe. "We were going in to get our lunch buckets and she was right in front of me and she started to wet the floor. Do you wet the floor when you have a baby?" she asked Rose.

"You wet the floor sometimes if you're just sick," Rose said kindly.

"Well, Myrtle Mae said she saw her in the privy the other day and she had her stomach all wrapped 'round and 'round with rags." So there was a topic that was a handy distraction, although it was horribly sad. Cole Sutherland came down that evening, still shaking, and told me very privately that he had delivered a baby, a stillborn little boy, on the floor in the school house just minutes after the kids had started home. The mother, who was fourteen, had gone through months of agony wrapped in rags.

But I admit I thought of something else, in the night. I kept an ear to the road. Were I Ben Aaron Steele, I thought, I would come in the night and take what was so blissfully given. Once, sometime, I thought I heard somebody coming. I listened, not breathing, until the quiet put me back to sleep. In the morning, when I went out to the lot, the pig was in her pen. She was a quiet, serious pig, either sulking or penitent. I don't know. There were big rocks jammed in her exit under the fence, and the prints of horse-hooves in the mud.

～26～

RAPIDS

ALL DAY THAT NEXT DAY I KEPT MY EAR COCKED. YOU CAN'T believe the things that will sound like a horse coming, when you want that horse to come. And then I thought maybe it will not be a horse next time, maybe it will be the wagon. Maybe an old truck. I was good for not one thing all that day. I just sighed out to the hog lot and dawdled to the woodpile and the spout.

Along in the afternoon there was a rumbling up on the ridge. I knew it was a truck. I ran up and brushed at my hair and flipped on some powder and got down the stairs just in time to meet Bat Dung; he came to the door to let me know he was putting some bags of guano in the barn.

That evening I sat out on the banister at the side of the porch and watched the sun go down, in the cold. The kids thought I was odd. And in the night, once they were gone to bed, I went out several times and stood, and looked off into the dark, and listened. And the hoofbeats that stopped my breath were nothing but my teeth chattering.

The next day it was a Saturday. I remember it by how awful I felt. I hadn't hardly got to sleep; I had troubles that got me up in the night. And by day I was just miserable and I didn't know what to do. Well, I was sitting out on the edge of the back porch in the sun, all doubled up, and Rose came riding up across the field with a jug of milk. She got down and looked at me and didn't say a word, and I didn't say one either, and she came and sat down by me and put her hand on my forehead.

"Little bit warm," she said. "You got the sore throat?" No, I said. I told her the problem. I could feel that intent look, the look that could see all things. I couldn't look back; I studied the moss in the cracks of the old rock steps.

"You got the gravels," she said finally. She said it with no doubt, like she expected me to have the gravels. Honeymoon piss-itis. Oh, God, it was awful.

She went in the house and got the bucket and dipper. "You sit right here and drink water," she said. "That's what you do for the gravels. You drown 'em. It it was summer I'd fix ye some corn silk tea."

"I think maybe I ought to get Ans, if I can," I said. The idea of going over the ridge to the Forks gave me another chill. Rose got up and got the mule bridle in her hand. "We'll get him if we've got to get him," she said. There was something dubious about the way she said it—it was like her Uncle Ans would be the last resort. I felt so rotten she annoyed me. If you felt as rotten as I do you would holler for a doctor, I thought. I felt too rotten to say that. Or anything. Anyway she was getting on the mule and going off. Leaving me.

"I'll be back directly," she said. "We'll dig up somethin'. Now, you drink." I drank, resentful, and ran groaning to the privy. Several times. But here she came back, soon, with a bundle of some kind of vine; she washed the woods-dirt from it at the spout, broke off a piece, little pink flowers and all, and ordered, "Chew it."

"What is it?" I said, pouting.

"Trailin' arbutie," she said. "Mama used it." It smelt sweet. I chewed. Tasted . . . weedy. I had to drink water to get rid of the taste. Rose went in the house and I heard her stirring around in the kitchen. She came out and filled the water bucket and I heard her and the kids washing dishes. She brought out some hot "arbutie" tea; she had put honey in it so it wasn't so bad. Before she left to tend her own house, she had cooked food to last all day.

In an hour or less, I began to get easy. By the next day I was really all right. It was a good thing; there was so much that had to be thought through with a clear mind. I wondered whether Ben Aaron might know I had been sick. If by chance he did, he paid no attention. I did go up to the Forks and spent a day with Nam, made it a point to go around to the stores for little things. Nowhere did I see Ben Aaron. Nam said she thought he was on a round of the furniture plants. She didn't really know, she said. He had been strange. She hadn't seen him.

Coy Ray came down and put in the tobacco seed in the beds. I thought about telling him not to bother, we were leaving. But instead I stayed inside and didn't talk. The days were getting warmer. Everything was budding and greening.

I remember all too plainly the torment of that spring. On the one hand I was tempted to go to the Forks and sit on my cousin's doorstep till he came in. Or out. What would I say to him? I would say, "I will do anything in the world if you will just have me." Or, I would say, "You have treated me absolutely wicked. I would not have you on a Christmas tree unless you were hanging from the top limb, by a good stout rope." I thought about that a lot.

And on the other hand, I knew. I knew what I had to do was get my kids and myself out of here, as quickly and quietly as I could. I would have to give it up. I remember leaning on the porch post in the evening, watching the shadows fall on the road. It was so beautiful. "Der Mai ist kommen," I thought to myself. But I knew quite well that it just was not so.

Coy Ray plowed the cornfield, and the garden, and he went to the Forks for the seed. School turned out early so the kids could all help at home. They went as wild as bucks in May, anyway; it was no use to keep them. Mine were so happy I didn't know what to say to them. Rose had brought down a bunch of guinea eggs and a little hen to set, and they hatched out the prettiest little diddles, they ran like spiders. The Wilcoxes had a jackass colt they were breaking to ride. Hugh was crazy about it. I weighed in my mind every way I could tell them we were leaving.

One morning when the lilacs were just out I dragged out of bed, for I was not feeling very good. I came downstairs, and when I went to make up bread for breakfast there were bugs in what was left of the flour. We were about out of sugar. I knew I would have to go to town. It seemed like it was awfully warm for that time of year; the heat from the stove made my head swim. I fussed at the kids for bringing in eggs out of the fence rows. The ones I was cooking smelt like they had stayed in a nest way too long.

I left the kids to do the chores and took the mule and rode up to the Forks. It would have been as close to go down to Red Bank but I fooled myself that I wanted to go see Nam a little bit. I figured on it half-heartedly on the way up. I rode up to Tatum's. And when I went in the store, who should be leaning on the counter with a drink bottle in his hand but my cousin Ben Aaron Steele. I could feel the blood all leave my head. My knees got weak as water. I had to lean back on the door frame to keep from falling down. He raised up, like somebody had put a coal in his pocket, and stared at me, struck dumb as I was.

He looked bad; he looked hollow in the cheeks, and weary about the eyes. He had fallen away a noticeable lot, in that six or seven weeks. He left it to Grover to speak to me first, before he found his voice. "Well, howd-do, Miss Cousin," he said, at last.

"Howd-do sir," I said weakly. There was this silence. "What can I get ye t'day?" Grover said. And I told him what all I needed, measuring the money with my fingers in my pocket. And Grover went about to gather up the stuff. We just stood there looking at one another. "Have you been doing well?" said my Cousin Ben Aaron politely.

"Very well," I said. I knew I looked like death warmed over. I fought with myself. What I wanted was to fall on him; I wanted him to just hold me and let whatever had gone wrong be forgotten. But my feet had taken root. Grover laid the stuff up on the counter, and rang up what I owed, and shakily, I paid.

"You got a load, there, Cousin," Ben Aaron said. "You think you can get home with it?"

"Oh, yeah, I think maybe so," I said. I felt him not looking away. I didn't breathe, wondering what he was wanting to say. And he said, then, "Well, I could have one of the boys drive that stuff down to you, this evenin' sometime."

I can't tell what I felt right then. It was a fury like I never felt against any human being ever in my life. The bare nekkid rotten despisable idea. I didn't even say, no thank you. I seized up the flour sack from the counter, and slung it over my shoulder, and poor old

Grover, not knowing what was going on at all, followed meekly behind me with the rest of it in his arms, and he put the sugar over the mule's back, and then the flour, and handed me up, and the little bag of stuff, and I found my voice to thank him and rode off as fast as we could plod. Oh, I was so mad. I was so hurt. And so sick. Oh, Lord.

I got up as far as Boney Creek before I got off to puke. And I liked to have never got back on. I had a while to think about things, on the way home. I had a while to put things together. Dark thoughts came from all sides, like vultures. It was the blackest pit I ever was in, when I had to throw up in the chamber pot the next morning, before I was hardly out of bed. I told the kids I had eaten something that didn't set right with me.

After about a week of that Pet got real uneasy. I heard her tell Rose she thought they should get Aunt Nam. Or Ans. And Rose said maybe, later on, but she was sure it would work itself out. I had felt Rose looking at me. The blanker her face, the more I knew the wheels were grinding. I was too distraught to care. But she was so kind. She cooked and brought things. She taught the kids to help more than I had ever been able to. She went to the Forks and brought back a bottle of camphor, from the drugstore. When I smelled it, to please her, my daddy lay dead on the steps in front of me again. But I gritted my teeth and said it made me feel better. And later on, it did.

We went ahead and put the garden in; I did not know what else to do. By the time we put the tobacco in the field, in June, I was able to stoop over without losing my breakfast. I was glad of that; Coy Ray was there most every day and he would not have long been fooled. It was getting to be summer, and I still didn't know what in the world to do. Except pretend things were all right. Nam came down and we canned cherries and made strawberry jam. I didn't want to; I didn't want anything to do with any of it. I was not hungry and that I guess was a good thing; when my clothes should have been getting tight they hung on me like sacks.

All I wanted to do was sleep. Sometimes I wished I could sleep and not wake up. But when the house was still at night I would lie awake and think. All kinds of awful things can go through your mind when you are alone, in that kind of plight. Some grisly thing about knitting needles came back to haunt me. Something that had been whispered behind their hands by the ladies on the piazza one time. I did not know then what they meant that some poor girl did with a knitting needle—or was it a crochet hook? All that was plain was that she had died disgraced.

I didn't know much more, at thirty years old, about what she really did with it. But it was hideous to imagine. Quinine did not sound quite so bad. Miss Lilah had actually suggested that I ought to take quinine, to get rid of Hugh. Can you imagine? Foots took quinine for his ugly spells. It didn't do him any good. I didn't think it would do me any either. The colored people believed in turpentine. Camp's sister Lizzie told Mit one time, in the kitchen, that she had sat three mornings on a slop jar of steaming turpentine. Lizzie had a baby every spring. She must have had a dozen babies that smelt like turpentine.

All of this was just so many dark birds flying through my head on long dark nights. None of it was of any consequence at all. No way on earth was I going to do this baby any harm, even if I knew exactly how. It was, after all, Ben Aaron Steele's baby. I could lie there and stew over how despicably he had treated me. And how I hated him. And I would think, this baby will have eyes like his, and hands like his, and a dimple in its chin. It will be the most beautiful baby in this world, even with a nose as long as ours.

One night after we had hoed in the field about all day I was so tired I thought I would die, when I hit the bed. I lay there and thought, well, maybe if I would just die of overwork or anything at all, it would solve things. The children were going to have to go back to Charleston anyway. It would be better if I died before I disgraced them. I thought after I rested a while I might get up and go to the Narrows. I closed my eyes and could see the foam. I could hear the water, when I listened. And while I was so still, there, very quietly, like a little wren stirring in its nest, there was this fluttering in my belly. And it was like every other thought, and every sound and feeling stopped. In a minute it fluttered again. I put my hand down on it and felt it, it was more like a little trembling. It was alive. It was mine. Nothing could take it away.

We worked like horses, all of us. We had planted two acres more in tobacco than we had the year before and we had to keep the weeds out of it, and the worms off of it, and we had to top it. None of us liked to squash tobacco worms so Coy Ray fixed us each a can with some kerosene in it to drown them in, even though he said it was wasteful. Every morning we went out with our cans to harvest worms. Pet swore she could hear a tobacco worm chewing a hundred feet away.

She was less hurt, by far, than Hugh, when I finally talked to them about going back to Charleston. Cole was going to start school at Shiloh when the crops were laid by, along in August. We had to settle something. We sat down on the steps one evening, and I told them, as matter-of-factly as I could. First I said we would all go back. But I knew that was not so; it would not work out quite that way.

"I will stay here till the crops are all in and we sell the tobacco," I said. But they should go and get enrolled in school.

"What will you do with my guineas?" Pet said. Rose would take them back, I said. And she began to talk at once, then, about seeing her friends she had missed. And going to the candy shop, and the picture show and things. Hugh sat too still, with his elbows on his knees and his forehead in his hands.

"Sofa is running us off," he said, in a quavery voice. I could see the tears making channels in the dirt down his arms. No, I said. Sofa had really done nothing. It was just time to go. I said it calm, and dry-eyed. And somehow they knew, by that, how very bad it was.

That night I sat down and wrote to Louise. "The children have done wonderfully well here," I said. "But they need to be in a better school. Would you get in touch with Miss Murchie . . . ?" I felt low as a dog writing something like that. There was never a better teacher on earth than Cole Sutherland. Or anybody who cared more about children. I lied a frightful lie. But I had to tell her something.

The next day we went up to the Forks and I put the letter in the mail. We went on to Nam's, then. We had seen her very little; for one thing we had been so busy. It was along late in the morning. You could smell the kraut and backbones cooking, before she opened the front door. Well, she hugged us and shooed us through the house and back to the kitchen.

"Aaron, you want some lemonade? The children are here," she said. Ben Aaron was up on a ladder in the kitchen, putting in a new stove pipe. The old one had burnt through and caught the ceiling afire, Nam said. He looked down at us, and smiled wanly, with the sweat streaming. I thought I would faint.

"No'm," he said. "Lemme get through." He went on working. Lacking her stove, for the moment, Nam had a fire in the kitchen fireplace and her pot of kraut hung over it, on a crane. It being the end of July, it was mightily hot. We took our lemonade and went to the porch. She had a basket of June apples out there that somebody had brought. The kids took some and went to the livery to feed the horses. Nam and I sat and rocked. She talked, and I squirmed like a worm in hot ashes. She peered at me and frowned and puckered up her mouth. "You lookin' mighty gant," she said. "What's the matter with ye?"

Nothing, only tired, I said. "Talk about gant, Ben Aaron looks dreadful," I said.

"Don't know what 'tis," she said. "I reckon that ol' hen done set on 'im about somethin'. She'll lay into him ever' now and then and he'll hunker about like a suck-egg dog. I'll swanny it makes me sick."

"How long has he been like this?" I said.

"How long since you seen him?"

I could have given her hours and minutes. "Two months," I said. She stopped in mid-rock. I couldn't look at her; I was watching a hummingbird in the hollyhocks. "He looked bad then too," I said.

"Two months?" she said. She was stunned immobile. "They law . . . What got the matter?"

"I thought you'd be relieved," I said. The hummer was right at the banister, whirring his little wings. He glittered in the sun like a little green jewel.

"Was it her?" she said. If the words had bitten Sophia they would have killed her instantly.

"I don't think so," I said. "No, I think it was him. I think he had too much to lose. I don't know." I was going to say of course it was best, but I lost the breath to speak.

"Well. Well, I'm glad you come to it before trouble got in somebody's britches," she said. "You know what was bound to come, the way it was a-goin'." I knew very well, by her face, that she was not glad. Nobody understood pain better than Panama McAllister.

"Yes, indeed, I am relieved," she declared, rocking again with vigor. "I thought we were a-goin' to have to give you up. Now if he'll stay away from down there. . . ."

"I'm sending the children home next month," I said.

"You don't mean you're sendin' 'em off to stay?" she said. She looked like I had hit her. "You don't mean you're fixin' to go?"

"I don't quite know," I said. I didn't know what to say. And I wouldn't have got to say it anyway. We heard Pet hollering, "Come on, sissy, you're not killed," before she and Hugh turned the corner, running. He was holding both hands over his nose. Tears were streaming through his fingers, but he was making no sound. He was being a man. Well of course I was scared out of my wits. However much she scolded, Pet was mortified.

"I don't think it got him in the eye," she said. "He put his dumb nose right into a wasper's nest." Nam jumped up yelling, "Lord have mercy get the Antiphlogistine!" And she trotted off to get it herself. Right in the middle of all this up drives Vicie Hambright, in her new Chevrolet coupe, 'course she didn't live but about two blocks away, but she would back out of her driveway and across the road to take Os his dinner at the feed store. And Vicie had Granny—that was what everybody called the dear old soul—sitting beside her and she got out and helped Granny out, Granny being poorly, and nearly blind. We settled them on the porch for the moment. Vicie had brought Aunt Nam a peck of red plums off her tree. Nothing would do, then, but that she and Granny stay, of course, for dinner. I finally escaped to the kitchen.

Ben Aaron had Hugh at the sink with a cold rag on his nose. I went and caught his arm. I don't know what I was going to say to him, right there over Hugh. When I opened my mouth I couldn't say anything at all. And Nam came in to make up her cornbread, and Vicie came right behind her, after a drink of water.

Cousin Ben Aaron handed Hugh the rag and eased away from me. "Keep it cool and maybe it won't swell," he said. "I've got to

go." He went. Nam hollered after him, "Don't you want your dinner?" But he was out the door and gone.

It was a case of "have to"; we stayed till dinner was over, and the
dishes were washed. And then we took off for home. Hugh's nose
hurt. I was half-killed. I never would forget it.

The next week, we packed their few belongings, and I went with
the kids to Red Bank, to the depot. I never forgot their faces, either,
looking out of the window of that train, as it pulled away. I didn't
know what the circumstances would be, when I would see them
again. I wondered really whether I would ever see them. It was a
time beyond description. It was the depths.

There was the thing of being alone in this place. I had never been
alone at night, not anywhere. That first night, I can't believe what I
did. It got so still, when the sun was going down. I went down to
the lot and caught up a box of biddies and brought 'em and put by
my bed. Just some live something. They whispered and pitted
around, in the night, and it was nice. I would have gone up to
Nam's. But I was getting conscious of how I looked. I was going on
five full months, at that point. I had made a couple of floppy cotton
dresses but they would not cover me up forever.

Being so skinny was beginning to work against me. When I saw
myself in my shimmy in the mirror I looked like a picked chicken
with a lemon in its craw. For all the dwelling on it that I did, I had
not the vaguest workable idea of what I was going to do, when I
had to do something. Which would be soon.

I just went on doing what had to be done about the place, sort of
oblivious. Sort of in a paralysis of fright. One side of my mind nagged
me that I ought to go see Ben Aaron; I was sure he had no idea I was
in this fix. And the other side said what would he do if he knew?
What would he say? It would be easier if I didn't see him. And I didn't.
As for the staying alone, it got easier. In a few days I got to where I
could sleep without the chickens.

And then one evening, a couple of men from the sheriff's office
in Red Bank came riding up in an old car driving along real slow,
looking all about. They said a man that had a habit of breaking in
on women had got away from the county jail. They had got him

for killing a woman down the county someplace. They had him figured to come up the river, looking for some isolated place to hide out.

"Pro'bly lookin' for some unperteckted womern," one said, to be reassuring. "Better lock up tight," they said, when they had decided I was not hiding him. And they moved on. And I locked up, as best I could.

That night I had hysterics into the pillow, till I wore out, and I hoped the killer would come on in, and it would be done with. The next morning I decided I would go to Nam's. Something had to happen. As I started up the road I noticed hoofprints, big hoofprints in the dirt. It looked like a horse had stood there, and shifted around, a very long time. There were about two packs' worth of cigarette butts on the ground. The sentinel was nowhere in sight; he had faded off with the night.

I picked up one of the butts and put it ceremoniously in my mouth, just for the contact, however cold. For the first time in months I felt human again. I wasn't scared. I went to the barn for a basket, I thought I'd go down in the orchard and pick up some apples. While I was down there rummaging around Rose came riding up the field. She wanted to tell me that Coy Ray had been out with a posse all night. They had caught a man in a laurel slick down the river a couple of miles. It was a man that liked to strangle women. We held one another and shivered. And then we took us some hampers and went down and got some apples.

I had not seen her in a while; she was getting over a deep cold and a bad cough. She had about quit hacking and it was a good sunny day. Good for her to be out, she said. We figured we'd get some pie apples out to dry. Mainly for her crowd; I didn't feel like I'd need many. We sat us down on the porch and peeled into our laps and sliced into a bucket between us.

Rose was a creature of few words, sometimes, and my mind being right occupied we worked along, not saying much. Every now and then a yellow jacket would buzz around the peelings and she would shoo it and flip the corner of her apron. By instinct, I guess, I kept my dress and apron bunched up in front and my lap full of distraction. Rose bent down and handed us up more apples; she could hold two at a time in each hand, with those long fingers.

She never looked at me, she was just working away on an apron full of fruit when she said, "I don't want you to worry, Cud'n Sen." I thought oh Lord, what now? She peeled on; the apple peeling made an *S,* on her lap, and she threw it over her shoulder to seal a husband whose name would begin with S.

"Mark that," she said, much too gravely for a matter so romantic. "I always helped Mama," she went on, directly. "I helped bring Fidel and Herman. I'll help you." I had no idea what to say so I said nothing. I dropped my apple and it rolled down to the banister. Rose got up and got it. She sat down and looked at me then, eye to eye. "It IS my daddy's. Ain't it," she said.

No question mark to it. She was positive. I was aghast. "NO!" I said. There was no way in the world I was going to convince this child of the earth that she was wrong on the one count. But I had to get her out of the notion that it was Coy Ray's. And that right then. I reckon it was a matter of low-down snobbery.

She set her mouth and ducked her head and went back to her apple peeling. We rocked in uneasy silence while she thought. "I never meant it was Pap's," she said at last. "I know better than that. I said it was my daddy's." I shuddered and squirmed. My mouth got all dry. "I thought you would have figgered us out by now," she said.

"Figgered out what?" I said.

"Pap and me ain't kin," she said.

"Nobody ever said a word to me about anything like that," I said. I was feeling kind of faint.

"'Course they didn't," Rose said. "Pap's not got the wildest idea that I know a thing about it. It was the longest time that I thought Pap didn't know it hisself."

"Do you think he really does?" I said.

"I think he does," she said. "Else why would he hate Mr. Steele so bad?"

Well, I thought, God in heaven give me breath. And I asked her then, "Who told you?"

"Mama told me. That was the last thing Mama told me. She said she thought she owed it to me that I know."

I can look back now and see that gold head bent over a lap full of apples. "I favor him, don't I?" she said. It was wistful and childlike, the way she said it, not looking up.

"I always thought so," I said. "I took it for us all just being kin. 'Course you certainly favor him more than I do." The bugs bummed back and forth and hovered.

"Celestine is my sister," she said, after a while. "Can you believe that? I have thought, how ought I to act to her? I've not been even let see her, but a time or two, in our lives. Nobody hardly sees her."

I sat there wondering how much Cleone had told, about Celestine's birth. And about Rose's. It took on a new weight, so to speak, a new irony, with this new chapter hickuping in my belly. It was like Rose read my mind.

"I think Mama, if she had lived, she would've kep' it the rest of her life," she said. "I think she troubled over it a lot, there at the end. I remember she was real sick, Pap was off someplace, he didn't know how bad off she was. Her face was all rosy with the fever. I wanted to go after Uncle Ans but I was scared to leave. So I was a-settin' up with her. I'd make her take a spoon of whiskey and honey, ever' little bit, for the cough. I watched her, and afterwhile she seemed to get real calm, and sleepy. I guess I dozed off for a while too.

"I remember, then, I heard her call me. Her voice was real strong, not a bit like she'd been. And I jumped awake and went and sat on the bedstead by her. She took hold of my hand and said, 'Rosannah, I have got somethin' I must tell you. I want you never, never to think ill o' your papa, whatever he may do. Never speak ill. He has been good to me in ways nobody knows a thing about. He's been good to you, too.'

"She turned her face to the wall and she was real quiet. A great tremble went over me; I was scared she had died. And then she turned back and looked me in the eyes, the longest time. And she said, 'Rose . . . Coy Ray's not your daddy. . . .' I felt like she'd hit me with a wet rag. You would've had to know Mama. She was the most beautiful, the most right-livin' person. I sat there with my mouth open, thinkin' what do I say? And directly she said, then, 'I want you to know, before I die, Ben Aaron Steele is your daddy. And I want that between you and me. And don't think ill of him, either. Give me your word . . .'

"Of course I did. I never asked her the circumstances. I just sat there thinkin' how good Mr. Steele had been to me, how he had loved me, and brought me play-pretties when I was little that Pap would never have thought of. How he had allus treated me like, well, like I was a person. He considered me. I sat there turnin' all that over, and I squeezed Mama's hand, and I said, well, I reck'n that ain't nothing to be exactly ashamed of.

"And she got this sweet look in her eyes, and she said real soft, then, 'Never sell it short.'

"She was so tired. I laid down beside her. When the rooster crowed I startled and rose up. Her hand was still in mine, only it was cold."

For the longest time, nothing could be said, at all. Then Rose said, "I broke my word to tell you for I thought you ought to know. I think Mama would wish it."

When I was able, I said, "Thank you."

"What did he say when you told him?" she said, then.

"I have not told him," I said.

"You mean he don't know?"

"If he doesn't care enough to come about me, I don't want him to know," I said. "All I know to do is to let it be born, here. It belongs to be born here. And I will take it and go. We will never tell him."

She was cutting dutifully away on an apple. She reached up, still clasping that little old thin-bladed knife, and wiped the tears from her cheeks with the back of her hand. "I'll help you," she said. The bucket was full. She got up and took it to the banister and poured off the brine, and she took the rack and knocked it and wiped the slatting on her apron and squatted down, then, to layer out the apples.

"Where ought we to put 'em?" she said. We looked around. "The chicken house roof?" I said. It was low and tin and I could climb up there.

She laughed. "Law, the flies would carry 'em plumb away," she said. "Let's put 'em yander on that stump." So we put 'em yander. And she said she reckoned she ought to go along home and get up some dinner, in case Coy Ray came home.

"Somehow it'll be made right," she said. "Mama used to say, 'The

Lord takes care.' The only thing that comes to my mind right now," she said, draping her arm around my shoulders, "is it will be lots better if Pap don't know. It really scares me to think, if Pap should know. He'll have a fit. He's goin' to be mad as thunder. Do you understand me?" she said, looking very serious.

"Yes, darling," I said. And I did. Oh, how I did.

~27~

THE FALLS

THERE WERE A COUPLE OF LITTLE BRANCHES THAT CAME DOWN off Wilcox Ridge into the river, just below the narrows. It was a curious thing that they seemed to have dried up. I wasn't up that way much, but I had noticed it one time before the kids were gone. We had walked up there when the river was up, full of a big rain, and there was nothing but trickles coming down the beds of those streams.

Hugh had said, oh, Coy Ray and the boys are building them a pond. It was none of my business; my mind wasn't on it anyway. But there seemed to be a lot of activity up on Coy Ray's side, much more than common. He was down with me a good bit, working. But I could hear saws and cracking timber into the dark, in the evenings. This was his time of big whiskey business; the corn was good and hard and the weather was cooling off. Whiskey, I thought, never made that kind of noise. I thought I would ask him if he was looking for a long hard winter, or why so much firewood? But I forgot it.

One day Rose came and asked me to wade the ford and walk with her. We went up the old road towards their place, and lo and behold, we had to skirt a brand-new lake. The road was gone, and the bottoms, all of it under water. What in the world? I said. Rose didn't answer right away. The way she looked, I could tell there was more than stumps at the bottom of it.

Finally, she said, "If you want to know somebody that their tail is in a crack, it's me."

"How so?" I said.

"You know Pap's land belongs to Mr. Steele," she said. "You know about that?"

"I heard," I said.

"Well," she said, drawing a big breath, "Pap's a-timberin' the ridge."

"You mean he's going to sell the timber?"

"He's done done it. He's sold it to some people that's done business with Mr. Steele. He's sold it for less." We walked along and on the back side of a big laurel slick there were the log-piles, big poplar and hickory and chestnut and oak. We passed by a couple of men coming down the ridge with a team. Coy Ray had gone down to Red Bank on some kind of business, Rose said. That was why she had picked the time.

"How's he gon' get it out of here?" I said.

"He'll pick him the right day, when it's comin' a good rain, and into the pond these logs'll go, and then he'll bust the dam," she said. "If they don't jam, or go to splinters in the sluice, way down the river there, the falls, you know, he's got 'em clear to the railroad at Red Bank."

Well, I stood there weighing that, I didn't see any way that Ben Aaron wouldn't find it out. The next thing was what would he do when he did? "I've told Pap it's low-down wrong," Rose said. "I told 'im the nicest I could and he said to shut my mouth. I see nothin' more to do. But to let it come to what it will."

I said yes, that was right. It was another thing that would just take care of itself.

We had come to the time of cutting tobacco. We went through the field and cut it and poled it, and it was good sunshine, and a couple of days later we commenced to barn it. We had just about got it up one evening; Coy Ray had sent his kids home to do the chores and it was just him and me, then, to finish up. I was on the wagon and he was up in the rafters and I was handing up to him. I wasn't feeling too well. I guess I looked sort of peaked. He kept giving me long, piercing looks. It made me uneasy. And then all of a sudden he hopped down on that wagon bed like a cat. Boy, he looked like a firecracker about ready to pop. He was too mad to do anything but draw long, shivering breaths, with his elbows stuck out and his fists made up. He was white as paste.

"Well," he said, finally, almost under his breath, "the righteous Mr. Steele finally got ye in the straw, eh?"

I stepped backwards, speechless. And he moved forward. It was not what I had expected at all. He talked very softly, matter-of-factly. He clenched his jaw and with a sweet voice began to list all the creative things he was going to do to the glorified and elevated Mr. Steele. The awfullest things you could imagine. No, worse. He grabbed me by the shoulders and shook me with every threat. I thought he would throw me off the wagon but he did not; he only jerked me up and set me on the ground.

"Git outta my sight, Mistress Goody-Britches," he said. "In-na house. Go. Git! That (filthy-wordin') bastard'll never do this stunt again."

Well, I went. I flew. I wasn't scared for myself, I was just scared. I ran in and closed the door and ran upstairs and hid myself in the chimney closet, panting. I slipped out directly and went to peep out the window, and Coy Ray was whipping the mules down across the field at breakneck speed, going to the ford.

I didn't know what to do. I leaned in the window, trying to gather my wits, trying to guess ahead of him. When I made myself think it came over me that Coy Ray was bad to pop off like that; that all that was threatened would never materialize. Lord, it could-n't. How many times can you kill a man, no matter how many ways you have in mind? That was not consoling enough. My heart just pounded. The veins in my temples pounded. My knees shook. The sun was going down, and if Coy Ray was going to Caney Forks (like he said he was) he had a good start on me.

I ran out to the barn and bridled the mule. I kept thinking I could walk a lot faster, but I was too faint, by spells, to walk at all. So I rode and the mule went picky-plod, and all the way I kept thinking what to do. What if I went to see Ben Aaron? How would I begin what had to be said? By the time I got in sight of the Forks it had occurred to me that I might get lucky and have to say nothing.

It was dark. I would simply return a favor. I would simply stand watch. If Coy Ray had not already done his deed, please dear Lord, I would stand between him and Ben Aaron. He would have to chop me up into stew meat for the buzzards, before he got to the righteous Mr. Steele. And I didn't think he'd do it.

So that is what I did. I stationed myself in the shadows on the lawn of Sophia's palace. And I watched. I did not blink. Every leaf that fell, every bird that stirred, I was ready to do battle. Time passed slowly. My seat on the mule hair was not the most comfortable, and I squirmed. I was curious too. Quietly as we could, I rode in closer, and looked in the windows. It made sense that if I were looking after Ben Aaron, I ought to know where he was. There was a racket coming from what I guessed was the parlor. Somebody was tormenting a piano. We peered in, the mule and I. Sophier was spraddled on the piano stool, plunking doggedly away. She was studying a new piece, it was "The Glow Worm," with her tongue sticking out the side of her mouth. The same few measures, over and over, never quite right. *Plunk-plunk-plunk-plunk-plunky-plunk.* . . .

Around the corner of the house light came from another window. It was a window with pink ruffled curtains. Against the far wall Ben Aaron was sitting on a divan, with Celestine curled up beside him, her head on his shoulder. He was reading to her. I don't know what it was, but he would stop and show her the pictures, and she would smile, and once she clapped her hands and laughed a great coarse laugh, out loud. It was getting cool. When he had finished, he came to close the window. I almost spoke to him, he was so close. But I did not, and he drew the shades, and I only saw his shadow leave the room. And in a little while the house was all dark. And I was left to wait, and to wonder so many things, not all to do with murder, and to shudder over them.

I remember I would doze, sometimes, and jerk up, and yawn, and watch some more. And the sky began to pale, and in my sleepiness I knew I had to get moving or risk discovery. Nothing was going to happen, anyway, in the light. Just to be sure something had not gone by me, unseen, I watched the damp and sandy patches in the road, going down, and there were no fresh tracks of mule or man but ours. I thought I ought to feel some relief. But somehow even the quiet and the fog were heavy with dread. The sun was just coming over the ridge when I rode around to the back door and got down off the mule onto the porch. I was most too stiff in the back and legs to creep but I itched too and I got a rag and soap and went to the spout and washed, and sat down, then, too tired to go inside, and watched the morning. I was asleep, leaned over against a post, when I heard the shot. It was just one shot, far off, but it might as well have been a cannon the way the echo bounced off Hogback and back and forth from every hill and crag coming down the river. Behind it, I knew I heard a woman scream. If I had been reasonable I would have known somebody was up there hunting squirrel. I was not reasonable. I was too weary. I knew better. There was a sort of resignation that went with it. With knowing.

I sat there limp, listening to my heart thump slowly, like a dirge. I thought I heard men hollering, a long way off. Somebody came hollering, and pounding at the door. I dragged up and went through the house. When I opened the door it was some old rough boy I had seen once over in Shiloh. When I looked at him I almost fainted from relief. But he was white as cotton. The front of his shirt was covered with blood. "Was it you got shot?" I said. Obviously he was not dead.

He didn't answer me. "Miss Steele, have you got ary quilt to spare?" he said.

"What is it?" I said. "Is somebody hurt?"

"No ma'm," he said. He looked sideways, away from me. "We need another mule," he said. "You got ary mule to let us have?"

"Did somebody shoot your mule?" I said. It was all not right. And he looked at me, then, and his mouth commenced to quiver.

And finally he said, "Miss Steele, I'm sorry. . . . Mr. Steele is down yonder in the road. We got to get him home." He didn't need to say another word to me. I just sort of fell forward, on him. And he held me up, shaking. He was mortally afraid. "I never seed a dead man speak. I never seed a deader man than Ben Aaron Steele. I don't know how he rode that horse this far. We seed him comin' down from Wilcox Ridge. We seed him fall. We got to him, and turned him over. I'll swear to you ma'm, I'm sorry, but he didn't have no face at all. And when I laid him back, he spoke to me. Miss Steele when a dead man speaks it marks your life. He said, 'My sin. Oh, God, my sin.' I'd swear that's what he said. . . ."

Well, I would have sworn it wasn't. Not quite. I patted that poor man, just by reflex. And I straightened up, and turned loose, and took a deep breath, and said well, I would get the quilt.

He and his logging partner had a team of oxen working, way back up Wilcox Ridge. The mule and wagon would be quicker. He went to get it. I went and got that blue quilt down, and took it out to him. "I don't think you ought to come," he said. "I'll send somebody down."

"I'll come directly, on my own," I said. And when the wagon had rattled off, I went out and fed the chickens, and the pigs, and went about the little things I had to do, and I left the house and started up the road. It was full of butterflies, they would float ahead of me and light. It was so beautiful along the road. The joe pye was blooming so pretty, such a pretty shade of dusty pink. And the touch-me-nots, and the asters, and things. There were a few sassafras leaves fallen. I sang myself a little song, walking along. I didn't cry at all; my nose was bleeding, but I just wiped it on my skirt. Up just a few yards this side of the road that turns off to Coy Ray's, there was a puddle of thick, sticky blood in the road. I stopped and looked at it, curious. There was a black and white beetle crawling in it. I flicked at the beetle with my toe, I hadn't realized till then, that I had gone off without my shoes, and now my toe was bloody, and all sticky. I walked on. In the sunny patches, the goldenrod was so pretty. On up the ridge the sourwoods were red. So he had been coming home to me. He knew. Oh, he was so surprised. That was why he spoke to me, after he was dead. My head felt light. Very shortly I will get to you, I said. I will tell you it's all right. I'm going to be fine. I was holding onto a tree, to keep from falling. I didn't really hear the buggy coming. I don't know how Nam got me in it, all by herself. I remember her hollering at the horse, turning it around, and her turning loose of me just to crack the whip. I remember coming down into the Forks, at breakneck speed.

"Where did they go with him?" I asked. "I want to see him."

"No, no," she said.

And I begged her, and I pleaded.

"They've got him at Sophier's," she said. Against her judgment, we went to Sophier's. Jack Garner was there, in the front yard, and Os Hambright. They helped us down. They led us, leaning on one another, up the front steps to that columned porch. We could hear Sophier inside screaming. She was just screaming and screaming, like some kind of wounded thing. There were ladies in there with her, they said. There were a bunch of men in a cluster on the porch. It was like the talk turned off with a switch, when we came through, when they stood aside and let us into their circle. On a chaise, there lay the body of Ben Aaron, still under the quilt. Somebody had draped that with a sheet. But even so, one of his hands hung down from under it. The fingers were waxy and stiff. Blood had dried between them. I reached down for that hand, and then I don't know. I didn't know anything, until I woke up in the bed at Nam's.

I woke up and heard people coming in and out, talking low. Some woman, I never did know who, was sobbing so pitifully, like her heart would break. I know Myrtle Shuman, Ansel's wife, was there. She and Nam were talking. The sheriff had called Ans from Red Bank and said be was going up to the ridge after Coy Ray. Ans had gone down to get Rose and the boys. Myrtle was as good a soul as ever lived. I remember her broad, good face and her padding about, fetching and helping, always so quiet.

"If I were not here, I would have to go to Sophia's," she said, sort of wryly, when we thanked her. Not once in all of it did Nam waver, or take on. Neither one of us had shed a tear. The matter of her moment seemed to be looking out for me.

But then, she did a real peculiar thing. I heard her tell Myrtle, "Sit here and meet people for me, will you? I've got to go t' the bank." And off she went. Her mind's off, I thought. Imagine thinking about money. And after what seemed like too long a while, she came breezing in, where I was, and rustled around in the little old bookcase, with her back to me, and I noticed her put two books up in the shelves with the glassed-in front, and lock the doors, with a key. At the end of everything, you know, I am curious, nosy; I wondered what was so pertinent, today, in *A Memoir of the Reverend*

Sydney Smith. And I studied the garlands of pink flowers on the wallpaper, and it began to come on me, what had really happened on that day, and all else fogged and faded.

Snatches of stray talk floated through the rooms of that old house like strands of spider web, looking for something to hang on. "They had a fight out here in the road one time," a man was saying. "It was just a cuss-fight till Coy Ray jumped up in the bed of a wagon and come down on Ben Aaron's head with a demi-john."

"Sheriff got 'im 'at time," another one said. "Took 'im down to jail and locked 'im up for 'tempted murder. Next mornin' Mr. Steele he come down with his head all bound up and the money in his hand to bail ol' Coy Ray out. Rode off with him, peaceful as a dove."

"They've had some strife about whiskey. . . ."

"It was some bad blood over a woman, I b'lieve, one time . . ."

"Well, I don't know, I heared that Coy Ray's been pirating some timber. I heared that just last evenin'. . . ."

Out of all of it I got only this much of what had happened: Ben Aaron had come down right behind me, that morning. For some reason he had gone to Coy Ray's. Somewhere up on that ridge he had been shot, point-blank, with a shotgun, in the face. Somehow he had lived to get down almost to The Birches. What did he go to Coy Ray's for? Sophia, they said, was totally incoherent. He probably hadn't told her anyway. And of course, I wondered, did he know somehow about me being there, that night? Did he see the mule's tracks in the road, as I had looked for Coy Ray's? Was he going to Coy Ray's, in the first place—or did he come on signs of Coy Ray's private enterprise along the way, and get side-tracked? As long as I live, I'll never know.

The reality, that it had happened, was mercifully blurred by the niceties of death. The whole of Caney Forks was in that house sometime that day. By late afternoon a lot of Red Bank came. Over and over, the women asked Nam, "Where ought we to bring the food?" And just as calm as she could be, she'd say, "We're goin' to Sophier's . . . we'll all be over there. . . ."

When she could get away she brought a wash pan, and got me up. I still had on the clothes I had hung tobacco in the day before. She went off and came back with a black skirt and a gray checked waist, and she rounded up some shoes as long and sharp as needles, and left me to get myself together. Of course the plaquet of that skirt would not close; I left the shirt tail out to cover it. I smiled to myself and said out loud, "Ben Aaron, I need another apron." I looked in the glass and I looked like a haint.

The undertaker had been, when we got to Sophia's. There was no sign of what had been on the porch. There were little knots of people everywhere, talking in near-whispers. The preacher's wife brought us in and took us up the stairs to a room where a couple of other women were sitting with Sophia. I would have known whose room that was, anywhere. The walls were painted lavender. The furniture was buff. A pair of plaster cupids smiled down benignly from a gilded shelf over the bed. On the dresser there was a huge brass jardiniere of peacock feathers that no doubt framed her image, while she combed. In the bed, under a lavender-flowered silk comfort, Sophia lay snubbing fitfully in her sleep. Ans had given her something for her hysterics. I went and stood over her. Her face was blotched and swollen just grotesque. Her hair was matted from tears, at the temples. She had been so lonely. She had suffered so much pain that she could not communicate, except that it came out uglinesss. This was only the final spasm. She had been, I thought, so miserably and gracelessly and lovelessly in love. How sad. I felt this strange detachment from all of it. I thought, "My sympathy, Mrs. Steele."

Across the bed, on the night stand, there lay the pipe with the curly-wood bowl. And a book, lying on its open pages. Ah, had he been reading Gautier and Mallarme to the romantic Mrs. Steele? I was compelled to look. It was *Candide*. I picked it up, keeping his place with my finger. He had been close to the end. How eloquent, how ethereal and dreamy he would have made those passages sound, for his love who understood not one word. It was a page that in English would read like this: "I wish to know which is worse, to be ravished a hundred times by Negro pirates, to have one's behind cut off, to run the gauntlet among the Bulgarians, to be beaten and hanged, to be dissected, to row in the galleys, in short to go through all the miseries we have suffered, or to stay here and have nothing to do . . . ?" All of a sudden I could not contain myself. I commenced to laugh uncontrollably. I laughed and the tears ran. I buried my face in my hands. The ladies jumped up, all flustered, to comfort me in my hysteria. Sophia tossed and moaned. Nam grabbed me by the arm and ushered me out and kept me cornered on the landing until I wore it out and hushed.

"For God's sake, what was that about?" she said.

"I must tell you later," I said, and I was nearly seized again. But we forgot it; there were so many people in the rooms downstairs, to be comforted by. We were making our way out through the parlor when Cole Sutherland saw us, and came up and took me to his heart, without a word. He had brought Rose. I looked around for her, and there she was, on the arm of an overstuffed chair in the corner, with her arm around Celestine. I wondered if anybody else would see one as the carnival mirror image of the other. We went and kissed them. I held onto Rose, for an instant, like she was life itself. And then I knew I had to go.

By the grace of God, Nam went to sleep that night. The truth was, neither of us knew yet what had hit us. My back had begun to hurt, at Sophia's. It was an irregular throbbing that came and went. That night I could not lie still. Finally I got up and went to the bathroom. I was in labor. Nothing mattered then but to get home. The mule, I supposed, was over at the livery, shut up for the night. I couldn't dare wake anyone. I got on my clothes and wrote Nam a note: "I am gone to feed the pigs." And I crept out, and headed down the road. The lights were still on, when I went by Sophia's. But it was a dark night out; the road was dark and foggy. I went mostly by feel, and sound. I could hear Boney Creek. I could hear the sighing of the hemlocks on the mountain top. I could hear the river. The pains had run together, they were constant. Near the end I had to stop and lean on rocks and trees and pant. I got to the front steps and got myself inside, and somehow got into the bed.

That is where I was when Nam arrived, splitting the wind. She had got up and found that note. "Run out on me, did ye?" she said. "They's folks'd come and feed them pigs." She got a towel and wiped the sweat off my face. "Is it a-comin'?" she asked. "Is it gone too far to stop?"

I just nodded. Babies that are ready to come are hard enough. This one was fighting every inch with every ounce, to hold on. I know unconsciously I fought to hold it. It took us a good while to lose. Nam took the horse and buggy around to the barn and hid it, in case some-body should come looking for us. She threw out some corn and let the chickens and the pigs out to forage. "Let the pigs go live with their daddy," she said. They were slick enough to make it till the chestnuts fell. There was nothing she could do, then, but sit and hold my hand and wait.

"When did it happen?" she said. She was weighing our chances.

"The middle of March," I said. I watched her whisper off the months on her fingers. "Not quite six," I said. "We're not going to make it."

"I know it," she said. She dug around in a bag of necessities she'd brought and got out a bottle of brandy and doled it out with a spoon. I hadn't eaten in so long it went to work at once. It eased the cramp a little and thickened my tongue, and loosened it. "I killed him," I said. "As sure as if I had held that gun, I killed him."

And she said, "Hush. We can none of us say why this thing, or that thing. The book was done written when the characters were born." She got up and went to the window and looked out, think-ing whatever she was thinking. Ive's clock began to strike ten. There was a break in the fog and the sun poured in, and the little flecks of dust danced in gold spirals around the room. The room went in spi-rals, round and round. I remember hollering once, and asking Nam to forgive me, and hollering again. The next thing, there was this little mewing. In my craziness I thought, where in the world did Nam get that kitten? That's what it sounded like. She had it wrapped up in a towel, holding up against her.

"Can you hold it?" she said. "It's a little boy." She laid it on my chest and draped my arms over it. She pulled me up with it, a little bit, and propped up my head. It squinched up its eyes and cried a little wispy cry. It was the tiniest thing, it was purple and wrinkled and it had its little hair, and eyebrows. It clutched at my finger, fee-bly, with its perfect little hands. Its little mouth was blue. It was making a raspy noise when it breathed. Nam had gone and fixed a pan of warm water.

"Do you think we ought to wash it?" I said. "It looks so cold."

"No," she said. She took it up, and held it on one arm, and with the other hand she patted it on the head with that warm water. "I baptize thee Benjamin Hamilton Steele, in the name of the Father, the Son and the Holy Ghost," she said. She laid it back with me, then, and turned away. I could see her shoulders shaking. "Was that all right with you?" she said finally. "I never even asked you what its name should be."

That was perfectly right, I said. I held it to my face. I could hear its chest bubbling and struggling. And then it stopped. I could feel the life twitching away. Nam went to take it, but I said no. She went out, then; I heard her go out the back. I knew where she was gone. When she came back, after a while, she had to untangle its fingers from my hair. They had gotten stiff.

"Get my shawl and wrap it in that," I said. She did, and laid it back on the bed. "What can we put it in?" she said. I couldn't answer her, so she went to look for something. She came back with what could have passed for a neat little coffin, lined with red plush cloth. She laid the baby in that old fiddle case, and we prayed over it, our own quiet prayers, and she said Amen, and closed the lid and latched it, and went out with it, in her arms. When she came back from the hill she said she had put it in the grave with Hamilton Steele. "The first and the last," she said. And then she didn't even sit down to rest.

She got more warm water and a rag. "I've got to clean you up," she said.

"Oh, let me rest," I said.

"Oh no," she said. "I can't. I've got to get us back to the Forks. Thank God, I doubt Soph can get that funeral up until tomorrow or next day. They've sent for her sister."

"Oh, I can't go," I said. "There's no way I can go like this."

"Indeed you must go," she said. "I've got to go and you've got to go with me. We've got to make on like nothin' in the world has happened. Only death and destruction." She was already scrubbing away on my face and arms and hands.

"I can't go," I said. "I cannot go to that church and sit there. I cannot see him put in the ground." She squeezed out the wash rag and dabbed my bloody self, and washed my legs and feet.

"You have got to do all that," she said. "You have got to give that body up." She went to the wardrobe and got clean clothes then, and pulled my feet off the bed, and got me up and dressed me like I was a child. Even to a diaper, out of an old sheet. And she went and got the horse and buggy, and drove it up, and helped me out to it, and came back and shut up the house, and we went flying off to the Forks, with me lying in her lap, until we got nearly to town and she made me sit up. When we passed the Episcopal Church there were a bunch of men out digging a grave. "She won't let us bring him home?" I said.

"Never thought she would," Nam said. To everybody who had panicked in her absence, she explained, "We had to go down and feed Sen's stock. And I had one o' my sinkin' spells; it's just I've not slept good." I thought please nobody look at her too close. She had blood splatters down the front of her dress. After we got in the house, not much got through the fog to me at all. I remember waking up, I know it was that night, and Rose was sitting there, tending the fire in the room. It had turned off real cool. Or else I was in a chill. I started to say something to her and drifted off again, with my mouth open. I remember her feeding me milk toast with a spoon, I guess it was the next morning. I know she and Nam got me up that afternoon and put clothes on me, and they put a hat on me, with a long veil, and lifted me into the buggy and we went to the church. They took us in the side door, I know, and sat us down in the pew behind the "family"—that was Sophier and her sister and Celestine, and some queer people I never saw before nor since. I remember us all getting up and the people singing "There's a wideness in God's mercy, Like the wideness of the sea; There's a wideness in his justice that is more than liberty. . . ." And I remember that casket being brought down the aisle by strangers, pale, well-to-do looking men in expensive dark suits. Sophier was all got up in black, of course, but she was peculiarly quiet, sort of all drawn up. I'll tell you, though, when that coffin got to the front of the church her sister Patience turned loose a screech and wail to raise the dead. She shrieked and sobbed for I reckon what in her mind ought to have been. And Celestine was sitting there between Patience and her mother, all bewildered and upset anyway, and it scared her so bad, all that taking on, that she commenced to howl and cry out of pure panic. And then some women behind us took it up, and the preacher stood up there with his hands folded, waiting to be able to talk. Whatever it was he said, I don't remember it. But we sat there, and it was like the Lord's hand I guess was on us. It was serene as sitting on the riverside. The sun was coming through those stained glass windows; it made shadows, I thought, like those water-dapples it makes on the rocks above the river. There were a lot of flowers in there, there was a solid blanket of red carnations over the casket, but that was not the way it smelled, in there. It smelled like fresh sap and sawdust and warm wild grass. And when we went out to the churchyard, and watched them put that carved oak showpiece down into that hole in the clay, and watched them shovel that red dirt in on it, I thought, well, Ben Aaron, the ground has won. You always did belong to it and now you always will. But not I, sir. No, not I.

I remember Ans's arm around me, very secure. And after that, nothing. Not much, at least, for days. Vaguely I remember being very sick; I remember Ans's face, and Nam's rocker creaking, creaking by the bed. And Rose holding my hand. The only thing that stands out plain from those days was once when the sheriff came and Rose got up and went out in the hall to talk to him. That I remember. "Rose, we got your daddy," he said. And she said nothing. "We got 'im in Knoxville, to his sister's house," he said. Silence.

"He come right with us, no ruckus atall."

"He never put up a fight?" she said, not quite believing.

"We told 'im what you said," the sheriff said. "He throwed up his fist, said, 'The hell you say!'"

Silence. "When you gon' tell us the truth, honey girl?"

"I told you the truth. Mr. Steele had a row with Pap. And I killed him."

～28～

DUE PROCESS

YOU KNOW THEY USED TO HAVE A JUDGE COME IN JUST A FEW DAYS of the year, up here; I don't know how it is now but then when something happened, some crime, it had to wait on court day. If the wronged parties didn't just take care of it in their own premeditated way.

Good luck or bad, whichever way you looked at it, court day was about three weeks away. They had Coy Ray in jail, no matter how much Rose protested. "I know she is an honest youngun," the sheriff told Aunt Nam, "but on this score I don't believe a word she says."

"Nor I, on this score," Aunt Nam said. What the Law had was two people, the only two witnesses, adamantly confessing to a crime. Rose, and her Pap. Harmon Garrison had been away when the deed was done; he had been in Michigan on some of Ben Aaron's business, and got home just in time to read the will. I had no call to hear that will; nothing that Ben Aaron had could he anywise have left to me, nor would I have wished him to.

But it was not without surprises. Some people whose land he got for taxes, or for a roll of loaded dice or a deal off the bottom of a deck, got their losses back intact, except for a little timber. Coy Ray did not, quite; the entire of Wilcox Ridge went to Coy Ray's boys, with Harmon as trustee until the least one came of age. To Rose alone went her mother's half of the old Shuman tract on down the river, south of Wilcoxes': 320 acres and several empty tenant houses.

He had bought that from Cleone one time when Coy Ray was in a tight, and she was scraping up money. And he left Rose a little money, too, to see her and the boys through school.

The bulk, of course, Sophia got. Her lawyer came down anyway, to make things troublesome for Harmon as he could. Harmon and Sophia were never what you'd call in love. Well, in the midst of this Harmon had to decide what to do about something else. "Please talk to Rose and make her have some sense about this thing," I said.

"What am I going to do about Coy Ray?" he said.

"You are going to defend him," I said.

"He's not asked me."

"I'm asking you," I said.

"'Y God, that puts me in a pickle," he said. "That man killed my best friend on earth."

"And your best friend on earth, what do you think he would want? Would he want Coy Ray to hang?"

"Hell no," Harmon said. "He'd want him staked to the ground and left for the piss ants. And then just before the last breath left the bastard, he'd ride up and grab him and tote him off to get a drink of likker, and pick a little tune. Oh, I'll go see Coy Ray, I'll do the best I can."

But then, "By the way," he said, "has Rose talked to you about it? Has she told you anything?" Not a word, I said. And I never asked her. I didn't even know if I wanted to know. Tell the truth, none of us kin had talked about it, hardly at all. We wouldn't admit it happened.

"I doubt that she'll tell me," Harmon said. "We may just have to see what she does when they put her under oath." And he was right. He went down to Red Bank to the jail and saw Coy Ray, said he was sitting on his bunk, staring out the window, wouldn't talk to him, wouldn't even look around at him but once. And that was to say, "I killed the son of a bitch. I don't give a damn to tell the world I killed 'im. Now what the hell you think you can do for me?"

It was about the same speech Coy Ray gave in court when the hearing came up. I would not have gone for the world except Rose asked me. She asked me to go and sit with her, until she had to testify. Certainly Myrtle and Ans would go. Ans had to describe the body, the cause of death and all that. But quietly, Rose asked me to come, and I was getting around some, by then, and I said yes I would.

Nam begged off that morning, said she just didn't believe she could bear to hear it talked about. But everyone else in the county and a hundred miles was there. It was Model T Fords and mules in the road as far as you could see. The courthouse was just swarming; there was a line of deputies on the steps, they made way for us, and got us in, and they took Rose off to an anteroom behind—what do you call it? The pulpit? I guess—the bench. Whatever, anyway we saw Harmon go back there to be with her and I felt better about it.

I'll tell you who else was not there: Sophia was not there. I had wondered whether she would have to be a witness and I guess I dreaded hearing that, or maybe I dreaded it for her, in a mixed-up way. I sort of rolled my eyes without obviously craning and she was nowhere in sight. It was like Myrtle read my mind. "Ans had to beg off for Sophia," she said. "She's threatening nervous prostration."

The judge was an old man named Hollowell Spence. He was little and dried up and bald-headed, and he had a little bristly cow-catcher mustache. It was sort of a distraction that he was cross-eyed. He couldn't hear real good and he leaned forward with his hand behind his ear, making X's with his eyes on whoever was doing the talking. One thing I thought, it would be hard to lie to him.

I don't know how these things are supposed to go; it was the only time in my life I was ever in a courtroom. There was this brassy, cocky lawyer that must have come from outside, too. I never saw him in Red Bank and I never thought to ask Harmon who he was but he seemed to be the grand inquisitor or something, he strutted back and forth with his thumbs in his pockets and his belly stuck out, and a furrow of wisdom on his brow. He was playing to the crowd; a hanging would not have drawn a bigger one. They trotted out those loggers, one by one, the ones that had found the body, so to speak.

Now, you won't find many people up here anytime that will tell you more than you ask, not even if they like you a whole lot. What that pouter pigeon got out of those boys he got word by word. Yes, they worked for "the deceased." No, they were not working for him that day. They were working for Mr. Coy Ray Wilcox. Not for pay. On the shares. Cutting chestnut. Did they know it was stolen timber? No. Wilcox Ridge was Wilcox Ridge. First and last. No, they did not see the shooting. Yes, they heard the shot. Thought it was a hunter. They were on their way down the ridge with a team of oxen pulling a log when they came to the road and saw "the deceased," still sitting in the saddle. And the horse seemed to be ambling along, at its own pleasure.

What was the state of the rider? "Bloody," one said.

"I b'lieved at the time he was dead," said the other. And they had left their team and started after the horse, and caught up with it, just as it had come to the main road, and paused, and headed south, toward The Birches. And just as they caught up to it, the rider fell.

I sat there frozen, as the second one testified, waiting for him to tell what he had come and told me. "And what did you observe to be the condition of the deceased, at that point?" that lawyer said. And the witness held his chew in his cheek and stared back kind of blankly. "Dead," he said. "Plum cold and dead."

Ans testified then that certainly, by the time the body arrived in Caney Forks, it was quite dead. The cause of death was blood loss, from a ruptured artery in the neck, and massive head injuries, undoubtedly caused by a blast from a shotgun at close range. No, Ans could not say why "the deceased" was not unseated by that force. Or how he could have ridden horseback some undetermined distance though dying, or possibly dead. "It is not the first thing I have not been able to explain," he said mildly. And he stepped down, and the deputy went back and brought in Rose.

Until she came out there, and stood to take the oath, I had not really noticed how thin she was, and how hollow-cheeked and pale. She seemed to have fallen away, even in that hour. She had on a light blue flannel dress I know Myrtle had made for her; it had long sleeves and it was gathered onto a yoke and had a little round collar, right pretty, but it hung on her like a sack. She had braided her hair and wound it round and round; she was all gold hair and eyes. Oath-taking was a very serious matter; she put her hand on the Bible and did solemnly swear and the judge leaned further forward and pushed his ear nearly closed, and fixed her in that cross-wise stare and she stared back, unintimidated. Where was she on that morning in September, that cocky lawyer asked.

"At home."

Was she alone?

"No."

Who else was there?

"My pap."

"Who is your pap?"

"Coy Ray Wilcox."

"Where were the other members of the family?"

"Gone to school."

"And on that morning did you see Mr. Steele, the deceased?"

"Yes."

"Where was he?"

"In the yard."

"Whose yard?"

"Pap's."

"Under what circumstances did you see him?"

"He rid up on his horse."

"And did you go out to meet him?"

"No."

"Did Mr. Wilcox go out to meet him?"

"No."

"Nobody talked with him then?"

"Pap."

"But you said Mr. Wilcox didn't go out."

"He was already out."

The jerk made a flourish with his pink hands and rolled his eyes at the judge.

"What was he doing?"

"Goin' to hunt squirrel."

"So Mr. Wilcox was armed!" Rose sat silent.

"Was he armed?" the lawyer said, sounding annoyed.

"You said," she answered in all innocence.

He puffed and blew his nose. "Was Mr. Steele armed?" he said.

"Not as I know of."

"But you did observe him. You did go outside."

"Yes."

"What prompted you to go outside?" Rose didn't answer that right off. "What prompted you?" the lawyer said, getting huffy.

"You must tell us, girlie," said the judge.

"I heard cussin'."

"Was Mr. Steele cursing?" the hateful thing demanded.

"No."

"Then your father was cursing." Rose sat looking blank.

"Was your father cursing Mr. Steele?" the lawyer said.

"Pap was cussin'," she said.

"Did Mr. Steele reply?"

"No."

"Why was your father cursing him? What was the cause?"

Silence.

"Was it an argument over timber?"

"No." There was not a breath stirring in the courtroom. Outside the breeze had picked up, rattling branches and flinging dry leaves against the windows.

"Then what was the argument about? You said they were arguing."

"No, I never."

"All right! Your father was angry with Mr. Steele. What was he angry about?"

"He was cussing, what was he cussing about?" the judge put in. He was leaned clean out of his chair. Rose looked down for the first time, and clasped and unclasped her hands.

"A woman," she said. There was a breath-drawing of delight among the spectators. A few wise murmurs. I noticed old Chick Aleywine down in the very front row. She had turned around and was grinning, showing her gums, proud as punch. Her day in the sun.

"A woman," said the lawyer. "What about a woman?"

It looked like poor little Rose grew down into her chair. "Pap eat him out," she finally said, "because he bigged a woman."

"He did what?"

"He bigged a woman. Bigged her with a baby." Of all the whispering and craning around and aha-ing there has never been the like. The judge glared and hammered it down.

"Bigged WHO with a baby?" The lawyer was delighted. Rose took her time, raised her chin and looked at him squarely.

"I never kep' up with their wimmen," she said. It was almost impudent. Titters rippled across the room. And it made that lawyer mad. You could just see the wheels grinding, along with his teeth. He got a glittering look in his eye.

"Tell me, young lady," he said, thrusting his leering countenance right up into her face. "Did YOU have a relationship with Ben Aaron Steele?"

She flinched like she was struck. She looked at me beseechingly.

"Did you have a relationship?" the slime thought he had drawn blood.

"Yes."

"Ah!" Gleefully, "What was the nature of that relationship?"

Silence. Rose stared at the tormentor.

"What was your relationship with Mr. Steele?" he said again. The judge shifted uncomfortably in his chair, frowning. It was so still in there you could have heard a gnat buzzing. Rose, literal little soul, bit her lip.

"He was my daddy," she said, simply, and perfectly clear.

There was no order in the court for quite some time. No matter what else came out of court that day, there was a winter's worth to talk about. The judge rapped and the lawyer went on.

"Mr. Steele was your father? Was this known to anyone else? Was it known to Mr. Wilcox?"

"I don't know," she said. "It was never talked about." She started to cry.

"How did you know it?"

"Here, here, that'll do," the judge said. "We're off the subject. Let's move along." The lawyer looked down at his feet.

"Mr. Steele was your father, you say. And I believe you told the sheriff you killed him. Is that correct?" She sat still, getting back her calm, with her hands folded in her lap.

"I did," she said.

"Did you have a weapon?"

"No."

"Mr. Wilcox, your, er, he had the weapon. Did you take it from him?"

"No, sir, I tried to."

"You tried to take the weapon to kill Mr. Steele?"

"I tried to take it not to."

"Young lady," the judge said, "was Mr. Wilcox aiming that gun at Mr. Steele?"

"He was jis' foolin' around," Rose said. Her voice was cracking.

"He was pointing it though," the judge said. "Where was he pointing it?"

"And Mr. Steele he jist set there, on his horse an' he wouldn't move, an' I hollered at 'im to go, go, get away an' he wouldn't move . . ." Rose said, on the brink of hysterics.

"And Mr. Wilcox fired that gun. . . ."

"I jerked it is what did it," Rose sobbed, "I jerked it up t' get it away, Pap never meant to kill 'im, he was jist mad, jist crazy, he never would of killed Mr. Steele, God knows. . . ."

Harmon jumped up and they let him take her out. Myrtle flew out behind them. I was too limp to move. When things had calmed they brought in Coy Ray. They had him in handcuffs, with a deputy on each side. It liked to have killed me. And that pile of chicken-doo commenced again.

"Mr. Wilcox, where were you on the morning of the third day of September?"

Coy Ray was looking out the window. He was white and cool as cornstarch. "I was killin' Mr. Ben Aaron Steele," he said to the wind in the trees. "I was fixin' his ass for good." I guess there was nothing else the judge could do, then. Coy Ray had admitted to murder. They put him back in jail to wait for the next court day, in December, to decide what to do with him.

I pulled my shawl up over my head and got out of there as fast as I could go and went looking for Rose. Harmon had her out in the back, away from the crowd. I had just got to them when the sheriff brought Coy Ray out through that back passageway to the jail. That was a jolt. Rose sobbed out at him, "Oh Pap, will you please forgive me!" holding out her arms. He never even broke his stride. He turned back once and looked at me. Years after that I'd wake up wondering; in my sleep I'd see that face. The last thing, as the door closed behind them, Harmon hollered at him, "I'll be to see you in a day or two, whether you want me or not!" I don't know if Coy Ray heard him.

Ans had found us all by then and we stood there sort of stunned, getting our bearings before we started home. Ans was driving his big old touring car. And then Rose said, "If y'uns don't mind I'd like Cud'n Sen and me to go back to The Birches, for this day." They looked at me, puzzled, and I nodded yes. I hadn't been home but the day the baby came in all this time. Yes, I wanted to go, I said. Well he would probably do best to go around the highway and come in from the Forks, Ans said.

"No, Uncle Ans," Rose said, "if y'll let us out at the road, up yonder, it'll suit us well to walk." Ans looked at me, pretty concerned; I had not hardly walked from Nam's to town. I said yes, it would be good to walk. It was sort of blustery-looking out, windy, clouds flying. But at the turnoff he and Myrtle let us out and said goodbye. We promised to come on, in a day or so and begged them not to worry, and we went on our way.

It was then a little bit before noon, I guess. But cloudy and really cool and the wind was damp and fresh on our faces, and we needed that. We needed to walk with the silence of one another; nobody on earth could share the things we didn't need to say. We had got up just past Barz's house when we saw some figures coming down the road. And they began to run, coming to us. And Rose took off running to meet them. It was Cole Sutherland and the Wilcox boys, on their way to Red Bank. "This thing was on my mind so bad I couldn't think," Cole said. "I turned the school out at dinner. I told the children just to go on home, that I had something to take care of." He had figured us to be in Red Bank all that day. The boys had pleaded to go; they had it in their heads their daddy might be getting out and they would see him home. Cole said he had hoped at least they'd get to talk with Coy Ray. "I know how lonely he must be," he said. While we were standing in the road talking though the bottom fell out and it started just pouring rain on us. I said let's all go on to the house and get a fire and dry out, and eat something, and then we would think from there. So we did, we got home and made up bread and fried it fast in the skillet, and made coffee, and got our wits together. When the deluge let up to just a drizzle, Cole and the two bigger boys took off for the Forks, carrying all kinds of messages, and left Rose and the two littler ones and me to come when it was dry.

Along in the gloom late that afternoon we heard this whining and whimpering and then a scratching at the back door, and Rose went, and it was one of Coy Ray's old coon hounds that'd been out of pocket for weeks, ever since the trouble. I told her to let it on in, and directly here was the other one, wanting in too, so we had 'em both in the kitchen gobbling cornbread, and then they went to sleep behind the stove.

And mercy, did it rain. It seemed so much worse after dark. The wind picked up and howled. I went out and got more wood off the porch. Coy Ray cut this wood, I thought. He chopped it and split it for me, and piled it by the back door so I'd always have some dry. I couldn't bear it. As I started in the door there was this horrendous roar, it was like an explosion first and then it rumbled louder and louder like the mountain was coming down on us. I threw the wood inside and yelled for Rose; she was in the front room putting down some pallets for the little boys, by the fire. She didn't hear me, the roaring drowned me out; she heard it and came running. "Oh, before God!" she screamed. "It's Pap's dam is busted."

Dear Lord, we had forgot that whole business. I had no idea what kind of flood it would make, how high it would climb or anything. "It'll not come up here," I said. But we took a lantern and ran upstairs and tried looking out the window. I don't know what we thought we'd see in the pitch black dark. There were, though, little flutters of lightning now and then. Ordinarily we couldn't see the river from the window, even in the light. But now in the flickers we could see a fierce swirling sea coming up at the barn. "That is the worst," I said. "It won't come any further." What we heard, I knew, was the booming echo of it going through the Narrows. There was cracking, now and then, too much like a gun. That was big logs busting up on the rocks, and on each other.

We went back down and huddled by the fire. "Hit's a sign," Rose said, too weary to be anxious. She lay down on the quilts and draped her arm across those sleeping little boys, and she dozed off, breathing soft and fitful, like her sorrows plagued her even in her sleep. And I lay down too then, but I did not sleep. I kept thinking, if Ben Aaron were alive he'd have Coy Ray out of jail by now.

The hounds heard a car before I did and set up a terrible racket. I took the lamp to the kitchen and threatened them with a stick to make them hush and I heard it myself, rattling down the road, groaning and shimmying in the mud. Directly headlights shined in the window and feet thumped up on the porch.

I went and opened the door. It was the sheriff. "Ans says Rosanner's here with you," he said. "Get 'er up, please ma'm, and get 'er dressed warm. I got to take 'er with me." I got a horrible, rattling chill. "Coy Ray's a-dyin and he's beggin' to see her," he said. "I swore to him I'd get 'er there."

I turned around and she was right behind me, her face was drawn as death. "I'm comin'," she said. She had one arm in her coat and her shoes in her hand. "He tried to come home, didn' he," she said.

"Yes, honey," the sheriff said, "and he's shot clear through." They would have to go back up by the Forks, and around, he said. He had tried to come in from the south but the river was over the road, down near the highway. Rose turned her face for me to kiss her good-bye. And they went off into the fog, about the business of death. Herman woke up as they went out the door. He cried, without a sound, when he saw that Rose was gone and I took him on my lap and we rocked by the fire while he slept, again. I looked into the fire, thinking. I was beginning to understand that the love of my life was dead and buried. Our baby was dead and buried. Now a man who loved me was dying; this child that I loved so much was on her way to his dying, and it would haunt her all her life. That hideous night I thanked God for those freckled little boys who slept so peacefully, by the fire. I thanked God the room was bright and warm when those old hounds set up a howl. I took it for a sign, like Rose would have done, and put more wood on the fire to make more light and warmth. And I thanked the Lord again that the breaking clouds were rosy and the kitchen fire was dancing and the dogs had hushed when the sheriff's A-Model came rattling down the road again. And we all went back in the kitchen and drank a pot of coffee, while the little boys slept on, oblivious.

"I let Coy Ray down," the sheriff said. Rose stirred her coffee very slowly, looking down into her cup. When they had got to town, the bridge was out. A wad of broken-up logs had hit it like a freight train. They had to go on, way south of Red Bank, to cross the river and come back up. When they got there Coy Ray was dead.

"He wasn't even cold. I kissed him," Rose said. "I b'lieve he knew."

The next morning we had a quiet little procession up Wilcox Ridge, out to that spur where a hundred and fifty years of Wilcoxes lay under rocks and wooden crosses. They put Coy Ray down by Cleone, and the whole matter then was left to God.

We straightened up, then, Rose at her brothers' domain and I at mine. Or Sophia's. Their place had been spared, at least, the wreckage of the flood. The birch grove was a shambles of broken trees and washed-up logs and mud. The ferns and things I thought would never come back; 'course they did, a lot, anyway, in the spring.

Now you'd never know it, except there are these logs, about; chestnut, most of them, upholstered with moss. You might could still see they were sawed. They weren't sawed here. Nothing, only a little firewood, was ever sawed here.

The water never bothered the house, or even the barn. I just "redded up a little," as Nam would say. Neatened up. But we neither one of us had any heart to stay down here alone, right then. So Ans came and got us, and took us to the Forks. He said it was best anyway, for a while. Nam was not doing any good, he said. For the first time ever he could remember, she had taken to her bed.

"She's old, Cud'n Sen," he said, sort of stricken, as if he had just noticed. I'll tell you I had a dread about going in there and seeing that, myself. I was getting clear-minded about all that had happened, and on account of me. I didn't see how she could stand to have me around.

She was by herself when I got there, lying up in her big old four-poster, with her night cap on, tied under the chin. As I tipped in, I thought, well sort of hoped, she'd be asleep. She raised up though and squinted at me and she said, "Well the law have mercy. I thought I was forsaken."

"No, ma'm," I said. "Not while I live."

"Well, stir around then and get us up some dinner," she said.

"I've not had a bite t'eat but some little old broth since I laid down here the day before yesterday. Make speed 'fore somebody comes." While I was down in the kitchen Vicie Hambright came in the back door with a bowl of soup with a dishrag wrapped over it. She didn't see me right off. When I spoke to her she looked like she'd seen a snake.

"Howd-do," she said, and she showed me her back—I must say it was considerable—and stalked off up the stairs. Vicie had put one and one together. The sum I am sure had been shared all over Caney Forks.

Well, anyway, when Vicie had gone out the front door, to avoid the kitchen, I went up and took a plate and asked Nam if there was anything else she wanted, and she said yes, to call up to the drugstore and tell 'em to send her a bottle of calomel. "I've got this sour stomach," she said. She pressed her fist into the middle of her chest. "It's commenced to pain me even in my sleep. I'm so weak I can barely make it to the chamber. I told Ans I had to have a dose of calomel and there was none in the house and that wretch said he was glad to hear it. Wouldn't bring me any. Bull-headed snip."

I said well, I would just walk down there, if she would be all right. And I did; I went up to Ans's office and told him what she wanted and he laughed a sort of sad laugh, and got out some milk of magnesia tablets and said tell her the drug store was cleaned out of calomel and to take a couple of these.

"You know it's not her stomach," he said. I didn't think so, I said. "Her heart's just gone," he said.

"Yes," I said, "it's lyin' over there across the road."

Ans was not the most demonstrative creature on earth. He kept a kind distance, you might say. But he got up, then, and came and held me and kissed me on the forehead. "I'm so sorry for it all," he said. "So sorry. And it's not over yet."

I borrowed a piece of paper from him and wrote the children a quick note. Somehow, in the fog, I remembered I had written them once in the past month. I had written, "Our Cousin Ben Aaron has died. There is so much to do it will be a little while before I can come home. Remember that I love you."

Now I wrote them again. "Aunt Nam is very sick and I must stay until something changes." I went on down to go to the post office with it. When I came out of the drugstore there was a big Packard automobile coming out from Sophia's. As I walked on up the street it passed me; there was a trunk strapped onto the running board and one on the back. I couldn't see who was driving. There was a pile of hat boxes in the front seat, and two dressed-up ladies in the back. I watched them up the road, up past the sawmill and the mill houses, till the dust closed in behind them.

It was the next day that the Bank of Caney Forks closed its doors. I didn't tell Nam that; I knew she had some money in there, like a lot of other people that got stung. It was one of the Sunshine Club that came in every day, with all the news of deaths and bread lines and Republicans; one of them told her about it.

I was appalled and then surprised. "Well, I thought it'd happen," Nam said philosophically. "I figgered it would go when Aaron's money left it. That 'us about all holdin' it together. That and the mill account. Sophier wadn' about to leave it there for charity's sake, I could tell you.

"As for me," she said, "I'm an old woman; money'll not long be of use to me. I feel bad, 'course, for you other folks that's lost. . . ." I thought she took it terribly well. When the bearer of bad news was gone, Nam raised up and reached a key from the little dresser by her bed. "I want you to go in that old bookcase yonder and fetch me a couple of books," she said. "I want you to know what they are, so you can get 'em, when you need 'em."

But before she could say what she wanted I heard the front door open, and one of the neighbor women hollered from the foot of the stairs. I hollered back to come on up, and stuck that key down in my apron pocket and went on about my business. That night when all the company was gone, and I took up her supper, she seemed awfully droopy. Her color was bad, right gray, and she didn't eat. I sat by her and tried to feed her with a spoon. "I know it's good, Daisy darlin'," she said, "but I just can't, I'm just too tired."

Now, that rocked me. I can't tell you what a sinking feeling came over me. I sat there just devastated, watching her, till she closed her eyes and her breath got fairly regular and slow, and I flew downstairs and called Ans.

"This is the way it will go," he said. He came by and looked at her, but she was sleeping blissful as a baby. And that was pretty much the way it was, from then on. We watched her slipping farther and farther away, and there was nothing we could do. When she was able to speak, she called me Daisy all the time. Bat Dung went down and got the tobacco out of the barn and took it to the auction for us. When I got the check it came to about $350 apiece for Rose and me. She divided with the boys, of course, and I sent some home to Louise for the children, but I had to keep some to run our household on, for I guessed Nam's nest-egg had gone down with the bank.

Well, one day I was feeding her some breakfast, and the light came back on in her eyes, and she said, "Daisy, I want you to have something. I think I told you a while ago to fetch me Papa's books out of the bookcase."

"What was it you wanted?" I said.

"Bring me the *Memoir of the Reverend Sydney Smith*," she said. I got the key and unlocked the glass doors and looked. There were two of them, two volumes. They were uncommonly fat and bulging. I took 'em and handed 'em over.

"Read!" she said impishly, waving her hand. I opened one at random, to a hundred-dollar bill. Nam put her fingers to her mouth and smirked. "Right interestin', eh?" she said. Both books were stuffed as tight as ticks. "We beat Sophier to it, darlin'," she said.

"Lord have mercy," I said. "What do you want me to do with these?"

"Papa'd want you to have his books," she said. She was fading off again. Sometime during those dreary days I was aware, just for the moment, that it was Christmas, and I felt wretched about the children. I called them on the telephone and we had this wooden conversation that ended up in a three-way crying match. That night Cole Sutherland came by, to say goodbye. There were no men working in Shiloh, hardly any kids left in school and no more money to pay him, and he was moving on. He had an offer back in Virginia; not much more than room and board, but he was going. "Look after

Rose," he said, with a tremble in his voice, "She's the most valiant human being I will ever hope to know."

Into January, Nam mostly slept. She would stir and I would drip a little soup or custard into her mouth with a straw or a spoon. She lay gray and sunken on her pillow. Her eyes got hollow. Her little fingers curled useless like bird claws on the counterpane. She took on the unmistakable look of death. One night, I remember it was snowing something fierce, I had pulled a chair up beside the bed and had gone to sleep in it, and I heard her calling, "Daisy! Daisy!" just as happy as a girl. That time I knew she was not talking to me.

We had to wait for the road to clear to make that trip to The Birches. We put her beside Daisy. It was where my daddy would have been, if he had ever come home. It was where she would have wanted to be.

~29~

THE GRAVE ROBBERS

IT IS PROBABLY JUST AS WELL THAT IN THE FEW WEEKS AFTER NAM died and was buried there wasn't much time to sit and mope around. We had business to look after. Nam was not what you'd call a pauper. Most everything a McAllister had ever owned was still there at the Forks.

She left the house to Rose and me, together. That was some relief since it had not left my mind that I was Sophia's guest at The Birches. Anyway, Nam apparently had done some latter-day figuring. She knew that Ben Aaron had left Rose a little money, and a place, so Rose was far from destitute.

So Nam left her savings to me. And she left me an interest, that Lord knows I never knew she had, in the Caney Forks Lumber Company. Now that was bound to be a burr in Sophia's hide. Not that it was going to amount to anything, the way things were going. It was 1931 and nothing much was going anyway but down. And if we had been in the middle of a boom it probably would have been no livelier, at the sawmill.

The last day Rose and I were at Nam's, going through and sorting out, Jack Garner came by. He came and stood in the parlor, with his old felt hat in his hands, and told me goodbye. Jack Garner had, for all purposes, run the lumber mill for close to twenty years. A couple of the sawyers had done been and told me goodbye. Most all the hands I knew were gone. Now here stood Jack.

"I'm not a-goin' to work for that Orpington bunch," he said. "Them people treat me like hired help. I feel like I'm supposed to go 'long wipin' up behind 'em with a rag." He had stayed till he had worked out every contract Ben Aaron had left behind. Nobody had gotten any since. He had a job offered to him up in Tennessee, at a pulp mill. So he kissed me on the face, and went out into the gloom.

That afternoon, Rose and I loaded up a few quilts and pictures and things I thought she ought to take with her, and closed up Nam's house and left it. On the way out, she took Nam's bonnet off the peg by the back door and put it on her head and tied the strings under her chin, as I locked the door behind us. Rose became, by that gesture, the queen of a falling realm. The future of the Forks was as gray and cheerless as the fog we went out into, on that day.

As we went down the road in the buggy, we noticed for the first time (we just hadn't been looking) that there was no smoke at all from the mill. No noise. No trains. There was a light in the office window; the carpetbaggers were in there going over accounts. But no industry at all. We went by Ans's then, and Myrtle fixed us tea. The boys were all dutifully at school. Rose said to her aunt if it was all right, she would just as soon go on down to The Birches with me. It was, right then, an awful lonesome road ahead. And the truth was, of course, there was nothing left to keep me there. My days as a squatter on one of Sophia's favorite properties were bound to be numbered. So Myrtle said by all means go. She could make do. She had a wondrous quality of having things always under control. We started down, then, bundled 'round in a woolen blanket apiece against the cold and wet. We went past Sophia's abandoned castle. No one had raked the leaves that fall. A tree had fallen, full of ice I guess, across the "brook" and toppled the little windmill. The creatures of the cement zoo stood dismal in the rain. And we went past the churchyard, with thoughts too heavy to speak of. Little splatters of red mud pelted the base of that monstrous, lonely marker. The blanket of fake grass was all mudded and matted down. We went on; there was nothing to stop for. All the way home we didn't say a sentence between us. But things improved, as they always do, when we got a fire in the stove and the kettle on. We opened a quart of soup and made up some bread.

Rose was being awfully quiet, still. We were sitting at the table and she was not eating; she sat there staring at the stove, with her elbow on the table and her thumbnail between her front teeth. I wondered what she was thinking. It was something that almost made her smile.

Finally, she said, "Sen . . . ?"

"What, darlin?" I said.

"I think it's time we brought my daddy home." Something, I think it was life, stirred in me for the first time in a long time. I remember I smiled, and it felt like something altogether new. 'Course if I had had a lick of sense I would have said, "How?"

"I think you're absolutely right," I said.

I can't say we sat there and planned how to rob a grave. We did talk somewhat about physics and found it most too weighty. We were not born engineers. But over several days we gave it thought. More than that, we took action.

We went methodically about our project, working backwards. We took our shovels and went up on the hill, inside the wrought-iron fence. Where would we put Ben Aaron? At the foot of Aunt Arie and Uncle Dave or by his sister Lucy, and her little baby? (Her Gillespie man had married again, long ago.) By Aunt Nam? She would treasure that.

"No," I said, "that's too close to the fence. I want room for me, next to him."

"I'd like there to be room for me, on the other side of him," Rose said softly. So we decided to start a new row. We decided to put him cornering on Nam, at her feet. We went about it like we were fixing to plant roses. With the point of a shovel we laid off a grave. It crunched in the spewed-up ice. We whacked and stood on the blade and worked up a sweat, in the cold. We even talked about laying his box right there on the ground and building a cairn of stone. And we laughed out loud. But then we dragged up brush and punk and built a fire. We laid on big stuff and let it burn, and burn. Over the next couple of days we dug. We put our minds to it and dug a fine grave, that I could not see out of. And then we set about the bigger operation.

We had to wait on nature to help us; we needed the Lord's lantern, since one of our own, bobbing along in the graveyard, might have set off the alarm. As a bonus, the sun shined bright a couple of days, and it was really warm, a false spring. We were counting on that Episcopal clay not being impossibly hard, at least where it had already been dug five months before. Digging would be one thing; lifting, quite another. One arthritic mule was not going to do it. "We need us a good stout team," Rose said. She had been back up to her uncle's and seen about the boys and had brought down a pile of mending. She had also, I gathered, spent some time in the cemetery, for more than mourning. "We might borry a team from Barz," I said.

"Might," she said, "but he'll ask questions. He'd hockey his britches if he had any notion what we're doin'." She rocked and sewed. If you saw her face in the firelight you could have seen the wheels turning. "They's oxen up at the livery that ain't got Sofa's name on 'em, no more than they got mine," she said placidly, with a certain set to her mouth.

"We can't get to 'em," I said.

"Can," she said. "Pap worked 'em all the time. Had a key to the gate. It's a-hangin' on a big long strop, right now, up at the house."

"We gon' steal 'em?" I said.

"We goin' to borry 'em," she said, not looking up from her work. We talked all we knew about fulcrums and winches and blocks and tackles, and the like. That didn't take us long. Even if we knew anything we couldn't hardly go up there in the daylight and build some fancy rig over that grave. And we wouldn't dare wake up the town dogs.

So in the end, we set out by the rising moon one night, with the mule and an old sled and a little dragpan and some shovels and harness and odds and ends, and a backbreaking set of logging chains. We went about this business with light spirits, walking on light feet. The clock in the church spire struck one as we came down into the Forks. There were no houses, I am glad to say, directly on the road where we would pass. We passed the Presbyterians who were all long past hearing. Just this side of the Episcopal Church, Rose left me to go on alone. She fished the magic key out of her pocket and slung two halters over her arm and melted off like an Indian into the shadows, leaving me in a little grove of trees to wait. It was not cold; it was unusually warm for a winter night, but I stood there shaking, huddled to the mule, listening to my heart go *thunk . . . thunk . . .*

thunk . . . Little clouds began to pass over the moon, just flying, making spells of total dark. Down at the end of town a jackass brayed. I guessed Rose had waked him up. I held the mule's mouth shut with my arms, in case it tried to answer.

And then, almost as quiet as she had gone, Rose came into sight with a huge, lumbering ox on either side. I hoped she knew what to do with them. I had never been on speaking terms with one. But as easy as I might put on my petticoat, she yoked them up. "One could probably do it," she said, "but I think we'll do better with two, to get us home." The sled was frightfully noisy on the road so we went across the field, and around the far side of the church to spare the lawn as best we could. The moon came out and there our duty lay before us.

We took our shovels to it, first. We dragged back the remnants of the rug of "grass," and dug in. The ground was fairly loose and soft. We struck a determined rhythm. It picked up faster and faster. The dirt was flying. It was like I was hearing a fiddler in my head playing some old reel, with a little whiskey on his breath. It was intoxicating. We were not ready when we heard the thud. It came too soon. Our loved one, it turned out, had not been buried very deep. If it was a shock to him, this intrusion (I don't for a minute think it was), it was sobering as the devil to us. We stood there in the grave, wordless, leaning on our shovels. And then, deliberately, we went ahead.

We were working in more dark than moonlight. We cleared the top of the casket and climbed out to plot our next course. What we had to do was to cut out the end of the grave, slanch-wise. The ground was harder, of course, where it had not been dug before. We hacked away at it with the shovels. And then Rose hooked up the pan. Talking softly as she could, leading them by the halter while I stood on top of the casket, precariously guiding the pan, she led the oxen forward, and backed them, and forward, and back, scooping out an exit ramp. It was not what you'd call going smooth. But it was working. I thought, if a locomotive could be moved this way, thank you Lord. . . .

A few little drops of rain fell on us, as we dug in the dirt with our fingers, clearing the handles. We barked our knuckles bloody on rocks and felt no pain at all. Triumphantly we looped the chains through the handles, and unhitched the pan, and fastened the chains to the harness. And softly Rose coaxed, and the oxen moved ahead, and strained, and wood and metal creaked, and the end of the casket tipped upward, and moved toward freedom. Now I could only watch and listen and hold my breath. There was a horrid possibility; what if it came open? What would we do? What would it be like? And then there was this splintering jerk and clatter of chain.

A handle had come off. We couldn't see a thing; after we came back down to earth we gathered the nerve to feel around and found that's what had happened. "We've got to get a chain round it," Rose said. We got the loose end and slid down into the hole and brought it around the box and hooked it. She spoke to the oxen again, and they moved slowly. The coffin inched up, and out, and was clear. And there it sat. There sat the prize. I couldn't help what happened. I drew the biggest breath I had allowed myself in almost a year, and all the hollering I had not done, when it needed so bad to be done, I did right then, when we could afford it least.

"Damn you, Sophier!" I heard myself yelling, "Damn you to hell. You get him back now! Let me see you get him back now!" It was awful. "Hush, hush," Rose said, smothering me into her shoulder. "We can't have nobody hear us." She patted me like a baby, rocking back and forth out there in the drizzle. But Providence helped us again, I guess he forgave that blasphemy, there in the churchyard, for he sent us a great wind that blew the weeping and wailing away, toward the mountain. It blew a regular gale and then it set in to really rain. We had to move along. We pushed the sled into place and set down some little boards for runners. And after a lot of jimmying and tugging and praying we got the end of the casket started toward the sled. Rose spoke to the oxen and they moved again so slowly, and the chain tightened, again, and up it came. And we chained it firmly in place, as best we could.

One last thing: we had to fill the hole. Which we had just made so much bigger. We stood there watching the rain fall into the blackness. The churchyard was so cussed neat there was not a pebble to help us. We didn't have half enough dirt. Yes, we thought of it. The empty casket would have done it nicely. We would have gone to almost any length, but we drew the line, finally, at that. I left Rose then and went scouting. I went across to the drugstore. There was nothing loose. So I went around behind the row of stores. Back behind I reckon it was the cafe, there was a trash barrel about half full of garbage. Something, I guess a rat, jumped out of it while I was toting it along. Years later, when someone dug into the grave of my cousin Ben Aaron Steele, in the churchyard of All Saints, we would have loved to see their faces when they dug down to that old drum and pitied the great man so casually put away. The rain battered us as we laid the funeral grass back on the mound. It followed us and smoothed our tracks. We piled on our tools, and Rose got on the mule, and I, by my choice, climbed onto the casket, and we started out for home. We moved very slow; the road was rough, and we were in no hurry. At the Boney Creek Bridge we stopped and rested out of the rain. Ben Aaron was making his last night ride. If we had met some travelers and scared them half to death, he would have loved it.

When we came, finally, to that open bend above The Birches, where my children had seen him that very first time, there was a streak of pink across the sky. I had never felt the kind of love for anything, or anybody like I felt for this piece of earth, right then. And for what we were about to add to it.

~ 30 ~

ROYAL FLUSH

ON THE HEELS OF OUR ESCAPADE IT TURNED BITTERLY COLD. ROSE had a terrible cough from being outside all night in the wind and rain. Ans sent two of the little boys down to see about us, when we had been out of pocket for a couple of days, and I sent him word that Rose was too sick to go home, that I would bring her when the weather eased.

My conscience hurt me terribly about letting her get in that plight, but between spasms of smothering she was absolutely gleeful over what we had done. I could only delude myself so much. That was still Sophia's hillside where he lay—if, as Ben Aaron had once said, a deed ever meant real ownership. I did not feel like a trespasser when I walked up there. When I squatted by that mound and replaced the roots of violets and strawberries I was not moved to think, "This is Sophia's mud."

My mind was clearing. One thing, I realized for the first time since Nam died that I might have the money to buy The Birches; she certainly would have wanted that. Land prices were sinking. I figured on the basis of what Ben Aaron had paid for places, and I figured I might have enough. Only, I knew this: Sophia would never sell. Not to me. But I could try.

When Rose and I went back up to the Forks, the end of that week, I went by the mill to see if I could catch Harmon Garrison. I thought it would be better to take it up first with the company lawyer. Oh, that is not so; I just didn't want to confront Sophia, even in the mail, and give her the chance to make me so mad I would go after her with the axe.

I went up to the office and had to knock. The door was locked. Directly one of those outland people came strolling up from behind a rotting slab pile, looking annoyed. "We are not open for business today," he said.

"We are not?" I said. It just popped out. He looked at me like I was trying to be funny. Well, of course they were not open; they had no orders and nobody to saw anything. "I thought Mr. Garrison might be in today," I said, "but I don't see his car. I'd like to leave a message for him, when he comes by."

"Mr. Garrison does not represent the Caney Forks Lumber Company anymore," the fellow said. "Our attorneys are in Boston."

"Our attorneys, eh?" I itched to smack him hard with a slab. "Man," I said, "Your ass is cravin' stovewood." Neither the voice nor the saying were exactly mine. I don't believe the man got it, anyway; he was puzzling on it when I thanked him all sweet and humble and went to the road.

Going back over the mountain I realized I was alone, on that road, for the first time since the morning after Ben Aaron died. And I thought about things. I had not seen my children in six months. I missed them something awful. It came down on me like a rock that what I was going to do, I was going back to Charleston and close the door on what had become my life. There were things, of course, that had to be taken care of first. I had to make a home, somewhere, for a few things from The Birches. Nam's house was crammed, and its future was uncertain. What were we going to do with it? Rose and the boys could move into it, but they were well fixed where they were. In my mind, as I rode along, I inventoried Daisy's attic. The furniture the Steeles had made. The dolls and books and dishes. Daisy's clothes, and all those family portraits. I would see Sophia Orpington in hell before she should set my daddy's cradle out to rot. I could hear her going room to room, dickering with some mincy antique dealer. I would have to do something.

At least it was a pretty afternoon. Mild. The trees had that rose-gray look that is hopeful about spring. I unhitched the mule down in the barn lot and got on its back and rode up the field, before I went to the house. It was like checking on a child in the night. I wanted to see that Ben Aaron was still there, and undisturbed. Someday, I thought, when the coast is clear I shall have a stone made, more to our taste, and put it up here. Until then, only Rose and I would know.

I rode on back down to the barn, then. I did not feel alone. I was putting the mule in the stall when I thought I heard an automobile coming over the ridge. Who in the world? Directly here came Harmon's little roadster, grumbling along. I ran out to meet him, and flung my arms around him. "You must have got my message," I said into his neck.

"Where did you leave me a message?" he said.

"I stopped up at the mill and talked to a sum-bitch," I said. "I told him I wanted to see you."

"I haven't been there in weeks," he said. "I have to talk with you about that.

"No," he said, "what I really came down here for, I came to see if you would marry me."

"I would marry you instantly," I said, "if I were not so awfully much married already."

He looked at me intently. "I know," he said. "I know. And in the state in which you are married, there is no such thing as divorce."

He was a good man. It was the most comforting thing that could happen to me, to be hugged by him, right then, very long and very tight. We climbed up and sat down on the steps, then, in the sun. "You didn't go by the mill?" I said.

"No, I went by Panama's. I thought I would see you, but the house was all closed up." I told him how we had left it, and how vague our plans were, for everything.

"So what is this?" I said. "Have you dropped Miss Sophier as a client?"

"Miss Sophier most decidedly dropped me," he said. "You don't think she would keep somebody so firmly devoted to you to do her legal work, my dear. No, she got a little bit impatient with me. We parted our ways back right after Nam died. We parted through her lord chamberlain and pages and footmen over there, of course; I have not seen nor heard from Mistress Steele, direct, since she went back to her folks."

"Well," I said, "as her minor partner in that business, I am a little bit depressed. From what it looked like in there this morning, I think we are going broke."

"You mean," Harmon said smirking, "that you have not been consulted as a partner?"

"Never," I said. "I may as well not exist."

"Ah," he said, "that is why I came to see you, really. Because you DO exist. Would you like to hear something interesting?"

"Tell me!" I said.

"Are you my client?"

"Yes! Yes!"

"Well, then. The Caney Forks Lumber Company is for sale. In fact, it may be about to be sold. Before I left there they had a bid from Intermont-Atlantic — that's a tremendous outfit. Big in hardwoods. Not much of a bid, near nothing, considering what that mill and standing timber ought to be worth, in decent times. But apparently it looked good to Sophier."

"Is she broke?" I said.

"Oh, she's not hurting," Harmon said. "Don't you worry about her. She just don't know how to run a sawmill. None of her friends and relations know how to run one either and that's all she's got left up there. This is one time she's smart enough to make a sensible move."

"Oh, I think she might have made another, time to time," I said. He smiled and picked some burrs off his britches. I was suddenly ashamed I had let the weeds grow right up to the front steps, while I was so distressed.

Directly, he said, "You talking about this place?"

"Yes indeed," I said. I realized then he must know something about its circumstances. "That's why I wanted to see you," I said. "I wanted you to help me out a little bit. I want to buy this place."

"Oh, Sophia won't like that," he said darkly. "Did you really think I could get her to sell The Birches? To you?"

I was looking into my lap. The flowers in the goods of my dress were beginning to swim about, a little. "In fact," he went on, "this place is part of the package she plans to sell Intermont."

"What?" I hollered.

"While you were up at the Forks you didn't see them out here measuring your trees. Why, they liked to have gone wild. There might not
be a big market right this day, but eh, law, honey, them birches, them
walnuts, maples, big oaks, they just keep a-growin'."

"Harmon!" I said.

"However. . . ." he said, savoring the pause, "however, like I say, I
have something interesting to talk with you about. The last thing I
did for the Caney Forks Lumber Company, or more specifically, for
the estate of Ben Aaron Steele, I had to inventory their holdings.
Now, I want you to know, that was a job. I was in the courthouse
for five weeks, checking over deeds and tax books. Do you have any
idea how your cousin operated? He would 'acquire' a few acres in a
card game somewhere, and forget to tell me, although I was supposed to be keeping up with his business. Sometimes he would buy
something—pay real money—and stick the receipt down in his
pocket and forget it. Oh, HE didn't forget it; he just didn't tell me.
Now," Harmon said, "there are serious questions on which the estate of Mr. Steele is in the dark."

"It is not all settled?" I said.

"Nowhere near," he said. "Because it is not, it has been taken out of
my hands. Do you remember—did he ever say anything to you, or did
your mother say anything, about your grandfather's part of the mill?"

"Yes," I said, "Ben Aaron told me about that. He said he had
made some kind of settlement with my mother about it."

"Do you know if she signed anything?"

"She never told me anything about it, at all," I said. "She never
mentioned selling this place, either. I never knew there was a house,
or a mill, or my own people, until I came up here."

"Well, it was a long time before I came into the business that some
disposition must have been made. Or I assume it was made," Harmon
said. "The problem with the mill—Sophia's problem—is that there
was never any record of any payment to you—you would have been
the heir, when Daisy Steele's estate was settled. No, I shouldn't say
there was never any record. I don't know that. All I can say is, when I
went through Ben Aaron's deeds and papers, there was no record of
any such transaction."

"What does that mean?" I said. I was not going to have it mean that Ben Aaron had lied. But I didn't say it. I didn't know what to say.

Harmon sat and studied. Finally, he said, "It could have been any one of several things. One thing it was not," he said, looking straight at me, "he did not lie to you about it. It could have been," he went on, "I think it might have been that the deal was made and nothing ever signed. You can ask your mother. Or," he said, "and I know Ben Aaron. . . . if something was signed, for some reason all his own he destroyed it."

"What do you really think?" I said.

He paid no attention. "The thing is," he said, with a satisfied sigh, "there is no record at the courthouse, either. There ought to have been a quit-claim filed. But I have had the books searched from the day your grandfather died to the day Ben Aaron died—twenty-one years—and there is no record."

I wondered, did Harmon do all that because he loved me, or because he detested Sophia? Who'll ever know? "Now you asked me what all this means," he said. "Practically, it means that unless somebody can come forth with proof otherwise, you own two-thirds of the Caney Forks Lumber Company. Nam's part, and what would have been your father's.

"And I will tell you a little something else that's kind of funny," he said. "But not till you make me some good hot coffee." He got me up, for I was weak in the knees, and we went into the house, and he made the fire in the stove and I put on the pot, and got out some fried pies left from breakfast. After a while I was able to stop shaking.

"If you are worried about Sophia coming to put you out, don't," he said happily. "The tax collector will probably dump you first."

"How?" I said. "Did she not pay her taxes?"

"Oh, she never did a menial thing like paying bills. She left that to Mr. Steele. Mr. Steele tended to be meticulous about those matters. His debts were paid. His taxes were paid. He even was quick to pay the taxes of others—that was not one of the things that made people love him. He watched the tax sales like a vulture. Not to dispossess people, or anything like that, but just to get a lien on their land; a foot in the door, so to speak. Mr. Steele was a most acquisitive fellow. That is why it was so odd that the taxes on The Birches are two years in arrears."

"Do you think he simply forgot it?"

Harmon looked at me like I had asked if roosters lay brown eggs. "Your cousin, and forgive me for saying so, could be petty as a piss ant when he was of a mind," he said. "I don't think he thought he could get this place back from Sophia with a tax deed but I do expect he wanted it to come up for sale, to needle her. He probably figured to ship her off to Europe one spring, at tax sale time, and when she came back he'd have at least a tax lien on The Birches. I think he thought of everything, some time, to try to get it back."

He went out and brought in more stove wood. The sun was getting very low. "How do you feel about being here by yourself?" he said.

It would be the first night I had spent here by myself since Ben Aaron died. I had thought about it. "I'll be all right," I said.

"I don't like it," he said.

"No, don't worry," I said. "I'll be fine. I have a lot to think about." And then I told him how I didn't feel so much alone. Harmon was my friend. I told him what Rose and I had done. I didn't expect him to be so undone by it. He looked at me with his eyes this big. In spite of himself he shuddered and groaned out loud. And then he said, when he had caught up with himself, "If you had asked me, I would have helped you."

"I knew you would," I said. "I think you have helped me fairly well as it is."

"You won't let me stay with you?" he said.

"No," I said. "You need to get over that road out there before it gets good dark." I helped him get his coat on, and kissed him, and he made me bolt the door behind him. Part of me terribly wanted him to stay. I nearly cried when I heard the motor crank and the car go off up the hill. But there was a part of me that rejoiced right then in that sort of morbid solitude. I made a fire in Daisy's sitting room. I had got the time from Harmon's watch and had set and wound Ive's clock. I sat and rocked and ran things through my mind. It was perfectly still, except for the clock, and the fire, and the creaks and rustles an old house makes in its sleep. When I listened I could hear the river. What a year it had been since Ben Aaron Steele had held me, there in front of that fire. And it melted away, like nothing, and I closed my eyes and was wrapped up, again, in the warmth of him, and the strength of him, in the depth of love that doesn't die. And I slept.

Early as the larks, I got up and washed and got dressed as best as was prudent, considering I was going to ride a mule down to Red Bank. When I got down there I went by Harmon's office to let him know I had come to town. He went over to the courthouse with me, then. We went down in the basement where all the little cubicles of welfare and crop advice and records of birth and marriage and vice and death shared a dungeon-like placidity, and the smell of wet tobacco.

We passed the door marked TAX COLLECTOR and went into one marked REGISTER OF DEEDS. They opened into the same dim, brown-and-mustard room. Arvil Hatcher, who Registered, was leaning over the counter talking to Philo Spivey, who Collected. Philo was sitting by the coal heater, thoughtfully whittling his fingernails with his barlow. The courthouse dog lay asleep at his feet.

"I want to show my client, here, something that is not in the deedbook. We want S through V," Harmon said, straightening the knot of his tie. Arvil produced the book dutifully and went back to his conference. The dog startled and bit at a flea. Harmon leafed through the pages, holding it for me to look. There were pages and pages of transactions, inscribed in careful, confident penmanship, between this Steele and that, between Steeles and everybody in the valley, going back more than a hundred years. A lot of them involved the Caney Forks Lumber Company. Of course I was interested in every word. But none seemed to apply, in our immediate situation. And then a matter entered on record in March of 1912 grabbed me: "Steele to Steele; Natalie T. Steele, trustee for Mary Seneca Steele, to Benjamin A. Steele. . . ."

"That was The Birches," Harmon said quietly. "Do you see?" My eyes clouded. But there was nothing else to do with my mother, or me, on that page, or the next, or anywhere. Harmon turned back to the beginning and we went through again. That time I noticed something and showed Harmon. A page had been torn out. He didn't seem at all surprised.

"Mr. Hatcher," I said, "what do you suppose went with this page? There is a page missing."

Arvil looked sort of sidewise at it, over his glasses, casually. "Lost in a fire, I 'spect," he said.

"Did you have a fire in here sometime?" I said. I wondered how the damage was held to one page.

"Got one about ever' day, when it's cool," Arvil said. He looked at me like I didn't have much sense. We searched through "Grantors" and "Grantees." Nothing. I began to get the thrilling feeling it was hopeless.

"You satisfied?" Harmon said.

"I guess," I said, bewildered.

"I want to be sure about the tax," Harmon said. "Philo, has Mistress Sophier Sweetheart Steele paid her property tax this year on that boundary up in the cove?"

"Not as I know of," said Philo. Reluctantly he got up and rubbed his back a couple of strokes and shuffled off to the shelves for the current ledger, and licked his thumb.

"No, she ain't," he said with obvious pleasure. "That's two year runnin'. Hmm. Might put it on the courthouse steps this year," said Philo.

"Could!" said Arvil.

"Have you notified the owner?" said Harmon, being officious.

"Oh, yeah," said Philo.

"Might ort to again," said Arvil, solicitiously.

Philo took out a printed form, from under the counter, and filled in the blanks with studious scrolls and flourishes, and put it in an official envelope.

"Where does the high and mighty Madam Steele live now?" he said. "I don't even know where she's at."

"Send it to the Caney Forks Lumber Company. They'll see that she gets it," Harmon said. So Philo addressed the envelope and stamped it, and whistled through his teeth. The old dog rose and blinked and stretched and bit at a flea on his back.

"Here," said Philo, sailing the letter to the floor. "Run 'nis over to the post office." The dog nosed the envelope about, a little bit, and rolled its eyes. I could see how a slip-up could happen, time to time, in even this efficient operation. We thanked our hosts and took our leave.

"Harmon," I said, while we were walking back to his office, "I don't want to fight Sophia hand to hand. I don't want to cheat her, nor hurt her in any way. She has suffered terribly. And I am sorry." (I couldn't believe my own ears, either.)

"I am not expecting to fight Sophia at all," Harmon said. "I don't even expect to fight her lawyers. I think they can be shown very simply where they stand. Where she stands is that she is going to have to do about whatever you want her to, if she wants to dispose of the company."

"I want The Birches," I said. "I want that house and those woods. I want that cemetery. She can have every inch and every dollar of the rest of it. I want her to have it."

"You are my client — you said," Harmon said. "I am not going to do that poorly by you. I promise we'll be fair. But remember, my love, Ben Aaron was my client, too. In what I do with this, I represent him, above all."

So I went home, and Harmon went to his office and wrote a letter. I never heard from Sophia. No cross words ever passed. There was no tax sale. On the same day the Caney Forks Lumber Company passed on to Intermont-Atlantic, The Birches passed quietly to me. When the violets uncurled their leaves among those fresh clods on the hill, this land was ours, again.

≈31≈

HIATUS

SO WHAT I HAD TO DO THEN, I COULD DO WITH PEACE AND acceptance, and it would not break my heart. I went up to the Forks and spent an afternoon with Rose, telling her goodbye. I think it would have gone harder with us both except that when I came, she had a letter from Cole Sutherland in her hand and a dewy glow on her face. She read part of it to me, where he said he had saved the train fare and would be down for the weekend.

Part of it she did not read out loud, and while we talked she kept the letter folded in her hand, inside her apron pocket. She still had a little cough, but she looked much better, and when I kissed her and left I did not feel that I was forsaking her.

The next morning I went up on the hill to watch the sun come up. The jonquils were up. Little blue hepatica was blooming in the shade of the stones. Almost matter-of-factly I said goodbye to Ben Aaron. I heard myself say to him, like I was someone else, "Well, I have to go now. But only this once — when I come back I shan't go again." It was so strange. And then I turned and left them all and did not dare look back.

I hitched the mule to the wagon, and put in my things. And I checked through the house, one last time, and went out and closed the door behind me. I put the key on a nail behind the steps where Rose knew where to find it. My ears were ringing, like I was in a vacuum or something. I got on the wagon and drove away. I could not have looked the old house in the face; I knew it looked resigned, and I would cry.

I turned off the road on the lane to Barz's place. He had the oxen hitched, and we unhitched the mule and put it in the lot and transferred my stuff to the "taxi" and we trundled off to Red Bank, in the same vehicle, somewhat modified, that the kids and I had arrived in. On every rock and stump and tree, every bend and overlook along that road, some memory was pinned, of something said or something felt, full of private sweetness and yearning and pain. I passed them as casually that day as if I might have been going down to Trotter's for a spool of thread.

Harmon came to the depot to tell me goodbye. He had one last bit of lawyerly advice to offer: "You know, as long as you are married to that girly-man down there, what you have here is in jeopardy, if he finds out you've got it. You don't HAVE an ugly-sister partnership to stand between him and The Birches. Act poor. The less he knows the better."

He brought me some magazines to read along the way, and helped me onto the train. I remember waving to him and wondering why he didn't smile or didn't even look, while the train pulled away. I settled back and listened to the whistle marking off the crossings. Directly the news butch came through, and I realized I hadn't eaten anything all that day, and I bought a bar of that awful sticky coconut ribbon candy, and watched sort of blankly out the window as the hills slipped by, and away. And it was cotton land, and pine land, and swamp land and we were on trestles over dark water. And it was sundown, on liveoaks with beards of gray moss, and it was night.

Louise and Uncle Camp were at the station with the children; Uncle Camp had my mother's touring car. It is awful to say, but I might not have known the kids right off, for Pet had grown so much taller, and slimmer and yet rounder. Female. And Hugh's legs had grown so long, and his face was thin and serious. They both had an "indoors" look, not like the way I had sent them back, brown right out of the tobacco patch. There was a way Pet looked at me, up and down, quickly so as not to be noticed, that made me realize I wasn't very stylish at the moment.

But Louise clasped me to her heart. She apologized for Foots not coming; "Hubert has a little touch of the grippe," she said. His mama thought it best he not come out. Aunt Mit was home cooking a big supper, since she was sure I hadn't eaten in two years. So we got in the car and started for home, Louise in front with Camp and I in the back seat, with the children. I felt like I was ready for anything, just to have my arms around the children again.

"Mama, it has been so awful," Hugh said into my ear. "You don't know. He talks about how bad you are, every time he can make us listen. He told us at Christmas that you never would come back, that you had just wanted to get rid of us. We thought about running away and going back to you, but then we didn't know. . . ."

"Hush, you dunce," Pet hissed. "Don't ruin things for Mama. He's just a fool." I guess a good wife and mother would have pinched her. I was neither. I gritted my teeth. I couldn't wait to get to our happy home.

The night was sweet and warm and full of wisteria, and the ocean, and decay. It was the hundred-years-past-rotten smell of musty aristocracy, of old houses so close together the sun never shined between them, and old furniture, and old families, and old grudges and old prides. Oh, I loved it. I didn't know I had missed it, until I smelled it. All those piazzas, lit up like Christmas. There was a ship coming up the inlet, as we went along, with its lights all on. The street lights shined in the crowns of the palmettoes. I had forgotten there could be so much light at night. Camp pulled up on the street, by the house, and helped us out before he put the car in the garage.

We went in the gate, and I stood on the steps of my father's house, again. I said to the children, "Your grandfather died here on these steps, in my arms, when I was younger than you." I had never told them that; I don't know why. I think maybe I had never come to terms with it, myself. Under the light I noticed Louise looked awfully drawn and pale. "Have you been well?" I asked her.

"Oh, yes." But as she opened the front door for us, she said warily, "I hope things are pleasant. We have had some hard times here, I must tell you. Please, Sister, don't be hurt if Hubert shows himself tonight." I patted her shoulder and bit my tongue.

We went straight back to the kitchen and Mit flung down her

egg beater and we were all hugged up when Foots came flouncing in, with Miss Lilah a few respectful steps behind. I remember he had on a red brocade dressing gown over his pajamas, with a slightly rumpled hanky in the pocket. "Well, well," he said, "Mittie, have you had our visitor sign the guest book?" He snatched me backwards and gave me a fish-kiss on the cheek. I could feel my gut knotting.

"Ummm-UMMM!" he said, "How lonely I have been for my dear little wife."

"Put de supper 'pon de table," Mit said to Camp, not a bit impressed. When we had all sat down, and Hugh had been pressed to ask the blessing, I began to notice things. There were candles on the table, in little dimestore glass holders. When I picked up my fork I noticed it was very large; I turned it over and it had U.S. stamped on the back of the handle. I glanced at Louise's silverware, next to me, and saw I had fared better. Her fork had tines so snaggle-toothed it wouldn't pick up rice. Now, I was not proud, or anything, just curious.

"Aunt Mit," I said, "Is the silver put away? "

"No'm." she said, hustling off to the kitchen.

"Hubert, where is the silver?" I said.

"Where is my car?" he said impudently. And he did his eyebrows up and down, with meaning. That infuriated me.

"I sold it," I said.

"Precisely," he said. "We had to eat here, too."

I didn't need to look at her to know Louise was in a panic. "Tell us about your visit with your people," she said, with a tremble in her voice.

"It was a revelation," I said. "There were some sad times; my cousin died suddenly."

"We read about it in the paper," Foots said. "Such a scandal! It must have been exciting!" That was a complication I was not prepared for. I decided to ignore it.

"And then my father's aunt was sick for several weeks, and died," I said. "But it meant more than I can ever say that I was able to know them."

"We've had sad times here too," Foots said. "I have been very sick. VERY sick. But I am sure that didn't matter to you."

"Hubert . . ." Louise said, barely audible.

"Hubert has been very sick!" Miss Lilah said, glowering at her. "You know he has been under de doctor fo' six months!" Well, the image tickled me so I nearly spit my tea. Hugh and Pet looked at me and struggled against giggles. To make bad matters worse, in that moment of levity, Hugh picked up a fried shrimp with his fingers and put it in his mouth.

"Young man," Foots yelled, with his face all purple, "That will be enough out of you. You think because your mother has come back you've got a ticket to behave like hillbilly trash and get by with it. I will thrash you, that's what I'll do!"

He hunched his chair back from the table and started to get up. Pet beat him to it. She jumped up like a cat. "You touch him again and I will kill you," she said, brandishing her fork with its two lonely sharp tines.

Uncle Camp was standing beside me with a pitcher in his hand. The white bones were shining in his knuckles. Hugh sat immobile, his mouth stalled in half chew. I put down my glass, and folded my napkin, and rose and clasped my hands in front of me, and all eyes turned.

"Uncle Camp," I said, "will you be so kind as to show Mr. Lamb and all his belongings to the door? If he is not out of this house within an hour, I shall kick his sorry ass across the bay." Foots bounced up like his spring was overwound, and botted off up the stairs. Of course Miss Lilah threw back her head and gasped, and clapped her hands over her face in horror. Pet and Hugh looked radiant. Louise looked down at her plate.

"Yes, mam," said Camp, and he went off to put the pitcher down. I sat down, then, and said, "Please excuse me, I am sorry I was unpleasant," and I commenced to eat my supper.

Well, Miss Lilah was all adither. "Louise!" she shrieked, "Don' let this give you a heart attact."

"My heart is fine," Louise said. "I won't let it give me a fit, either." And Miss Lilah, her world undone, leapt up with more energy than I had ever seen her expend, and flew upstairs to comfort Hubuht. Mit came in with a bowl of floating island, then, and Louise and the kids and I finished our supper in pretty good cheer. There was considerable slamming and bumping around upstairs, but we ignored it.

We were still sitting there, talking placidly, when the invalid came barreling down the stairs, again, with Uncle Camp struggling along behind with two suitcases. They went out the kitchen door.

"He has no money. Where will he go?" Louise said, very flatly, dawdling with her spoon.

"I 'spect he'll go to Denby Turnham's, won't he?" I said.

"He won't go to Denby's," she said. "Denby got married."

"Denby Turnham got married?" I said. "When? To what? "

"I didn't write you? It's been maybe four or five months. He married Fant Carson's widow. Everybody was talking about it. She's so much older, you know. She has a lot of property, I hear. Hubert was incensed about it," she said. "He wouldn't even go to the wedding. He's been on his high horse, really, ever since. I don't understand him. Why can't he just live and let live?"

Poor Foots, I thought. His only port in the storm, and it closed.

"Oh, I wanted to tell you," Louise said. "I'm so sorry about the silver. I knew he had sold it. He told us Mit stole it. 'Course I knew it wasn't so; that was just so he'd have an excuse not to pay her."

"She's not been paid?" I said. I was mortified.

"Well, she finally quit coming. For months she didn't come. She came back this week when I told her you were coming home. She came to clean up and get ready for you."

"What else do you reckon he's sold?" I said. "Have you looked into the jewelry?"

Louise smiled. "I know he's sold all of mine. That birthstone ring that Daddy gave me when I was twelve and my locket with the baby curl in it. You better see about yours. But what good will it do? What if it's gone?"

"I'm sure it's gone," I said, "but that's the least of our worries. It's not gone far."

Neither had Foots, of course, as I was sure it would turn out. I had sent the children to bed; I had promised to come visit each one before they went to sleep. Louise went up to comfort her mother, who had prostrated herself in grief. After a couple of hours of riding up and down every street and cobblestone alley in Charleston, Uncle Camp came driving home, with Foots and his suitcases still in the back. He parked out front and came in.

"What must I do wid 'im, Miss?" Camp said. "He ain' got a dime fo' stay in no boardin' house."

"Bring him in," I said. "Put him back upstairs. I shall have to make it clear to him exactly how he is going to behave, as long as he lives in this house."

And I did. Plainly. And that was the beginning of the rest of my life with Foots, in what I am sure was a thoroughly wondered-about arrangement. From that night on we saw each other at meals, spoke when necessary, and never, never lived together again like married people. After a few days, when I got around to it, I consulted the memoir of the Reverend Sydney Smith for a little help and went downtown to Siggie Bonenblume's jewelry shop. With great delight, from the dark dusty chambers behind the store Siggie was able to produce exactly what I was shopping for: a silver tea service with the Twyning coat of arms on it; a set of silver flatware, candlesticks and trays and jewelry I hadn't even missed, even a little birthstone ring and a locket with a baby curl inside. All of it was redeemed for very little, "Cost plus nothing," Siggie explained. "I hope you don't think I'd give that bastard what it was worth when I knew you were going to want it back."

Things settled down, day by day, month by month, to the normal Charleston turtle-pace. It was like I had not been gone. The ladies of our house put up a united front and went forth to teas and meetings of the Daughters of the Confederacy. Sometimes we were the hostesses ourselves. Louise was, as always, my dearest friend. Miss Lilah prudently held her tongue, which must have been a struggle and a half. Foots spent most of his days at the Bon Homme Club, in the company of others who did not earn a living.

It was no grand situation. But the children relaxed and did fairly well. In some things they did remarkably. Hugh began to lead his class consistently at school. Louise taught them both music; she had several students who came regularly for piano lessons. When Pet was fifteen, she began to study voice with a teacher at the Latin School. First it was one of those niceties our parents make us do so we will be ladies.

Then it was in earnest. By the end of that year, Mama and Dr. Rehnwissel had come home to stay, and it was everything. "Papa," as Pet called him, had a new cause and new life in the refinement of my child's vocal cords.

When there was news of some import, I would hear from Caney Forks. Rose was not exactly a fount of chatty prose; she wrote when she had something to say and said it. Like about six months after I was gone, she wrote and said, "The new big man at the lumber co. wants to buy Aunt Nam's house. He is nice but sort of braggy. What do you think? I think no. All well here. I miss you."

I took her word and thought no, too. We decided to rent to the braggy man instead. And I missed Rose, in a way there were no words for. When one of those rare letters came, I always got tears behind my eyes. She wrote once, "Cousin Barz wants to pasture cows down at The Birches. I think you might ought to let him, it would keep the brush down. I told him I would ask you."

I had the letter in my hand, with my head down crying, and Louise came in and got terribly concerned. "Oh, Sister," she said, "is it something bad?" I raised up and couldn't help but laugh, and said no, it was just that an old man wanted a place to run his cattle. And I told her a little bit about Barz, how scared he had been of me, and I told her the truth about the car, and how it got traded for a mule we nearly had to chew for, and about the cow we called Miss Murchie. And we laughed. But there were tears in her eyes, too, and I loved her for it.

It was the next spring, a year gone, when Rose wrote again. "Dear Cousin Sen," she said, "The last Friday in May Cole is coming here to marry me. It would be real nice if you and Pet and Hugh could come." I let out a joyful shriek although of course it was no surprise. I wrote back yes we would, with bells on. It didn't occur to me at the time that Pet was going to sing at the Latin School commencement that same day. And then, that week, after I had made peace with Pet about it, Louise had her first bad spell in a very long time, while she was pressing the ruffles on Pet's new dress. She grabbed at the iron as she went down and burnt her arm so bad the doctor had to graft new skin.

So, at the last minute, I sent a telegram full of regrets and loving wishes. It was no lie when I said my heart was right beside her, when Rose came down the stairs to Ans and Myrtle's parlor, so happy.

As I suspected, and Rose chose not to say, Cole was going to be out of a job at the end of the term. Rose was in no financial straits of course. But I wrote and suggested that they might want a place to stay and some crop land that wouldn't need clearing, and that they ought to think about moving to The Birches. It was the most fitting thing, and they accepted. I could see Rose keeping order there; she would not let the weeds grow up to the door, nor have the mice take over the kitchen. I could see her rocking pretty babies there, in front of Daisy's fire. I dreamed about these things, and that sometime I would go see them. I would go home, and there would be life in that house. Someone living, who belonged there, would come to the door.

The years slipped by; I guess it was the third winter after Rose and Cole were married that I had a letter in a strange hand from the Forks. We had been down to Savannah for a wedding, one of Foots and Louise's cousins got married and there was close to a week of parties and all that, and the day we got back there was this letter from Myrtle.

"My dear Sen," she said, "It hurts me so to tell you that Rosannah slipped away from us Sunday. You knew, I am sure, she had TB. Ansel thought she was doing so well, she had just come through pneumonia and had gone back down to The Birches, saying she felt just fine. She had a hemorrhage and was gone before Cole could get here with her. We tried to telephone you all that day, and the next, but got no answer. So we laid her to rest in the Steele cemetery. I believe that is what she told me the two of you had once decided. We have Cole here with us, for a while. He is so lost. The boys are heartbroken. All of us are — She would want me to tell you that she loved you very much. I know, for she told me so. Many times."

There wasn't any duty to stand in the way of grief. I took to my room and closed the door and the curtains. I simply could not bear it. It alarmed the household. Aunt Mit and Louise would bring up trays of the nicest food I couldn't begin to eat. Even Miss Lilah came and looked in on me, in the dark. I knew they didn't understand, and how could I tell them? I couldn't hardly say what that regal, golden child represented to me. How could I say that in the color of her eyes, and in the cleft in her chin, and in so many attitudes and gestures her father had still lived. Through her, alone, the family had still lived, in all its inbred peculiarity. I couldn't tell them any of it. But they accepted it, that it had been some private devastation. And they were kind.

My mother was a godsend in that time. My mother took most matters of consequence very lightly; the things she took seriously were parties and flirtations and social intrigues. She was always on the move, into something; she was always leaving a little breeze behind her, full of some perfumer's notion of spring bouquet. And my mother, as I well recalled, was not one for long mourning.

She gave me a week and then she and Pet came in and packed my clothes and strong-armed me to the train and we went to New York, to the opera and the ballet and the stores. My unusual non-living arrangement with Foots did not embarrass Mama like it did me, I mean about having big parties and things at the house. So she began to plan some for me. It was not really all that rare for people to wholly ignore (and abhor) each other, while happily married—if we only knew what went on beyond the piazzas and the fan lights, she said, with a knowing lift to her brow.

As for Dr. Rehnwissel, he was never young, I am sure, when he was young, and he was growing more frail and fretful in his island exile. He lay in his hammock a lot, when it was warm, fanned by moss and seabreeze, reading his papers and cursing Adolph Hitler, whom he saw inevitably ascending. He yearned for the more decorous days of Der Kaiser, upon whose printed visage he once had been moved to spit.

But we began to have music at the house again. The Saturday musicales, little recitals by local "talent," some of which would have been totally unpalatable (and unattended) without the little cakes and punch. The doctor himself was down to one pupil. He would have only one, and it was Pet. He had made a tolerable—no, a very good singer of my mother. He had a better voice to work with, and a much more single-minded creature, in my daughter. The Saturdays he had her sing for us even I looked forward to, though Lord knows we heard her daily, and near around the clock.

On the other hand, Hugh was very little seen or heard. He had his own pursuits. He had a paper route, for one thing, and besides a

little money he made friends. And a lot of them didn't live on our
street. One night while Pet and Papa were doing Mahler in the music
room, I went back to the kitchen to see if I could help Mit cook supper. Just as I went to push the swinging door I heard something I
couldn't quite fathom. This utterly ecstatic sound. And I listened, and
it stopped my breath. I looked in and Hugh and a couple of colored
boys were in there, sitting in the corner in kitchen chairs. They had a
beat-up banjo apiece; they were bent over them, with their heads together. They were playing "Blackberry Blossom." I let the door close
back, quietly, and cried into the wall.

There were times like that, that the darkest, deepest loneliness
rose and bubbled over. Those times belonged mostly to the night.
Sometimes I would dream about The Birches, some wistful, un-
graspable, undefinable dream, full of morning light and fog, and I
would wake up, trying to bring it back.

Years went by after Rose was gone that I heard nothing, except a
Christmas card or so, from Red Bank or the Forks. I did get a letter
from Galveston, Texas, an engraved announcement that Irvin Harmon
Garrison had joined the law firm of something and somebody. He
had written across the bottom of it, "If you get in dutch in Texas, call
on me." That was one of those low moments.

Then I got a letter from the Caney Valley Power Company. That
was something I had never heard of. It said they were surveying for a
hydroelectric project, and they wanted to verify ownership of properties in Big Caney Township.

I wrote at once to Ans. He wrote back that this was some big new
thing backed by the federal government and that the word was out
that they were intending to dam the river, just above Boney Creek.
It would back water over the Forks and way on upstream, nearly to
the river's source. He and Myrtle were distraught. I wrote back that
though I owned very little there I was with them, against it, as long
as we could fight.

It was a lost cause; the lumber company announced it was moving and that left no industry to keep the Forks alive. And very few
landowners; most of the people in the valley had by one means or
another become Ben Aaron's tenants.

So Ans had the best of Nam's stuff moved to The Birches. It crossed my mind that they would consult Sophia about moving that solitary grave. I wondered where she would tell them to re-bury that old drum of fish scraps and chicken bones. I thought about the displaced Presbyterians, too.

But I did not go back. I could not bear the destruction. I never saw Caney Forks again.

We had all kinds of anxieties and sadnesses that year. Pet had been away at school; she and Papa had decided between them that she would go to Philadelphia. Partly he wanted her to study there with somebody he knew. Partly he wanted her out of the reach of one of the most-eligibles, a big, soft, flushed and sweaty young man named Algernon Pinckney Templeton, Jr., who was known among the girls as Pinky.

Pet was not real nice to Pinky. She was barely pleasant enough of the time that he decided he would persist. Three summers he met her at the depot with roses. The last summer he pressed his suit to the point that Dr. Rehnwissel could have felled the burnt-out pillars of Valhalla with his fury. Pet teased the doctor about it. "Oh, Papa," she said, "why do you worry about that old pig-track?" Papa worried about several things till it made him sick, that summer. He took to his chaise, at the cottage.

Pet was sitting by him, trying to feed him some ice cream when he heard the news on the radio that Hitler had marched into Poland. The old man raised his fist and swore a German oath and died. He would not be made The Enemy by politics again. My mother took on terribly for her customary three days, before she settled in before the mirror and chinked the few new mourning lines with powder and touched up her curls with brass and took up life, again, to the fullest.

Only after he was beyond telling did I realize how much that blessed, funny old man had enriched all our lives. Or how much I really loved him. But Pet had simply and openly adored him. He was the first great loss of her life. She was bereft. Pinky, who was not a bad fellow at all, was all sympathy, all patience. And always underfoot. Hugh deviled the life out of Pet about him. He would sing to her in a high, quavering voice, "Pinky Shaftoe's fat and fair, Combing back his yel-low hair. . . "

I said at least if she married Pinky she would never, ever have to worm tobacco again. I doubted she ever told him about worming tobacco. Poor Pinky, he was caught up in the first registration for the draft. He was fatally healthy, not terribly employed and too available. He pondered earnestly about it, and went and volunteered. On his first furlough home, Pet married him.

The year the war started, Hugh was in his third year of college. He had made up his mind to study medicine. He went on and finished out that year, and in the spring, when school was out, he went and joined the Navy. And then he came and told me. Well, at that point, I would as soon he had come and whacked me with the sledgehammer. I cried and carried on and made the child feel terrible. I needed killing.

The matter was this: we'd had several years of strained calm in the house; Foots was not changed, he was just being wise. But lately he had developed an identifiable vice: he would get into the whiskey, and it would give him courage to be himself. He commenced again to indulge his tastes and run up bills. When he was drunk, or pretending to be, he would threaten us. I kept my door locked, and a stick by it. Pet, more than anybody, had been able to keep matters straight. Now she was with Pinky, at a base down in Mississippi. With Hugh out of reach I would have it alone.

Of course Hugh had already been gone a lot; he didn't know a lot of what went on. I shouldn't have laid it on him, either. But I did. And he sat very quiet, for a little bit. He looked like he would cry. Finally he said, "What do you stay here for? What do you owe him? Why did you ever come back here, when you had perfectly well got away?"

I just sat there and twisted my ring around. "Do you not remember," Hugh said, "that you were a thousand times happier up there on Caney River, out grubbing with the hoe barefooted, than you ever have been here? Or than I certainly ever saw you here. I was certainly happier there. Do you remember the day you took us and put us on the train and sent us back here? You didn't know how furious I was with you. I thought I would die. Why did you do it?"

I guess it was my last Mother-Knows-Better speech. "Because it was the right thing to do. At that time," I said firmly.

"May I ask why?" he said. "How did he make you come back?"

"Your father had nothing to do with it," I said. "All the whys are buried."

We sat and looked out the window, at the gulls dipping and flapping. "I hope someday you will forgive me, Hugh," I said. "You're right. We were so lucky. I wonder all the time how things would have turned out for us, if I hadn't ruined it."

"You can always go home," he said. "You can take Aunt Mit and Uncle Camp and go."

"It's changed," I said. "There's no more Coy Ray and Rose. No more Aunt Nam. No Caney Forks."

"No Ben Aaron," he said, very gently. He got up and came and put his arm around me. "But all the things he loved are right there."

Not quite, I thought. "That's right," I said. I didn't know how to tell him that the time to go would simply be the time to go. That the matter would take care of itself.

Hugh was gone and Pet was gone. Aunt Mit was getting old. She couldn't half get up the stairs; she would groan, blessing Jesus, tears in her eyes. Aunt Mit was mortally afraid of woods and rats and snakes. Uncle Camp had got thinner and more stooped over. His hair was just a little cotton frizz around the back of his head. You had to talk to him very loud; "Muh eahs done gone, chile," he said. His eyes were going, too. He had to quit driving.

Uncle Camp's life, outside that house, was the Second Beulah Land Baptist Church. Sometime I would have to leave them, if they didn't leave me, first. I could not ask them to go to this far country. It helped in that time that we were preoccupied with simple existence. We lived by the newspapers and the radio. We stood in line for the commonest things, like sugar and meat and shoes. We rolled bandages one day a week. Sometimes, on Sunday, we would have a dining room full of sailors.

Pinky's mother died, she had been delicate for some while, and the Sunday after the funeral, when Pet and Pinky had gone back to Mississippi, we asked his father to dinner. He was a delightful man, even in mourning. He came almost every Sunday after; he was real family, in the most comfortable sort of way.

A.P. Templeton the elder was especially good for Louise. The war made her awfully nervous. She had bad dreams about foreign planes and bombs. Mr. Templeton was interested in planes; he took her walking in the evenings and pointed out things about them to her. She learned, as he had, to know them by sound. It was the strange ones that made her turn pale. And the thought of submarines coming up the river. Any little ripple that used to mean a school of mullet became a periscope, she was sure, ready to emerge. Mr. Templeton never said, "Oh, that's dumb — what would it want with us?" He just held her elbow securely, and walked on calmly, while the dreaded thing swam by.

The only explosions that rocked our domicile came strictly from within. We got a young woman to come help Mit and me with the spring house cleaning. Mit told her (I didn't) to go in and take down Foots's curtains to be washed, and while she was up on a chair he threw a vase at her. It didn't hit her, thank the Lord, but it broke the window. After that I tried to make sure he didn't get any whiskey.

Not that I think whiskey had all that much to do with it. When the likker ran out, in the cupboard, I wouldn't buy any more. I kept the money hid. I prevailed upon the storekeepers as best I could not to let him have any on credit. But then somehow he would get hold of some, time to time.

Late one afternoon there was the most horrendous to-do up in his room. The awfullest screeching and cussing and pounding, and a female yelling. Louise had a piano student in the music room. I ran upstairs as fast as I could go. Now this sounds like I am making it up but I declare it was so. Foots had Miss Lilah by the throat, pinned back against the wall, and he was beating her on the head with his patent leather dancing pump. He was hollering, "You stingy old bag, I wouldn't drink that piss at a dog fight." Her eyes were all bugged out and her tongue was sticking out. There was a bottle of some kind of pore-bucker whiskey rolling about on the floor. I grabbed it up and popped him on the head, not hard enough, I'm sorry to say, to break either one. But he sank dramatically to the floor, clutching his skull. Having been delivered, Miss Lilah sort of spindled backwards, onto the bed.

"The very idea!" I yelled. "The very bare idea!" Well with the first breath she caught, Miss Lilah hopped up and went to the rescue of Hubert.

"You killed him!" she shrieked. The victim wanly fluttered his eyelids.

"Excellent," I said. "Hooraw."

"You KNEW he was sick!" she said, cradling the corpse.

"Shit," I said. "Get up from there, Foots. Get up right now." Very meekly he shook off the bonds of death and arose and sat in a chair. His mother was speechless. For a moment. The halting measures of the "Minuet in G" floated up the stairs.

"He's not even crazy," I said. "He's the smartest trick around. He has learned to get by on meanness instead of work and decency."

"Meanness!" she bellowed. "You vulgah hussy. You tell ME who has been mean in dis house? Whooo walked out an' lef' us wid hardly enough to eat? Who made us nearly beg fo' evah penny?

"Whooo," she said, glaring and running out her jaw, "Whooo shut dis po' boy here out of her room—to keep him out of her bed—till he got so flustrated . . . he wets . . . his . . . paints!"

Foots just sat through all of this with downcast eyes, rubbing his head. All of a sudden I started to laugh. I laughed till I thought I would pop. I went over and picked up that patent leather shoe and threw it in his lap. "Please pardon the interruption," I said. And I went out and closed the door.

I went down to the library and got The Reverend Sydney and took him to my room. I withdrew the deposits from his pages and divided them into three piles. One I returned to the Memoirs and put under my pillow. The others I put into envelopes. I went at once with one of them back into the alley, to Mit's. Camp had been sick. He was sitting in a chair in the sun, with a quilt over his knees. His eyes looked sunken and dull. I went into the house with the envelope, and very quickly kissed Mit, and put it in her pocket, and when I said goodbye, as I had come to do, I was on my way out, where she couldn't catch me. I went back by Camp. I took his thin old knobby hand and kissed his fingers. And then I ran back through the hedge, just wracked. I ran inside the garage and leaned on the wall and got it over with, as much as I ever would, before I went in the house.

Louise's pupil was just gathering up her books and going out the door. "Louise, come up," I said. "I have to talk with you quick." She came along behind me, and we shut ourselves in. "I am leaving and I think you should come," I said.

"Oh, Thank God!" she said. "Go! Before you calm down!"

"Run pack your belongings," I said. She beamed back this mysterious smile.

"I mustn't," she said. "But I'll help you pack yours."

"What do you mean you mustn't?" I said. "You're not married to them."

"Go and don't give me a minute's thought," she said. "I shan't fare so badly." She was more tickled than I had ever seen her. She helped me get a few things in a suitcase, just a few clothes, and a few pictures and a couple of books. I called a cab.

"If Hugh should call, tell him I have gone home," I said. "I will write to Mama . . . I will write Pet. . . ." I handed her the other envelope. She glanced at it absently, as we went to the door. "Oh, but I forgot — you'll be there all alone!" she said, as I was getting in the cab. I threw her a kiss and was gone.

The farther away from Charleston the train rolled, the cleaner I felt, and the more weight rolled off of me. I let back my seat and half-slept. There's no way to say the blissful anticipation I felt. Going home.

The lights of other trains flew by; we stopped at little towns and let soldiers off and took soldiers on. Two of them, I wondered who they were, got off in Red Bank with me, and helped me with my suitcase. There was a taxi out front, this time with the motor running. It was not Barz. I considered, and then I smiled and shook my head no, and took up my suitcase, and started up the road, in the dark.

~ 32 ~

HOME

IT WAS ALMOST MORNING. JUST BEFORE THE LIGHT, I WALKED UP past Ollie Trotter's; I recognized the sound of the little branch when I crossed the bridge beyond the store. I went striding along, swinging my suitcase, over the rise and down into the dip where the river runs.

The sky was getting pale and I could see the bridge ahead. I kept my eye out for the road; I didn't know but what it was completely grown up and I would miss it. But no, there it was, clear ruts, like somebody still used it. I stopped there and put my suitcase down for a minute, breathing as raspy as a crosscut saw and got a good long smell of the morning, and the river damp. The cool of it tingled in my nose. The air was so still my ears were ringing.

A little panic fluttered through my mind. Desperately, I wanted the children with me. I wanted Louise. Why had Harmon deserted me, when he certainly knew someday I would need him? I can turn back to Red Bank, I thought, and stay in the hotel awhile, until I get someone to go up with me—God in heaven, what am I doing? There's nothing but dead people up there. And then the little sigh of morning floated up over the grasses, and into the trees. It was a warm little breath; it wrapped itself around me. I picked up my suitcase and faced that dark hulk of mountain that lay between me and The Birches, and put my foot on the road.

I remember a bird waking in the brush beside the road; it said, "We miss you we miss you we miss you," and others answered from up the slopes. It was reassuring. I saw the river, then, for the first time; I was afraid to look, but there it was, rolling, that cold gray-green of spring, and the mist rising, like spooks departing. It was deep and full and barely whispered.

The road left it and got steep. I pretty soon felt how many years it had been, since I walked up here. I had to stop and rest a lot. I will stop at Barz's, I thought; he will be up, and I will sit with him a minute. He will have a pot of coffee. I kept watching for his turnoff. It was farther than I had ever thought, and then I almost missed it; weeds had grown up in it. The gate was fastened with a chain and a lock. Signs on it said POSTED: NO TRESPASSING. There was no sign of life. So I walked on.

A little way on up I stopped and watched the rim of the sun clear the ridge across the river. It was a new day; I caught my wind and got up speed. From the top of the ridge I looked across to Hogback and took up fairly trotting. It was easier going down. I remembered how it is that the road closes behind you there. The world closes behind you. All that I didn't want to bring, I was leaving behind.

My feet made echoes on the planks of the bridge on Seven Mile Branch; this morning the branch was lively but perfectly benign. I saw that the orchard was grown up in brambles. The field had pretty badly gone to brush. Bird tracks criss-crossed the bare spots in the road. I came around the bend into a herd of deer and they sailed and scattered and startled me nearly into a faint. My heart was pounding. I walked along slowly, then, until I saw the chimneys, with creeper climbing all over them. I saw the house, with the sun in its face. The lilacs were bent down of their weight, around the porch. And I ran. I ran up and flung myself on the steps and of course commenced to wail. I was exhausted. The steps were warm and almost soft. The birds were singing, I had never heard so many. The bees were working the lilacs, they were humming, and humming, and they were a woman singing, in the lightest, sweetest voice. When I roused it was up in the day; my arm had gone to sleep. There was a bluebird feeding right beside me, in a white lilac bush. It turned its head and looked at me, like, what is that strange thing? And then it went on flitting and pecking.

It was like I had not been away. I reached behind the step and the key was there. I went up and put it in the lock, but when I touched the knob the door came open. It was like the Sleeping Beauty's Castle, inside. The furniture was there, as Rose had left it. Someone had covered it with sheets and quilts. There was a coat of fine dust on everything. I had no idea what time it was but the sun was overhead. I wound Ive's clock, and set the hands at noon. I opened the window by the sweet bubby bush and went on slowly through the house. It was dark and cool in the kitchen. Cole had left a stack of stovewood. A pail of cobs by the stove had all but gone to dust; the mice had worked on them. Daisy's bonnet was a fragile tatter on the nail by the kitchen door. Nam's hung on a nail above it. I opened the back door and heard the trickle of the spout, although it ran under years and years of leaves. The brush was so high I could barely see the barn. I had my work cut out for me. But I had all my life to do it.

It occurred to me I was half-starved, and there was nothing this side of Red Bank, unless I fished or rocked a rabbit. I went back in and went to the pantry room and found some matches. There were shelves of jars of things Rose had canned. I took one down and took it to the light, and wiped the dust off on my skirt. It was blackberries; they were sort of pallid. It had been at least eight years. They were not bad; they tasted pretty winey. Old blackberries will not kill you, I decided. I sat out on the porch and drank them out of the jar. While I sat there a deer came and drank at the runoff of the spout, paying me no mind.

I thought what I must do; I must get the scythe and clear paths, at first, to where I would need to go. Before much of anything I would have to go to Red Bank and bring back food. The prospect was horrendous. I was not the limber kid of thirty anymore. It would only take more time, though, and I had it. One thing I had now was time. I went in and knocked on the flue, to warn the mice, and fired up the stove. I rinsed the kettle and filled it at the spout, and put it on and went and picked some wintergreen and made a cup of tea. Then I gathered up my skirt and started off up the hill. Halfway up I stopped and looked back at the smoke coming out of the chimney. I was home.

As I went on up I was thinking, does Ben Aaron know I am Home? I called him—Ben Aaron . . . Ben Aaron. . . . It was a silly thing to do but I couldn't help it. It came back echoing from the hillside. Everything was grown up in saplings. There were little trees inside the wrought iron fence. The gate was nearly rusted down. It groaned when I opened it, and a rabbit ran right between my feet and I let out a yipe. There were stones that were broken and stones toppled. There was one that had not been there; a beautiful one with wild roses carved into it. It said, ROSANNAH WILCOX SUTHERLAND AUGUST 15, 1914– FEBRUARY 2, 1936 HOW SWEETLY BLOOMS OUR ROSE IN HEAVEN. The grass and brambles were so thick I didn't see the one next to it, at first. It was a discreet little marker, just a little polished wedge of granite. It said on it, only, B.A.S. AT HOME.

There was a rustle of that warm wind. I sat down on Rose's stone, I felt like she had asked me. And I talked to them. I had never felt less lonely, or more loved. After so long a time I went back down, gathering deadfall on the way and started a stack on the back porch. And I sat down and picked the burrs out of my skirt, thinking. I was thinking about the first time I had come down from that cemetery, with a skirt full of burrs. I had to think stern thoughts to myself. For the sake of this place I was going to have to stay sane. The squire would not come riding anymore. But I sat there, and listened to the voices of the house, and the field and the woods, and there was no way I would believe that I would not see him again.

There were earthly matters to think about. Somewhere I was going to have to sleep, and that before long. Rose had moved the beds upstairs. I went up and settled in the big front room   this one   on the morning side. The bed had been neatly made; when I lifted the covers they were stiff with age and dust. There were clean ones in the bureau drawer, with little yellow age-specks, and quilts folded and stacked in the wardrobe. I fixed the bed and flopped down to think some more. I thought I ought to go find a candle. I ought to go fill the wash-pitcher at the spout. I ought to wash myself and lay out my clothes so I could get up and get a start back down to the store, in the morning. I thought with half-closed eyes. I could faintly hear the narrows roaring, and the birds. I saw the clouds over the ridge turn pink and I floated off on 'em, dead to the world.

When I cracked my eyes again the sky was getting light. I got up and went to the window to look. The deer were feeding down in the

field, a good herd; it felt good not to be alone, the one quick creature, of sorts, among the dead. I figured at that point that I might
be barely quick enough to get to town for groceries. Another morning without coffee and it would be all over. So I went down to the
spout and cleaned up and trotted off, thinking of reasonable, tem-
poral things like what I would need to survive and whether I could
tote it seven miles mostly up. Flour. Coffee. Meal. Lard. Salt and sugar.
Candles would be lighter than coal oil. Staples alone were going to
weigh a ton. I would have to buy seed. Once a week I would have to
make that trip. How wearying it was going to be to live here. How
wonderful.

Ollie Trotter's I found was all done over. Nothing but feed and
seed anymore. More's the horror, somebody had painted it white.
Ollie was not there, nor Mrs. Ollie. It was being run by grandchil-
dren. I bought some seed beans and corn and some okra and
tomato seed, just little bags; I would plant more later. Ollie's did
still have a dope box and a rack of crackers. I bought a dope and
crackers and went back up the road a way, to the branch and sat on
the bridge rail and swallowed them whole. I took off my shoes and
sneaked down to the branch to wet my blisters. There was a new
Piggly Wiggly over beyond the depot. I went over and shopped. I
bought stuff by weight, not by what I liked a lot. When I came out
there was a big black cloud coming up. The wind was gusting; I
knew everything was going to get soaked. So I took up my sack and
went to the hotel and rented a room. It had an iron bed and muslin
curtains and a nice view of the hosiery mill. It was luxurious. I went
down to the cafe and got a paper cup of coffee and a sandwich and
brought it back and sat and wrote letters to Louise and the children
and listened to the rain. I decided it might become a weekly event,
coming to town and spending the night in the hotel. That night I
went down to the dining room and felt kind of odd being alone but
I ate everything they would bring me. I had seen nobody yet in town
that I knew.

There was an older lady waiting tables, though, that kept looking
at me. Finally she stationed herself, hand on hip and said, "Are you
not one of Mr. Steele's people?" I said yes indeed. "Did you not come
in here with him a time or two?" she said. I know one time, I said. "I

remember when he used to come in with a bunch o' men," she said. "The courthouse bunch, you know. They'd set and eat and talk, all of a sudden he'd get tickled about somethin' was said, and he'd th'ow back his head and laugh. Lord, that man would laugh. I loved to hear 'im. It was one dark day when he died . . ."

Yes, mam, I said. It was.

"Said it was over a womern," said she, sort of wistfully. "Most things like that'll generally be over a womern, or over likker. I never did know Mr. Steele to be bad to drink . . . Where you livin' now? You been away."

"I been away," I said, "but now I'm back home. I'm back up at the old Steele place. I had to come get groceries and couldn't get back home without gettin' wet."

"What you a-drivin'?" she said.

"I'm a-walkin'," I said.

"They law! You a-walkin' by yourself? Who's up-pair with you?"

"Nobody," I said. "It's only me."

She threw up her hands. "They law! In 'at ol booger-house? They law have mercy, honey!"

When I got up I hugged her. I couldn't say how much I thanked her that she remembered, kindly.

I waited for the fog to lift a little the next morning; sometimes you know you can't tell if it's bad weather or not. But it was a pretty day and I took up my "budget," as Nam would say, and started out. There were some croaker sacks out on Trotter's trashpile. I took up one and put my provender inside and slung it over my shoulder. People talked about hoboes. Here I was one.

Every day, then, it was work to do. I cleared a little garden with the scythe and then the shovel and the hoe, and planted seed. The next time to town I got some flower seeds too, and cleared in front and planted four-o'clocks and things. And a nice little thing happened. Just as I came to the fork in the road, a little brown dog came out of the bushes and started following me. It was like a little shadow; when I would look around it would be gone. It was afraid. But then there it would be again. I had some crackers in my pack, I laid a couple down and walked on, and directly I heard it coming along behind, going *crunch-crunch-crunch*. When I would stop to rest I'd lay down more. When I hit the steps at The Birches there it was right behind me, with its little tongue hanging out. It plopped down in the shade of a bush and stretched out its little sore feet. It had come to live. If it had been a party of a hundred, it would have been no better company.

And then one day when I was in town I passed a sad mule tied to a post. Its head was hung down; it had bad spots where the harness had rubbed and the gnats were worrying its eyes. I was real tired of walking. I stood there scratching its ears till the man came out. "What's she wuth to ye?" he said, all smiles.

"What you need?" I said.

"I need $28 to pay m' taxes," he said.

"Lemme see 'er teeth," I said. "I don't ever want to chew for another mule."

He lifted a mule-lip with his thumb. "Lookahere," he said, "Ain't but eight yurr old. Lookit t'em pearls."

Eight yurr my foot I thought. Eight yurr three times over. But I bought her and draped my sack across her back and led her home. There was the warmth of life in the barn again. We would have to make corn, she and I, to sustain it. I had never plowed. It took me half a day to figure out the harness. I never did plow too good, I'll have to say. But we put in a crop of field corn in June. And it made.

It might have been lonely here at first, except that the summer just consumes you, if you are working to survive. Like something possessed I fought the brush with the scythe. Day by day, lick by lick, The Birches came out of the scrub. There was nobody to talk to, most of the time, of course. I talked to the dog. I talked a right smart to the mule; we were good friends. I talked to the trees and the birds and the bugs and the wind. I talked a lot to the house, and all the time to God. The house came out from under the dust. I bet I put a thousand spider webs outside with families in them. I felt worse pangs when I cleaned the pantry. All those jars of stuff Rose had canned to last till a spring she never saw. A few of 'em had blown and leaked. I carried all of it way out in the lot and dumped the stuff out. The garden was coming in, and the blackberries, and I needed the jars.

There was plenty of everything and it was a blessing. On account of the war there was not plenty of anything, hardly, in the towns. If somebody came it was nice to put a big bait on the table. The day they came with Cole there were a dozen at supper here I guess. Oh, it was so sad. I had not heard of him in years; not since Ansel and Myrtle were run out by the dam. Well, I was on the porch with a lap full of beans when a soldier and another man, turned out it was an undertaker, came driving up in a jeep. Got out and looked sort of puzzled to see me sitting there. Took off their hats and came up.

"We didn't think this home was occupied," the undertaker said. And the soldier said they had come to see about burying Cole Sutherland. Well, of course that started something up again. I started to cry. "Are you one of his people?" he said. I shook my head yes and no at the same time. They stood and looked uncomfortable. They wanted to find the cemetery. Cole died on a hospital ship coming back from the invasion of Sicily. He had asked to be buried by Rose. His parents understood. So we went up and saw where it would be. The ground was just white with daisies up there, right then. It was just lovely. And the next morning the gravediggers came. And that afternoon, it was the funeral. I had never met Cole's parents, and his two sisters, but they stayed with me that night. Oh, it was sad. But there was a sweetness about it. That wistful, soulful sweetness that you felt and could no way describe.

I heard from Hugh every week. There was always a letter from him; sometimes one from Pet or Louise or Mama. And then one week in the fall I went to town and there was no letter. I didn't wait another week to go; it got to where I went nearly every day. I was in a panic. I was on my way down one morning, half hopeful there would be a letter and half petrified there would be one of those awful telegrams, like Cole's people got. I would hurry the poor mule a little bit, and then I would slow her down. And I came to a place where I could see the road below, and there was a figure walking. It was somebody in a dark blue uniform, toting a duffle. Well, I jogged that mule in the sides with my heels and got her to honestly trot. And Hugh dropped his bag and came running. We met each other with the tears just streaming.

"I've been scared to death," I said, "it's been so long since I heard a word. Don't tell me you let the cow get lost again." We went on back to the house and he stayed a week. He spent most of it chopping wood. Splitting stove wood. In between he walked the place, swinging away with the scythe. I had never been up to the lake. I couldn't bear to face the grave of Caney Forks alone. So we walked up together. From the top of the ridge we saw it spread out below us, with its blue-green fingers reaching up every branch. We walked on down to see the dam. It rose up like a fan between the hills. The power plant was on the right, with towers full of big lines going every which way. Electric lights were there if we wanted them. We agreed we didn't much care. They had built a new road on the east side that joined the highway, somewhere. We noticed trucks coming over it, moving along like ants. Our road stopped now at Boney Creek. The bridge was gone, there was just a big mound of dirt pushed up where the road used to be, across the creek. That was fine. We had gone far enough.

I just wanted to put the Hogback between me and that humming, whining drone of death. We made tracks for home. At night we sat by the fire and talked. We talked about what he wanted to do, here, when the war was over and he was home. We could grow beef cattle, he said. We could raise lots of chickens. We would have a money crop of some kind. He would finish school and set up his doctor's office in Red Bank.

I wished, but I knew. You will find a nice girl, somewhere, I thought. She will want a more modern house; you will have to have a phone. Of course you might want this place; it would be nice to have a young woman and children take it over. I could build something little, a sensible distance away. I thought these things while he talked about others. I went with him to Red Bank, to the train. He was going back to Charleston to spend a day or two and then ship out again. It was deadly to see him go. I had to tell myself that it wouldn't be long till he'd be back. But I carried that image of Cole's casket, with the flag. I guess I was not rational about these things. There was a special loneliness about the place when he was gone. One thing, it was getting cool; the days were shorter and there was less work pressing to get done. I added to Hugh's woodpile on the porch. The fall of the axe bounced across the cove. It was good; it was evidence of life and plans for living.

And then, bless Pat, in just a few days company appeared again.

Honeymooners. I had been given not a hint till Louise and Algernon Pinckney Templeton the elder were let out of a steaming old truck at the steps, suitcases in hand. I was dumbfounded. We hugged and kissed and danced each other 'round and 'round. They were the beamingest couple I ever saw. Her mother had been quite buffaloed, Louise reported; Miss Lilah could not fault Mr. Templeton because he was Somebody. Since Louise was now fifty-five years old, her children would be unlikely to come into the world with "heart trouble," a horror Miss Lilah could never stress too strongly when Louise spoke to a man on the street.

Louise had used some of the money Rev. Sydney Smith provided to get a good but firm-willed couple to tend to our joint responsibilities. It had gone beyond her capabilities, she said. Foots was staying soused. "I think Mama aids and abets that," she said. "It's the only way she can control him." When they went home Louise would be the mistress of the Templeton house, one of the grandest places in Charleston. But they stayed here several days. Louise had only heard tales of how we lived, here. A.P. had no warning, but he was very jolly about it, he fell at once to cutting wood. He loved to fish and spent a lot of time at the river. And Louise seemed to be enchanted. The color that fall was just beautiful. The field was thick with asters and goldenrod. The Birches put on all its charm for her.

We went up to the cemetery one afternoon and I told her about these people and I told her, as best I understood it, how it was we came up here, about the wreck and finding the house and that morning up on the hill when I found all my folks were dead. I told her a little bit about Ben Aaron. Or a little more than I had ever told her. I even told her how Rose and I stole the body. And as we started out and she closed the gate behind us, she had the most thoughtful look on her face. "There is something awfully—rare—about this place," she said. "I feel it. Do you know what I am trying to say? Do you feel it too?"

"I do. It is something very—rare; it is so rare," I said, "that I know I must never leave it again. Oh, maybe for a day or a week. But I can never take my life away from here." I would have been so glad for them to stay much longer than they could. The day before they had to go I rode to town to make a date for their truck-taxi to come back for them. And I went by the post office and picked up a letter from Pet. When I got home I was able to tell them that we were all going to be grandparents. Louise was going to be a great-aunt besides. Reminds me of the Steeles, I said. We were all delighted.

After they were gone and I had time to think about it, I thought about being that baby's granny. Hmph. Well, you are not Shirley Temple, lady, I said to myself. It made me get to work on baby clothes, on sacques and bonnets and little gowns and got right enthusiastic. The winter passed before the fire, a lot of it. The dog and I sat by the stove and talked about our baby. I would talk, and the dog would pretend to be interested, it would cock its head and raise one eyebrow and one ear.

Hugh wrote in every letter to please be careful in the cold. He remembered about some old man who went out to feed his cows and fell and got snowed over and laid out there till spring. I remembered it too. I fed the mule good once a day and stayed inside in bad weather, as best I could. The hardest thing was getting to town. Or not getting to town, for weeks at a time. I worried about Pet. She had asked me to come stay with her when the baby was due. And I was going. They were still in Mississippi; Pinky was blessedly overlooked and worked at the same desk most of the way through the war. And I was worried about Hugh. No, it was more than that. I was sort of numb about it. I had too many eggs in that basket, out there on an aircraft carrier, somewhere at sea. It got much worse after I had this dream one night. It was the plainest dream, I was looking down the road and it was morning and here came Hugh, striding up out of the fog. He looked happy as a lark. Radiant.

I expected that telegram. Every time I went to town I went in dread. It did not come, to me. It came to Charleston. Louise got it. She didn't send it to me; she and A.P. came, as fast as they could.

∼ 33 ∼

FACE TO FACE

SOMETHING TO BE THANKFUL FOR: NATURE IS JUST ABOUT oblivious to human tragedy and gloom. The jonquils and the quinces bloomed that spring; the orchard bloomed for us through its moss and dead limbs and brambles. The lilacs budded. The birds sang to us by day and the little frogs by night.

Everything else in my world changed. Hugh was gone; all that we had hoped for, looked forward to, went down on a ship hit by a torpedo, down to the bottom of the sea near the Marshall Islands. What could my boy be doing there, when our world dropped off beyond Shiloh?

I was confused. Louise and A.P. tried to get me to go home with them; A.P. tried reason, and Louise cried. As it turned out none of us would see Charleston for a while. A couple of days after they got here, the telegraph woman made her way up with a message from Pinky that Pet was in labor, and they wanted me to come to Mississippi at once. I knew I was far too wobbly to go. I would be nothing but a liability. So, not knowing what else to do, Louise and A.P. left me; we had the telegraph lady send the old truck up to get them and that night they were on the train, going to help the children. The next morning the lady was back with another telegram; the baby was here and it was a little girl, named Sarah Natalie.

It was right then that a lifetime of contention with my only living child was set in motion.

It never occurred to me how hurt Pet would be with me for not coming. The next time I went for the mail there was a letter from her. "You have got to pull yourself out of this," she said. "Nobody can do it but you. You will not ever feel better staying up there in that dreadful old house in the middle of nowhere. Hugh would not want you to be living like that. It has been awful not having you here, I wanted you with me, you know. You must learn to face awful things sometime without going all to pieces."

I think it was not so much that she hated this place. No less than Hugh and me she had found some happiness here and some people whose memories she surely must still love. I could never say this to her children, but I have had a feeling that it was a little bit of "Mama always did love HIM best," a notion that this place was more home to Hugh and me, and somehow it, and maybe we, cared less for her. Unlike her brother, Pet had not caught on to some other force at work up here, for me. I have never known romance to move my daughter; I think about that voice, of the Isoldes and Sieglindes and Salomes that never had a chance because Pet had to have security that art can almost never promise.

She did write regularly, though, and sent pictures of the baby. I thought she was beautiful. Along in the summer they did come through, on their way to Charleston. Pinky had a thirty-day leave. Pet wrote and asked me to meet them at Red Bank and I did. We all stayed at the hotel that one night and I got to hold the baby.

They left early the next day. Pinky asked me to come with them. I wanted to, so badly, in a way. But the garden was in. I had nobody to tend anything. What it was, I really didn't want to go bad enough to just go. Even Pinky, who was the essence of tolerance, thought that was strange. Of course it was.

And then, the war was over. When I went down to Red Bank one Monday morning the newsboy was hollering on the street corner, "Jay-Pan surrenders! Jay-Pan surrenders!" I bought a paper and thought how wonderful, the kids would be free to come when they pleased.

Of course they went back to Charleston as soon as Pinky was let go. They bought one of those big old houses that had been in his family, sometime, and Pet settled down to become a celebrated maker of aspics, a pillar in the Episcopal choir and a rising matron in Charleston society.

It did not make anything better between us when I missed the next baby, too, because the day I was set to go, several days before Pet's due date, a storm brought about twenty inches of snow and I simply could not get out of here. Ice crusted on top of it, and it was over a week before the mule could make it down to Red Bank. I called from town to explain. Pet said she and the new baby girl were fine, they had plenty of help and not to "strain myself" to get there. The baby's name was Anna Frances, for Pinky's mother.

I should have got on that train and gone right then. But honestly I was so relieved I was ashamed. My living arrangement here had not made me very pretty or stylish or clever, not at least as such things are valued in Charleston. And, truth to tell, Pet was well taken care of. She had cooks and maids and nursemaids, and she had Louise, who was, in all truth, a better mother to her than I had ever been.

Over the years, when the girls were still little, Pet and Pinky did come a couple of times, they got me to meet them in Red Bank and took me on to Flat Rock, where they had rented a big fine house for a few weeks in the summer. It was terribly social, all parties and folderol. I didn't have any Flat Rock clothes. The first time, I didn't know that skirts were nearly to the floor. I did go to the Red Bank Salon de Beauty and get Eloise Brock to fix my hair. It had gotten right ratty, I will admit. I didn't know till I saw it in Eloise's mirror that I had got so gray.

But year by year, the visiting got sparser. The girls got busy lives of their own. Their parents took them to Europe and on excursions in the summers; they were, in fact, about as involved in this place, here, as I had been at their age.

So, time passed, and things settled here more and more into the way they were going to be. In cool weather I spent whole days chopping wood. We sat in the kitchen a lot, the dog and I. I made Christmas presents, I had ordered a how-to-crochet book and after some awful flops I made things that actually passed for doilies and booties and caps. I made quilts and knitted socks and dwelled upon the catalogues. Pet and Louise sent boxes up. It was, for a while, a novelty to spend Christmases alone. I made a sort of ceremony of going up to where the brightest holly grew, and cutting some, and I draped the mantel with it. I made a fire, on Christmas Eve. And the dog lay down on the hearth, and I sat and drank some old wine and rocked and saw all kinds of things past in the fire, before I fell asleep.

Now and then, over the winters, somebody would come by; a dog would come up, say, and maybe a day or so later a hunter would come by, looking for it, and maybe sit by the fire a little bit and tell some news and drink coffee. As long as they were fairly sober I was glad to have them come. Of course drunks showed up; there was a bunch that roared up in a Jeep one day while I was out replanting the dahlia bed. Shot out a parlor window, before I let 'em have it with a couple of fat rocks and some dirt clods and broke their windshield. They would've shot me but they were too drunk to aim; shot the little dog, instead. He cut a somersault and they drove off. When I picked up his little limp corpse he reached up and licked me; it just barely parted the hair of his head, barely skinned him.

I carried him inside and bolted the door, knowing they'd be back. But days went by, and no sign. Tracks still went only one way, in the road. I wondered if somehow they had found a way out up at the dam. Finally, curiosity got me. The dog and I went for a walk up the road, and not more than a couple of curves away there sat the Jeep. Its hood was smashed plumb into the ground with the boulder still sitting on top of it. No sign of bodies or anything; the riders had escaped. But I looked up the bank, where that rock would have had to come from, and nothing was disturbed, not a break in the fringe of laurels it would have had to roll through.

Word got out. This was, as the lady at the cafe had said, "a haint place," with a witch in residence. It brought out the drunkers and the daring. One night I heard cars on the road and a ruckus up behind the house, and there was a gang going up the hill toward the cemetery, with lanterns and all sorts of gall. I was not putting up with that. I went behind them to watch; when one of them stuck a shovel in the ground I got behind a clump of junipers and hollered, "You get off of my graves!" It was kind of scary, to tell the truth; sounded weird and tremulous, like a screech owl. Boys, it got their attention. One of the brave hollered something really ugly, and they began shining lights around looking for the witch, who began right then to look for a quick defense. I found it in my apron pocket. I had boiled wash that afternoon and I still had a box of matches. With my back to them I commenced to strike matches; the matches kept going out. Finally I struck one, lit the whole box and dropped it in the grass. The brush just exploded. I ran for dear life. The visitors ran too, cussing and yelling. The field was just blazing. I fell back behind some big rocks. My conscience smote me. Lord what have I done? How could I stoop so low? I said. That mess of trash could all be killed, I thought, and it would be my fault.

Well, while I was lamenting, a flash of lightning lit up the field, and hail began to pelt us and torrents of cold rain came down. I squatted there so grateful, and unbelieving, and I would have sworn there was a big laugh in the thunder that echoed back and forth across the cove. All that was left of the grave-dirt collectors was a string of tail lights, headed down the road. One old truck was still there the next morning, and for days after. Finally I went out and cranked it up and drove it down the road, out of my sight. It's down there yet, I expect.

One adventure like this followed another. One day while I was in the hardware store I picked up a shotgun and held it, looking at it, thinking I really needed it. Then I remembered what it could do, and put it back.

The state of my mind did concern me, time to time. Now and then I went up to the cemetery and sat beside Ben Aaron and talked to him, told him all the troubles and little crises. I felt better for it, especially that the only answers came from the birds and the wind.

Much as I needed to hear from the outside, the mail brought jolts and dilemmas along with the day-to-day news. I treasured spidery little notes I got from Louise, always cheerful even though she was growing frail and A.P.'s heart was failing. Occasionally I heard from Mama, wherever on the globe she was with the man of the hour (which was about as long as some of 'em lasted). Then I got a letter from Pet, mailed from the airport in New York, saying she and Pinky were on their way to France to Mama's funeral; she had died suddenly of pneumonia and Pet knew, rightly, that I would never get there.

A while later Pet wrote again, "Our old house is standing empty. Of course it is yours and it would be so wonderful if you were in it, safe and comfortable near me . . ." That nearly did it. It would never be quite right, though; very soon after Mama died Louise wrote that Camp was dead. Mittie was gone to live with her sister in Summer-ville.

But I thought about it. I had learned not to be complacent about some things; I asked Pinky to take over Mama's estate and secure it so that nothing could fall into hands that still, even in pitiful in-validhood, could grab and squander. I thought of Foots and his mother in the way that I thought about a dead jellyfish; step on it and it would still sting you.

The thought of going back was tantalizing sometimes, the idea of being with those beautiful girls and people I loved, of being warm without working at it, and buying from the vegetable man, and smelling the sea. I might have done it. But one day I came in from hoeing, it was hot, and went to get a drink from the bucket and sud-denly the kitchen just went dark. When I woke up days had passed, I don't know how many, but the dog was licking my face and whining, just starved. I crawled and got a chair to pull up on; one of my legs was asleep, that arm was weak and I had an awful time getting up. Then, there was a commotion coming from the barn. The mule was hollering and kicking down his stall. It was perishing for food and water. I used the chair as a crutch, stumped out there and opened the door and just stood back. The mule came out kicking, overjoyed at the pasture grass and stream.

I really did not know what had happened to me until I rode to town a few days later, and the first little child who saw me turned and hid her face in her mother's skirt. When I saw my reflection in a win-dow I saw why; my left eyelid drooped and the corner of my mouth was pulled way down. It was mortifying; I grabbed up a few necessi-ties and fled for home as fast as I could go. The next time I went to town I wore a bonnet hiding all it could. Any idea I had of going back into society was squelched, the way it looked right then.

I felt so ugly. And yet. . . . One day I was out doing the wash, I'd made a fire under the pot and was stirring in soap when a paper flut-tered down, dropped by the wind, it came slowly, turning over and over, and landed at my feet. I picked it up and thought now, where in the world did you come from? It was a page torn from some old children's book, a picture of a rosy little boy and girl on a swing, looking happy. It had been printed over with a pencil, in block letters, a poem: "Forget if you must / Forgive if you will / I love you yet / From the top of my hill." Now, what in the world? Of course my eyes went at once to the top of the hill, that crag on Hogback. There was nothing I could see. Still and all, I felt wonderful.

But after the little dog did not wake up one morning in the fall, the loneliness seeped in like fog. There was still plenty of life; we'd had a fine crop of sunflowers, and there was plenty wild grain and thistles, and I cracked a good bit of corn, so the birds and smallish creatures came bountifully. I would put out feed and holler, "Thank the Lord for dinner!" and nearly get blown over by the rush of wings.

Still, the house was awfully empty, give or take a mouse or a blacksnake or so. I was out picking wild grapes one morning and noticed something wiggling in the weeds. It wasn't like something was trying to run away. I went and looked, and there was Bird. He was sort of crouching there, all rumpled. Even with his wings half spread, he was the biggest thing I nearly ever saw. I had never seen anything like him, except in a picture book. Well, and on a dollar bill. There was a raw place on one of his wings, and some bloody speckles on the white feathers of his head, like he maybe had been in a fight. He glared me in the eye and hissed.

The sight of those claws and that snapping pruning hook of a bill made me really humble. But I couldn't leave him for the wildcats. I thought, I will wrap him in my apron. That was like tying up an alligator in a doily. At the end, I took off my old dress and wrestled it around him, getting a few bloody marks for my trouble. He in that sling, I in my underpants, we went to the house.

He was not permanently hurt. But he was sore and outraged, and hungry. Bread nor fatback were remotely to his taste. This was a radical problem; I was not sure I liked the way he looked at my exposed hide. Whatever I did was going to go against my grain but so much for that. I went to the chickenhouse with the axe, and brought back a faithful laying hen. He all but snatched it from me, and the feathers flew.

That of course could not go on; it was good fortune to learn that he loved fish. The river was a Godsend. Bird had free run of the

house; there was no confining him. He had a lot of confidence
about his place in the world. This was not what anybody could call a
standard relationship between beast and human; I was as wild a
creature as Bird so I guess was less a threat to him. Very soon when I
came in with a catch, I would say, "Thank the Lord!" and he would
be right there for dinner. He even got more polite about how he
grabbed it. And, he took to following me around. He would perch
on anything big enough to hold him. I would talk to him, and he
would listen.

We had lived several weeks like this when he seemed perfectly
well, and I opened this window, here, and he flew out. What a sight,
those tremendous wings. I watched him soar off across the field, and
then he turned north, over the Hogback, toward the lake where he
really was at home. It was painful. But it was right. It had gotten
cold, but still, I left the window open; I had the idiotic notion he
might come back. It took him three days; he came back that time
with a goose, just swooped in and made a dreadful mess. After that
he came and went. Sometimes he would spend the night perched on
the footboard of the bed. Like he is, right now. Soundly sleeping.

I got down with a heavy cold; maybe it was from sleeping in a
blizzard with the window open. But it got really bad; I could not
get to town and everything was running out. Bird had been away
for several days; I had sadly just about given him up. Here I was, on
my last legs. And then here he was. In he sailed, and dropped a great
big fish on the floor beside the bed. It was still flopping. But he did-
n't eat it. Out the window he went again, and shortly here he was
back with another one. Then he was gone again. I was too weak not
to believe what he was doing. I crept out and went downstairs and
made a fire in the stove, and fried fish. Things got better very fast.

It was something else that really made me wonder, though.

I was cutting brush one day that spring when a young man came
walking up the road. Not anybody from around here. Not a bad
looking kid, nice-looking towny clothes, recent haircut. But he looked
sort of vague, the look of the truly lost. He was trying to get to the
dam, he said. Said he was supposed to talk to somebody there about a
job. Wanted to know how far it was, which way to go. I told him,

but he sort of shuffled around, nervous, before he went on up the road.

I worked on a while till it got late afternoon, and I went up to the house. Went in the front door and started back to the kitchen. And there, right beside me in the hallway, was that weird boy. He had dumped out the bureau drawers, had stuff scattered all over. He had big old knife from the kitchen, holding down by his side. My jig was up.

"So what are you doing in here?" I said.

"What are you gonna do about it, old woman?" he said. Then he grabbed my shoulder. "You got money, old woman. Where is it?"

I never even thought. I stood just an instant, then I threw back my head and loud as I could, I hollered, "THANK THE LORD FOR SUPPER!"

The kid stepped back, astonished. There was a dark shadow then that filled the stairwell. A whoosh of wings. Bird descended, and hovered. The kid screamed, terrified, and bolted. I thought Bird was only curious. It was not until I was cleaning up the trail that boy left behind him as he made for the road that I noticed drops of blood, along with a stream of poor thin hockey. I have wondered whatever happened to him, actually it was kind of pitiful, but we were not apt to see him ever again.

Sometimes the tiniest things take hold of our lives. Like losing a pair of dimestore glasses. I figured they must have been in my dress pocket when I gathered up Bird, and fell out in the struggle. Several days I went back down in the field and kicked around the weeds, looking, but no luck.

The fact was, I could read but mighty little anymore without them. Mail came that I could not interpret. The situation got worse after the mule went off and died; getting to the post office was so hard that several weeks sometimes went by and I would not have any idea what was happening. A nice thing, an old guy who drove a logging truck took to looking out for me; he was hauling out of Barz's old place and he would just come on up, bring the mail, sometimes flour or coffee, whatever occurred to him I might be out of. I would open the letters out in the sun; that helped, also if it was Pet or Louise I knew the handwriting and it was easier.

One time he came and brought a tax notice. I had him wait while I looked at it, and then consulted the Rev. Sydney Smith. When I counted out the money into his hand, and asked him to pay it for me, I had thirty dollars left to last the rest of my life.

Of course there was money enough in Charleston. That amounted to a carrot on a stick. No way could I imagine my daughter sending the wherewith for me to stay here. Something else was going on too—and here is something I guess I have just chosen to forget—one day my blessed courier drove up in the yard and hollered, "I see the power company is atter you agin!"

"I don't want anything they've got," I said.

"No, but I b'lieve they want somethin' YOU'VE got," he said. Fact was, several letters had come that had gone unopened. I finally confessed to the man that I couldn't really read, so he read this latest epistle to me.

"Mrs. Lamb," it said. "Since we have had no response from you about our need to acquire your property on Big Caney River we must remind you that we have applied for a permit to dam the river at a point one-fourth mile above the falls of Big Caney. When that permit is secured we will hold eminent domain. If you wish this acquisition to occur other than through the courts, please respond at once. We are sending a copy of this notice to your daughter, Mrs. A.P. Templeton, Jr., in Charleston, in case you have not received our communications."

As the road signs say, The End is Near. Something is about to happen. I know the children are coming now. Maybe it is time. Maybe it is time. Fly south, beloved Bird. Raise a family.

Here! I see your eyes. I have waked you with all this talking. It's not day yet; that light is just the moon come out from the clouds. What's the matter? You want to go? Well, hold on, I will let you out. Oh, my, I don't blame you. How beautiful it is. How other-worldly that smell of moss and woods. You hear the narrows?

And what is that? Bird, do you hear it? I'll swan.

Good God, Ben Aaron! Play on, joy of my life. I'm coming!

Don't you leave me.

ACKNOWLEDGMENTS

I am grateful for this opportunity, at long last, to thank a few of the dear people who have helped with this book over so many years, in so many ways.

I thank, first, the sainted relative whose adventure of the heart was such a family disgrace that her story would not pass the lips of a solitary soul, until only a couple of old ladies, then still among the living, knew of it—and one of them told—in a whisper, with far fewer details than I would have liked.

I would like to thank an unknown young woman who, back in the early 1960s, rode the Park Road bus I caught each day to work. She always sat behind the driver and talked to him about nothing I remember, in a voice as light and haunting as the smell of moonflowers. For over a decade after the job was history and the bus ride no more, that voice lingered, as Sen's, to narrate this story.

I thank and will ever love the encouraging, supporting people, and the people whose knowledge, from the tides along the Battery, to how to rob a grave in plain sight, to making a computer work and other arts of publishing, combined to save me (somewhat!) from my own ignorance. Among them, but by no means all: Eleanor Parker; Mary Beth Gibson; Jerry and Linda Bledsoe; Pat Borden Gubbins; Bea and Ed Broadrick; Mary Liles Gravely; Suzanne Kirk; Angelica Cranford Hastings; Jim Scancarelli; Dannye Romine Powell; Barbara Webster; Tom and Mary Layton; Frank Guldner; Sharyn McCrumb; H.J. "Doggy" Hatcher; Charlotte Ross; Anna Simon; John Ware; Frances Marvin Mauldin; Pat Edmunds; Olivia Fowler; Karen Swann; Sandra Woodward; Hazel Ritch; Greg Brock; Gayle Edwards; Starkey Flythe Jr.; Tom Johnson; Louis Henry; Perry Morgan; Novello editors Frye Gaillard, Amy Rogers, Ann Wicker and Carol Adams; book designer Bonnie Campbell; my agent Michael Congdon—and my children Tom, Katharine, and Fred and his beloved Mary.

To those, listed and otherwise, who have passed beyond my expressions of gratitude, I hope with all my heart that you somehow know it, anyway.

NOVELLO FESTIVAL PRESS

Novello Festival Press, under the auspices of the Public Library of Charlotte and Mecklenburg County and through the publication of books of literary excellence, enhances the awareness of the literary arts, helps discover and nurture new literary talent, celebrates the rich diversity of the human experience, and expands the opportunities for writers and readers from within our community and its surrounding geographic region.

THE PUBLIC LIBRARY OF CHARLOTTE AND MECKLENBURG COUNTY

For more than a century, the Public Library of Charlotte and Mecklenburg County has provided essential community service and outreach to the citizens of the Charlotte area. Today, it is one of the premier libraries in the country— named "Library of the Year" and "Library of the Future" in the 1990s—with 23 branches, 1.6 million volumes, 20,000 videos and dvds, 9,000 maps and 8,000 compact discs. The Library also sponsors a number of community-based programs, from the award-winning Novello Festival of Reading, a celebration that accentuates the fun of reading and learning, to branch programs for young people and adults.